Vengeance. Now.

Habu would not be diverted.

    –No. *Heed me!*

    They killed Alexandra. Distaste in Habu's thought.

    –*Do not take that from me,* Reubin demanded. –*You were against Alex; she was a civilizing influence. A humanizing influence upon me. Us. You wanted nothing to do with her.*

    No response.

    –*I wanted her.* Reubin was becoming angry.

    Habu must have sensed Reubin's building anger. *The man Nodivving. He is a killer. I sensed it.*

    –*Certainly he is amoral. Most people of tremendous power are.* Reubin didn't want to think about applying the same criteria to himself. His anger exploded. –*Would that I could purge myself of you.*

    And then die. We are symbiotes, you and I.

JAMES B. JOHNSON
has also written:

DAYSTAR AND SHADOW

TREKMASTER

MINDHOPPER

HABU

JAMES B. JOHNSON

DAW BOOKS, INC.
DONALD A. WOLLHEIM, PUBLISHER

1633 Broadway, New York, NY 10019

DAW Book Collectors No. 780.

First Printing, May 1989

1 2 3 4 5 6 7 8 9

Printed in the U.S.A.

DEDICATION:

For Rich Johnson—always ready with help and answers.

1: REUBIN FLOOD

Reubin rode the tube from the shuttle apprehensively. There had to be an explanation. What had happened to Alex?

He'd been lucky to make it to Snister. This starliner was the last scheduled to and from the planet for months.

Other passengers stood or sat, waiting to arrive at central processing. Reubin guessed they used a shuttle here on Snister to better control the arrival and departure of people and cargo. Which meant too much governmental control and some sort of closed society.

When his wife had failed to arrive on Webster's as planned, he'd dropped his business in the sector capital and hopped a starship for Snister. Alexandra was supposed to join him, then they were to take the Long Life treatment, and ship out for the frontier, ending their previous lives and beginning new lives together.

Supposed to, he thought.

The tube bumped and stopped. The far end opened and people filed off in the usual disorderly manner of civilians.

When the starship had neared Snister, he'd tried to radio Alexandra. No luck. Snister's central locator contained no record of her. He'd remembered Alexandra's daughter: Tique Sovereign. Yes, there was a listing for Tequilla Sovereign. "Put me through, please." No response. "I'll leave a message." Reubin gave his name and the message, "Am arriving 1500 local on shuttle. Where is Alex?"

Surprisingly, the processing agents at passport control were efficient.

Walking up the concourse afterward, he came out into the waiting area. Scenes he'd witnessed hundreds of times before. Families reuniting. Businessmen threading through the throng.

With little hope of success, he scanned the crowd. No sign of Alex—wait . . . no, not her. Against the far wall, he saw a woman leaning in the shadows, staring out a bubble toward the landing area.

Tique. Alex had showed him a holo of her daughter once. "Pronounce it like 'Teak,' " she'd said. One of the things Reubin liked about the Long Life Institute and their dictatorial policies was that by definition everybody was forced to speak Federation English.

Tique had turned to survey the new arrivals and obviously spotted him at once.

She was a woman with curly auburn hair, quite as attractive as her mother but in a different, more angular way. Her eyes were quick and intelligent. She wore one of those half jumpsuit-half skirt things Reubin didn't understand. The height of fashion, no doubt. She shook her head and moved toward him.

He searched her face for some clue. Words and greetings bubbled around him as he arrowed toward Alexandra's daughter. His subconscious was sending warning signals to his other self.

He stopped.

She stopped. "You would be Reubin Flood?" Her words were cool.

"I am. Where's Alex?" Something was dead wrong.

"You didn't receive my message on Webster's?"

"No. When she didn't arrive, I headed here. We've been in transpace."

"Let us get out of the crowd," Tique said as a man jostled her, looked at her and twice at Reubin and mumbled an apology.

A nameless dread began to seep through Reubin, outward from his gut, grinding through him like a throbbing poison. The beast within him came to a higher level of awareness. He followed her, asserting his control.

Tique stopped at the bubble, glanced out, and turned to face Reubin. "My name is Tique—"

"I know. It was that or your mother would have gotten a tattoo. Where is she?" His voice was rough, demanding.

"I . . . she's dead. Mother is dead."

He'd known it. He could smell death from afar. Not again. Not now. "How?" The word sat harsh between them. A familiar, deadly tremor began deep inside him.

"Heart attack." Her face was impassive. Did she blame him for her mother's death? How could she?

But Reubin didn't care. It had been centuries since he'd felt about a woman the way he had about Alex Sovereign. Why was he so awkward about the term "love?" They'd met under strange circumstances and forged a friendship which quickly turned to romance. A comfortable feeling of well-being and togetherness. A long buried rage boiled and rose and rose. He spent a moment controlling the now familiar feeling, and forcing it back. Control. Now was the time for control. *Can you not let me have my grief?* he asked. The lurking presence did not respond.

The shock was still spreading through him, stunning him. Dazed, Reubin looked at life going on around him. A child dragged a Raggedy Ann doll across the tile. People swirled in groups or alone, some talking happily, others hurrying, anxious to be home and away from this place.

Not again, he thought. A bitter taste rose in his throat. A primal slithering began in his soul. His first response wasn't the grief, the sorrow he knew intellectually would assail him later. Rather, outrage grew in him like gorge rising. It threatened to overwhelm him; the serpent within recognized the trigger and fed on the outrage and the internal chaos that outrage produced. Reubin struggled for control, all the while watching the woman Tique catalog the emotions running across his face.

She stepped back.

The tremor peaked. *Let me out,* the serpent urged, already close to the surface.

—*No. Not now.* Reubin's emotions were being ravaged by the realization Alex was dead and his control had slipped.

Reasserting control, he swiveled to face Tique. "Nobody diess of a heart attack. Not anymore." He was aware his voice had turned to ice. Alex was dead.

"Yes, they do," Tique replied. "It is not frequent, but it does occur. Especially in people who haven't had a treatment in over eighty years standard. And especially in people who've had a lot of LLI treatments."

He shook his head. He didn't want to believe it.

"Look," Tique's voice was accusing, "you've got me *defending* my own mother's death! I don't want to do that thing. Don't do this to me."

Reubin saw how close to the edge Tique was. He reinforced his control. "Let'ss get out of here."

She cocked her head at his sibilance, then turned and walked off.

They went down the concourse. At the baggage drop, he punched in his pax code and his single case appeared in the mouth of the chute.

Her back was stiff with resentment. At least she'd had some time to reconcile her loss.

Tique led him outside the terminal, her movements mechanical. Reubin knew that this was her first life, so it stood to reason that her mother's death might well be Tique's first experience with death. Not that many people died these days. Except on Karg and a few other places he'd been.

Snister's atmosphere was humid. Clouds swirled. He thought it might rain and wondered idly what the rain was like on Snister. Anything to stop thinking of Alex; anything to occupy his mind so that the other part of him could not use his grief to grab control and wreak the havoc he so desperately desired. Reubin was a strong man, but the serpent scared him. Indiscriminate response was not civilized, not right.

Tique put a card in a slot and soon an elevator arrived with her groundcar. They surged out along the route.

They drove to the outskirts of Cuyas, Snister's capital. Reubin remained quiet, yet his thoughts were boiling. A different idea occurred to him. "Can we visit her grave?"

She glanced sharply at him. She shook her head. "Mother was cremated."

"Oh." He tried to recall the data that the shipboard tape had spewed out about Snister. He remembered that the population was not at all large for a planet its size. In other words, they wouldn't begrudge the burial space. "It was her wish?" He asked the question not so much to know the answer, but to find out more about his wife. He knew so very little.

Tique shrugged and maneuvered the car under a large, pyramidal building. "I don't know. The government pathologist ordered it."

"Why." Not a question, but a statement.

"Something about the rarity of the cause of death. In case it was a bio-organism, they didn't want to take a chance on the infection spreading."

Typical governmental bumbling, Reubin thought. They could have put her in a safe coffin—casket, he corrected. On the other hand, perhaps they had saved tissue samples. The officials at the port of entry had seemed efficient, so there was no reason to think that others would be less so.

When they arrived in Tique's apartment, she showed him to a bedroom. "I'm sorry. I closed out all of Mother's affairs, sold her home, all of that."

"Oh?"

"The government thought it best."

"Oh?"

Tique looked exasperated. "Look, damn it. She was a high government minister. There were considerations."

"Oh?"

Tique placed her hands on her hips. "Of course. The

money. You can have the goddamn fedcreds. I'll give you an accounting balance sheet to go along with it, too. *If you can prove you married her.*"

Reubin set down his case. He looked her in the eye. "Keep the money. I don't need it, I don't want it."

"Then why—?"

I want Alex, he thought. "You got any liquor in this place?"

"Yeah, sure." Tique was obviously annoyed at his brusqueness.

He followed her into the main room. She pointed to a wet bar. "Help yourself. I'll be back in a moment." She left through a door on the other side of the room.

Reubin looked around. Tique's apartment was nothing spectacular. She was not filthy rich, but certainly well-to-do. The furnishings were warm and comfortable and the environmental control cut Snister's humidity in half. A lot of beige in the room. Smell of fresh cut flowers. View from about four floors below the top of the pyramidal building.

On a hunch, Reubin checked the control console, and punched in to display the current memory.

A side wall darkened and there was Alexandra Sovereign. He turned up the sound, but not loudly enough that it would alert Tique.

Alex. She wore her favorite silver jumpsuit. Large silver earrings dangled from her earlobes, looking like rowels.

"Hello, Silver Girl," Reubin whispered.

He punched "START."

Alex laughed, certainly not a tinkle. "I'm telling you, Tique. You should have seen him as I first did. Half the planet ablaze, and he cut across the sky ahead of me in a hijacked barge, for goshsake." Alex sipped a drink. "Enough firepower lancing through the skies at him to run the city's power requirements for a hundred years. I have diplomatic immunity, so I wasn't really worried. But he reached the starship before I did, and stepped off into the entry port and the barge barely hesitated, it shot off somewhere while his rear foot was in midair."

Tique must have replied, but that had been deleted or the pickup was targeted on Alex only.

"I put my aircar in the cradle, stepped into the air lock and the door was closing and the ship was taking off and this crewman was bowing and escorting me down the corridor and all I could think about was the man. Tique! You wouldn't believe it. He was half-scorched from some battle. Dried blood on the other half. Weapons, my God! On his back, on his hips, protruding from his boots. Twin bandoliers crisscrossing his torso like some bandido of olden times, carrying God knows what.

"My first view of Reubin Flood, Tique. Grim and exhausted—but wary and alert. The sight of him hit me right between the eyes and in my womb. He followed me down the corridor and I could sense his eyes boring—"

Reubin froze the frame, staring at the image on the wall. At his core, he knew it wasn't over. He would never, ever get over this woman. He was angry with himself for being so coldly analytical about her, him, them. Must history repeat itself? He hoped not. But the rage flamed, right there below the surface. A killing urge grew inside him. No, he thought. Not again.

Yes. This is my function.

It was easier to contain the serpent this time; at the spaceport it had been a real struggle.

He hit the "HOLO PROJECT" button and the frozen Alex leaped from the wall to the middle of the room. For one second, then he punched it back onto the wall. The holo was too real, evoking Alexandra's presence almost sacrilegiously.

"That's private," Tique said from the doorway.

Caught, Reubin started.

Tique was staring at him. "My God. Your face." She shuddered.

Reubin killed the image and turned to the bar. "Sorry for the intrusion," he mumbled. He found some 150 sour mash and poured it over ice in a tumbler. He would mourn later. Freeze his sorrow just as he'd frozen Alex on the wall. He lifted his eyes to Tique and she shook her head.

Her words rasped in her throat. "For a moment, I saw in you what she saw that first time, the rawness she described—"

Reubin had regained his control. "You don't need to patronize me to cover the awkwardness. I'm all right now."

She came over to him. "I wasn't, Reubin Flood. It was my opportunity, perhaps my only one, to find out what you are really like; what Mother saw in you. And I didn't want to waste the chance."

"Sure. Look, kid. If you'll help me, I'll be on my way. Can you show me a frame or two of her . . . uh, remains? I mean before cremation? And the death certificate. And I'll take my leave."

"You are not very trusting."

"Nope." Not when they cremate without checking with the family. "Since, as you said, it was a rare death and the pathologist specified cremation, perhaps they'd have the film of the autopsy."

"My God! You'd . . . you'd *watch* that?"

"I'd dig up her corpse if I had to," he said. He drained his drink and refilled it.

Tique was looking at him with a combination of suspicion, awe and horror.

"I take it that you didn't see any of the evidence," he said.

"I'm not a doctor." Tique went to the command console, punched keypads, and read a list scrolling on the inset screen. "There." She touched another pad and waited. "Doctor Crowell, please."

Reubin went back to his room to shower and change.

When he returned, Tique shook her head. "No good. Doctor Crowell is gone for the day and his office will not release any of the information without his permission."

"Even though we're next of kin?"

"Well, she was a government minister and entitled to confidentiality." Tique shook her head.

"First thing tomorrow, then," Reubin said.

It had long since occurred to him that if you inquire

about a recently deceased person, the central locator should refer you to the next of kin, a doctor, or at least some minor functionary.

They don't simply report "No listing."

2: TEQUILLA SOVEREIGN

Well before the start of business the next morning, Tique's comm chime woke her. Instead of the pathologist, the Prime Minister's office contacted her: Would she and Mister Flood kindly attend the PM?

Tequilla explained to Reubin.

"Why?" he asked.

"I don't know . . ."

"You know something."

Yes, she did, but she didn't want to show it. She looked at him frankly. His face appeared rested, yet his eyes were dark and dangerous. She shrugged uncomfortably. "It's rather personal."

Reubin cocked his head and set his coffee down on the table. "Death is personal. Alex and I were married, that's personal. Now what is it?"

The man was like a weed-burr under your saddle harness while riding: irritating. "Fels Nodivving was, uh, shall I say, pursuing Mother in a, um, romantical way."

"A bureaucrat would have chosen those words. But I see your point." He thought for a moment. "Even after Alex returned here to Snister a married woman?"

"Yes. Or so it seemed to me." Her mother had rolled her eyes upon a similar question from Tique. "Maybe even more so." Tique recalled her mother saying, "It's worse than ever, hon. Fels is persistent. I'll be glad to close out my affairs and go off with Reubin to start our new life together." Tique hadn't paid much attention. As this was her own first life, she'd been in the midst of an emotional struggle. The coming permanent parting from her mother promised to be worse than the forced separation from her father when he'd left to take the Long Life treatment and head for the frontier. And her mother had been strangely reluctant to cut the bond between them, too. "You've been closer to me than many of my children," she'd told Tique. "You've never had to leave your folks or your offspring; I'll tell you it's difficult, sometimes—sometimes it's a blessing. This time, well, regrets beat at me like waves on the beach." Alex had smiled. "I oughta be a poet or something, huh?" Now, Tique felt a wave of sorrow.

Interrupting her reverie, Reubin responded. "Even so, if the man Nodivving desired your mother, why does he want to see us instead of allowing us to visit with some minor official, like the pathologist?"

Tique shook her head. "I don't know. It's possible that the Prime Minister wants to meet the man who won the woman he wanted."

"Take my measure?"

"Something like that."

"Perhaps," said Reubin, "he thinks I know something. That explanation fits more than others."

Tique rose from their breakfast. Reubin followed, carrying dishes to the slot. "That's a solid answer," she said, "but it doesn't make sense."

"It makes more sense than a lot of other things here which haven't made sense more."

"What?" Tique asked. Who the *hell* was this man? A man whom she'd resented as much as she'd ever resented anyone. He had been going to take Mother away. Not only Tique's mother, but her best friend, too. Reubin Flood hadn't known Mother for more than a few real-time weeks and he was taking her off. The anger and resentment Tique had felt even before Mother died returned.

Reubin went to look out the window. "Never mind. Tell me about this Prime Minister."

"On the way. Don't want to be late." She was glad she could put off talking to him even momentarily.

As they drove across the city, Tique talked, interrupting herself on occasion to show Reubin special sights. Anything to occupy her mind and keep her anger and resentment down. "The city, Cuyas, is rather modern. In the outlands, however, things quite contrast."

"We can talk wormwood later," he said. "Tell me about Fels Nodivving." Reubin's eyes never rested as she drove. They reminded her of a wild creature: always assessing.

A sheet of rain hit the aircar and she activated the blower to clear the forward and rear portions of the bubble-canopy. She allowed the road's computer to control their pace. As long as they were on a major thoroughfare, the road would do the driving for them.

"How do I explain the Prime Minister?" Tique said. "It's all tied up with economics. Fels Nodivving is the Chief Executive Officer of Snister Wormwood, Inc. This is a Company planet. As CEO, he is automatically the Prime Minister. He runs the planet, business and government."

"Prime Minister," Reubin said, "by definition, connotes a variation of the parliamentary system. Which, in turn, usually means a democratic system, more or less. True?"

"Oh, we're free enough," she said, checking her weather radar. "It's just that the Company goes in for the necessary window dressing. We're free personally. We just don't have much say in governmental affairs."

"Sort of self-contradictory," Reubin said.

Tique glanced at him. His face was neutral. "No. Not when you understand that the Company *is* the government."

"That's how they used to explain it, the party theorists."

There was no rancor in his voice. Tique guessed—mostly from hints her mother had dropped—he was another of the Original Earthers who "had seen everything, been everywhere." One of the few remaining who'd been through the entire history of Earthe expansion to the stars, one who predated the Long Life Institute. Which reminded her: "There is perfect historical precedent and justification for the Company ruling an entire planet. How about the Long Life Institute? For centuries it has been an entity to which no laws apply. The LLI exists Fedwide and no one dares touch it. No one outside the Institute has any influence over it whatsoever, regardless of the circumstances."

"Are you sure?" he asked enigmatically.

"What?"

"Nothing."

She would have liked to pursue the topic, but they arrived at the Government Center. They took a bubblevator up to the Prime Minister's suite. When she introduced Reubin to Fels, there was a subtle change in the room. Tension. It wasn't outright dislike. More in terms of challenge. Fels Nodivving was a strong man, a man to whom everyone gave great respect and deference. There was none of that give in Reubin Flood. No acceptance of domination.

It seemed to shake Fels momentarily. Physically, Fels Nodivving was shorter than Reubin—but wider at the shoulders and hips. Fels had been an accomplished wrestler a life or two ago. He had thick, curly black hair drooping to cover his ears. He was clean shaven and sartorially correct, wearing the corporate uniform of Wormwood, Inc.: coveralls, with a small logo on the right breast. The deep blue coveralls reflected in his eyes, making them dark, but Tique couldn't determine a color.

Now they sat, Tique reviewing the day so far, Reubin and Fels scanning the autopsy results.

Tique leaned back in disgust as the Prime Minister and Reubin Flood studied the autopsy. She was on the couch which obliquely faced Fels' desk and the wall screen. Reubin rested lightly on a hard chair. Fels was on the edge of his executive chair, running the info onto the screen from his desk console.

They saw the video replay of the autopsy. Tique refused to view it. She watched Reubin as the gruesome thing expended itself on the wall. His face was rock hard, as if under rigid control. Now Reubin and Fels Nodivving scanned the analytical results of the autopsy. Data scrolled in columns and neat little paragraphs and subparagraphs. Reubin's face was intense with concentration.

Had Tique not been closely watching the two men, she'd never have known that moment was when it all began.

"Oops," Reubin said. "Too fast, I missed that one."

Fels touched a keypad and the frame leaped back onto the wall. His face froze and his eyes locked onto Reubin for a fraction of a second. The enmity between them grew exponentially then; and it certainly wasn't because Reubin had failed to "sir" the PM.

Reubin's shoulders tightened, then relaxed. His voice was normal. "Okay. Thanks. Go ahead."

Tique glanced up. What could have been a holo-scan of her mother's brain disappeared from view.

The rest of the audience with Fels went predictably. After reviewing the entire autopsy, Reubin asked, "Was there no chemical analysis of the blood? I saw other tissue analyses, but not blood."

Fels turned in his desk chair and tapped on his console. "Ah, there. An appendix to the other findings. I didn't think it worth showing."

"Show me." Reubin's voice was commanding.

"Certainly."

The antagonism between the two climbed another level.

Data filled the wall and Reubin studied it. Then he waved a hand. "Through."

Fels killed the images. "Are you satisfied, Mr. Flood?"

"Yes." Reubin rose, though Fels had not indicated the interview was over.

Fels regarded him. "It is quite unusual for a bridegroom to study an autopsy so closely." An edge appeared in Fels' words. Was it residual jealousy? Or something else?

Reubin stared down at him. "It is quite unusual for the CEO of a company and planet to run the results of that autopsy for that bridgegroom."

Fels stood. "Perhaps I simply wanted to measure the man who won Alexandra Sovereign."

"Perhaps," said Reubin.

Tique got to her feet. Neither of the men was aware of her.

"Will you be staying long on Snister?" Fels asked Reubin.

Reubin shrugged. "It could be that I'd like to see the planet. Play the tourist."

"It could be, also," Fels enunciated slowly, "that memories on Snister would be overwhelming to you and you'd want to depart soonest."

"That could be."

"In fact, I suggest it," Fels said.

"Noted."

Tique could feel the strong undercurrents rushing about the two. Though not at all used to any sort of overt or subtle challenges, she couldn't help but shiver internally. Hostility fairly leaped between them.

On the way out of the Government Center, Reubin Flood was strangely quiet. In the car, he was the same, fiddling with his wristcomp. It gave Tique the willies.

Then he swung the Heads Up Display from the driver's view to the passenger side. He toyed with it for a moment.

"This promontory," he said. "It offers a good view of the countryside?"

Tique nodded. She had questions to ask him. "Some call it 'Lovers' Leap.' But the actual name is something like 'Scenic Overlook #18.' Reubin, I—"

"I've punched in the coordinates on the HUD if you need them."

"I know the way. But—" She realized he was looking at her with a strange intensity. Slowly he shook his head. He didn't want her to talk, to question him. That much was obvious. But why?

"Tell me what you do for a living, Tequilla." Reubin looked at her and settled back. Danger boiled in his eyes.

Tique couldn't begin to categorize his reaction to Mother's death. It was as if he weren't . . . human.

Wind pushed clouds off the sky above them as she drove into the mountains above Cuyas. "I'm an aquady-namacist."

"I know that much. What does one of those things do?"

She felt self-conscious again. "It's what it sounds like. A variation of an engineer and program designer. I run computer models of water dynamics. Irrigation. Dams. Since we have to have dams for irrigation sometimes, we use them for power, too. Underwater drive-vanes require just as much engineering as configurations for aerody-namics, for instance. Especially if you want to maximize profits and minimize expenditures, which is the middle name of the Wormwood conglomerate." She thought of the "wetlands" where wormwood grew. "During the monsoon season, which is much of the year, we've got to control floods. I'm kept pretty busy."

She hesitated, then continued. "They've planted all the wetlands with wormwood, not simply allowing nature to grow it at her own pace and where the ecosystem dic-tates. There's a great plain where man-planted worm-wood trees are already being harvested." She waved angrily with her left hand. "Wormwood, Inc. has planted wormwood damn near everywhere now." She cautioned herself to keep her opinions out of the conversation—for now. "Anyway, because of all that, I have as much work as I can handle. Though, right now, I'm on leave because of Mother."

As she drove, she told him of the various projects she'd worked on. As wormwood became more important throughout this sector of the Federation, new wormwood forests were needed. The production spread out from Cuyas and other cities. The major wormwood production now came from Company-grown groves on that distant riverine plain as opposed to harvesting the original, nature-grown wormwood trees. In the other areas, the trees had not yet matured. But they were increasing their harvesting capability: manpower being hired, machines being built, processing centers under construction; all targeted for the projected harvest in a few years.

"The expansion from harvesting natural wormwood trees to man-grown ones was, in fact, the reason Mother was offworld surveying markets and soliciting business." She went on to explain how the particular combination of climate, humidity, flooding, root nutrition, and light filtered through Snister's atmosphere created the odd conditions in which the worm could live in that particular tree, acting as a symbiote to the tree itself.

Tique was proud of her profession. It was unique, as far as she knew. "To become an aquadynamacist, you have to become an expert in all phases of computers. I can make the company's mainframe tap dance if I have to."

Into the mountains, she followed the single route up; at the 3K level, just below the crest, was the promontory. She ran the car into the turnaround. No other groundcars were stopped. Occasional traffic went up or down the mountain behind them.

Tique had always loved this spot. Her mother had brought her here often—on the way to their mountain cabin—when she was a child. Lately, she hadn't come as frequently as she'd have liked. Briefly, she wondered whether Reubin was psychic and had asked to be brought here because it was Alexandra's favorite place, too.

The wind blew strongly, hinting of rain even at this height. Tique led the way into the protective bubble toward the viewers.

Reubin fiddled with his wristcomp again.

Tique looked out over the mountains and valleys and forests of wormwood trees. She pointed. "See that peak at about nine o'clock, just below the horizon?"

Reubin activated a viewer and swung it around.

"Flaag Peak," Tique said. "Perhaps 4K to the west and down on that shoulder is the cabin Mother gave me. It was her departing gift. She, well, she was gonna go off with you to start a new life and uh, well—" The memory assaulted Tique. Mother. Dead.

"Got it," Reubin said, diplomatically still glued to the viewer. "Can you get there from here?"

She nodded though he wasn't watching her. "Aircar, or a long ground route. It's alone out there, a blip on the side of a mountain, surrounded by forest and rock and mountain and a lake."

Reubin had stopped looking through the viewer. "It's in your name?"

"Yes." Was Reubin after Mother's money? Every time she thought she had him figured out, he surprised her.

"Good. Listen, Tequilla Sovereign. We have a problem. I am going to tell you about it for one simple reason: they will never believe I *didn't* tell you."

"Tell me what?"

"First, your car is bugged. Are you aware of that?"

"No. Why—"

"It was clean when we drove to Government Center, so they must have installed the bug while we were with Nodivving. It may be tied in with the autosystems, but it's there."

"You know this for a fact?" Tique sat down heavily on a bench. Wind blew leaves on the ground, which rustled in the comparative shelter of the bubble.

Reubin touched his wristcomp. "Special design. One of the functions is a signal locator. Your car registers one—surely in case your built-in transponder is inop or perhaps gimmicked so it doesn't broadcast. Doubtless by now, your apartment has been doused with listening devices." He put a foot on the bench and leaned on his knee, watching her closely.

"But why?"

"Your mother. More specifically, my questions this morning to Nodivving. The questions alerted them. Which, in turn, means it's likely they killed her."

"Mother? Murdered?" Tique was bewildered by this turn of events. "I don't understand." Could Reubin possibly be serious?

"Me, neither, but I'm going to. Think about the circumstances of Fels Nodivving himself showing us the results of the autopsy."

"Mother was a government minister—"

"Certainly. But Wormwood, Inc. has some kind of stake in your mother's death, as near as I can figure."

"But why, Reubin? I mean—"

"I don't know. Yet."

"How can you *say* this?" Tique felt strangely empty. This interloper was mixing up her feelings. Emotions she thought dead rose again. Her forehead burned.

"Recall the autopsy. Did you see the chemical analysis of her blood?"

"I wasn't paying that close attention. Frankly, it was rather odious to me, all that—"

"You didn't see it." Reubin sat down and stretched his legs. He interlaced his fingers, twisted his hands inward, and snapped his knuckles. "It wasn't there. Until I asked, remember?" He laughed dryly, with no humor. "All they had to do was to dummy one up, but they didn't take the time and effort. Or, perhaps—"

Tique waited, watching him think. Not wanting to think herself. "Perhaps what?"

"Perhaps they purposefully failed to include it so that I'd notice. If I noticed and left the planet quickly, that meant that I was privy to Alexandra's secret—and making a panicked run for it. But I studied it."

"What secret?" Tique was more at a loss as each moment passed.

"The secret they killed her for. The secret they wouldn't have gotten from her, else they wouldn't leave the sucker-bait of the incomplete autopsy." Reubin breathed deeply. "I've always loved high mountain air. There's something primordial about it."

"I say again, Reubin, *what* secret?"

"I don't know. Do you?"

Tique shook her head. "Not only that, but I'm not sure I know what the hell we're talking about right goddamn now." More anger seeped into her voice. Was this man toying with her?

"Nor am I." Reubin's voice was strong, decisive. "Did you notice the color cross sections of her brain?" He didn't wait for her response, but continued. "It was difficult to tell because the autopsy got into her brain and the pathologist could have conceivably caused the damage—"

"Reubin? You are frightening me. Will you please start to make sense?"

He looked at her, scooted closer and snaked his arm through hers. She stifled her recoil. "There is a little tuck in the cerebrum, right under the front of the corpus callosum—which is the big band of commissural fibers that connect the hemispheres. Anyway, in that specific brain matter is close access to the pituitary gland and the hypothalamus." He tightened his arm against her. "Bear with me. This physiology isn't important, but it's necessary to understand. They made a mistake. They showed us color frames of the autopsy. There was some discoloration and tissue damage."

"And?" Tique decided she didn't want to withdraw her arm from his right now. More confused emotions.

"You don't know?"

"Damn it, Reubin. Stop asking me if I know. I don't."

His smile was grim. "Right. It is not commonly known. But some people have an implant, a biochip attached to points in the brain, the pituitary and the hypothalmus."

Tique removed her arm from his. "Sure. You should be a professor. You know physiology. Why haven't I ever heard of this implant?"

"Only the Long Life Institute knows about it. And those involved."

"And you, Reubin, and you. Or so you say."

He rose and paced the short space behind the viewers inside the bubble. "I know because I have one of the implants myself. Only those people who worked on the original development of the Long Life Institute, or one of its ancillary projects, have them." He stopped and stared at her.

She didn't let the fierceness of his gaze inhibit her. She returned his stare. "Go on."

"The biochip," he said, "contains a couple of simple programs which you can trigger. One is to defeat drug or hypnotic interrogation. You trigger it and your cover story, hypnotically placed there by the most skilled experts in the Federation, is at your demand. You respond with your cover story, no matter what drugs they use. You actually believe the story, too. You don't fess up about your role with the LLI. So drugs and hypnosis cannot be used against you.''

Though she didn't want to, Tique asked the logical question, dread flowing through her mind. ''And physical torture?''

''The second function of the implant. Suicide. It tells your heart to stop functioning. I'm not certain whether it is a hormonal-directed action, or simple electrical impulse to the appropriate location in the brain. Maybe both. But the autopsy should have showed something out of norm in the chemical analysis. If the biochip launches hormones to the brain function to stop your heart, it would show up. The people at the Long Life Institute are the most expert in hormones in the Fed.''

Tique ignored his words. Suddenly the world changed. ''You just told me that someone tortured Mother and she committed suicide?''

Reubin sat again. ''That's the way I figure it. And the autopsy revealed the biochip and your pathologist, Dr. Crowell, removed the biochip thinking it might hold a secret or two. Once brain activity stops, electrical energy ceases and the chip is useless. But she was dead when they dug out the implant. It fits my definition of murder.'' His head dropped and his jaw muscles rolled, giving Tique the impression that he was undergoing some sort of internal struggle.

''Why? Why, Reubin?''

He lifted his head. Something flickered in his eyes and was gone just as quickly. Eerie. ''She knew something they wanted to know.''

''Connected with the LLI, right?''

''It must be.'' He paused. ''Those who knew any of the LLI formulae or had any access to the original projects were implanted with the chip. It works off the brain's own electrical activity.''

"I'm beginning to see," she said. Her voice sounded weird even to her. "The greatest secret in the known human experience, in history. The Long Life treatment."

Reubin shrugged. "It could be. If someone solved that, he could bust the Long Life Institute monopoly and name his own price. People wouldn't have to follow the strict rules of the LLI and its founder."

Tique was still baffled. "I don't think I understand fully, yet. You, Reubin Flood, *you* know the Long Life secret?"

He shook his head. "No. And your mother probably didn't, either. I was involved only peripherally. I had a part in the R and D of the computer systems for the LLI."

"God. You're *old.*"

A strange look passed through his eyes. "And you're young. Neither one of us should die for a few more centuries. But Alex did. On the other hand, she might have suicided to keep them from using you or me against her—hostages to her knowledge. Whichever, they killed her and stole her from me . . . ." His voice trailed off.

Tique waited a few moments for his emotions to calm. Another glimpse of him with his mask down. He had really cared for Mother. Tique softened her voice. "Why now? She'd been on Snister since Wormwood, Inc. pioneered it. She was going off with you—"

"Yep, you got it. She was leaving. It was their last chance."

"I'm dumbfounded. I don't know whether to believe you or not. It doesn't make sense, not in this universe, not these days."

"The oldest motives in the book, Tique. Power and wealth. Unlimited power over all human beings. More wealth than trillions of people can even dream about."

"You keep saying 'they,' Reubin. Who are they?"

"I don't know, but I'm going to find out. Offhand, I'd say the hierarchy of the Wormwood Company is both the most likely suspect and the only current suspect."

"Fels Nodivving?"

"It's as good a place as any to start."

"I'm cold," she said and shivered.

"Nodivving virtually ordered me off planet," Reubin said.

"I remember."

"I've told you what I've figured, because it is possible that since Alex is dead, I'm their only link. They might think that Alex told me her secret, whatever that is."

"Uh-oh." She began to see where he was leading.

"And you might be next, but they have you here on planet with no plans to depart. I'd recommend you maintain your normal schedule for a while, then grab an opportunity to visit Webster's or somewhere and don't come back."

Thoughts of her own personal safety had not entered her mind. Considering the stunning blows she'd received in the last few minutes, her own safety didn't seem important.

Tique rose and went to the bubble wall. She looked out over the mountains and forests. She wondered what type of man this Reubin Flood was. She'd seen several different Reubin Floods—or at least manifestations of different people. She'd yet to see the one which her mother had seen.

Mother had chosen him. That was one thing. Mother had told her about first seeing Reubin, amidst battle. He'd been the classic warrior then. Mother had married the man with little time in between the meeting and the deed. Unusual for anyone these days when life was long and marriage taken seriously. Resentment built in her again. But Mother generally knew what she was doing. Tique wondered if Fels Nodivving's pursuit of Mother had driven Alex to marrying Reubin Flood, with the Long Life treatment next and all it implied. Anything was possible.

Clouds were lower now, boiling right in front of her.

Reubin stepped up beside her and a swollen, gray behemoth of a cloud rolled over a snowcapped mountaintop. The peak seemed to gut the cloud, tearing it asunder. Tique shivered again.

"Me, too," Reubin said empathetically. "I'm going to try to make a run for it. If I reach Webster's, I'll do some research and return here; then we'll teach 'em how the cow eats the cabbage.''

"What's that mean?''

"Just an Olde Earthe expression.''

She cocked an eye at him. "You really think that Fels and his people will try to stop you?''

He shrugged and wiped fog off the inside of the bubble. "It's all speculation. Remember, if I was right about the autopsy, then . . .''

Tique grimaced. "Snister has no army or navy, there is no need. It's all unified under the corporate auspices of Wormwood, Inc. But the Company police force, the 'Constabulary' it's called, is quite efficient. The Constabulary also runs the port of entry.''

"We'll know right away, then, won't we?''

"When your ship gets underway,'' Tique said, "will you send me a message telling me you made it? Something innocuous.''

"If you wish,'' Reubin said.

"Thanks.'' Here she was worried about the safety of a man whom she resented. He had given her a different perspective about events, though. Perhaps she was being caught up in the intrigue.

"Be advised, when I return I might be disguised. I haven't decided which yet. As somebody else, it would be easier to investigate. On the ninth hand, I might have to be myself and use me as bait—''

Lightning flashed far off. "A lightning rod?'' she asked.

He nodded. "It might be the only way to smoke them out.''

She traced a pattern in the condensation on the inside of the bubble. "Reubin? When Mother came back from Karg and announced she'd married you and was leaving to go off pioneering, I didn't see much of her at all. Then she was dead.'' Tique felt awkward having to do all the explaining before she asked the question.

"What is it, Tique?'' One of the few times he'd used her name.

"Would you tell me about Mother? And you?'' They'd

always been close and Mother's affair with Reubin had made Tique feel left out—for a change.

"We met on Karg and married on the starship in which we escaped."

"More. What was the war about? What was your job? *Who* are you?"

"No." His voice changed abrubtly. He'd been cooperative, but now—? The word "No" had been pure ice. She'd been close to reaching him, and at the last minute he'd withdrawn again back into himself. Back into his mask. Damn him!

So far he'd shown little grief. What kind of man was he?

She saw him watching her with an animal cunning that made her terribly uncomfortable. Without looking at him again, she walked through the rain to her groundcar.

It was well past midnight when Building Security woke her.

"Ma'am, it's your guest, ma'am," said the voice over the speaker on her bedside console.

Tique shook sleep out of her eyes. "What? What about him?"

"He's on the roof, ma'am."

She sat up. "What's wrong with that?"

"He's retracted the bubble."

"Oh." Oh! She linked into the building's weather radar and her screen was cluttered. "I'll go up and take care of it."

"Just thought you ought to know, ma'am, since it's not really illegal—"

"Thanks." Tique disconnected and dressed quickly in a waterproof jumpsuit. She punched in outside visuals. A storm played over Cuyas, lightning streaked and wind lashed rain sideways.

She chose the internal stairway and soon came out on the roof.

Rain drenched her immediately.

She wondered when the bubble had last been retracted.

It was something Mother would do. A sheet of lightning lit her immediate world.

Where—? There.

Reubin sat on the edge of the roof, legs dangling over and out of sight. He lifted a bottle to his lips and drank for a moment. Lightning hit the diffuser pole high above them and cracked. Tique jumped involuntarily and smelled burned ozone. Reubin didn't move.

She walked toward him, strongly aware of the missing security of the bubble. She stopped behind him, apprehensive of the distance between them and the ground far below. Though the building was pyramidal, it was still a dangerous fall during a storm. Right now the fall appeared damn near vertical.

Reubin Flood turned and looked at her. How had he known she was there? Some animal instinct, probably. The glare of lightning illuminated his eyes.

And they were not human.

Even as she watched, fascinated by the alien phenomenon, his eyes milked over; after a short time, human intelligence looked out at her.

A strong gust of wind and rain threatened her, taking her balance away.

Reubin steadied her with his left hand. It wasn't just the possibility of falling which frightened her.

She motioned him back with her.

He took a drink from the bottle of 150 sour mash he held, then rose slowly. Tique backed against a strong wind to a double seat near the center of the roof. Reubin followed her.

She sank onto the seat, found the controls, and raised the bubble until Reubin stopped her halfway. At least it was on the upwind side, blocking the shrieking wind.

Reubin stood in front of her, soaked, the water streaked on his face mimicking tear streaks. He was breathing heavily, as if interrupted during some physical feat.

Overcoming her initial revulsion, she signaled him to sit next to her.

For a moment, he resisted. Then he shrugged and sank beside her. He held out the bottle.

She wasn't going to, but she changed her mind. She took the bottle and tipped it to her lips. The strong sour mash burned her throat. She held in a cough and gave it back to him.

"What are you doing up here?" she asked.

His face contorted and he didn't answer. In that moment she saw he was vulnerable. No mask. Another Reubin Flood.

She sat with him for a while, not pushing it.

Finally, he said, "Challenging the elements."

"The weather or the universe?" she asked.

He looked surprised. "Both, I suppose."

A sheet of rain whipped around the partially closed bubble and blew over them.

Suddenly she realized it. "You were up here grieving." Her voice rose to overcome the roar of the wind and she worried that it sounded accusatory.

He took another drink and didn't answer her.

That was what he'd been doing. Maybe he wasn't so . . . frightening after all. Or would the term be disconcerting? She found herself constantly revising her opinion of him.

Lightning flashed over their heads and immediate peals of thunder throbbed through her body, threatening to turn her insides to liquid.

"I had to do something," he said, not raising his voice so that she had to strain to hear him.

A strange cathartic, she thought. A strange man. "I understand."

"Do you?" he asked. "I have sorrow, I have grief. Those have been my only companions in times past." His face fell. She knew he was grieving for Mother whether or not he admitted it. She had to read his lips to understand what he next said. "It isn't the first time for . . . for me." He finished lamely and Tique knew that he'd been close to confiding in her.

He drank again and so did she.

She felt that finally they'd reached an accommodation—an uneasy one, but an accommodation nonetheless.

All the more difficult because of his strangeness. What tragedy had struck him?

"Something in your past?" she asked, mesmerized. "*This* happened to you before?" What *was* he talking about?

Again he drank deeply and stared off into the storm.

The silence stretched between them, punctured only by the chaos of nature awry.

"Would you tell me about it now?" she asked gently, changing the focus of her questioning. "You and Mother? About you?"

He shrugged and looked off into the storm.

"Who are you and where do you come from?" A last try. She'd speculated before that he was one of those closemouthed Original Earthers.

He drank and remained silent.

"I'd like to know about Mother," Tique said awkwardly. "I know the story as she told it, but there are gaps." She felt she was exposing some of her inner self to this strange man. And immediately realized that was probably what *he* was afraid of. She threaded her right arm through his left.

He sat there, staring into the night.

Tique waited. After a while, she said, "You know, I resented you from the start. You were taking Mother away from me. Then you came in here like some sort of self-appointed bigwig, demanding, taking, not giving. I hated you because you intruded upon my loss. Then I thought about what you said. You said that Mother was going away with you, so Fels Nodivving or somebody killed her. You admitted it was your fault she's dead now. What am I to think? Tell me, Reubin Flood. What the hell am I to think?" At the end her words poured out. "And you didn't even show grief or sorrow, no pain or distress, or even remorse at allegedly having caused all this." Until now, she amended to herself.

"I mourn differently than mosst humanss," he said without looking at her. "For I have had more practice. More opportunity. But I do sso in my own fashion." His voice had taken on that strange sibilant manner. He seemed to realize this and shook his head as if to clear it. He upended the bottle once again.

Tique felt an unusual chill travel through her body when he'd spoken thusly. The chill, she felt certain, was an atavistic fear of something deadly, something unknown. She took the bottle from him and swallowed several gulps of sour mash. Then she looked at him and he seemed human again.

Vulnerable again.

She returned the bottle to him. She'd pried too deeply into him, his makeup, his past.

"I find I can talk about Alexandra," he said. The dissonance was gone from his voice.

Lightning flashed and the skies clashed, providing an eerie background to his story.

3: REUBIN

Reubin remembered it all and told little.

He had first met Alexandra Sovereign on the planet Karg. Specifically, hastily leaving the planet Karg.

Reubin leaned into the wind. The airbarge he'd hijacked buckled from enemy fire. He slewed the ungainly machine so that it flew with the left front quarter panel facing forward. Thus the rear of the barge and its cargo acted as a buffer between him and the enemy fire.

An energy beam ignited a crate of Leninist Army manuals on the edge of the barge. The wind whipped the flames into a trail behind them. The craft shuddered as a missile struck somewhere below.

Habu was awake fully now, figuratively leaning over Reubin's shoulder, observing and biding his time. The serpent had lurked just under the surface, no longer somnolent for the battles they'd just been through. Sometimes Reubin had called upon Habu and his abilities.

I am here. Ready.

–I know. Not yet. I might need your reflexes shortly, Reubin told the other.

I am ready.

Reubin didn't want all of Habu. He never wanted all of that creature. But over the centuries they'd reached an accommodation. For survival. Of both. Because of Habu, Reubin, at the end of his lives, courted danger. Thus, in turn, he needed Habu. An unbreakable cycle which Reubin would gladly escape. Habu in full control frightened him. But Reubin respected Habu's talents and abilities and, when necessary, used them.

Down deep, Reubin was worried. For the compulsion to court danger had been limited to the tail ends of his lives. However, during this life and part of the last, he found himself drawn to perilous situations.

He forced his attention back to flying the barge.

Reubin's hands flew over the controls to compensate for the gaping hole in the bottom of the barge. The aerodynamics of the aircraft, never perfect to begin with, were almost obliterated.

Reubin's sixth sense told him that they'd found his range and that more missiles were being programmed to follow the first one.

He hit the "PALLET RELEASE" button for positions one through twenty, wrapped his legs around the pilot seat, tested the seat restraint, and flipped the barge over ninety degrees. Twenty pallets full of Leninist supplies tumbled into the Karg skies, with the burning army manuals making a nice trail of fire toward the ground below.

A series of explosions told Reubin that his timing had been good as the supplies intercepted energy beams and missiles which had preferred flaming army manuals to the scarred hull of an airbarge.

Reubin dumped 2K of altitude in a free fall before sliding the barge back onto straight and level. Perhaps the falling debris would mask his own descent.

The lights of the spaceport loomed in the distance.

Would he make it?

With the fall of the IPs, the rest of the offworlders in IP territory would have already been long gone. And, from what Reubin understood, the rest of Karg was into a boiling frenzy of warfare, at such a high pitch that not even Karg could sustain.

This time, he'd been careless. In his never-ending effort to disappear and resurface in a different life, he'd chosen the wrong situation. The trouble is, he thought, just such chaos is tailor-made for my purposes. Not to mention *his* compulsion for courting danger, especially toward the end of his lives. And Karg had provided more than enough chaos and danger to sate his desire.

It was almost time to change his life again. So, to bury his trail further, he traveled to Karg and enlisted as a mercenary. His intention was to spend some time in their internecine wars and come out with a different identity. That way, when he applied at the Long Life Institute on some world he'd arbitrarily choose, he'd already be one additional identity removed. The LLI computer would never figure it out—though, admittedly, one of these centuries it would start correlating people, files, and codes and come up with some interesting discoveries.

The people on Karg simply didn't like each other. Religious fundamentalists of several types: Christian derivatives, Moslem offshoots, Leninists, and even a smattering of Intellectual Philosophists. They fought all the time.

Reubin Flood enlisted in the IP Army under the name of Teale. This time he'd guessed wrong.

He wound up commanding the troop guarding the City of Death, being promoted to the rank of comajor mainly because the Leninists had killed off the higher echelon of the IP field grade officers.

The City of Death was appropriately named. It was a graveyard of epic proportions which illustrated, if nothing else, the dedication the inhabitants of Karg gave to their hate and resultant warfare. The City of Death lay at the center of IP territory. Wealthy Intellectual Philosophists (Reubin thought much of their nomenclature and terminology to be contradictory) buried each other in the City of Death. Periodically they visited the graves of the deceased. To do this in style, atop the gravesites, they had erected huts, shrines, cabins, all of which they used only when visiting.

Because of his past, Reubin felt a kinship with the City of Death.

Over the years a living city of poor and disenfranchised had grown up in and around the City of Death. It was a waste of covered space to leave the veritable homes atop graves unoccupied for most of the year. Inevitably, a sub-culture took hold and flourished.

Reubin Flood and his unit were to guard the graves of deceased IPs, not the live peasantry who parasitically survived atop the dead city.

Enjoying the fruits of an extra heavy birth cycle some twenty planetary years earlier, the Leninists over-whelmed the miserable IP force and flooded the land with young men trained to kill the enemy without quarter.

Reubin Flood fit their criteria of enemy.

The only thing Reubin had going for him was the fall of the IP. Any off planet visitors would be considered suppliers of the IP by the conquering Leninists. Thus, any starships in port would be leaving like the proverbial rats.

Two preprogrammed drones with nightview eyes buzzed the barge and hovered overhead.

Reubin hit "EMERGENCY JETTISON ALL." Ex-plosives sheared bolts and retaining straps. Compressed air fired the remaining thirty pallets of cargo straight up in the air. Reubin tilted the barge on its side again and flew sideways out of range of the falling cargo.

He saw no more drones.

His panel showed him to be nearing the spaceport.

"IDENTIFY" lit up on his screen. He punched in his code as major sector commander and the screen blanked.

A worried face popped up on the screen. "Comajor Teale? State your purpose."

"Who are you?" Reubin demanded.

"Flight control—"

"Patch me through to your sector command, this equipment isn't doing the job," Reubin snapped. Time to write your own invitation to the party, he told himself.

Eyes flickered. "The unit has moved west—"

"Who's the senior officer present?" Reubin put steel into his voice. He touched the power control bar to insure it was at max.

"I am. Colonel Burak . . . sir."

"You confirm my code, Burak."

"The computer does."

Reubin took a deep breath. "I am assuming command. I will land at the base of the tower and join you shortly."

"Sir, I remind you that Flight Control is not under the Ministry of Warfare and therefore not subject to your command except through specifically authorized circumstances."

"We'll get it straight when I arrive," Reubin told the IP colonel. His face was the IP sickly white and Reubin knew instinctively that Colonel Burak had tabbed him as an offworlder. It would be difficult to cajole him into turning over his command. "Is it safe for me to land? I don't want to get in any starship takeoff wash on my inbound."

"The Starline cruise ship *Al Latalia* is ready to launch."

A cruise ship? Reubin couldn't imagine anybody visiting Karg for mere vacation purposes, though he did remember something about the City of Death being a tourist attraction. And the City of Garbage, too, he recalled.

"Well," Reubin said, thinking furiously. He needed to board that starship. "I don't see his sequence lights yet. I think I can be under cover before he launches."

"It's your funeral," Burak said.

"Your mouth, Colonel, is overreaching your rank," Reubin snapped. "You'd best call up your evacuation programs and start memorizing." Keep the colonel guessing. He might take offense to Reubin's last minute changes. What he intended came under the category of desertion in military regulations. He flipped the monitor off.

No ground traffic at all below him. The lights of the spaceport sprawled ahead of him. A solitary spaceliner sat forlornly on one of the central launching pads. Warning lights began the five minute countdown.

Reubin snapped on the comm link. "Burak. Hold that ship until I'm clear."

Burak came on and grinned wickedly. "Sorry, *sir.* The captain of the vessel is anxious to leave. I have no control."

Just what Reubin wanted. "Gimme his freek."

Burak reached out and touched a keypad. "Info is in your comm link. You'll never talk her out of it."

Reubin killed the link and called up the spaceliner *Al Latalia*.

"Unidentified barge, clear the area," said the voice and the picture leaped onto his screen. The face was female and angry.

"Spaceliner, hold your takeoff," Reubin said.

"Hah."

"Are you the captain?"

"That's a fact, barge. In about three minutes you're gonna be fried like the rest of this forpin' planet."

Reubin fumbled the casing off the ammo belt which crisscrossed his chest. "My credentials, madam." He leaned closer to the pickup and increased the lighting momentarily.

"Um. Captain Kent at your service, sir. Of course you realize that if those gemstones are not real, I'll have you scrubbing the hull while we're in transpace—from the outside."

"They're real."

The woman nodded. "They look it. Passage one hundred thousand fedcreds, and one thousand fedcred bonus to each member of the crew."

Steep. "Done."

Her eyes narrowed and glanced aside. "There appears to be a war following you. Our east entry port will be open for two minutes, no more." The comm link died.

With fifteen seconds to spare, he sidled up to the east entry port. He set the barge controls to fly north with a two second delay. He climbed out onto the stabilizing cradle and into the entry port as his barge surged away.

Habu faded back into the darkness.

A crewman stood waiting. Reubin walked wearily ahead through the airlock into a corridor. The outer door did not close. What was this?

Reubin turned to ask the crewman and a one person aircar settled into the cradle he'd just vacated. A woman with silver hair stepped out. She turned and pushed the aircar away with a shapely leg no jumpsuit could disguise.

The crewman bowed quickly and escorted her inside. The outer door snapped closed.

As the two passed Reubin and the airlock closed behind them, Reubin thought that Captain Kent had snookered him: she was waiting for another passenger anyway.

Without a word, Reubin followed the pair. The crewman showed them into a nearby lounge cabin. "Use the cushion seats, please, in case of inordinate acceleration." He disappeared.

The woman looked at Reubin. "Inordinate acceleration?"

"Perhaps he's government trained," Reubin said.

"Lift off," a voice from an overhead said. A small buzzing repeated three times.

Reubin looked at the woman. She was dressed in a silver jumpsuit and her silver hair was long and windblown. She was staring at him.

He knew what she saw. An exhausted man carrying an energy rifle on his back, a laser on his hip, a projectile weapon in an underarm holster, not to mention the handles of several other weapons and knives protruding from his clothing and paraphernalia. The bandoliers crossing his chest and around his back were full of charge packs, explosives, and ammunition that wouldn't fit into or onto his combat vest. The gemstones were concealed again.

The woman's eyes flashed as her teeth showed in a tight grin. "You didn't stop to shave?"

"Hello, Silver Girl," Reubin said against his will. He didn't want to get familiar with this woman, but he couldn't help it. "Traveling light?"

"The skycap will be along with my luggage directly."

The ship jerked upward. "We could share my toothbrush," Reubin said.

She ran her eyes along his body again. "No, thanks. Doubtless it'd turn out to be lethal." She turned and strode to a seat and sank into it thankfully. Reubin couldn't miss the sigh of weariness.

"Me, too," he said and lowered himself into the ad-

joining lounge. "My name is Reubin Flood." Which it
wasn't. He'd appeared on Karg using the name Erdenhaer
and enlisted under the name of Teale. Reubin Flood was
the identity he planned to use for the purpose of changing
life. He was due. The pressure within his mind was
growing.

"I'm Alexandra Sovereign." She regarded him for a
moment. "They vectored me in from a different direction; but I watched the trail of fire behind you. Indeed,
Reubin Flood, you are a lucky man."

"I am now, Silver Girl." Habu wouldn't like that.

She smiled in acknowledgment.

Acceleration increased. The ship's own field would kick
in soon with a single standard gee.

"You're from Snister?" he asked.

She nodded, forking more spinach onto her plate.

"Nobody's from Snister."

"I am."

It was hours later and they were sharing a midnight
meal. The dining room was empty. Reubin was considerably poorer, his load of gems lightened.

Alexandra Sovereign eyed the platter. "I wonder if
that's real or mock liver?"

"The onions are real. If you don't want to know the
answer, don't ask the question."

"What'd you do with all your weapons?" Alexandra
asked.

"Captain Kent quoted some arcane rules, laws, regulations, and took them away."

Alexandra regarded him. "You don't look the man to
bow to authority."

"Rules are rules," he said, and was glad they hadn't
x-rayed or scoped him. Not to mention a couple of weapons he'd concealed in the room they'd occupied during
takeoff.

Alexandra's silver jumpsuit had ben cleaned and glistened in the dim light. Reubin wore slacks and a tunic
from the ship's stores.

* * *

Later, in a lounge, they had an after dinner drink together. While they weren't in synch with shipboard time, Reubin felt his body and internal clock becoming accustomed to the change.

"Now let me get this straight," he told Alexandra. "You're a coffin salesperson from Snister."

"Casket," she corrected automatically. "And I am no salesperson, though, in essence, that was my business upon Karg. My title is Minister of Wormwood, principle export of Snister. Death is a way of life on Karg. It was my intention to pitch the benefits of interment in wormwood caskets."

"The corpses care?"

"Loved ones," she corrected. "Yes. Wormwood is highly sought after in this sector of the Fed. It lasts longer than other wood. It is of much higher quality." She sipped her drink and Reubin wondered if the liquor was synthetic. He could never tell.

"And the worms?" he prompted.

"The wood is harvested at a specific time in the growth process. The worms are the natural symbiote. The worms' activities while the trees are growing insure that the wood will last longer after it is harvested. They eat their way through the wood so very slowly—their metabolism is geared to two speeds: slow and stop. Their, um, processing of the wood leaves a faint sweet, pleasant smell which is why the wood is so popular."

"I don't think I'll ask about the worms and the deceased." But his mind was serious. He knew about symbiosis. Day after day, year after year, century after century. Would he never get any respite?

She smiled and leaned back. They sat in silence for a while.

And it took awhile, but finally the thought occurred to him that he was growing an affinity for this woman. Something he hadn't felt so deeply for a century or two. Maybe longer. The feeling was more of a comfortable empathy than a physical attraction.

He had volunteered nothing about himself other than his name. Nor had she pushed him about his background, his past. As it was, he felt that he'd talked more than he had in the last year.

Her eyes on him and a slight smile, she said, "You are much used to silence, no?"

"If I don't have anything to say, I don't say it."

"Cryptic," she said. "A man accustomed to living alone."

"I am about due for a trip to the Long Life Institute."

"Oh." She studied him for a moment. "Me, too. Is it bad yet?"

He shrugged. "It builds. You get used to it."

"I know."

Eight hours of sleep and now they faced each other in the splatter ball room.

Gravity could be adjusted from zero up. They wore thin coveralls of some paper material. When the balls of colored water struck and burst open, the paper changed color from white to whatever color the water was. The first one to completely change color was the loser. Reubin was throwing blue and Alex was throwing red. The longer the game lasted, the more the paper coveralls disintegrated.

They touched hands in the traditional beginning of the game.

Alexandra hurried back to the dispenser on her side of the court. She punched the start button and snatched water balls from the dispenser tube.

Reubin had walked back to his dispenser slowly, observing Alex to try to figure out her tactics.

Her arm snapped and he stepped aside—but she'd thrown a second quick one, guessing he'd step to his right.

He'd automatically stepped to his left.

He smiled a challenge and dodged her volley for a moment. Perhaps she'd tire soon. But he did not underestimate her craftiness. It occurred to him that she was showing him less than full power and shot accuracy. Which probably meant that she was waiting for him to approach his dispenser.

She stopped as if winded.

He moved toward his dispenser and reached out.

She threw several water balls quickly and accurately. He dodged, but water splattered off the back wall and he felt wet on his back.

''Wallflower,'' she taunted.

He stuck his tongue out at her.

He braved the distance to his dispenser and collected half a dozen water balls, taking only one hit on his shoulder. The paper began to disintegrate.

A bell toned.

''My gee,'' he said and grinned wickedly. He went to the control and punched in zero.

''Oh, no. No fair,'' she said.

He floated, pushed off, and threw underhanded. It was a direct hit on her thigh. Blue splotches appeared all over the front of her suit. The paper began to deteriorate.

The force of the throw twisted him up and sideways.

Then he was busy contorting, dodging in midair zero gee, a veritable hail of red water balls. Alex had thought ahead of him, guessing that was what he'd do. As the gravity had disappeared, she'd anchored her legs around her dispenser and began pelting him as fast as she could.

The entire left side of his paper suit was gone and he was drenched in red. Not only that, but the globules of water hung in the gravityless room, adding additional obstacles.

Reubin dispensed half a dozen, as many as he could hold, and pushed off toward the gravity control. He punched in two gees and Alex fell off her dispenser tube. He nailed her on the way down.

''Hey! Not fair,'' she said and rolled along the floor toward him, firing her last salvo.

He dodged aside.

''You move quicker than a snake,'' she said as the tone sounded.

He froze. He watched her but could read nothing as she went to the gravity control. She switched it back to point seven and they continued. Surely she couldn't have guessed his identity. Were her words on purpose or merely a common metaphor?

Reubin decided her comment held no deeper meaning. He admired the flesh which was appearing through her costume in great gaping blue bits. He planned his next shots, deciding to make the game last as long as possible. No more zero or two gees.

"Pizza and beer?" Alex said.

"I bribed the cook," Reubin said.

It was midafternoon and they'd managed to cleanse the stains—supposedly no more involved than using soap and water, but Reubin always found that some remained. Under the fingernails. In the crook of the elbow or knee.

"Big spender," she accused, wrapping a string of cheese around the slice in her hand. "I can pay my own way."

He shrugged. She was saying that he was a mercenary on the run, bailing out of the mess on Karg with only the clothes on his back. And that she was a high government official with a commensurate salary and/or other holdings with which she could adequately afford to pay her own way.

"I'm taking the Change anyway," he said.

"Haven't you heard? You *can* take it with you."

"I heard."

She looked at him over the mug of beer. "You are a study of contradictions, Reubin Flood."

He drank his own beer.

"A real man of mystery," she continued.

He shrugged again and felt self-conscious as if that was all he'd been doing.

"If you're taking the Change, I guess the past is no longer important."

"It's gone," he agreed. "Not worth going over anyway."

"Sure."

He was uncomfortable. He didn't want to talk about his past. Nor admit to the dormant killer serpent deep within him. He was going to take the Change and the past would no longer matter again. On the other hand, her interest was certainly promising. He knew himself to be a cold man, one who usually didn't respond to a woman without long exposure to one. Alex was different. Why now? Now that he'd severed his ties and was going to take the Change? Could he postpone the Change? No. Madness and death would follow.

"I've been up front with you," Alex said with more than a little zing in her voice.

"You have," he said. "Actually, I'm wanted in every sector of the Federation."

"For mass murder, no doubt," she said. Before he could respond, she went on. "I saw you come on board. You can and have killed. But I don't believe you would do so unless it was absolutely necessary to your survival. Or perhaps with some higher purpose."

"Tell me about your daughter," he said. He cursed himself for a bumbling fool. That awkward line about being wanted was amateurish. And he'd long since reconciled the deaths and, though some considered it mass murder, he did not.

"Here. I've got a holo-chip in my wristcomp." She punched tiny keys on her wristcomp and a holo appeared alongside the pitcher of beer. "Tique," Alex said. The holo showed a woman with auburn hair. She had the sensuous body of her mother. The tiny head swiveled to the right and an eye winked. Then the holo recycled and began again. After the next wink, Alex snapped it off. "Short for Tequilla. Tequilla Sovereign."

"She is truly attractive. She takes after her mother," Reubin said.

"Why thank you, Reubin."

"Her father?"

"Her father took the Change twenty years ago, so she's just out of the first stage." Alexandra's face softened. "It's been eighty years, but I still remember her babysoftness. I'd never borne a daughter before—only sons, so the experience was unique. We grew quite close over the years."

"You didn't take the Change with him?"

She looked at Reubin. She understood that he knew she hadn't taken the Change else she wouldn't be here. "It had about run its course. It was the best way to part." She hesitated and Reubin could tell she was fighting some inner battle. "My daughter and I didn't want to part. And at the time my job was new and important to me." The Change, taken without your spouse, was automatic divorce.

"I can tell Tequilla was your choice of names." Reubin smiled.

"It was that or get a tattoo."

"Oh," he said, remembering the last tatters of blue-stained paper clinging to her body earlier. "Would have been a shame to cover such natural beauty."

Her look matched his boldness. "You have a way with words."

Again he felt uncomfortable. Other people were coming into the dining room now, looking jealously at the pizza and beer.

He looked into her eyes and saw it. "Well, Silver Girl. I no longer feel awkward. Thank you, madam." She knew what she was doing.

"No charge."

His hand went to her head, threaded through gossamer silver hair, and scraped a smudge of blue from behind her earlobe.

They sat in the viewing lounge. Since the bubble which capsuled the *Al Latalia* was opaque for transpace, there was nothing to see. Thus the lounge was empty.

Alex was silent, looking into the murk between the spaceliner and its bubble. Reubin appreciated the fact that she didn't need conversation; sharing silence mirrored his own feelings of the moment.

He wondered what was so different about Alexandra. Something undefinable attracted him to her; not specifically the comfortable silence, not their compatibility, not her good looks. Something.

Beware.

That was it. On his elementary level, Habu sensed something, maybe something instinctive which threatened the serpent. Was Habu jealous? No. Habu usually exhibited only basic emotions, and those were mostly geared to his survival mechanism. Yet Reubin sensed Habu's disapproval. The fact highlighted Reubin's awareness of that difference in Alex.

You'll never know the answer unless you ask the question, he told himself. "Alex?"

She turned toward him, a far away look in her eyes.

Concerned about being blunt and too forward, he stumbled for words. "Um. Look. There's something extraordinary about you. I can sense it. What *is* it about you?" He felt as awkward as a kid on his first date.

She leaned back, raised a knee and rested her foot to the seat cushion. She circled her knee with locking arms. Her face was framed with silver hair. "Me, too. It's like being a freak at a side show—"

Reubin knew immediately. "Are you really?"

They were called "Original Earthers" or "Olde Earthers." So few remained that they didn't advertise the fact. People thought Original Earthers rather clannish—which they weren't because they seldom gathered. And when they did, they were careful to avoid arousing resentments. Reubin remembered bitterly the pogroms on Tsuruga. He ripped his attention away from the past and back to the present.

"I am." She was nodding enthusiastically. "I should have figured you out sooner, Reubin, but your mercenary trappings hid it from me. People can just look at you and know you're different, far out of the ordinary."

Again they fell silent.

Reubin thought about what she'd said. He knew he was different. Sometimes he couldn't help physically reacting to something Habu had said or done. Another mask: being an Original Earther helped mask Habu.

Most of the Original Earthers were now dead. They had selected death over continuation of life through the Change and the Long Life Institute and its processes.

Centuries wore them down. They suicided. Most just lost interest in living. But not Reubin. Not with Habu deep inside him, Habu and his survival compulsion. Reubin didn't know whether he'd be alive today without Habu's internal drive preventing him from taking any activity such as suicide in order to die. He did know, without wondering, that he would be long dead, killed in action or captured by those who wanted Habu dead—there were individuals as well as governments who wanted Habu dead—without Habu's survival instinct and his killing persona.

Being an Original Earther made Alex Sovereign all the more special. She must have some personal drive, a strength over and above that of a normal human, to keep her going so long. She could be like Reubin himself, one who took to the Long Life treatments well.

"How long?" she asked the ritual question.

Reubin smiled and refused to give the traditional answer "Damn near forever." Instead, he said, "I don't really know. I've done so much traveling through transpace, I lost count of the math a long time ago. My rough guess would be something in the neighborhood of twelve hundred Fed standard years. But it could be as high as two thousand. At any rate, I've undergone the Change maybe twelve times."

She was nodding, her chin bouncing off her knee. "I'll never understand the mechanics. Surely, I've stayed on planets I've helped pioneer or grow into self-sufficiency longer than you have. I was fortunate in the worlds they sent me to. Generally, I stayed past the mandatory requirement I owed the Long Life Institute." She paused. "Just like Snister now. Eighty-five years. My time lines are straighter, easier to figure. Ten changes."

The natural attraction he'd felt for her was growing, and growing quickly. It's been so long, he thought.

"How many years has it been since you encountered another one of us?" she asked.

"Too long. Since the beginning of the Change before this one."

She whistled. "A dwindling few, no?"

"Yes." It was like an exclusive club, being an Original Earther. Of course, by definition, that club would be spread out over the entire Federation, and heading farther as the frontier expanded on all sides. "Where were you from?"

"Part of the North American Federation," she said. "Canada."

"I know it." Though he'd been born well before they ever had a North American Federation. "I'm from Virginia." He still remembered foggy mornings and varicolored leaves and mountains and crisp, clean air.

Reubin felt rejuvenated. Thus it wasn't difficult to force an unhappy and disapproving Habu farther back. He had more success controlling Habu than he could wish for; that success made him feel closer to Alex.

But, like him, she had a reserved attitude. They became closer, but did not discuss the past.

Maybe Reubin wanted her companionship too much. Maybe it was his overactive imagination. Maybe it was his chilling thought as they left the lounge. He realized that Alex bore a certain resemblance to his massacred wife. She'd been from Olde Earthe and had died on Tsuruga. Her high forehead, a turn of her shoulder, her quick smile.

The realization was so intense, the image so vivid, that it triggered Habu.

Habu shot to the surface poised, ready to kill.

It stopped Reubin physically as he stepped into the corridor.

Alex continued on for a few meters until she realized he wasn't with her. She turned. She saw his face. "Reubin? What's wrong?" She came back to him.

Habu was clouding his consciousness.

–*Goddamn it, leave me alone!* Reubin breathed deeply.

Habu peered about, questing for control, looking for the enemy, an enemy, any enemy. Reubin felt adrenaline gallop through his body. He would pay later for any movement now. His body could move superfast, faster even than the human body was designed to go. Such speed and extra strength was difficult to handle unless Habu was in total control. His human persona could handle it, but cautiously, by moving in an exaggerated slow motion. He froze himself as Alex stopped next to him.

Where is the enemy?

–There is none. Go back. Do not interfere.

No.

–We are on a starship. In transpace. You know that. Take no action, for you will kill us all. Reubin fought for control. He ran a biofeedback operation to cleanse himself of the adrenaline. The concentration helped him to shut Habu out. He was winning the battle. Habu retreated, still emanating disapproval of the woman.

"Reubin? Tell me. What's wrong? Are you all right?" Alex was looking with concern into his eyes.

She touched his arm and he had to restrain himself from jerking away and hurting them both. A few more moments, just a few more.

She watched the struggle going on within him and grimaced in sympathy. "It passes." Her voice was reassuring.

She'd mistaken his symptoms. She thought he was going through the mind-bending mental torture which occurs when you haven't had a Change in too long. When you were overdue for the Change, the pressure built and built and ripped your brain apart with excruciating pain. It was why people suicided.

"Sss—okay," he managed to get out.

"I'll comm a medic for a painkiller," she said and moved to a wall comm unit.

"No, pleasse. I'll be all right in a minute." He moved slowly to dissipate some of the accumulated energy.

Ironically, he realized that pressure, in fact, was building within his mind, reinforcing the point that he was overdue for the Change. But it wasn't bad. Yet.

When he recovered, he went to the recreation deck and ran for two hours on the treadmill. He set the machine on the maximum resistance and at a forty-five degree angle. It was the equivalent of running uphill with twice your own body weight.

As he ran, Alex sat and watched him.

Occasionally, people would come over and observe, marveling at the almost impossible physical feat. Reubin ignored them. The more he ran, the more energy he burned. Sweat rained from his body and with each drop he was more and more free of Habu. He was purging himself of adrenaline inspired energy and at the same time of Habu.

Alex got tired of watching him and worked out on weight training machines while he finished up.

"I need a beer," he said when he was done.

"You need to replace fluids," she told him.

"Make it protein beer, hold the alcohol, then." While emotionally and physically drained, he felt like his old self.

"I've read of therapeutic effects of inordinate physical exertion," Alex said, "but that's more than I can handle. Did it really work to relieve the pressure?"

"Yess," he said.

The romance progressed.

Being Original Earthers brought Reubin and Alex closer together. Reubin overheard the purser calling them "very conspirational."

Reubin decided that Alex Sovereign was hiding something. Or didn't want to address something. No matter how much she discussed the past, it was her current life to which she referred. Nothing about her previous lives, if any, prior to her last Change and other Changes before that. It was common courtesy and protocol not to inquire too deeply into previous lives.

Also, there were little things. Alex was highly intelligent. Reubin detected a hint of dissatisfaction with her work; he thought that some problems had occurred lately in her job. But he didn't ascribe too much importance to these thoughts because she was a government minister, and in any government—especially in a high position, there is bureaucratic infighting, political pressure, cliques, cronyism. Reubin always thought that governments should be run as businesses under the free enterprise system.

On the other hand, he liked and respected her. Her values were similar to his, her judgment faultless. Reubin respected her privacy. After all, *he* was hiding something and did not wish her to pry into his past—and she hadn't.

All of which made Reubin sad—for once—that he was changing lives again. Another giant step from his past. While there were ways you could trick the Long Life Institute, when they gave you the Change, they arranged your passage to new or even soon-to-be pioneered planets. This was their basic charter, and one of the reasons governments seldom tried to interfere in LLI business.

But no matter what he did or where he went, he could never, ever lose Habu.

Reubin had no answers. He had arranged passage to the sector capital, Webster's, where the liner was heading. He had business (mostly financial arrangements) to take care of before he took the Change. Alex would tranship back to Snister.

The passion of their affair surprised Reubin. He was happier than he'd been in centuries. Not only was Alex Sovereign compatible with him sexually, but they shared an intellectual niche which made him comfortable and frightened him at the same time.

Frightened him because he didn't want to lose her. And he was due to take the Change.

He was busily scheming how to outwit the LLI again when Alex surprised him as he'd never been surprised before.

One shipboard day, they were floating in his cabin at zero gravity shooting rubber bands at a reading disk floating in the middle of the room.

"And they say the ancients were the best writers," Alex said.

Reubin's next shot scored and the disk spun aside.

"*The Last of the Mohicans.* Too bad that didn't occur one generation earlier."

"Don't blame the Mohicans, Rube—"

"Reubin."

"—it's the writer." Alex floated around collecting rubber bands.

"How in hell could such trash last so many centuries and remain acclaimed literature?" Reubin scratched his head. "Trumped up plot, illogical choreography, major characters with the brains of dinosaurs. And I still don't understand that business about the fog and the bodies and the lake and—"

Alex came back toward him, grasping his knee to steady herself in midair. All that happened was that they both began a slow spin. "The whole thing's a matter of theme of national definition. See Hawkeye as a messiah, or a legendary mythical persona, such as Audie Murphy, Captain Danjou, Habu."

He winced and grunted.

Habu mythical? Not when he was alive in this very room. It was always disquieting when people talked about Habu in front of him.

But her next words made him forget. "Reubin?"

He wrapped a rubber band around the base of his thumb and snapped the end on the tip of his pointy finger. "Um?"

"If I take the Change with you, would you marry me honest and true and could we go out to the frontier together and pioneer and explore and live happily ever after together?"

After a moment of looking into her eyes, he said, "You'd do that?"

"In a Manhattan minute."

"No questions asked?" he said, face burning.

"I already know what I need to know," she said contentedly.

"Your daughter? Tique?"

"She's been taking care of herself for sixty odd years now. It's the relationship I'd miss." She paused. "We've some friction now. She thinks I'm a corporate mogul

who rapes the land. I think she's an eco-freak. But regardless . . .''

He let out the breath he realized he'd been holding.
He grasped her hand and steadied them by a handhold
of the ceiling. "I haven't felt like this in two or three
hundred years." The more Changes some went through,
the more precipitate their decisions. The more they were
wont to do offbeat things. Reubin hoped this romance
wasn't a result of too many Changes. He wanted it to
be real.

"Me neither. You gonna answer my question?"

"I love you, Silver Girl." His words surprised even
himself.

"Me, too, Mystery Man. I want to spend a lifetime or
two with you."

"I suspect it'll be an adventure," he said.

In the big lounge with a hundred wealthy tourists from
the sector capital looking on, Reubin Flood and Alexandra Sovereign were married.

Captain Kent, in full uniform, said, "Do you, Reubin
Flood, take this woman to be your lawful wedded wife,
in this life, through a Change or two, unless necessary?"

"Yes, I do," said Reubin.

Captain Kent turned to Alex. "You don't have to do
this, my dear."

"I want to."

"Do you, Alexandra Felicity Partmandahl Sovereign,
of your own free will, take this man to be your lawful
husband, in this life, and through a Change or two if you
don't get divorced?"

"I do."

"By the power vested in me by the Federation and its
laws, I now pronounced you matrimonially linked. Steward? Champagne, if you will."

Habu observed the ceremony unhappily. Reubin was
able to force him back into hibernation.

Alex was to return to Snister, wind up her affairs, bid
her daughter good-bye, and join Reubin on Webster's,
where they would go to the LLI together.

Reubin had some business of his own to tend to on Webster's. While he'd been essentially a nomad for the last twenty years or so, there were still things he had to do: consolidate bank accounts, prepare false identities in case of emergencies, and illegally access the LLI computers. The latter was for him to use programs he'd installed secretly when helping to build the system. He was able to add his new fake identities and their histories to the LLI database, thus effectively covering his trail. For a few centuries, his Habu instinct had warned him when the Fed authorities occasionally were closing in on him. He didn't know if the infamous Habu would be reason enough for the Fed to prevail upon the LLI to help them find him legally or illegally; if so, his preemptive raid into the LLI database would preclude that and his trail would dead-end. Another reason for sneaking into the LLI system was that he could preselect his destination afterward—if he wanted to.

While the LLI process could be accomplished anywhere, it was done on sector capitals so that mandatory one-way transport to the various frontiers could be arranged. Occasionally, for those who could afford the LLI treatment and could not afford the expense of the trip to the sector capitals throughout the Federation, the LLI maintained roving ships that made planetfall all over the galaxy at random intervals. Or a local or planetary government could request one of the ships by paying costs. Sometimes this was accomplished to reduce population.

Two vastly different things contributed to people living many centuries.

The first, and the easiest for Reubin to understand, was that because of star travel, people zapping back and forth throughout the explored portion of the galaxy, people aged differently. Added to that, medicine and preventative aging (PA) contributed to long life.

But the major contributor to long life was Silas Comfort Swallow. Silas Swallow invented FTL—or his Project I did. Swallow controlled it. Being the first to come up with FTL, he was the first to explore the galaxy near Olde Earthe. He also sold FTL to most of the rest of the Earthe. For cash and a percentage. He became the wealthiest man ever known at any time in the history of man. Every off-Earthe enterprise paid into Swallow's accounts. He also owned all the nearby planets which could be settled by humans. More money.

He could afford the research. He spawned Project II, allegedly based on the mythical man who never aged, or aged in reverse, Pembroke Wyndham.

Reubin knew a few more of the particulars of Project II than most citizens because of his minor consultant role in setting up the resultant Long Life Institute after Project II had developed the formulae for insuring that long life.

Hormones give chemical orders to the body. At that time, there were only forty-five known hormones. Endocrinologists were able to locate either four new hormones or four synthetic hormones within the system of Pembroke Wyndham. Additionally, they found that Wyndham possessed *no* free-rads. Free radicals, Reubin understood, were an atom or a group of atoms as parts of molecules, which contained one or more unpaired electrons. Free-rads disrupted molecular activity which the body needed to function properly. The example Reubin remembered was that free-rads damaged DNA which raised probability of out of control mutations or cellular divisions—cancer. They caused wrinkles in skin. Cataracts. Impeded the body's immune system.

Something about Wyndham's system. The researchers allegedly synthesized hormones from his pituitary, thymus, gonads.

Reubin wondered if Wyndham was still alive after all that testing.

At any rate, Reubin knew that the bigger and most important secret in the known human history was the recipe of the synthetic hormones. The secret of long life was locked within the Long Life Institute.

With as many people as possible receiving the Long Life treatment, the Change, life itself had altered. Ages were no longer important. You were "Young," born, growing up, starting a new life. The next stage was called "Intermediate," something a scientist would think up, nothing creative to match the new realities. Just about everybody was Intermediate. Reubin, Alex, even Tique. In this stage bodies were reparable and women were still able to bear children.

The third and last stage of life was known as "Indeterminate," when someone had been around and through so many Changes that signs of aging showed, and weren't reversible. This happened to people at different times in their lives. The body began failing here and there, no longer receptive even to transplants of cloned parts. Women no long could bear children. At the end, people suicided, an easy-go proposition these days.

People aged differently. Some lived twice as long as others. It was a matter of personal genetics and how well the treatments took. Reubin thought he was probably an extreme example of this. He didn't want to consider what Habu's contribution to his long life was.

However, anywhere from eighty to one hundred and twenty plus Fed-standard years, most people's brains could not function sanely with the accumulation of knowledge, experience, and memories. The LLI treated these symptoms and people were able to renew their lives. It was part of the deal with LLI. Nobody knew whether the treatment was separate or a part of the original hormonal treatment. Another LLI secret. So, to live longer than your brain could stand and before it went insane, you had to have LLI treatments.

The treatments allowed the mind to store all the excess information, experience, knowledge, memories. Some theorized the treatments merely opened more access to the unused but available space in the mind. Unfortunately, the process rejuvenated him physiologically. It never altered his fragmented persona. Personality remained unchanged. Reubin often wondered if the process didn't open enough extra room in his mind to fit Habu. He also thought that if Habu was a mental defect in his mind, then it well could be that the process reinforced that defect.

Silas Swallow was a visionary. He built the LLI charter around this fact. You had to donate all your worldly goods to LLI (thus enhancing the LLI position) and LLI would send you off to the frontier, expanding man's universe. You'd stay for a predetermined length of time, dictated by the situation and conditions. After a while, you got your money back from LLI as shares in the Institute. So if the LLI failed, the entire structure of the Federation would crumble. Everything was designed to further the LLI.

In actuality, most people taking the LLI treatment were ready to begin new lives. If not, they went mad, or suicided, or died.

But Silas Swallow had insured the survival of humanity by forcing its expansion to new worlds.

Expansion, almost by definition, brought on technological progress, keeping humanity technologically equipped to further its reach to the stars. Sounds poetic, Reubin thought, then remembered Karg and wondered if humanity hadn't had a few too many failures along the way.

Reubin would take the Change and thus be good for another hundred years or so. And be able to remember his past lives. Alex would take the Change with him and they would begin a new life together, just as Silas Swallow had foreseen would become the custom.

Reubin and Alex. Reubin wondered where they would be sent. It made life seem worth all he'd gone through before.

Reubin and Alexandra together. He'd really looked forward to it.

Yeah, sure.

Webster's Departure Central was full of people going everywhere in the known galaxy.

As a planetary minister, Alex was accorded VIP treatment. From VIP processing, a single aircar was to deliver her to her ship.

Reubin and Alex had said their good-byes earlier. Reubin gave her a perfunctory kiss on the cheek. "See you soon, Silver Girl."

"High mountains and raging seas and bleak space could not keep me away, Mystery Man." She searched his eyes one last time. "Until then."

Yeah, sure.

The raging beast within him grew again upon the remembrance. The killer serpent threatened to burst through and take control.

4: TIQUE

She paced her apartment, worrying and deciding what to wear tonight.

She had taken Reubin Flood to the shuttle at Port of Snister two days ago. *The Lady of Angorra* had left the system thirty-four hours ago.

Since then, Reubin had neither called her nor left a message. Had the possibility he raised about the government not allowing him to leave been correct? Had someone intercepted him? How would she find out? She thought about calling Fels Nodivving, but decided against it.

Bilge, she thought, then changed her mind.

Who was Reubin Flood anyway? He'd told her a little about meeting Mother on Karg and their ensuing romance. But that was it. Other than the implied military ability; he had served on Karg as a mercenary. He'd told her what happened, but not who he was. Not of the sorrow he'd hinted at, nor of his strangeness. She knew he possessed an odd implant—or so he said. At one time he had something or other to do with computer systems, possibly in the genesis of the Long Life Institute. But she still didn't know who he was. A mystery, she decided. She'd asked him about himself, but he'd neatly deflected the question into a quick outline of his and Mother's romance on the starliner.

Tique sat at her makeup console. She toyed with a composite to see how it would look on her before she applied it. She didn't like makeup, but a dab or two strategically applied and a little color kept up with conventions.

Before she'd left him at Passport Control, she'd decided that Reubin was being paranoid. His innuendos, half-charges, and suppositions were shotgunned, void of proof.

On the other hand, she liked him. Something she couldn't yet articulate drew her to him. He was strange, very different, at times even haunted.

People had swarmed about them at the entrance of Passport Control. The shuttle would be full. Tique felt awkward. She didn't know how to respond to Reubin, so she decided to let him take the lead. After all, he had been her mother's husband, albeit briefly. She found she no longer resented his intrusion into her life and her grief. She remembered the unspoken, clumsy accommodation they'd reached. Maybe because of their shared experience on the roof.

Reubin leaned forward and murmured to her. "Remember what I said."

Tique nodded, aware of his overwhelming maleness. If he returned to Snister, he'd be disguised as somebody else with appropriate travel and identity papers. Tique didn't know how that was done, but she was certain Reubin could do so.

He stayed close to her for an extra second and Tique thought he was going to kiss her good-bye. But he pulled away and grasped her hand. His hand was strong and dry. He gave a quick squeeze, a sympathetic smile, and walked through to Passport Control.

Tique had wondered if she'd ever see Reubin Flood again. He was a strange man. Was he in danger as he'd speculated? She tried to watch him, but there were too many people in Passport Control. When passengers checked in, they went through a farther door and down corridors.

She'd have to wait for his call from the starship.

Now here it was two days later and she didn't know what the hell to do.

She finished her face. The man in the storm seemed so very far away.

Perhaps she could make some inquiries.

The place to start might be this evening. Right now she was waiting for Josephine Neff.

Josephine Neff, the Interior Minister. Tique wasn't certain what to make of her sudden celebrity status. Tique knew Josephine personally as an acquaintance of her mother's, but Tique never saw Josephine Neff in her own social circles. Once last year, though, Josephine had judged a fog-shaping contest which Tique had entered. Her work with water had taught her how to develop and use heat differential off water. While she hadn't won, Josephine Neff had awarded her an "Honorary Mention."

All Tique's friends, especially those in the Cuyas Fog-Shaping Club, jestingly accused Tique of improper influence because her mother was Wormwood Minister and Josephine Neff the Interior Minister. But that had been fun: honorary mention in a worldwide competition. Plus, Tique hadn't been fog-shaping as long as most of the others. Her fog-shaping was more mathematically derived as she'd used the computer and computer models more than others. The fog-shaping went right along with her other passion: nature.

Which made their engagement this evening that much more strange. What could the Interior Minister have in common with Tique Sovereign? Tique was known for her opposition to the Company's indiscriminate planting of wormwood. They were deforming the world, killing off animal and plant species by the dozens. It was turning Snister into a giant greenhouse; already rainfall averages were climbing—and this on top of the almost constant rain now. Tique felt strongly that Wormwood, Inc. ought to return to harvesting nature-grown wormwood trees only. Mass-reproducing the rare trees did not justify the ecodamage.

She was aware of the odd contrast of her beliefs and her vocation. It had been one of the few areas of disagreement with her mother. Josephine, too, was aware of this.

Maybe Josephine wanted to offer a belated sympathy about her mother's death? Perhaps. When Josephine had called and suggested that Tique join her at the Corona, Tique had tried to beg off. Barbarity wasn't on her menu. But Josephine had insisted. And one doesn't lightly turn down the second most powerful person in the government—and therefore the Company.

Tique saw it was nearly time and took a bubblevator down ten levels to the landing. She told Security whom she was expecting and paced alongside the landing ramp.

The Security man in the control bubble waved at her and a long, fancy aircar slid onto the landing grid and came to a stop. A side door swished open and Tique climbed in.

She joined Josephine in the back as the door behind her closed and the car accelerated and lifted into the air.

While the car had no markings, it was obviously a Company car with a Company chauffeur.

Josephine held out her gloved hand as Tique settled down. "Hello, my dear."

"Josephine. Thank you for inviting me."

"Think nothing of it." Josephine spoke almost in a whisper. Tique had always thought her voice affected, a mere tool which caused the listener to pay closer attention. In her high-level position, though, she could get away with it. Josephine was dressed in formal evening wear, ruffles and lace and full length skirt. Tique had dressed in basic black which could be construed as still mourning, or semi-formal. It would pass okay at the Corona.

"It is my understanding," said Josephine, "that you seldom attend the Corona."

Tique had to strain to pick up her words and wondered how she would be able to hear the Minister at the Corona with all the people and the shouting and cheering and jeering.

Tique shrugged. "It's just not something I'm comfortable with." Actually, she'd never attended.

Josephine smiled. "Many people share your aversion. Yet the Corona serves a necessary function. I'm not talking about pabulum for the masses which doubtless some blame on the Company.''

The Corona. A stadium outside Cuyas holding a couple of hundred thousand people. Activities broadcast throughout the world.

The old, old, old idea: take a man sentenced to death, put him in the middle of the stadium and two hundred thousand people and tell him he can have his freedom if—

If. If he can outfight other prisoners. Defeat wild animals drugged into a killing state. Outwit computer-directed killing machines. Sure, sometimes they allow someone to win free to keep the mystique of the Corona intact; there had to be some hope of success, the one-way ticket off planet was a great enticement. Those who had lived through the ordeal had ostensibly beaten the odds; however, the odds could be manipulated, opponents and beasts drugged. Tique thought that most planets probably had their own version of the Corona.

Tique became aware that Josephine was studying her face. "You're thinking the Company uses the Corona for its own purposes."

Tique turned her head to hear Josephine better. "The Company, just like people, has flaws." Tique was trying to be diplomatic. It occurred to her that she might be undergoing some type of loyalty test. Which didn't make much sense. Who cared what a lowly aquadynamucist thought? Tique could make a computer system dance and hum a tune and design her models, but her loyalty to the Company shouldn't matter. She did her job. Wormwood trees grew, were harvested, and sold. Regardless of her concern about the fate of nature.

"Quite delicately put, my dear. Your mother was quite a bit more outspoken."

"I know."

"Yet Alex climbed the Wormwood corporate ladder to the ministerial level. She was quite good at her job."

"She was," Tique agreed. Why are you telling me this?

"On the other hand," Josephine waved a hand negligently, "your mother was a strong willed and independent woman." Josephine paused for a moment, all the while staring into Tique's eyes. "But it has been brought to our attention that Alex Sovereign held out on us." Her voice trailed off.

Tique wished she knew what Josephine was talking about. Though, it was possible what Reubin said—

"It occurs to me," Josephine continued, "that your mother might have left with you something that didn't belong in her portfolio as Minister of Wormwood."

"What do you mean?" Her stomach rolled and Tique knew it wasn't because the aircar was dipping into a descending turn.

Josephine pitched her voice stronger. "A legacy, for instance. Some record, recorded, written, spoken, concerning past projects."

There it was. Tique scrunched her face as if thinking deeply. Josephine's words lay like curdled milk in the air between them. She lifted her eyebrows curiously and shook her head. "Nothing I know of. The Personnel Office ought to have records of what Mother did for the Company through the years." She'd responded as if misunderstanding Josephine to deflect from her actual knowledge, that which she'd garnered from Reubin Flood.

"There is some information," Josephine said looking out, "which we'd like to obtain. I am certain that if you ran across it you would recognize its importance. Further, I am certain you would share that information with us."

"You're sounding very mysterious," Tique said, trying to say what she would be saying if she didn't know anything.

"We're almost to the Corona." Josephine smiled, but her eyes remained cold and penetrating. "Perhaps the stimulation of the contests will trigger your memory."

"If you say so, Josephine."

"We can talk later."

It was becoming obvious to Tique that she should be alarmed. But she wasn't. Mother was dead. Reubin had disappeared. The person second only in power to Fels Nodivving was questioning her bluntly.

Maybe Reubin had forgotten to call, or the ship's comm section refused to send his message. Maybe not. She'd figure out how to approach it diplomatically with Josephine after the contests.

The car settled on the Corona's VIP ramp and soon Tique found herself in the VIP suite. The room had a bubble front which overlooked the arena and had the best view in the stadium. She'd never been here before and looking out over the crowd, she felt a group anticipation, a gut-level expectancy. The place was packed.

Josephine nodded to a man at the rear of the suite. He stood at a command console. Tique guessed VIPs must require immediate access to communications and control and data systems at all times. The man keyed a speaker. "Proceed." So they'd delayed starting the activities until Josephine Neff arrived. Rank Hath Its Privileges.

Josephine walked to the front and sat in one of the command chairs. She waved Tique over. "You don't want to miss anything."

Tique followed dutifully and sat on Josephine's left. The bubble was so thin it was almost as if it wasn't there. Atop the stadium at each cardinal point, giant viewscreens sat so that people not close could see as if they were standing next to the action.

She knew what was to come. While she held no brief for murderers and criminals who volunteered for the contests, she still did not approve. But it was entertainment, and cheap at that, she realized. She began to understand. Hundreds of thousands of tickets were sold each week, almost all profit. Not to mention the revenues of viewing it all worldwide on video.

On the console to the right of her seat, Josephine punched a code. "A slave unit to the master console," she explained, tossing her head in the direction of the command console. "I have to let Operations know where I am almost every minute." She turned her head back to the arena.

Tique wasn't surprised. The top government officials

in the entire world, not to mention Company officials, must have their command and control elements. A similar console sat to the left of her own command chair.

Josephine held up her hand.

The man at the rear of the suite came forward. "Madam?"

"Wine," Josephine said.

Tique saw the man leaning toward the Interior Minister. He was used to her soft tones.

"Red," Josephine said. To Tique, she said, "Red for blood. Would you care for something?"

Tique didn't want to witness the following action, but she knew she was being forced to. "Tequila," she said. "On ice."

The man withdrew.

Tique saw activity beginning below in the bright glare of lights.

The steward returned with their drinks, placing them on the table between the chairs.

"That will be all," Josephine told him. "I'll call if we need you."

He bowed slightly and left through the rear door.

"Three challenges this evening," came a muted voice, obviously a public address announcer.

Josephine leaned forward. "Get on with it!" Then she seemed to realize her position and leaned back. "I understand they've come up with a beast called a snarv, from a perfectly barbaric planet named Bear Ridge, wherever that is. A natural killer. Ah, it's about time."

Tique turned her attention to the arena. It reminded her of a clip she'd seen about the ancient sport of bull-fighting.

A side panel swung up and an animal she could never have imagined appeared in the opening. It slunk out into the arena on six legs. The giant vision screens showed its eyes darting about; they chilled Tique. A long snout topped a mouth full of razorlike teeth which angled backward toward the beast's throat. The six legs were powerful and the feet showed a gripping ability, telling Tique the animal was most likely a mountain creature. The short legs gave it a crocodilian advantage. Rock-gray fur rippled. The beast was silent and thus more menacing. Tique knew that microphones were aimed at the combatants to provide the accompanying sound to the audience, both at the Corona and those watching on television.

"A murderer," said an announcer. "His name is Hosiah Hence."

Another door opened and a man stumbled out. He appeared dazed. Like all combatants here, he wore only shorts and boots and his head had been shaved. He looked at the sword in his hand and surprise etched onto his flat face. The camera got a close-up shot as Hence saw the snarv. Tique read desperation in his face as Hence swung the sword tentatively and awkwardly. He stepped to the side against the wall.

The snarv eyed the man and crouched even lower.

Hosiah Hence spat with determination, stepped toward the snarv once, then twice.

Suddenly, quicker than Tique could follow, the snarv was airborne and Hosiah Hence was gutted by talons, half his shoulder torn off by the snarv's rows of murderous teeth.

The crowd drew a collective breath and emitted shouts of surprise and awe.

Tique tasted sour bile rising in her throat and into the back of her mouth.

The snarv crouched atop the corpse and surveyed the crowd far above it.

Tique noticed Josephine. The woman had pushed her face up against the bubble and was glued to the action. Her jaw was slack and her eyes gleamed. Tique thought that she could have left the room and Josephine wouldn't have noticed.

Another door opened and a robot snaked out, attached clamps to Hence's body and began to drag it off. The snarv sniffed the mechanical servbot and roared a challenge. The snarv leaped upon the robot and carried it to the ground. Its paws slashed at the machine and Tique saw scratches in the metal.

The snarv returned to its prey and the robot armed its way upright and rolled out of the arena.

A door on the far side of the arena opened and another man strode out.

"A murderer and repeat rapist," intoned the announcer. "Donald Simon."

The man carried a double-bladed ax.

Tique shifted her vision to a screen to view him close up. Her breath caught and her face began burning. Reubin! Reubin Flood! My God—

Tique's eyes swung wildly around and saw Josephine Neff watching her with amusement.

"Josephine," Tique said, alarm shooting through her, "that's Reubin Flood. There's been some kind of mistake—"

Josephine raised heavily etched eyebrows. "Has there?"

It all fell into place. Tique understood now. Reubin had been right. He hadn't been able to answer their questions, maybe because of his implanted biochip, so they had sentenced him to death. The interplay between Reubin and Fels Nodivving had been a deadly one, she now realized. And they couldn't afford to let Reubin off planet.

Tique remembered the quiet confidence Reubin had exuded. She took a deep breath and spoke the most difficult words she'd ever spoken: "Well, I *thought* it looked like Reubin Flood. Now I'm not so sure." She gave what she hoped was a nonchalant smile but which felt weak and ineffective.

"Maybe, maybe not," Josephine said. "I'm certain that you would remember if it really *were* him—just as you would remember anything your mother might have told you. What I referred to earlier."

Tique shrugged and her shoulders ached from the act. She doubted she was fooling Josephine one little bit.

Josephine turned to the arena. "Let us watch. There may well be a lesson to be learned."

Tique sank back into the luxurious chair. She wondered if there were any way in which she could help Reubin. Then it occurred to her that she was in danger, too. They were playing a different game with her, obviously. Neither Mother nor Reubin had told them what they sought; that left Tique herself as the final link. Perhaps they feared the same thing would happen to her as had to her mother: death, and thus the end of the trail.

What had been Alexandra Sovereign's secret?

Tique's eyes riveted to the arena, jumping between the screen and Reubin.

He held the ax lightly on his shoulder. His face was dazed as had been that of Hosiah Hence. Drugs?

As if to answer, Josephine said in her whisper, "The drugs wear off. We wouldn't want to cheat the paying customers, would we?"

The snarv still crouched over Hence's body. It made no move toward Reubin.

"The combatant will have to kill the snarv to go on to the next challenge," Josephine said conversationally.

The snarv jumped as if startled.

"Ah," whispered the Interior Minister, "they've shot it with a stimulant."

The snarv tried to bite at its own flank.

Tique watched understanding creep across Reubin's face on the split screen as the side shot showed the snarv trying to twist its short neck enough to bite at something stuck into its right flank. Two of its right paws flailed at the foreign thing.

Reubin wore a simple pair of shorts and boots. His body was sun-browned. His head had been shaved since she'd last seen him, shaved bald like all the other combatants. He certainly looked different than the Reubin Flood she'd known. A wild light appeared in his eyes and Tique thought she could see the realization hit him solidly.

He leaped forward and ran toward the preoccupied snarv.

At the last moment, the snarv noticed him bearing down on it. Its snout whipped around and its teeth glistened in the lights. It started to scurry off the corpse and Reubin launched himself through the air. As he went over the snarv, Reubin sliced the ax down and into the snarv, obviously aiming for its neck. But the snarv had moved and the ax cleaved into its left front foreleg.

The snarv roared in pain, a deep and chilling sound, reaching into Tique's atavistic fear-place.

Reubin landed on his shoulder, rolled in the dust, and came up with the ax held in both hands. His eyes were fierce, totally concentrating. Tique saw no more traces of the drugs.

The snarv attacked Reubin, coming in low where it had the advantage. But its injured front leg made it stagger and Reubin had no time to reposition his ax; he simply thrust the weapon down the snarv's long throat.

The snarv snapped its mouth shut and backed off quickly. Then it stopped and opened its gaping maw and began what Tique could only describe as a series of coughing motions. Blood from the snarv's throat and that from Hosiah Hence expelled from the creature's mouth and splattered Reubin.

Reubin jumped aside, lifted Hence's body, and came up with the slain murderer's sword.

As the snarv barked, trying to remove the ax from its gullet, Reubin slashed at its throat. Ichor erupted and Reubin hacked away.

Then the snarv was dead.

Reubin leaned heavily on the sword. He turned slowly around, surveying the arena as if he hadn't had time to do so before. His breathing was easier. His body gleamed with sweat and blood; dust stuck to the wetness.

Tique thought she saw a satisfied look on his face as he took inventory of the dead snarv. Some sort of metamorphosis was taking place *inside* Reubin Flood.

His eyes searched the crowd and the arena. An anticipatory silence ruled the night.

Reubin flung a defiant single finger at the hundreds of thousands present. His browned body bent and the visual effect was of a serpentine statue. He dropped his hand.

Josephine shivered, her shoulders continuing to vibrate for a moment.

A far door opened and Tique watched in horror as Reubin ignored it. He bent to the dead snarv and pried its mouth open with his sword.

Three gnurls trotted into the arena. While they were herbivores native to Snister, their disposition was to hate and attack anything alive and standing on two legs.

Reubin still did not look up and see them. His arm pulled the ax from the mouth of the snarv. Arm and ax came out crimson and black and green, glistening and deadly.

The three gnurls bounded toward Reubin and circled him as if they'd ganged up on humans before. While their mouths could bite, their teeth were flat for mashing vegetation and could not tear and rip. But their hooves were deadly sharp, nature-designed to cut and scoop ground cover for food. And they were quick, their long legs allowing high leaps and sideways movement.

They began closing in on Reubin Flood.

Reubin twirled the ax in his right hand, spinning it faster and faster until it was a blur.

Swiftly he stepped forward into the path of one of the gnurls. The spinning ax bit into the animal's shoulder and Reubin jumped back as the second gnurl lanced in with its hooves. Reubin ducked and slashed at the underside of the animal's forelegs. The second gnurl collapsed, muscles cut and unable to use its front legs. The first gnurl ran out across the arena spewing blood from its wounded shoulder and screeching a high-pitched whine.

The third gnurl hesitated and then attacked Reubin. Reubin leaped over the second gnurl on the ground and avoided a kick from its rear legs. The third gnurl trotted around its fellow to get at Reubin. Reubin jumped back on the far side of the grounded gnurl, this time dodging snapping jaws. The last gnurl trotted back. Reubin jumped again.

Tique realized she wasn't breathing properly and sat back to catch her breath. Josephine was plastered against the bubble, oblivious to anything outside the arena, eyes locked onto the action.

Reubin was still jumping back and forth, leading the

remaining gnurl back and forth around its downed companion.

Tique's fingers lingered on the console beside her, and she wished she could help Reubin. Though to what end, she did not know.

Reubin began another leap over the fallen gnurl, but pushed himself sideways instead. The third gnurl was turning to run around the dying gnurl one more time and was surprised. Reubin's sword severed most of its head. He stepped aside. His eyes sought the last gnurl, the one he'd wounded. The beast lay dying against the far wall.

Reubin breathed deeply.

He spat at the camera and raised his sword. Slowly, he turned around, challenging the crowd.

Tique didn't understand why Reubin was baiting the crowd. But she didn't blame him. She realized that he knew he wouldn't leave the arena alive.

Jeers and shouts of derision turned to scattered applause and some cheers. Those regulars must realize something extraordinary was happening. After all, the almost naked man in the arena had bested two murderous challenges, and the crowd was beginning to appreciate his accomplishment.

Three men stepped through an opening near Reubin. The door closed in a blink and Tique wondered who was controlling the activities. The three were dressed as Reubin. But all three were heavily armed with an array of weapons: knives, swords, chains, throwing stars; one carried a shield.

Reubin saw them and the crowd inhaled collectively. They were aware of the inequity.

As the announcer began, "Three child-molesters—" Reubin launched his bloody sword like a spear.

The move surprised everyone, especially the new combatants. The sword struck the one holding the throwing stars. The weapon pierced the man's chest and killed him instantly.

"—who gain their freedom if together they best this one man—" Tique couldn't hear the rest over the roar of the crowd.

Reubin attacked. He spun the ax in his right hand again, as he had before. He ran straight for the man with the shield, but shifted toward the other man and changed the arc of the ax. Again surprise was on Reubin's side, and his opponent died, the chains he'd held poised to strike crashing down on his decapitated body.

It seemed to Tique that she'd never seen anyone move so fast. Ever.

The man with the shield waved a sword and backed away in horror. Reubin continued his movement, the ax building momentum again, twisting and flinging the weapon sideways as if its weight were negligible. The weapon clanged onto the shield.

As the frightened man danced aside from the ax, Reubin picked up a chain and swung it around twice, and whipped it about his adversary's legs. The man tripped, his shield banging awkwardly on his stomach. Reubin pounced on him and his arm pistoned twice. The man sank back to the ground unconscious.

Reubin crouched there, apparently trying to regain his breathing, swinging his head to and fro, searching for new threats.

People throughout the crowd climbed to their feet applauding and whistling.

Tique realized Reubin had survived the three challenges. According to the rules, Reubin should be freed. Tique drank from her tequila and it was warm, ice melted. She drank long anyway.

Josephine's mouth hung open. "Magnificent." She seemed to tear herself from the spectacle. She touched the button activating her command console on the right of her chair.

"Operations," said a voice from the speaker.

"Continue as outlined," Josephine said.

"Enter command code," the voice responded.

Josephine punched in NEFF 69696 FFEN. Her eyes flicked back to the arena and Tique read the code on the screen.

"Acknowledged," said Operations.

Josephine turned off her console and scooted up close

to the bubble again, her demeanor reeking of anticipation.

Tique felt a growing horror. She'd faced the shock of Reubin being in the Corona arena. The extent of the conspiracy was still sinking in. She'd seen Reubin sent out to die and acknowledged to herself that he *would* die. She'd watched him win his three challenges and hope had been reborn. What a warrior! She hadn't thought he had it in him, the well dressed man in her apartment, the vulnerable man on her roof pouring his grief into the storm, even though her mother had told her the fantastic tale of his escape on Karg. Now, Tique had just witnessed Josephine Neff pronounce his death sentence. Her empathy went out to him. Frustration built within her. She felt helpless.

From directly underneath the VIP bubble out rumbled the killing machine.

"Slaybot," said the announcer.

The crowd stared in horror. The slaybot was seldom used. No one had ever bested it. Some in the crowd muttered and many booed. The challenger had won his three matches and therefore should be set free.

Reubin definitely had the crowd on his side.

The slaybot moved relentlessly toward Reubin.

Tique had seen enough about the slaybot on various videoshows. It was invincible. Short range antipersonnel laser. Mechanical arms with razor sharp extensions. Tiny, blinding phosphorous flares the size of a thumbnail; these last totally debilitated humans, blinded them, stunned them. The slaybot guided itself via infrared optical sensors and radar.

Reubin rose wearily.

Tique watched his face on the giant screen. Resignation.

Then an amazing transformation swept across Reubin's face. It turned hard. Tique had seen hints of the transformation before, but now there seemed to be a completely different man before her—not the one who started the contest in the arena below; but another who'd been growing a warrior-persona during his combat and was now totally changed into that killing visage. His eyes milked over. Muscles rippled, tendons quivered. His body was fluid in movement.

He lifted a sword from the dust and swiftly drew an elongated S with a burr on the top end.

Tique didn't understand.

Josephine, totally engrossed, whispered to herself, "A striking snake!" and Tique heard. That's what it was.

Reubin ran to the side where two bodies lay. He snatched up several throwing stars, planted his feet, and methodically threw them at the advancing slaybot. He flung them with such force that they smashed the radar scanner on the slaybot. This left the machine with IR senses only.

Immediately, the 'bot fired the short range laser to where Reubin had last been standing.

But he was no longer there. He ran crouched, zigzagging across the arena. He surged and slowed, turning while running. His movements were so fast Tique could barely follow them. His speed was even more than it had been before when she'd thought she'd never seen anyone ever move so fast. Energy beams followed him, but the slaybot couldn't turn or move as fast as Reubin. It ceased fire.

The slaybot rotated and followed at its same inevitable pace, stalking Reubin.

Reubin slowed and the 'bot began to catch up. Just as the laser fired again, Reubin went down in a long roll. He came up with the unconscious man in front of him. He held the man and untangled the chain from the man's legs.

Reubin stumbled toward the slaybot, holding his unconscious previous attacker in front of him. The man was large and heavy. The slaybot's laser snapped out and when the two humans were within range, Reubin tossed the body to the side and knelt. The 'bot swiveled, laser firing, tracking the tumbling body, scorching ground, and finally searing a path across the unfortunate man's hip and stomach.

Meanwhile, Reubin twirled the chain and launched it

at the slaybot. It snagged the machine, and wrapped around it.

Tique saw what Reubin was trying to do. He must know about slaybots, she thought. Part of the metal chain covered the laser portal and deflected the beam. The 'bot immediately extinguished the weapon. It turned to follow Reubin again, pursuit relentless, chain clanking against its left side. Its mechanical arm rose to push at the chain, but was not designed to reach backward sufficiently for the task.

It fired a phosphorous flare at Reubin. At the swish he dived and rolled against a wall, covering his head with his arms.

The bubble in front of Tique opaqued at the height of the brightness and then cleared as the flare died.

Reubin was on his feet, a knife from somewhere in his hand. He stumbled along the wall as if blinded, the slaybot following leisurely.

Reubin again left his feet. He burrowed behind a dead gnurl against the wall as if hoping the slaybot wouldn't find him.

The gnurl trembled as if still alive.

The slaybot trundled up and stopped. Its arms extended forward and down and, with its super sharp instrument, began to slice into the gnurl, as if digging for Reubin.

The gnurl seemed to erupt and Reubin was standing with the large gnurl held over his head, entrails and organs covering him and cascading to the ground. Blood and gore rained. Tique knew that gnurls weighed four plus times that of a large man, yet Reubin lifted this one effortlessly.

Reubin had gutted the gnurl. Why?

As the slaybot repositioned itself, Reubin slammed the gutted gnurl atop the machine, and pulled it down over the 'bot, covering it like a sheath.

Reubin sprinted away.

The cameras remained on the obscenely clad 'bot as its laser fired constantly. It also shot off flares and its extensions jabbed at the dead gnurl.

The animal's carcass kept the flares from going any-where. Flare after flare was expelled and burned brightly between the carcass and the 'bot.

Tique thought she could smell scorched flesh even in the bubble. She'd bet, if nothing else, the flares would burn out the slaybot's IR feature.

It was better than she'd hoped. The heat must have damaged the machine's control components and it simply shut down, no longer firing anything, no longer moving at all. The flesh of the gnurl continued to sizzle out there in the arena, and its hide curled and burned.

Reubin stood in the middle of the arena, gesturing. Come on, send something else. His face and animal be-havior were foreign to Tique. He was alien, not human.

He returned to the gnurl-covered slaybot and bent to retrieve something from the dust.

He lifted a bloody, pulpy thing high above his head.

"The heart," Josephine said, voice clear and filled with wonder and awe.

She must be attuned somehow to Reubin, Tique thought.

Reubin brought the organ to his mouth and tore a hunk from it with gleaming, white teeth. A red muck formed around his mouth and his chest and torso were covered with a sheet of blood. His eyes were alien, much more so than she'd seen on the roof that night. Then he stretched and threw the heart, blood slinging off it, at the VIP bubble. He must have identified it as the source of power. The fleshy mess didn't come close to the bubble, but his intent was evident.

"What a gesture," Josephine said. "He's challenging me—us." She keyed her console. "More."

"Code," said Operations, and Josephine input her code again, angrily. "Damn bureaucrats."

"Confirmed," the voice said through the speaker on the console.

Josephine turned immediately back to the bubble, all else forgotten, including the code on her console.

Tique had seen the passion in Josephine's eyes.

Below, Reubin was dragging one foot in the dust and sand.

Doors all over the arena opened and six slaybots moved out, oriented themselves and made for Reubin in the center of the arena.

Not even Reubin could overcome these. Tique's frustration and anger rose. Her original resentment of him was gone as if it had never existed. She so desperately wanted him to triumph here—as did the crowd, evidenced by their response.

Reubin barely glanced up. He continued to drag his foot, etching some odd design onto the floor of the arena.

The six 'bots all raised their extensions and razor edges slithered out. They advanced, closing in on Reubin. Tique guessed they'd been programmed to use their mechanical razor weapons and not lasers or flares.

Josephine's face was smashed against the bubble and her breathing was shallow and quick.

Tique looked around desperately. She fingered her now-empty drink on the edge of the console on her left.

Without even stopping to think about it, she activated her console. Two quick keystrokes and she'd slaved it to Josephine's console—along with the Minister's command code.

Tique's fingers flew. SCREEN ONLY. DISPLAY CORONA POWER SCHEMATIC.

Her screen filled with a myriad of different sized and color coded lines. She ran the demand light to the main power input line. DISCONNECT she keyed.

AGAINST FUNCTIONAL REQUIREMENTS, the screen responded.

COMMAND OVERRIDE, Tique typed. CONFIRM CODE.

CONFIRM, the computer system told her. POWER DISCONNECT IN PROGRESS.

First the environmental control went. No one seemed to notice as the hundreds of thousands of people present were screaming their displeasure at the new slaybots attacking Reubin.

Sections of lighting went out. Apparently the controlling computer would not overload and disconnect everything at once. Tique could see stars and clouds through the bubbledome.

Another afterthought hit Tique and she typed, OPEN ALL DOORS IN ARENA AND TO OUTSIDE OF CORONA. SAFETY OVERRIDE. Then she punched EXECUTE. She didn't know if anything she was doing would work, but at least the lights were going out.

Tique hit keypads swiftly. CLOSE DOWN ALL CORONA COMMAND CONSOLES. She did this in case some obscure failsafe backup maintained power in the VIP and Operations centers, precluding someone from countermanding her orders.

Josephine was sitting upright, just now realizing something was dead wrong.

The screen blanked and a green afterglow died.

Tique looked into the arena. The light faded as she watched. She'd seen Reubin leaping over the top of a slaybot and heading for one of the open doors in the arena wall. Had he been wounded? It was hard to tell in the growing gloom.

In the center of the arena surrounded by slaybots was the design he'd traced.

It took Tique a moment after complete darkness to figure out what it was. A stylized version of a snake's head, fangs poised ready to strike.

She felt a chill run from her bowels to the spot behind her eyes.

Josephine was slapping at her console. "When I find out what the hell is happening here, I'll have people's jobs."

A battery-powered emergency light illuminated the exit.

"Let's go," Josephine said.

Their car was just outside on the VIP ramp.

"We'll discuss your mother's legacy another time," Josephine Neff told Tique as they went out onto the ramp.

"What I don't understand, is the snake's head. First he scrapes up a snake, then a snake's head. What's that mean?"

Tique felt her intestines were water.

5: REUBIN

Reubin regained consciousness in a bubble-cage in some underground place. He remembered Passport Control and that was all.

Habu was clamoring, survival instinct giving off alarms.

A man stepped away and holstered an injection gun.

Rarely did Reubin ever welcome Habu into full awareness. It was infrequent that he relied on Habu. Most of the time he spent his effort trying to contain him.

The serpent was snaking through Reubin's mind, slithering past barriers.

Reubin clenched his eyes and opened them again. He found himself wearing shorts, boots, and nothing else. His mouth tasted like rotting corpses and his head hurt. He ran his hand over his head and discovered he'd been shaved inexpertly.

He sat up, groggy and disoriented.

Habu was struggling for control.

–*No.*

Habu did not respond. But the survival instinct was operating. Reubin was a strong man used to fighting his alter ego. He set his mind to a holding pattern and tried to take account of his circumstances.

He smelled animal excrement, sweat, blood, fear. He decided he was in the bowels of some cavernous place. A murmur came into the background.

A crowd?

Half the wall disappeared and harsh, man-made light speared in.

A double-bladed ax landed by his feet and the man who'd awakened him by injection motioned for him to pick up the weapon.

One glance out the opening told Reubin the story.

They must want him dead. Extrapolating swiftly with a cloudy mind, he figured they'd drugged him and—

"Up," said the man, and an energy beam lanced out and glanced off the concrete below him.

No choice. *–Be ready,* he told the serpent.

Wearily, he grasped the ax and rose, as slowly as he could, to buy time for his mind to recover.

Me.

–Maybe, Reubin responded. *–Wait.*

The short range energy beam creased the air behind his right ear and he knew he had to step out. When he was just past the opening, it slid noiselessly closed.

The background murmur increased. People. Many.

He smelled blood.

Habu snaked tendrils through Reubin's nervous system.

He took in the scene at a glance. Even through the haze in his mind, he knew a killing place when he saw one.

He fixed his eyes on the snarv crouching over a man's body. Must be the last combatant.

A surge more powerful than he could possibly control in his condition went through him and he attacked the snarv.

After killing the beast, he leaned on the man's sword, sated from the action. He breathed heavily. That wouldn't do. He worked on regulating his breathing. He surveyed the arena and the enormous crowd salivating for his blood.

He gestured at them. A challenge.

–Think, he told Habu. *–There will be more.*

Yes. I am ready.

–Give me room to evaluate. Reubin didn't want to lose complete control. If he did, death would be next.

Habu prepared for the next challenge.

Then came the strange beasts followed by the three men and the slaybot. And there was the satisfying blood and raw meat of the galloping-creatures. And the taunts to the authority above. Reubin slipped in and out of control. When outrunning the slaybot, he used more speed than a human's body could handle. He would pay with pain later—should he survive.

Blowers kept air moving in the giant arena and helped cool his overheated body.

By traditional standards, he should have won his freedom with wins in the previous bouts. No doubt they had more in store for him. They wanted him to die, never mind the rule of three successive victories.

His nostrils were clogged with blood and dust and absently he blew them clean. He spat.

Habu was more and more in control and enjoying the most freedom the serpent had had in years. Reubin fought for his own identity, close to being overwhelmed by the beast within him.

–I must think and evaluate or we will not survive.
Kill!
–We will not survive.

Habu was caught up in the heat of battle. Involuntarily, Reubin found himself tracing a snake pattern in the dust.

Six slaybots appeared and he kept dragging his foot in the sand, as if insane and trying to assure some legacy after his death.

The slaybots closed in on him. The crowd was screaming as if one, rocking the entire arena with their displeasure. And cheering him on.

He continued tracing.

The slaybots encircled him just as he finished the design. It wasn't like Habu to be creative in something other than survival, killing, or attack modes. His assessment of the situation mirrored Reubin's. Reaching out for a legacy was a facet of Habu new to Reubin. Of course, they'd never, ever been in such a hopeless situation before.

His animal senses immediately noticed the lack of blowing air. Some odd occurrence was taking place.

The slaybots had their cutting blades out and were advancing to the killing point.

He dodged. He decoyed. He ran at the circle of slaybots, faster than any human had ever moved in such a short distance.

Light began disappearing section by section. Reubin dodged one slaybot, whose extension shot out unexpectedly and sliced along his abdomen.

He faked the next slaybot to the left and somersaulted over it. Then he was sprinting for one of the suddenly open doors. Surprisingly, all the arena doors were open. What the hell was going on here?

—Give me control. I must think and move together.

A handful of the killer-herbivores trotted from another entrance along the wall.

The opportunity of escape and the bewildering events gave Reubin the mental leverage he needed for control.

Reubin ducked into an opening. Behind him, the arena was finally dark. The crowd had gone through its "What's going on?" phase and shouts of worry and panic pierced the air. Emergency battery powered lights illuminated the exits.

What had happened?

He didn't know; he didn't care.

Freedom was possible.

He knew he had to control himself. Habu had risen to the surface and taken over during his berserker rage out there; but after the heat of battle, he needed a clear head. Fighting skills were secondary now, escape was paramount—and for that he needed his mind to kick into gear. He had relied on Habu and survived; now he must contain Habu to survive.

He felt sticky. The gnurl's blood had dried over part of his body. The other part was slimy gore.

He trotted along, not wanting to go too fast: the slaybots would be trailing him and would provide magnificent disruptions of which he could take advantage—unless the gnurls or other humans sidetracked them. He didn't know if the 'bots had been programmed with his readings or a general program since they'd been supposed to face only one man in the arena.

His body was moving in real-time again.

Ahead he saw a light and he increased his caution. As he approached the pool of light, he saw a trainer checking locks on cages; obviously most had mechanical locks in addition to electronic ones.

The gnurls within were restive. The trainer stepped back as a hoof sharpened by clipping lichen off rocks lashed out. But the bubble material absorbed the blow.

Reubin saw his opportunity. While the trainer was recoiling from the attack, Reubin came up behind him and chopped viciously at his neck. The man went down instantly.

Reubin swiftly pulled off his trousers and tunic, searched the wall for what must be there and found it. A water hose for the animal cages. He prayed the power failure hadn't stopped the water pressure. He stripped his shorts and blasted himself with the hose. The cold helped restore his thinking. He began to feel he was in control again. The wound on his abdomen was still oozing blood. At least, he thought, the slaybot's razor was probably fairly clean. He set a biofeedback pattern in his mind to repair the damage and let it go to work.

Habu still lurked, but knew Reubin was correct in assuming control. Not for the first time Reubin appreciated that Habu could take control in degrees. Had Habu forced Reubin back into the dark, he would still be a berserk killing machine with little reason other than battle logic and experience. Only on one or two occasions had they reached an accommodation, a level higher than individual control, which melded them together, Reubin and Habu; not separate entities switching off control, but intertwined as one. The true Habu.

The pressure of the hose had cleaned the blood and gore from his body. He slaked the water off himself and pulled on the trainer's trousers and tunic. He slipped the knife he'd brought from the arena into the back of the trousers.

He ran his hand over his recently shaved head and wondered when they'd done that.

Though they were wet, he was thankful for the boots he'd been provided.

He moved swiftly and silently down a corridor which seemed to lean outward from the arena. At another emergency light, he spotted a set of double doors. Good. It stood to reason this was one of the routes used for bringing the animals in from the outside.

Behind him, he heard a shout. Someone had found the stripped trainer. Or had encountered the slaybots trailing Reubin. He edged one of the double doors open. An intersection. A larger corridor ran crossways to the animal ingress. A small pool of battery light. A group of attendants hurrying past: no public corridor this. A pair of men with weapons. A single man *wearing a hat*.

Reubin stepped out of the doors, snaked his arm around the man's neck, and dragged him back through the double doors.

He knocked the poor soul unconscious, and removed the man's shirt. With his knife he cut the shirt, lifted his own tunic and bandaged his wound.

A bearded man ran down the corridor and interrupted him. "Say—" The man saw Reubin's gleaming head, and turned to run. Reubin swept his feet from under him and slammed the man's head into the floor.

Neither man was armed, but Reubin took their identity cards and money. Even though the fit wasn't perfect, he wore the first man's hat. He was glad it was the full 360 brim, not the three-quarters one that seemed so popular here on Snister. Besides covering his shaved head, it would also shade his face.

He walked calmly through the double doors again and headed along the same corridor toward the outside.

Without running, he hurried and caught up with a woman.

They went through a large exit together. Starlight and vehicle lights provided sufficient illumination to see.

The woman tugged at her jumpsuit. "Whatever happened to the power?"

Reubin shrugged and lifted his hands. He would have liked to know the answer to that question, too. Any way he looked at it, there was only one beneficiary of that fortuitous event. Power failures did not occur, especially when a few hundred thousand people were gathered in one location. Engineers have programs that prevent and, if not prevent, then warn. Was this a continuation of some plan he couldn't yet fathom? Probably not, for if they'd wanted him alive, they wouldn't have chanced putting him in the arena with the opponents he'd faced.

He headed for the dark. Vehicles swarmed in the sky and on the nearby roadways. Doubtless there was a tube-walk underground somewhere to accommodate the great mass of spectators. But he didn't want to chance that.

The moist outside air tasted and smelled good, a welcome relief from the sand and blood and sweat and death.

Habu floated near the surface and observed Reubin with what he could only describe as professional interest.

It occurred to him that because of the circumstances, it was probable that the area would soon be swarming with police—what did they call them here? Ah, the Constabulary. A professional force would have begun to respond to the emergency by now.

Reubin walked slowly toward what looked like a parking lot. Mingle with people in the dark, he thought. That's the safest way.

He scanned the skies.

They looked like fireflies in the distance, all converging on the arena. So he knew where the population center was. When they came closer, he could make out the signaling strobes. The Constabulary was responding with everything from single-seat skycycles to armored aircars. They swooped from the night sky and landed wherever there was room. Their lights reflected slightly off the arena's bubbledome.

Reubin stood behind a large group of people watching the aerial show.

Constabulary poured out of vehicles all around the arena.

Though he'd been drugged and unaware of what they'd

done to him, he'd pretty well figured out what had occurred.

He assumed he was in or near Cuyas.

Anger built.

Reubin continued to the parking lot and began weaving through parked groundcars as if his were at the very back of the lot. Gradually he worked his way through the vehicles, then returned to the side closest to the arena. He tugged the brim of his hat down.

There. A Constabulary skycycle. Reubin would've liked to waylay a cop and take his weapons, but that might prove to be risky if the sergeant was monitoring body signals. On Karg, Reubin had an open comm link with all his troops. Each had worn a sensor which showed change of biosignals. He could tell if a soldier had been wounded, was unconscious, whatever. Reubin knew better than to chance technology.

But one thing he was pretty certain wasn't monitored on a peaceful planet like Snister: Constabulary vehicles.

He hoped.

He settled onto the skycycle and was thankful for technological standardization. While not exactly like a civilian vehicle, it was of similar design to military machines. Soon he was up and off.

Two women watched him with awe and understanding dawning on their faces. He tipped his hat to them. One gave him the thumbs up. Then he was airborne.

He smelled night air again and with appreciation.

He smelled freedom.

A little altitude and he oriented himself, locating Cuyas by the clustered lights, tall buildings, and occasional bubbledomes.

While they might not be monitoring their vehicles, the Constabulary wouldn't take long to determine one was missing. Especially now, for he'd glanced in the curved mirror and seen the arena lights come back up so swiftly it mimicked an explosion.

He thumbed the control and the bubble encased him.

He took another minute to force his Habu persona fur-

ther down. He needed to think clearly, not fight and kill.
Survival.

Then he reinforced the thoughts stemming the flow of
blood from his wound and was satisfied that his body was
responding. But for the first time he felt weak from the
loss of blood and the exertion in the arena. Where he'd
move as swiftly as a striking snake and turned just as
quickly and abruptly, residual pain seeped. Additionally,
whatever drugs they'd given him were wearing off and
making him groggy.

He didn't want to turn on the monitor as it might signal
Constabulary Control that one of their skycycles was
moving away from the action.

Judging from other traffic leaving the arena, he chose
a corridor at the proper altitude. If there were traffic computers, he would soon be in trouble as he hadn't activated
his gear. He accelerated, weaving past several larger air
vehicles.

Nearing the center of the city, he searched for a public
area. There. A landing alongside what appeared to be a
shopping center. The only way to maximize his survival
was to lose pursuit among lots of people and vehicles.
They could easily chase down a single man out in the
forests and on the plains.

That's what he wanted them to think that he figured.
That's why he was dumping the stolen skycycle downtown.

He swooped down and parked in a location marked by
a glittering ''OFFICIAL VEHICLES ONLY.''

No one was near enough to question a man dressed as
he was riding a Constabulary skycycle.

He headed for a concourse which looked as if it led to
a public tubewalk underground. He merged with the
crowds.

He only heard one conversation about the power failure
at the arena.

He stayed on the outside of the walk, where occasional
shadows hid the fact that his clothes were damp. He'd
had neither the time nor the ability to dry off. The ban-

dage and his biofeedback instructions had blocked the flow of blood.

For the first time he realized he was hungry.

Just before he was completely out of sight, he stopped and looked back to where he'd parked the skycycle. A large Constabulary aircar was settling in beside it. Reubin knew his instincts were right; his timing had been exact. But because of the swift Constabulary response, he knew he was in deep trouble. These cops were *good*, skilled at their profession. Not like some he'd encountered.

Well, it wasn't as if he'd asked to be in this situation. Anger erupted within him and Habu fought to emerge. –*No.* Escape now to fight some other time when the odds were better.

He headed for the walk above the road and aimed north.

Within an hour, he found what he wanted. A hospital. Open all night and full of strangers.

A machine took his red bill, gave him two green bills in change, and a hot stew. While that filled his hunger, he ate another meal for the protein. The future did not bode well for regular meals. He didn't dare use the ID-charge cards he'd stolen. That would be like waving a flag at the Constabulary. Save them for emergencies.

He found the last machine he needed in the lobby. The screen scrolled with TITLES AVAILABLE under the category of ranching. Nothing had been listed under survival. He figured a book on ranching on Snister would help him learn dangerous plants and animals. If food animals for humans could eat it, it wouldn't be deadly to humans. His objective was to research compatibility of Snister life-forms to the human organism. Germs, microbes, bacteria. He opted for a lightweight hard copy instead of a tape or disk. The machine spewed it out and he folded it into a pocket on his tunic.

Recalling tearing at the gnurl's heart in the arena, he thought ruefully that he'd learned the hard way that gnurl meat was human-compatible.

Using the name "U. Grant," he made a reservation

for vanity cosmetic surgery at an arbitrary later date—
one which could be changed. He could pose as a doctor,
tech, or patient as long as the computer had logged it
into the system. Reubin always liked to have at least one
fallback plan.

While at the public console in the hospital, he ran a
check of ships at the spaceport or orbiting. Nothing. Escape from this planet looked bleak—not that escape was
in his plans right now. Let's see. LIST SHIPS AS-
SIGNED PERMANENTLY. Freighters for shipping processed wormwood. Corporate spaceyacht. Slim pickin's.
LIST SHIPS SCHEDULED TO ARRIVE SNISTER
W/IN 50 DAYS.

NONE. Uh-oh. ONLY UNSCHEDULED GOVERN-
MENT/WORMWOOD, INC. COURIERS.

His trip on the spaceliner to Snister must have been
good timing. Not for Alex. Damn. He'd stroked the trigger again and Habu groped restlessly. It frustrated him
that when he thought of Alex, it drew the predictable
enraged response from his other persona. It was something Habu would have to get used to. It was also an odd
juxtaposition that Habu had resented Alex, but now became enraged because of her death. Perhaps it was indicative of how much the two had grown together over
the years.

He made a few more inquiries and quit the console.
Then he left the hospital, another exhausted man finally
going home.

He thought about sleep and guessed he could find
somewhere in the hospital that he wouldn't be disturbed.
But he knew he had to get as far away as possible. By
dawn the city would probably be sealed—if they were
really concerned about his being free. But would they
be? Obviously, he was expendable or they wouldn't have
put him in the arena to be killed.

He began walking north again, sticking to the shadows
and avoiding places where, if seen by the Constabulary,
he'd be questioned for being where he shouldn't be.

They'd taken him as he walked through the scanning
room to the shuttle. A blast of gas instead of disinfectant

and he was unconscious immediately. He had hazy memories of questions and drugs and more drugs. He was relatively certain that his biochip implant had kicked in properly with his cover story. Certainly it *had* worked, for if it hadn't, he would have told that he was, in fact, the notorious Habu, a much more valuable prisoner than one Reubin Flood. Thus they wouldn't have sent him to his death. They'd have held him for the Federation authorities.

Then why had they given him a false name and sent him to his death in the arena? They had nothing to gain from his public death, and some to lose. They should have simply injected him with a lethal agent and destroyed his body. Especially with the top brass in the government and on the planet having a role in his abduction.

It all added up to one thing. He was an example.

An example of what? Was there something, some conspiracy on this planet he knew nothing about? Anything was possible.

But the one thought that continued to run through his mind was that he'd been used as a lever against somebody. It was the only real answer. He knew only one person he could be used to pressure: Tique Sovereign.

A lot of trouble for a simple lesson. But, he admitted, he didn't know the dynamics between the brass who had killed Alex, and Tique Sovereign. He didn't know the politics or the personalities involved. So there could be dozens of legitimate reasons he'd been sent to die at the arena.

Therefore, he couldn't contact Tique. They'd be waiting.

He'd seen himself on the giant screens at the arena. They'd be fools if they weren't sending the signal to all televideos on the planet. Meaning, of course, that damn near every person on Snister knew or would know what he looked like, be familiar with his features. Well, at least he could grow his hair back and let his beard come out.

He was two hours north of the city and still worrying about Tique when dawn broke.

He'd been paralleling the roadway, but now he cut east and away. He found a hollow in the side of a hill covered with trees. It offered the best protection he could find. An aircar would have to be right on top of him to use IR gear to detect him.

He ate one of the meals he'd brought with him and skimmed the book on ranching, even though he was exhausted. Strange insects crawled or flew about and Reubin hoped fervently they weren't going to bite, sting, chomp, infest, infect, or drill him.

He tried to estimate the location of Scenic Overlook #18 in the mountains ahead of him. He would cut through the valleys and the passes. He thought about hiding on the back of a freight vehicle, but again didn't want to chance discovery.

He decided he had to hole up somewhere and figure out what he was going to do. He needed help, someone with connections, someone with the proper access to find answers.

Before he took his vengeance.

Only one person might assist: Tique, if she was still at liberty. He hoped she'd remember his inquiries about her cabin. He had the address and location from the central-info terminal at the hospital. The machine had thoughtfully shown a schematic map of roads and air corridors to that location. Then he'd punched in the fact that the computer had called up the wrong address in case the Company's system had logged that someone had requested that information. A good computer search might be programmed to tell if any inquiries had been made to or about anyone, in this case, Tequilla Sovereign.

He checked his wound and determined it was healing. He'd bathed his wound at the hospital and taken an antibiotic and strapped on a seven-day healant bandage. It's amazing what they sell at hospitals over the counter and from machines. He'd also purchased a more durable set of clothes, tunic and trousers designed for outdoor work, quick wash/dry undergarments, and a heavy jacket. He figured to be doing some mountain climbing. Flaag Peak. Or was it Flaag Mountain? That he couldn't recall a simple detail was a measure of his low ebb of energy. They must have put him through the wringer before they sent him to the arena.

Exhaustion flowed through him and he set Habu to hover near the surface as a sentinel while he slept. He nestled into leaves and foliage until he was comfortable and slept the day through.

Rain killed his ranching on Snister book. He'd gone to sleep reading and a light early evening rain had fallen. As he was accustomed to hardships, the rain hadn't roused him. But it had destroyed his biodegradable book. Cheap damn machine. He wondered if the tapes and disks available had been of as poor a manufacture. Somebody was always making money on cheap stuff. Though he did admit that the dissolvable books were better for the environment. He tossed the handful of pulp aside.

His skimming of the book hadn't told him much. He'd had to extrapolate his own conclusions. Apparently life on Snister, since it was carbon based, was more or less compatible with human requirements. The balance of vitamins, minerals, proteins, so on, was different, but deficiencies could be overcome easily. Food animals such as sheepaloe had no trouble growing on Snister vegetation—if you tossed in a few supplements. There were no inimical microbes, bacteria, whatever. If something wasn't nutritional, at least it wouldn't kill you because it was alien. There were a few dangerous plants you shouldn't eat—or at least the book had warned against allowing your livestock to feed thereon.

Fortunately, water was water. All and all, Reubin decided, for the short term he was safe.

He ate the remaining food, pausing to read the contents in case it would help him live off the land. Nope. Sheepaloe. Another Silas Swallow project. But the vegetable name was not familiar: whinless. He doubted he'd know it if he tripped over it.

He buried his garbage and made the hollow look as

though no one had been there. Then he struck out to the northeast, heading for Tique's cabin and wondering.

What in hell had happened to the power at the arena? The newscast he saw at the hospital had merely said "a sudden and mysterious power outage" had ruined the evening's sport and "resulted in the escape of one dangerous and armed prisoner." A still shot of Reubin followed, baldheaded, of course. There was no general alert, merely a warning to be on the lookout as "authorities expect to have him returned to custody soon" for something called "appropriate justice." Apparently they had to tread lightly as Reubin had, in fact, defeated his opponents and had earned his liberty.

Reubin tossed his jacket over his shoulder and felt the stubble on his head. Fifteen days, he thought, and he'd be a different person.

He realized that his Habu personality was pretty well submerged this morning. The rage had subsided with rest. It was time to plan.

He moved from a forest area into a valley between mountains. He spied what at first he took to be an aircar, but actually turned out to be a large bird with three smaller birds circling the huge thing. Strange ecology, this.

Which led his thinking. What would be the best method of taking revenge on Snister? They'd killed Alex and tried to do the same to him—not to mention humiliation, drugging, all their crimes. What best way to hurt a giant conglomerate which controlled an entire planet?

Economically.

It came to Reubin Flood that Snister and Wormwood, Inc. relied on a single solitary sole product: wormwood.

His mind clicked. Throughout the universe humans had engaged in ecoraiding in numerous documented cases. But he couldn't recall a single instance in which an entire planet, a product with such impact, had been the target. Though he had to admit, his own personal history pointed toward planet-wrecking.

Scope, he thought. That's the key. No penny-ante stuff

here. And if he did it right, then the resultant fallout should expose whoever was responsible for Alex's death.

Awright, Alex. It's settled. I shall bring this planet to its knees. Just for you. Then I will kill those responsible for your death. *In Memory.*

Habu stirred. He was becoming used to references to Alex. But Habu urged a different course upon him. Revenge was fuel to Habu.

Reubin increased his pace. His fragmented persona was driving him to extreme revenge. He had to fight the urge as Habu raised his awareness and surged. Damn. The trigger again. Alex.

After all, it had been radical, inordinate circumstances leading to radical, inordinate vengeance which had caused the genesis of Habu.

But Reubin was adamant. He would first see about removing the product these people depended on. Attack the economic structure of Wormwood, Inc.

Why? Habu interrupted his reverie, suddenly concerned.

—*Because I want to do the human thing first.*

Let us kill instead.

—*No. Reason will prevail this time.* Reubin could feel the dawning within Habu.

Kill.

—*I am human. I cannot live through another of these occasions. I don't know if I care to live after this, now that I think about it. But I will not die a nonhuman barbarian.*

Look what humans have done to you.

—*Good point. But not valid logic.*

My way works. Long ago you used me. Years.

—*No. Long ago I was . . . mad? They made me berserk. They made me kill. I did not want to, not after a while.*

We killed. We won.

—*We killed. No one won. We killed a world.*

Let us kill now. Disregard your plan.

—*This time we do it a different way. This time I have control.*

Already you have usea me much. Let us go out and kill them.

—We will kill the right person, Reubin replied desperately.

—First I want to make the system pay. Again he was being overwhelmed by the strength of Habu's response.

Vengeance. Now. Habu would not be diverted.

—No. Heed me!

They killed Alexandra. Distaste in Habu's thought.

—Do not take that from me, Reubin demanded. —You were against Alex; she was a civilizing influence. A humanizing influence upon me. Us. You wanted nothing to do with her.

No response.

—I wanted her. Reubin was becoming angry.

Habu must have sensed Reubin's building anger. *The man Nodivving. He is a killer. I sensed it.*

—Certainly he is amoral. Most people of tremendous power are. Reubin didn't want to think about applying the same criteria to himself. His anger exploded. —Would that I could purge myself of you.

And then die. We are symbiotes, you and I.

Reubin hoped that wasn't true. But he gave up the conversation anyway.

Through centuries of life it had been one accommodation after another. An eternal balancing act. Habu was right. They were symbiotes. Each relied on the other. Their peculiar, unique existence had inevitably required the talents of both to continue to survive.

Reubin wondered if Habu disappeared, would there be a tremendous empty space in his mind? An empty feeling?

He continued his journey.

Disinterested, Habu relinquished his hold on the surface.

Reubin guided his thoughts toward developing a plan of attack against Wormwood, Inc.

It occurred to him that he needed to learn a great deal about wormwood. You have to know the target, the enemy, to attack his weak points.

The time came when he should begin climbing, and the two moons were on the other side of the world. So he rolled under a rock and slept until dawn.

Not yet hungry enough to eat insects or waste time hunting, he chewed on a handful of rock lichen and continued on his way.

He gained altitude, climbing a lot of rock surfaces now. The air was cooler, and when it came the rain was cold.

Reubin took longer than necessary. He kept near cover in case of aerial surveillance. He had to wend his way carefully so as to not be visible from roadways winding along the mountains way above him.

The exercise was cleansing his soul of weeks of inactivity. Most of the aches and pains gained in his arena battles had gone away. He believed that the physical expenditures and his lower level of subsistence helped keep his mind clear, held at bay the pressure which would disappear once he took the Long Life treatment. On the other hand, he might not live long enough to enter the LLI for his treatment. But that pressure and a little pain edged into his mind anyway.

Toward evening, he decided he'd had enough of this starvation and followed his instincts up a branch canyon. He found a high lookout point and sat for an hour observing.

There. In the growing dusk he watched three feathered figures no longer than his arm dart out of shadows on the opposite side of the canyon wall. As if a team, they attacked and felled a small animal drinking from a rivulet below.

The three birds didn't seem able to completely subdue the animal.

Then Reubin understood.

The giant bird, or whatever the hell they called the monster, launched itself from a cave and fell—as opposed to flew—the distance to the ground. Almost at ground level, it sprouted great gossamer wings which caught air and snapped audibly in the canyon. It settled the remaining distance to the ground, waddled to the three birds and the small animal, and bit the animal's head off with his owllike beak.

Reubin climbed down from his perch. As he approached the scene, he saw the three smaller birds licking at the animal's blood which had pumped out on the rocks. The giant bird simply sat on its haunches and waited. So the relationship was more symbiotic than parasitic, Reubin realized.

He checked his knife, then picked up some rocks. He doubted he'd have trouble with these creatures, but you never knew. Most planets he'd been on, birds were of little or no danger to man. Any animal engineered for flying was usually delicate with hollow bones. Men were large enough to frighten them. He hoped the case proved the same here.

He tossed the rocks and shouted. The three symbiotes quickly scrambled into the sky. The large bird turned to face Reubin. It was easily taller than he, with a large belly. Its body was covered with dark brown and gray fur. Reubin tossed another rock and shouted again. The bird bleated, hopped a few times downhill, and snapped out his wings. The thin skin between the cartilage caught a current and the bird grunted and worked his wings, gradually gaining altitude, bleating unhappily all the way.

Reubin approached the decapitated animal. He couldn't have told what it was even if he knew the local flora and fauna.

He skinned the animal and checked it over for evidence of worms or disease. He knew that the more heat, namely cooking, was applied to meat, the less nutrition the meat would provide. On the other hand, he didn't want to ingest germs or parasites he could've killed by cooking. The meat smelled fresh and looked healthy. He never thought carnivorous birds were fastidious eaters, but he trusted this one mainly because he didn't want to stop, light a fire, and cook. He sliced a hunk of lean meat and chewed on it. Slightly gamy, but edible. He cut up the rest of the meat and buried the remainder of the carcass.

As he hunted a place to spend the night, he chewed on a small bone for the marrow.

He drank from the tiny stream and climbed to a shallow cave in the face of the canyon wall. No IR would find him here.

Chewing on the gamy meat, he regretted what he often regretted at times like these: the lack of something to read. No distractions of civilization, just peaceful nature. Then he remembered the time when he and Alex had read *The Last of the Mohicans*, and anger washed over him.

He settled down to plan.

Late that night a thunderstorm played in the mountains and overhead. A flash flood swept through the canyon. Reubin had noted the increase in water and knew something was amiss. He climbed up the side of the canyon until he reached the top and pulled himself over and onto a ridge running north. He squatted and studied the canyon below. But he could see nothing.

He found a downed tree and broke some leafy limbs. These he built into a top cover, inadequate, but the best he could do at night in the rain. He resigned himself to the discomfort and managed some sleep.

In the morning, he knelt at the edge of the canyon, estimating the height that the water had reached. He thought that his original cave had been safe. But he couldn't have known that. Though the episode was a lesson learned.

He continued into the mountains, eating plants or leaves he'd seen animals eat. Several times he robbed predators as he had the birds. It was an old habit: the meat wouldn't be poisonous, and it would be edible raw. He hoped. If he had one of those expensive, wide range laser weapons, he could set it low enough to at least singe the meat—whether to kill germs or to burn off fur. Or he could start an old-fashioned fire. The few eggs he could find he ate raw.

These were the things he thought as he worked his way above the rain level and snow fell upon him. Here he was worrying about cooking his food and all the while planning to bring an entire planet to its knees. Optimism, he thought with a wry grin. Two hands, one knife, and one mind (well, at least one).

Once, in late afternoon, he thought he saw aircars crisscrossing the land somewhere below him. Genuine business? Or a search pattern for a fugitive?

No way of knowing. But he increased his vigilance.

He reached the area of Tique's cabin on Flaag Peak the following evening. The sun was setting and the air was raw with cold.

He was skirting an iced-over lake on the ice itself because the wind would blow snow over his trail quicker than on land. Snow was less than a meter deep, more was piled in drifts.

Carefully, he slid his feet ahead, testing for thin ice. Occasionally, he thought the ice might be dangerous and changed direction. Snow began falling in thick, wet flakes.

While aircars are supposed to be quiet, they cannot be completely silent. The peculiar whistling reached him on the ice of the lake's surface. Two of them, he thought. The noise came and went, telling him that he had but scant moments before they covered the area of the lake.

No accident this, he knew. They were searching the area near Tique's cabin. He'd have done the same thing himself. And with infrared gear.

Damn. He groaned and leaped high and to his left. He slammed both feet down together. The ice cracked, shattered, and he went under the freezing water. He had his knife out, knowing he couldn't wait in the water because it meant death.

He jammed his knife into the intact ice and pulled himself out. Quickly, he rolled toward the shore, gathering snow on his wet body. He could feel his body temperature falling rapidly. He didn't engage his biofeedback mechanisms since he didn't want to generate the additional heat. Perhaps the snow and water—now frozen to ice—around him would fool an IR operator. Perhaps. If it didn't, then his lowered body temperature might lead them to think he was some animal or fish. He kept rolling, a giant elongated snowlog now, and crashed into a snowbank.

Shaking violently, he stopped moving. He tried to listen for aircars but heard nothing over his chattering teeth. How long could he remain motionless? How long would it be before the cold killed him?

It was an old trick: immerse yourself in water and roll in snow which, because of the water, stuck to your body. A mobile igloo. Insulation to save yourself until you could reach warmth and safety.

But he was too cold now. Hypothermia was killing him. He could hardly move his arm to clear his mouth so he could breathe.

Another minute passed and he feared he'd waited too long.

A lethargy overcame him. His limbs felt numb, then no longer there.

He *had* waited too long.

–*Habu.*

–*Come forth.*

–*Habu?*

6: TIQUE

"**W**ell, get a shot from the video," Josephine Neff told her office. "And if the information about the snakes is not available on Snister, I authorize funding for a data search on Webster's." She gave them the location of the funding code in the system and angrily stabbed fingers at the command console in her limo. "Wasn't he magnificent?" Her voice had risen out of its customary whisper.

Tique knew Josephine was talking about Reubin. While Tique's heart had been pounding about her own intrigue, a part of her brain told her that she'd just witnessed something extraordinary.

Josephine's orgasmic reaction was wearing off and anger was showing around her edges. Perhaps that was how Tique had gotten away with killing the power at the Corona.

"Go ahead Command Two," came another voice over the comm system.

"Priority," Josephine said. "The power went off at the Corona. I want to know how and why and who and when."

"Roger, Command Two. We're working the problem. The comm link with Corona Ops is down."

"Keep me informed," said Josephine, a whip in her voice. Her hand slammed and the link died. She snorted. "We're working the problem," she mimicked. "Damn bureaucrats." She slumped back. "What a man."

Concern about Reubin clouded Tique's thinking.

As if to echo her thoughts, Josephine said, "I wonder if he escaped?"

Tique did not respond immediately. "If he has?"

"I'd like to wager on the time it takes for us to capture him." Josephine flashed an uncharacteristic smile. "Likely, it would take us a while." She paused. "That would be some hunt," she mused. She began peeling off her gloves.

Unable to restrain herself, Tique said, "Is that all a man's life is worth to you? A hunt? Entertainment?"

Josephine looked up at Tique under dark brows. "Lemme tell you something, honey. That's all *any* man means to me." Her eyes swept the command console as if waiting for a report.

Tique breathed deeply and sank back.

Josephine looked under her brows again. "What's the matter? Did I offend your nonviolent sensibilities? You've a lot to learn, little Miss Eco-Prissy. There is a big wide universe out there and you only get what you're willing to take. Wake up, Sovereign. Hell, your own *mother* didn't even trust you with secrets, I about know that now. At the Corona, your face was white with fright. You couldn't hide anything if you wanted." Her voice had trailed off during her attack, returning at the end to its basic whisper.

Tique squirmed deeper into the seat, anger boiling inside her. See what you think, Tique thought, when your engineers figure out it was me who disconnected the power and comm links. Nonetheless, Josephine Neff's words stung. She did wonder how long it would be before her computer artwork was discovered. It set her mind to planning.

The limo dropped Josephine off at her office, then took Tique home. Tique fidgeted, knowing she had to do something. There were laws and regulations against tampering with power and comm links, disconnecting computer access, the like. They could also get her on a couple of hundred thousand "public endangerment" charges. Too, she could be billed for engineering work and the man-hours spent by the Constabulary.

She knew she had to become scarce. Once they found she'd been the one responsible, they'd also reevaluate their thinking that she knew nothing about her mother's so-called secret. And then she would be in real trouble.

Hastily she packed.

She wondered about her own efforts. She'd never done anything quite like that in her life. Certainly her mother had. Maybe those genetic traits came down to her, giving her the gumption to act as she had at the Corona. Maybe she'd gotten the inspiration from Reubin facing overwhelming odds.

What she knew about Reubin told her that nothing he did was frivolous. Nothing. Everything had a reason. So when he traced that stylized snake during the battle and the snake's head as the slaybots closed in on him, he had a purpose. It was almost like a challenge. His eyes had been practically burning. There was no doubt that he was a dangerous man. She recalled he had a mercenary past, and she thought of her mother's reaction when she first saw Reubin on Karg. A bitter taste came into the back of Tique's mouth at the thought of her mother's death. Alexandra Sovereign had been the one to tame Reubin Flood.

Tique added a thick coat and comfortable hiking boots to her bag and went downstairs. She had occasionally walked in the upper level forests of Flagg Peak with her mother or alone. It was where she'd first learned her love of nature. Her hobby of fog-shaping was a natural outgrowth of her conservationist views.

She punched for her car and waited. She knew that she could not hide anywhere on the planet. Period. They'd find her. But suppose she went to her cabin? They'd know she was there. Isolated. Far away from cities or the spaceport or whatever. But it would still be a problem for them to come and get her. So they'd know she was there and they could take her any time they wanted. As good as a prison. But on her own terms.

Not to mention the fact that Reubin knew of the cabin, had quizzed her on it. Unless the drugs had burned his mind to cinders. But his performance at the Corona belied that thought.

Her car arrived and she drove off.

As she passed Scenic Overlook #18, she thought about stopping, but did not. She was in a hurry and though the nightview scopes made the place and its panoramic view as attractive at night as it was in the daylight, she was in no mood to admire the scenary.

She was also worried about Reubin. On the screen at her apartment, she'd run a replay of the last few moments of Reubin's remarkable performance so that she could try to determine if he'd escaped while the lights were extinguished. She didn't know if he had, but it was painfully obvious that one of the 'bots had gotten to him from the sudden spurt of blood spraying as he'd somersaulted the killer machine.

Early that morning she reached her cabin. She punched in the combination of the bubble access and drove in. The bubbledome provided environmental protection for the whole cabin and perhaps an acre surrounding the structure. The computer controlled systems maintained spring flowers all year long.

On entering the cabin, she thought about increasing the power to the bubble's grid so that it would melt the accumulated snow and ice. Then she decided against it. It kept her world closed and made her feel as if she was in a giant igloo. Which matched the cold, gray of her emotions.

She put her things away. Her mother had designed the cabin, including the self-contained power source. So Tique didn't have to depend on commercial, Wormwood, Inc.-provided power.

The cabin was three levels high with a sun deck on top. When the weather allowed, Alexandra would retract the bubble and they'd sit out on the sun deck and talk. Her mother could talk on a great many subjects and occasionally surprised Tique with what she knew. Thinking of her mother, Tique felt an oppressive sadness overcome her.

The following day her computer beeped and told her, "In accordance with your program, I inform you some-one has attempted to contact you at your city residence." Ten minutes later, another beep. "A message from the Constabulary," the computer intoned. "You are to con-sider yourself under house arrest pending disposition of your case. Command Authority cited as approval source."

"It figgers," Tique said. They'd discovered what she'd done, but they didn't know what to do with her. Or per-haps they were using her as bait to catch Reubin Flood. She installed a quickie program to alert her of any news concerning Reubin.

Another program she worked on for two hours was a debugging sweep. Her computer would not allow *any* ex-ternal electronic source, never mind any "Command Override" crap. No Constabulary technician could out-program Tequilla Sovereign. So, she was safe from elec-tronic surveillance.

The following day, she saw aircars in the area for the entire daylight period. Intimidation? Searching?

A few days later, the airborne surveillance returned and continued through the early evening. Tique had been down in the cave below the cabin updating the food in-ventory. As she climbed back up the stairs, the computer began shrieking. "Intruder alert! Intruder alert!"

Tique discontinued the warning and checked her mon-itors. Something large had caromed into the bubble on the west side and continued to bounce off the bubble clumsily as it moved alongside the structure. Tique checked and found the aircars dwindling in the dis-tance—they'd given up for the day.

Her equipment showed her that whatever it was out there had collapsed near the front access to the bubble. Could it be an animal?

She knew damn well what she thought it might be, and cursed herself for useless speculation. Apprehension traveled from her womb to her brain. She took a pencil laser with her in case the life-form was a dangerous an-imal—or man.

Outside she found a huge clump of ice and snow pushing against the bubble, trying to rise. The shape was vaguely human, but looked more like a snow monster.

It was a person with only one eye visible, rimmed with crusted ice. She'd seen that eye before, on the giant screen at the arena. It wasn't an eye with which she was familiar from knowing Reubin Flood for a couple of days. There was an internal fire in that eye, an indomitable energy. It was also a window into which she couldn't see, a window into an uncaged beast.

She helped the figure up and together they stumbled into the protection of the bubble. The access closed automatically once there was no longer an obstruction in the way.

God! How was Reubin alive?

Somehow she got him into the ground-floor bathroom and into the shower. She had no experience with freezing and hypothermia.

She turned the airdry jets on hot and left him sitting on the ledge. She punched in emergency first aid onto the computer and chose the listing under hypothermia. She scanned it quickly. Insure breathing. He was breathing. Warm dry clothes. Warm drinks if victim does not vomit or cough. *No alcohol.* If severe case, a healthy adult can be rewarmed in a warm, but not hot, bath. Less severe cases, put in a very warm, heated room.

She rushed back to the shower and checked Reubin. The ice had cracked off and snow was melting. She closed the door and set the water temp at 37 since that was body temp. Maybe she'd raise it another degree later. She turned on all the faucets and nozzles and the shower responded as if for a whirlpool bath, filling quickly.

Ignoring the rising water, Tique undressed Reubin. It was awkward work in the confines of the shower. His face was gaunt beneath the stubble, and his poorly shaved head angered her.

His skin was still icy to the touch. As the water rose to waist level, she found it easier to undress him. His wound had been bandaged and the bandage appeared dirty though intact.

She tugged off his boots and trousers. She left his undershorts on. His torso showed a few old scars.

His lips were the proverbial blue. She shut off the water since it had risen to the level of Reubin's neck. He appeared as if in a coma. She scooped warm water in her hands and forced some between his lips. Finally, they opened of their own accord and she poured several handfuls down his throat.

His clothing was floating and getting in the way, so she hung them on the hook. His teeth were chattering now and she bathed his head with the warm water. She touched the controls and the water circulated like a whirlpool, maintaining temperature. She added another half degree.

She surveyed him. He really looked—well, terrible. Shorn like an animal, exhausted, sick.

His muscles began to ripple. Maybe he was returning to consciousness.

An odd expression settled on his face. His body tensed. His neck muscles stood out. His head swiveled from side to side, seeming to sway hypnotically. Gradually, it stopped and faced Tique.

She stood there curiously, not knowing what to think.

The one eye opened again and blinked. The eyelid drooped to make his eye look hooded.

Tique took an involuntary step back, slowed by the water reaching to her chest. The eye followed her.

An unreasoning dread flowed through her entire body. The eye flowed with menace.

Then she finally saw a human emotion in it: despair. Immediately, that was followed by bewilderment, then blankness.

She wondered if the cold had unbalanced his mind. She found herself pressing against the wall.

The one baleful eye closed and his whole body relaxed and slumped forward.

She moved to him and lifted his head and shoulders out of the water; she leaned him back against the wall.

She found she was breathing hard in the hot, humid stall.

Both of his eyes opened slowly and the fire leaped out

of them. His mouth moved and his tongue flickered. She felt his body tense and surge against her and the water. Then a light of intelligence came through and he relaxed. His eyes took in his surroundings and he dipped his head into the water and drank.

He lifted his head and croaked, then ducked and drank again. He came up spitting and choking. He stammered, "It would be more interesting if you were undressed, too." Then he rested his head against the wall.

At least he wasn't brain dead. She thought his flippant remark odd for the circumstances. It occurred to her that his words had disarmed her quite reasonable apprehension at being in a closed shower with some psychopathic monster.

She felt his neck and his ears. Still cold. And here she was sweating under her hair and the back of her neck.

"Very hot here," he croaked.

"Good. We're going to keep it that way." She was more or less calm, now.

She made him drink some more warm water.

Eventually, he warmed.

She flushed the water from the stall and turned on the airdry jets, regulating their temperature to forty degrees and decreased the force of the air to minimum. When she was more or less dry, she went to the kitchen and microwed some soup.

He was still sitting there when she returned. She stopped the airdry jets and turned on the sauna for a few minutes. The stall heated immediately.

She forced him to drink the soup.

He gagged. "Chicken soup. It figgers." But he drank it.

Tique began to sweat and turned off the stall. She helped Reubin to the lift her mother had insisted be installed. ("*I* sure as hell ain't gonna carry stuff upstairs.") Tique snapped the waist-high barrier around him and sent him to the second floor.

She got him into bed and he fell asleep immediately. She checked his temperature and it was close to normal.

But she did increase the heating in the bedroom and in the bed.

Then she went downstairs and drank a large tequila over ice.

When Tique awoke the next morning, something was subtly different. She activated the computer to check on Reubin. The screen showed a black-line diagram of her house. Red lines snaked through every room and closet, from the sun deck to the cave in the rock below.

"Per your program," the computer said. "The red lines indicate the man's routes. His travels occurred upon his waking, two hours and twelve minutes ago."

Including this bedroom, Tique saw. He'd come close to the bed, then checked the windows. Careful man, that Reubin Flood.

A sudden guilt overwhelmed her. Reubin must have seen what she'd done. She'd put him in *her* bed, and she herself had slept in her mother's bedroom. Was there something Freudian about her actions?

The hell with that. There was definitely something amiss with *him*.

She showered and went downstairs.

Reubin was sitting at her console, using her computer and drinking coffee from her favorite mug.

He glanced up at her. "It's blowing one hell of a blizzard out there. We're safe for now."

She stared at him. "You're welcome very much."

"Thank you very much," he said, "for defrosting me last night. Thank you very much for letting me have your bed last night. Thank you very much for your hospitality. Thank you very much for cleaning and drying my clothing. Tell me why you put me in your bed and not Alexandra's?"

It's not because I was jealous, Tique thought, like you want me to admit. "It was on the second floor."

"That lift didn't care how many floors it went up," he said, turning back to the console.

Tique was immediately flustered. "Well, excuse the hell out of me. I did the first thing that came to mind. Maybe there was a little bit of self-sacrifice in the back of my mind, I don't know. But do not, I repeat, do not, read anymore into it than you should.''

"Sure, kid. Look here." He pointed and transferred the image from the console screen to the wall screen. There he was: bald, torso gleaming with sweat, shoulders lifted, arm in the air, middle finger defying the crowd at the arena.

"They selected that shot," he said, "because it was the most pejorative. It inherently angers people. They forget that I beat the odds and should have been set free."

Reubin touched the console. The scene held, but a voice-over said, "—most wanted man on Snister. Authorities have confirmed that he escaped by kidnapping this woman, an aquadynamics engineer—"

Her photo appeared and she said, "Aquadynamacist, not engineer."

Reubin killed the display.

"What's it all mean?" she asked, fearing she knew the answer.

"It means they've written you off. It means they needed a legal reason to apprehend me. It means you done made somebody very angry."

She nodded absently. "They've found out I was responsible for the power and comm link outages at Corona during your, um, battle."

He looked up at her, understanding racing through his eyes—calm, thinking eyes, not the fire-breathing eyes of a monster. Not psychopathically threatening, hooded eyes.

"You were there," he said.

"I was."

"You took a chance."

"Compared to what you'd gone through in the arena? I had to do something. I've never liked the Corona and what it stands for. I—"

"Thank you very much for killing the power at the arena so I could make my escape," he said, not holding back a grin.

"You're welcome very much," she said.

"Tell me."

Briefly, she told him of the circumstances.

"Josephine Neff, eh? Interior Minister and Number Two on Snister."

"Right," Tique said.

"That's Number One and Number Two, both, whom we have identified as part of the conspiracy."

Tique felt a chill as if she'd just heard the death sentence pronounced.

"All of which means," he continued, "that we're safe until the blizzard is over. We're effectively incarcerated here, available whenever they want us. One pass over the place and their IR gear will tell them two people are here. We got a problem."

Tique was becoming bewildered. She went into the kitchen and got coffee and made breakfast. "Come and get it," she called after a while.

He came into the kitchen. "Thank you very much for the breakfast." He sat down at the table. "What is this stuff?"

"Breast of sanderling," she said. "A wildfowl and highly protected."

"So how come we're eating proscribed food?"

"One, it's full of protein, and you need a lot of protein, I'd guess. And two, it's a delicacy which we've had preserved in the larder since before the protection regulation was issued."

"How come it's protected?"

"It's one of the links in the chain which ends with the worms in the wormwood." She paused. "Since they've gone into mass wormwood plantings, they've found that the trees have outgrown the natural increase in other necessary parts of the cycle. One species of which is the sanderling."

"Oh. You realize you're going to have to go on the run with me, don't you?" He had a disconcerting way of changing the subject suddenly.

She pushed away from the table and walked around, looking at the expensive wormwood paneling she and her mother had installed a few years ago. She touched the wood, somehow knowing that her life was ending in some fashion. Never again would she be comfortable as Tique Sovereign, aquadynamacist for Wormwood, Inc.

"They've identified me as the culprit at the arena," she said.

"Not to mention harboring and sheltering a fugitive— thank you very much—the most wanted man, and so on."

"I'm pretty well sunk, aren't I?" It all came over her at once. It was so overwhelming, she couldn't even think about it. She sat down heavily. Never in her wildest dreams had she pictured anything like this happening to her. What would she do?

"There is a way out, you know." His voice was quiet. He was studying her, judging her. Watching her reactions.

"Oh?"

"As long as they think you've got your mother's secret, or have some access to it, you're in trouble. We simply remove, ah, the source of the trouble."

"What do you mean?" She took a bite of her food, tentatively wanting to believe Reubin that there was a way out.

"Josephine Neff. Fels Nodivving. Maybe even Wormwood, Inc."

"Kill them?"

"That's one option. This sanderling is good. Say we remove Nodivving and Neff one way or the other. The system still remains. The power base. The engine that drives the Constabulary which wants us badly. Never mind the hidden, personal reasons why top officials want us."

Tique sipped her coffee. She enunciated her words carefully. "You are telling me, Reubin Flood, that you intend to bring down the government? Wormwood, Inc.?"

"It had occurred to me," he said.

He'd said it matter-of-factly, casually, modestly. Tique said, "Oh, my God." Then she laughed. "Rather audacious. And right after breakfast. Also a big bite to chew. How do you plan to go about this?"

"I don't know yet. But I'm working on it."

"I was afraid you might have the answer," she said.

"Eventually. But you realize it will be much more difficult soon?"

"After the blizzard?"

"Right," he said. "We'll be on our own, out in the wilds, with little more than our wits." His look was piercing. "We'll be on the run, hunted by damn near everybody on Snister. We've got to maintain our freedom while we strike back."

She sighed in resignation. "From that platform you intend to bring down the officials, the economic system, and the governmental system of a planet?"

"Why not? It's the only way we'll straighten this mess out. Are there any more of those muffins? Ah. Thank you very much." He took a bite. "Think about what food you have that's nutritious and dry-preserved and that we can carry."

"I haven't decided whether I'm going with you or not," she said carefully.

"If you want an invitation, you're hereby officially invited. If not, say hello to the Constabulary and your friends for me. Keep in mind they have nothing to lose, now. You're a goner. When they get hold of you, your mind will be grits inside one day."

She'd figured that out, but hadn't wanted to admit it to herself yet. She wondered what a grit was. "But I don't know Mother's secret."

"They've probably guessed that by now, but they can't take the chance. See, you're their only link. Your father's gone off and taken the Change, severing any ties with this life. No way they can trace him through the Long Life Institute. If your mother had any other husbands or offspring in previous lives on other worlds, Wormwood, Inc. doesn't have access to them—and, frankly, shouldn't—according to the rules of the LLI. They have access to one person: you."

She shook her head. Her life, her existence, was crumbling at his every word.

"Look, doubtless Alex knew some secret of the Long Life Institute, but in the centuries she'd been around, she hadn't told anybody, so why should she be expected to tell you?'' Reubin cut a chunk of sanderling and ate it with relish. ''They probably have guessed that much, but they can't take the chance. Come with me. I'd feel a lot better, not having to worry about you.''

And be alone with him in the wilderness? ''I am not your charge, someone for you to concern yourself over.''

He was silent for a moment. ''I beg to differ. You are the only link I have to my dead wife. I want to know why someone killed her. Additionally, I feel an obligation to Alex to insure no one harms you in any fashion.''

''It's the least you can do, right?''

He stared at her. ''I was not patronizing you. Don't be so damn touchy.'' He grinned. ''Nor am I after your fair and attractive body.''

''Reubin? What did the designs you made in the arena sand mean?'' They seemed tied in with his unwillingness to discuss himself.

''I've thought a lot,'' he said, ignoring her question. ''I'm having a hard time expressing my anger properly; but it is my intention to explore ways to disrupt the well-oiled machine here. For that I need your assistance.''

''What are you talking about?''

''Wormwood, Inc. It, in the end, is responsible for Alexandra's death. I'm going to bring it down, all the way down. Destroy the company.''

''By yourself, of course.''

''With you, if you're willing. You can't stay here. I was thinking in terms of guerrilla tactics, classic eco-raiding, till we discover their Achilles' heel.''

She was already nodding. Her secret desire. Stop the indiscriminate planting of wormwood trees. ''You're saying wormwood is an agricultural product. Find a vulnerable spot in its ecosystem and attack?''

''Exactly. Or a variation on that theme. Perhaps the mechanics of the operation would be our focus point. To do any of this, I need you. You know Wormwood, Inc. You know its operations. You know about wormwood trees. You know about Snister. You know locations and geography. I need you.''

"Right." It was an exciting prospect. Strike a blow for nature. But she'd be alone with him out in the wetlands. Well, she was alone with him here and now, wasn't she? And nothing frightening had happened. "Okay," she said grudgingly. "I'm in."

He rose quickly. "I'll check the weather radar and the forecast. You hunt up some lightweight travel food. Do you have any weapons here?"

"A pencil laser."

"Great. I've got a knife. Now we're even."

"You've left one thing out," she told him.

"What's that?"

"You've got gall," she said.

7: CAD

Snister. A man named Reubin Flood.

Cadmington Abbot-Pubal stared at his screen.

The first possible clue as to the whereabouts of Habu—or whatever name he was going by now—in over a century.

Robert Lee was Habu's name when he lived here.

The man was careful. Cad had long since decided Habu had some kind of miracle ability to hide, change identities. Which all added to the myth. The more years went by, the more people thought Habu was one of the founding myths of humanity; Cad was one of the few who knew better.

Ironically, word had reached him here on Tsuruga, part of the Ryukyu Retto group in the Fukui Prefecture—which Cad's ancestors had pioneered and then abandoned after Habu had wreaked his havoc. Those who lived through the ordeal.

He was here for perhaps the tenth time, to the planet of his origin, at one of the two towns remaining on the once populated planet. Scientists ran the two bubble-dome settlements; and tourists and curious journalists paid enormous sums for the privilege of visiting what was now known as "The Planet of Snakes." The tourist industry supported the scientific observations and made somebody wealthy, Cad was sure, though he didn't know who. Well, that investigation could be done another time.

He stepped out of his quarters and looked through the

bubbledome. Yep, there was one now. A couple of meters long, big dark green spots and bands. *Trimeresurus flavoviridis*. Green of the snake merging with green of the jungle—perfect camouflage. A mutated viper from Olde Earthe—habu, from Okinawa, somewhere off the coast, he remembered, of Asia in the Pacific Ocean. The original habu from Okinawa had been poisonous—about the same as other vipers such as the rattlesnake or fer-de-lance, but somewhere in the transport to Tsuruga or in their caged zoo confinement, the snake had changed gradually over the years. Maybe it was the UV rays here, he thought. Now the Tsuruga version of the habu could kill a person instantly.

Thanks a lot, Robert Lee, Reubin Flood, or whatever your name is now.

Cad felt a presence and tore his eyes from the bubble.

"Hi, Cad." Jane Wakasa stopped beside him. She was one of the scientists and her face showed more Oriental ancestry than Cad's face did. Many of those original Tsurugan traits had been assimilated; the Japanese genetic pool had become absorbed and diluted by a mobile humanity. Giving Cad another reason to hate Habu: the man had killed off the Okinawan variation of Japanese. Some called it genocide.

Cad smiled at Jane and wondered if they could be related in some obscure way. "Going out today?" He nodded to the jungle outside.

"Nuh-uh," she shook her head. "I done my time yesterday." She looked at him in the way women did who were interested in him and had made inroads.

He smiled. A classic womanizer, he liked aggressive women. "I didn't want to go out myself." After the disaster—genocide—and the subsequent exodus from Tsuruga, scientists had decided to allow the habu snakes to reproduce, with no controls. Which, in effect, they had already done. The scientists simply quit fighting them. Since the snakes were already introduced and too numerous to do anything about, they'd decided, centuries ago, to allow them to continue to run rampant. Theoretically it was an experiment to determine what a foreign, or alien, life-form could do to a total eco-system. Since there were no natural enemies of the habu, then there remained only their own population pressure and availability of food source to limit their growth.

Now there were tons of snakes per square meter out there, he thought. No wonder the inhabitants—the few remaining after Robert Lee had wreaked his havoc—had abandoned the place.

Now it required bubbledomes and power grids to insure the safety of humans.

"Anybody home?" Jane asked.

"Oops. 'Scuse me, JW. I was lost in thought."

"And you claimed you weren't scientifically oriented."

"Well," he said, "us journalists have been known to crank up the brain on occasion."

"That's nice. Listen. About tonight. . . ?"

He groaned and sighed in turn. He shook his head wistfully. "Can't. Got to take the mail run out this afternoon."

"Oh?" Her eyebrows shot up.

He nodded. She knew his background; hell, everybody knew he was the most knowledgeable expert in the entire Federation on Habu. "A possible sighting on a planet named Snister."

Her face fell. "They ought to shoot people who give planets tacky names."

He shrugged. "Somebody made an inquiry as to background or meaning of a serpentine symbol to the sector capital. So it got into the system and my syndicate picked it up and passed it on to me."

"Somebody just asking about a symbol?"

"A drawing is more like it," he said. "Actually, two of them. One a simple striking snake, the other a giant, triangular head."

Jane shivered. "Ugh. I want nothing to do with it. I've heard stories . . ." She turned back to the bubble. "You always hear that Habu is a legend, not real, like

Davy Crockett, Mike Hammer, Valentine Smith.'' She put her hand on the bubble and shivered again. ''Not me. Not here. Habu was real all right. Anybody who's been here and seen the jungle writhing with snakes—agh!'' She shook herself. ''Do you think he did it on purpose?''

''Actually,'' Cad said, ''I've read where some scientists speculate that the snakes just got away from him. Simply crawled off into the jungle.''

''That's what I was referring to,'' she said.

''I've heard the behavior described as a psychotic break,'' Cad said. ''No contact with reality. Hallucinations. But I suspect the label psychopathic fits better; he certainly disregarded normal behavioral restraints. I'm convinced—and you know I've done my research—that when he did what he did, he planned it coldly and logically and executed his plan in a premeditated, murderous fashion. Genocide is not reasonable.''

She shook her head. ''One man responsible for all this.'' She waved her hand toward the outside. She shook her head again.

''I know what you mean,'' he said. ''How about lunch instead?''

She looked at him speculatively. ''Tempting, Cad. What time does the shuttle leave?''

Cad wished fervently that he didn't have to run off to some planet called Snister. But nothing would stop him. Nothing.

The first actual lead in a hundred and twenty or thirty Fed-standard years. The original habu from Okinawa was known to be able to fast for a couple of years before death. One had been observed to fast almost four years back in the late twentieth century before the experiment had been discontinued. Cad likened the Habu he sought to the snake in his ability to disappear into the background and gut it out for years, on a low level of energy and living off his own fat—outliving those who sought him. But once Habu emerged from the man in a high-energy burst, he was highly visible.

And lethal.

On Snister, they actually have a video of this person, Cad thought. Then he asked himself yet again, "If I ever find this chameleon named Habu, does the Fed still want me to kill him?"

8. REUBIN

"Ready," Tique said, coat and backpack in arms.

"Lookin' good," Reubin said. "Remember, do it just as we outlined. Somebody will be listening or hear a recording later." He hoisted his pack. "By the way, that's a very nice watchdog program you've got here."

"Thanks," she said. "I do computers a lot."

"I know. I've benefited." He was still impressed with her performance at the Corona.

He could tell Tique regretted leaving the cabin. She was taking it well so far. A person who'd been sheltered all her life, now the very fabric of her existence had been ripped apart. Mother dead. Now she was on the run with the most wanted man on Snister—and a hell of a lot of other places she didn't need to know about.

The blizzard abated somewhat as they drove down the mountain. Reubin shivered, thinking again of the lake and almost freezing to death.

Tique drove skillfully, though the terrain-following program helped and this road contained the magnetic strips which enabled the groundcar to follow automatically. They were going to take advantage of the more advanced road closer to Cuyas.

"I'm not sure I can go through with it," Reubin said.

"You can do it, Reubin, I just know it," Tique replied, voice stiff at first.

"It's simply not in me to surrender."

"Well," she said, voice more relaxed. "We've discussed it and discussed it and it's best. We can get the whole thing cleared up.''

"Dammit, they tried to *kill* me," Reubin said.

"That could be a result of underlings exceeding orders.''

"I'll grant that." He was getting into his role.

"What about the snake's head and stuff you drew in the arena?" she asked. He'd told her to ask, but refused to answer her real questions as the two had outlined this plan.

"Something I read in a book once," he said. "I was simply confusing the issue out there in the arena. Sort of putting a hex on the place." Habu's challenge. For the moment, he'd overcome his hate and suppressed his alter ego. He didn't need the publicity surrounding public awareness of Habu. Then he thought of Alex again and almost changed his mind once more. This planet needs Habu to tear it apart. But, he argued, more can be done anonymously. Otherwise, you'll have every Fed jerk in the sector down here like stink on manure.

"Maybe we can get hold of Fels—or Josephine Neff," Tique continued, playing her part well.

"That'd be the only way it'll ever get straightened out," he said, right on cue. He paused momentarily. "The more I think about that, the better I like it."

Tique swung onto a feeder route. "It might be that they'll listen to me."

"I don't know why. Dammit. You don't know what Alex knew. Hell, I didn't even know she *had* a secret. Maybe there's a way we could profit from this . . ."

"Reubin!"

The point was to convince Nodivving that he and Tique knew nothing, which would take some of the pressure off. What better way to make your point than to suggest something perhaps illegal, showing greed. That ought to help anyway, he thought.

"Disregard," he snapped. "We drive around Cuyas a while, and I'll decide. There's an apartment—well, let's just wait and see. Hey, conditions are better at lower altitudes, aren't they? How come you have a cabin so high up?'' He felt awkward playacting to some unseen present or future audience. And an unfriendly one at that.

From there the conversation went to normal give and take. The apartment gambit was to mislead. They might well believe he and Tique were holed up in town and expend their search energies there.

In two hours, Tique found a major thoroughfare leading to Cuyas. They drove through rain for awhile. Then the rain quit and the skies cleared a little.

When twenty kilometers from Cuyas, they pulled over at a rest stop. After a few minutes, they stuck their heads back in.

''Now I need a nap,'' he said.

''I'll be real quiet,'' she replied, punching instructions onto the control board.

Reubin thought he wouldn't believe it himself, but somebody might be dumb enough to.

They closed their doors and stepped back. The car surged out onto the route and headed for Cuyas. It would terminate in the largest, most frequented auto-park in the city. Let them try to work that one out, Reubin thought. The plan was to do it this way in case the bug was actually broadcasting and not simply recording. Anything to buy time.

A freight hauler was coming along the main highway and they ducked behind shrubbery even though the driver was probably asleep. If there was a driver.

They were in the foothills now, and crossed the highway to head around this mountain range. Their goal was the major Company-planted wormwood groves.

Once they were away from roadways and possible observation, Reubin slowed down to a pace comfortable for Tique.

When the writhing hit his mind, his face must have shown it, for he'd let his controlling biofeedback program drop—he hadn't thought he'd need it while doing the primarily physical activity of traveling across country on foot.

''Reubin? What? Oh,'' she said, understanding crossing her face. ''Is it that bad yet?''

"I'll make it," he said, and locked in a quickie biofeedback program to handle the lesser attacks.

"You really don't have the time left to do this, do you?" Concern filled her voice.

He took comfort in that concern. "Yes, I do," he said emphatically. He stopped and looked at her. Ordinarily he kept his own counsel, but this time he was completely honest with her. "I will *make* time. It's that important."

"You will go mad." Her words were a simple statement, not a question.

"Maybe, but first I will finish what I have begun."

They began walking again. "Jeez," Tique said. "Mother meant that much to you?"

More, he thought, but merely grunted. He realized the totality of his commitment. He'd waited too long this time to take the Change. The pressure was mounting too swiftly. He wouldn't be able to control it for long. Then his brain would burn and fizzle and it would be too late.

Then again, perhaps Habu would have some input into the situation.

Then again, perhaps he'd have to accelerate his plans.

Should he give it up? Just sneak off Snister and forget the whole thing? After all, he'd bitten off quite a lot, taking on an entire planet—especially while on the downhill slide of the mental consequences of living so many centuries.

It occurred to him that he'd really been looking forward to going through the Change with Alex and spending a lifetime with her. Right damn now, he decided, I am not interested in continuing my existence. I will take my vengeance upon this world, and the consequences be damned.

Habu stirred. *We will live.* The survival reflex.

Reubin responded. –You know I've lived too long past my time to undergo the Change. Most likely, it's your fault. It is my intention to finish this job before I seek the Change.

We will kill.

–Right.

Soon.

—Perhaps. But we will do it my way this time, even if it's too late. They might catch me and we'd be dead anyway.

We will kill many first. Habu settled back contentedly.

Reubin thought that at least he'd diverted his alter ego. That and he'd introduced the serpent to the fact they might die. They'd face all those questions when they arose.

He felt better for solidifying this thinking, but knew this attitude was brought on by the mental pressure—not by his natural judgment and 'druthers.

He cautioned himself that it wasn't just his own life he was laying on the line.

Tique. Yes, Tique.

"A sanderling," Tique pointed.

"Makes me think I'm hungry," he said.

"Not yet."

Rain began to fall lightly. "Not again," he said.

"You'd best get used to it." She took out a package not quite as big as her fingernail and unfolded it until the ultralite poncho shook free. She donned it.

Reubin did the same. He wished they weren't neutral in color, but camo. That would help—not with an IR scan, but with visual.

"Reubin? Will you tell me about the snakes? Really. You've been avoiding it." She shrugged her poncho into position. "There's something to it, more than you're admitting. It makes me . . . apprehensive." Her face was determined and her voice told Reubin he needed to answer her question. The thing is, he thought, he would not be reassuring whatsoever.

He didn't answer right away, sloshing along. "Who the hell would choose to live on this place?"

She moved up beside him. "Me. Tell me about *you*. Your performance at the Corona was something to behold. You had two hundred thousand people there rooting for you in addition to whoever was watching on televideo."

He ran his hand over the raspy growth upon his head under the poncho hood. He was uncomfortable discussing this. "I'm uncomfortable discussing this," he said as soon as the thought crossed his mind.

"Well," Tique said, "I'm uncomfortable out here in the wilds with a man I hardly know. I'm uncomfortable being chased by the Constabulary. I'm uncomfortable with a lot of things."

She had made the right decisions so far. Else she'd be drugged at this very moment with a completely emptied brain.

And she was Alexandra's daughter.

And there were excellent reasons to tell her about Habu.

He turned his head toward her. Drizzle fell between them. "You've a right to know." He stopped walking and she stopped beside him. He put a foot up on a boulder to stretch his hamstring. Or to stall, trying to decide how to tell her.

"Well?" Tique wasn't as patient as she'd been at other times.

"I'm going to tell you because I doubt I'll come out of this alive. Alex was . . . well, she meant a lot to me—"

"Not again," Tique said, exasperation showing in her voice. "What are you talking about *this* time? Another secret?"

"I'm leaving you a survival legacy. I suppose humankind will breathe easier knowing I'm dead. I owe them that much." He watched her face reflect an incipient fear his words were generating. "Plus it will give you such instant attention and fame to be the one to tell the story that no one on or off Snister will dare touch you. I'm giving you a weapon, a terrible one: knowledge."

Her look had changed to one of confusion. "You're going to tell me you aren't Reubin Flood."

"Correct." He sighed. "I am the one they call Habu."

Disbelief flooded her face. Her head moved backward. She stared at him.

He let the silence grow, broken only by the soft rain tinkling off of rocks.

No. Habu was alert now. His message was that he/they were exposed now and in danger.

–*It is my decision*, Reubin told emphatically.

It is our affair only.

–*Circumstances require this.* Reubin was determined to maintain control.

Tique was still staring at him with awe and dawning understanding. She was adding everything she knew and had seen. Her face was slack. "You're *him?*"

"Yes."

She stared at him for a moment longer. "Oh, dear sweet Jesus. I never thought he was real." She looked forward again, stepping around a large rock. "*You're* him?"

"Yes."

She searched his face.

"You know? I'm inclined to believe you."

He shrugged. "You asked, I told you."

"Habu is supposed to be a myth."

"Sometimes myths are based on reality. Just exaggerated."

"If even one tenth of what is said is true . . . ."

He shrugged.

At least her reaction wasn't one of fear. "It explains a lot." Well, she was Alex's daughter.

He nodded.

"Reubin? Would you tell me about it? Did you really decimate an entire planet? Have you killed and killed through the centuries?"

"Suffice it to know that I do not kill indiscriminately, nor do I eat little babies."

Abruptly, she sat down on a nearby boulder. "You just admitted to genocide."

"Not really," he said mildly. He leaned forward and rested his crossed arms on his upraised knee. "Genocide is a big, bad word. I refuse that label."

"Oh?" Eyes raised. She was angry now, forgetting for a moment her own position.

"Look, damn it. I'm not going to go over the whole thing again." He didn't want the memories which were not memories but years worth of nightmares. He forced his mind back to the present. "Tsuruga. The riots. The pogroms. They killed everyone from Earthe."

"Except you." The challenge was obvious in her voice.

"Except me." He fixed his eyes on hers. Water dripped off the hood of his poncho. "My family. Wife and child," he hesitated, "newborn . . . and friends and fellow workers at the Earthe Embassy. And all the other Original Earthers on Tsuruga—businessmen, students, tourists, immigrants. Most were killed in a barbaric, merciless fashion by mobs whipped to killing frenzies." The memory brought an agonized bitterness to his words. "It was so savage that I went berserk—insane—for years, I don't know how long, and when I came to my senses, here was Habu inside me—"

Incredulity spread over her face. She shook off her hood. "There's *someone* inside you?"

"Yes and no." How to explain? "Perhaps I went mad, schizophrenic or multiple personality or something. What happened during that long period was that I metamorphosed into something I still don't quite understand. At any rate, the result was that I depopulated Tsuruga; some I must have killed directly, some died as a result of my seeding the place with snakes. The remainder of the depopulation of Tsuruga they blame on me came from panicked people escaping from the planet. They left for fear of the monster I'd become, the monster who would kill them as he had so many before them. And they left at the very end because the planet was no longer habitable by humans." His anger had grown and grown and his voice turned brutal. "*Remember* those same people of Tsuruga turned me into Habu; and those same people were guilty of participating in the murders of all Original Earthers. The others were guilty of failing to stop those murders."

"Yet they died anyway. Was it your position to judge?"

"*No.*" The word was emphatic. "It was *not* my intention to kill all those people either on purpose or accidentally. Just the ones responsible: the rioting rabble and their governmental and religious leaders who had instigated the pogroms and worked the rioters into the frenzied hatred of all things and people from Earthe.'' He had to rein himself in. He was getting too wound up. He needed a clear head and he didn't need to make Tique angry with him. ''I carry the guilt of those actions. Yet it was something long in the past.''

Surprisingly, she empathized with him. ''It must have been terrible, what happened to cause all that.'' Her hair was soaked.

He nodded, remembering. He wanted to tell her that the trauma was worse, far worse, than any meager words could convey. ''No human being should have to go through what I did. Nor should any creature with any kind of awareness.'' He lifted his head and opened his mouth. Rain cooled his throat. ''It's why Habu reacts with violence. I try to control that reaction. Most of the time I succeed.''

She stood. ''And now you're dividing your attention in addition to fighting off the building mental pressure from not taking the Change.''

''Yeah.'' Leave me alone, please? ''Thanks for trusting me.''

This time she shrugged. ''I'm not sure of my judgment. But I trust Mother's.''

After many days of careful hiking and avoiding all people and places where they might encounter people, they reached the beginning of the uninhabited area.

At first, Tique was quiet and reserved, favoring him with frequent curious glances. Eventually she determined to accept him at face value: Reubin Flood as opposed to the legendary killer. Although she believed Reubin's story, ''Habu'' was not someone she felt ready to acknowledge.

On the second day, Reubin had had to move slowly because of blisters on Tique's feet. Though she was a hiker, her previous hikes had been day trips, and leisurely ones. He'd been forcing the pace, and they walked for more than half the day. While distance was important to him for safety reasons, he knew that he must hurry—

the pressure was becoming more insistent—he didn't know how much time he had left.

On the fifth day, their rations were gone. Reubin began hunting and trapping their food. Fish were the easiest.

On the seventh day, they crossed a line of rocky foothills. A storm caused them to seek shelter under a low overhang.

"Might as well stay here for the night," Reubin said. "Be too dark to travel soon." He didn't want to traverse hills at night and in a storm.

"I'm starved," Tique said. They hadn't stopped to search out any food that day.

Reubin knew foraging for something to eat wouldn't work, either—not that these barren hills offered much sustenance. "Here." He scraped lichen off a rock and held it out to Tique.

"Me? Eat that?" Tique's voice was both amused and astounded.

"Sure. It used to be called rock tripe. It will keep hunger away tonight at least."

"No, thanks. I think I'll fast tonight. It'd be good for my figure."

"You must've fasted a lot."

"Um, thanks, Reubin."

The next day they were rounding a mountain range, as they would for days, keeping within the lip of sparse woods. Reubin set a few traps and deadfalls. He captured several small animals. That evening, he made soup in their large container, mixing edible plants and chunks of meat.

"I never thought I'd enjoy something like this," Tique said, drinking from her cup. "Natural, fresh killed meat. Jeez, what'll it be next?"

Reubin was pleased with the way she'd adjusted to hardship. At first she'd been quiet, hurting from blisters. Then when her feet had hardened and become used to the incessant walking, she'd been easier to live with. He'd been afraid that Tique Sovereign would turn out to be a spoiled product of too much civilization.

He considered alternatives. He could have sought another city, and with a few breaks, obtained her a new identity, and eventually gotten her off planet. On the other hand, he knew he needed her and her knowledge of all things on and about Snister.

He went to sleep that night under a lean-to, wondering if he really wanted to destroy Snister's economy. This entire planet had not been part of the thing which had killed his wife. And there were people here whose livelihoods depended on Wormwood, Inc. Maybe he'd have to determine culpability in Alexandra's death. Nodivving. Josephine Neff. Officials of Wormwood, Inc. Which was sufficient for him to consider destroying the Company. He understood that Wormwood, Inc. was a subsidiary of a parent megacorp named Omend. Omend which did business throughout the Federation. Omend which most people in the Federation had heard of or done business with. Things to study upon.

"So this is a wormwood tree," Reubin said, glad to have reached at least the outskirts of the wormwood growing area.

"That's it."

Reubin stretched his neck. "No wonder it's so expensive." The tree was perhaps a hundred meters tall. "You'd have to set aside part of your day to walk around this thing." It promised to be a tough opponent. He discarded the idea of simply cutting down trees. The thing was of gray bark with broad limbs beginning halfway up the trunk. Some scrub here and there, dead limbs and smaller limbs which couldn't grow as wide and large without access to sunlight. Pods up there in the foliage. Moss. Animals and birds and insects. A world of its own.

It dominated the bank of a stream coming out of the mountains.

Tique walked to the stream. She tested the water. "Um, cold. But I don't care. I'm taking a bath." They'd hit a dry stretch with no rain for a couple of days and sweat attracted caked dirt.

Reubin studied the area closely. No sign of people.

Most of the stream was covered by several nearby worm-wood trees. "Go ahead. You don't know of anything dangerous in the water, do you?"

"Nah," she said. "Not on Snister." She dropped her pack and took off her boots. She looked at him. "I've lost my vanity somewhere along the trail. Be advised I'm washing my undies, too." She stripped her trailjeans and pulled her tunic over her head. As she walked into the stream, Reubin gave her the appreciative once-over she'd been soliciting. He thought that maybe she was angry with him; after all, they'd been in the wilds alone for how many days now?—and he hadn't tried to seduce her yet. Which she might take as a personal insult to her looks and charms. His eyes roamed the forest on the far side of the stream and continued roving, seeking any possible danger. Tique was an impressionable young lady. Quite an attractive one. She was her mother's daughter, wasn't she?

But Reubin was still operating on intense anger. They'd killed Alex and he had to be single-minded about his response. Not to mention the fact that his brain was slowly turning into genuine grade-A mush. He didn't want to estimate how long he had before permanent damage occurred. Madness. Constant debilitating pain. With death standing next in line.

Nor did it matter, for he did not expect to live through this.

"Damn, Tique," he said, words forced from him, "get into the water before I get ideas."

She looked over her shoulder, a glint of triumph in her eye. She slowed her progress into the water even more. Women, Reubin thought inanely, because he didn't want to admit she was getting to him.

For a while she cavorted in the deeper water, then came up and sat shoulder-deep in front of him. She began scrubbing out her underwear. Reubin could remember when there was no such thing as superdur, indestructible material which you had to attack with a laser to destroy or even inflict minor damage. This stuff could be washed easily and it would dry in a quick breeze or a little sunlight.

He put his back to the tree, looked up, and wondered just exactly how in the frozen *hell* he was going to interfere with this forpin' behemoth of a tree. "Tell me about wormwood. About these glaciers they call trees."

Tique held her underpants up and inspected them.

For some unaccountable reason, Reubin felt comfortable with the domesticity.

She began rubbing them together in the water again. "I'm not expert. Mother was the expert—"

Reubin had stopped feeling pangs of anger whenever Tique mentioned Alex. Which was often. He didn't think he was getting over the loss of his wife; he simply thought that it was something he was able to share with Tique.

"—but I can give you a quick layman's rundown. The wormwood, like much of nature, is at the hub of its own little ecosystem. The whole thing depends on an annual cycle. Believe it or not, there is a dry season and fire, sometimes, which surprisingly insures survival. Now—"

"Maybe you could start at the beginning?" Something? Something odd—what *is* it. Let the animal Habu out a little—there. Senses more wary now, more alert—

"The trees are so large, they'd kill each other off and never grow right if fire didn't occur sometimes, keeping too many of the seedlings—if not all the seedlings for several seasons—from growing. See, the—"

Smell! That was it. An odor which did not belong, but one with which he was familiar, at least somewhat. What? Where?

Habu flooded into his body.

He rose to his feet slowly, knife appearing in his hand.

Tique's voice trailed off. Her eyes were stuck to him, obviously seeing his immediate and total change.

He crouched. Where had he smelled that before?

The animal part of his brain was running full out, selecting and discarding possibilities.

Got it!

Gnurl. He began to speak, to warn Tique.

When the gnurl lunged past the tree and headed right for her.

Her face whitened, her eyes widened.

The gnurl was on its first bound, razor-hooves lancing into the air for Tique when Reubin launched himself at the beast. Had his reflexes not been Habu inspired, he wouldn't have made it in time. His left arm snaked around the gnurl's neck and he dragged alongside the beast, feet leaving the ground, the massive shoulder muscles bunching and pistoning against Reubin.

He wasted no time trying to mount the animal. He simply whipped the knife across the gnurl's throat as quickly and as many times as he could. His left arm pulled with all its strength, forcing the beast to its right.

They splashed through the shallows, barely missing Tique.

Blood was spurting all over his hand and knife, but he kept it up. Inspiration born of necessity hit him and he cut with his knife longitudinally, instead of from side to side.

The extra depth of the blow must have severed some artery, for the gnurl slid to a stop and attacked Reubin with its massive fat, but flat, teeth. One nip of the jaws at his face and Reubin dropped, rolled, and dived into the water. The stream was cloudy with blood and Reubin managed to swim around the gnurl underwater, dodging a few lashes of deadly hooves.

He erupted on the gnurl's left side and landed upon the animal's back. Deciding to do the safe route, he hacked at the gnurl's eyes with his knife. Blood, pus, pulp, and slimy matter squirted. The animal bleated and whined a primal scream of pain.

Knowing full well where the heart was on the beast, Reubin straddled the gnurl, his legs holding tightly, leaned down, and began stabbing at the heart.

By then, though, it had become unnecessary. The gnurl fell forward into the water, spasmed, and lay still. The carcass bobbed in the reddening water.

Reubin kicked himself away. He grabbed a back leg of the animal and began dragging it toward shore.

Tique was standing there half dressed. When she saw his face, she stepped back involuntarily.

Reubin reasserted control, and submerged the Habu warrior within him. Habu had enjoyed the diversion.

Tique looked mighty fetching, wearing only her tunic. That sight helped Reubin regain his humanity.

Her body trembled. "Reubin, I . . ." She took a deep breath and spoke more slowly. "It was as if you were possessed—"

"I'm human again," he said. "That I will prove manifestly if you don't get some pants on."

"Oh." She scrambled into her shorts and then her trailjeans.

Reubin dragged the gnurl's corpse partway onto the rocky shore. "Can you eat these things?"

She looked strangely at him as she adjusted her jeans.

It took him a moment to realize that she was thinking of the arena when he'd taken a bite out of the still-beating heart of a gnurl.

"Sure," she said, now fully dressed. "It's tough unless tenderized, especially a wild one not bred and conditioned to be a food animal. But it's a herbivore and has no organisms which will harm humans."

He looked at the giant animal. "I hope you're hungry. He's already bled."

Reubin scouted the area to check if there were any more gnurls. He found a salt lick on the far side of the stream. It was probably the attraction that had drawn the gnurl.

So he returned and hacked off chunks of gnurl meat, wrapped it in part of the skin, and they moved deeper into the forest until Reubin found a clearing suitable for his purposes. Great limbs covered most of the clearing, but enough sunlight made it through.

He built a fire and roasted gnurl steaks. After living on dried rations, fowl like sanderling, and fish, he craved real red meat. He burned his steak on the outside and ate while Tique was still cooking hers.

She looked at him with distaste as blood and juice ran

down his face, stained his ragged new beard, and dripped onto the ground.

He ignored her.

When he finished, he began cooking another "steak," actually a hunk of meat. While he did that, he cut more of the meat into long wide strips of about a half inch thick. He made some brine with salt he'd obtained from the salt lick. He placed the brine and cut strips of meat in a pouch made from the gnurl's hide.

"Whatcha doin'?" Tique asked.

"Soaking the meat in brine. Tomorrow, we'll make jerky."

He ate his other hunk of meat. Tique finally began at hers, chewing quite daintily in counterpoint to him. He didn't care. Sated, he curled up against a tree, set Habu as a sentinel, and fell asleep. The technique had saved his life many times—and allowed him the necessary sleep to stay alive.

"Permanent, like hell," Tique said, working her fingers through her hair, untangling.

What Reubin called "the frizzies" had died somewhere along the trail and Tique was letting her auburn hair grow. He fingered his own hair and said ruefully, "If my old first sergeant could see me now, he'd be proud."

Tique glanced at him, then understanding lighted her face. "Times change, we change, no?"

He nodded and smiled.

She frowned. "Darn. You've got me doing it now. Cryptic and reflective. Golly, Mr. Flood. I don't know what to think."

He did. She'd grown considerably since he'd first met her. A sheltered woman, never having any trials or tribs. Now she was on the run and adjusting to survival off the land. And had apparently reconciled herself to the fact that he was the infamous Habu.

Reubin turned to the framework of small limbs he'd built. He began laying the strips of gnurl meat he'd cut the evening before on the crosspieces. "Back to work.

This is going to take a couple of days, so you've time to tell me about wormwood, annual cycles and all.''

"Sure.'' Tique ran her brush through her hair continuously. "Hope this helps.'' She winced at a tangle. "I know, start at the beginning. During the dry season, the fires hit the area sometimes, benefiting the trees. Fire clears out the minor foliage which would steal the nutrients from the wormwood tree. As I was saying yesterday, it keeps most of the seedlings from growing. Kind of like a policing mechanism, keeping the population of trees at the right number for the land to support.'' She looked pointedly at him. "Until the Company began its own plantings.''

"The fires don't kill all the trees? Even those which need to survive?'' He began building a small fire under the framework.

"No. They are fire resistant because of their thick and sort of spongy bark. Thus, too, the fires don't travel *up* the trunk to the more susceptible growth.''

"I don't believe there is a prolonged dry season,'' Reubin said.

"Well, there is. Except it'll be shorter and shorter with all the new wormwood trees they've planted and are fixing to plant. The 'greenhouse effect,' you understand.''

"I do.'' Reubin adjusted a support. "Go ahead.''

Tique waved her hand toward the mountains. "All the growing ground for the wormwood trees is like here: a fertile flood plain. Lots of rivers and streams coming from melting snow above. What they call a riverine forest.''

"How do you know all this?''

"Remember my job?''

"Oh, yeah. Something I can't even spell.''

She continued brushing her hair. "Recall all these rivers and streams, for later in the cycle these overflow—but I'm getting ahead of myself. Okay. The trees produce flowers during the dry season when rivers are calm and not threatening to overflow. Animals and birds eat the flowers or the nectar and go from tree to tree pollinating. One prime fowl of which is the sanderling.''

"Which is why they put it on an endangered list.''

Reubin nodded to himself. Could he use this? "Without the sanderling, the process would break down?"

"There are other animals which perform the same function, but not as well and as often as the sanderling. Nobody knows the answer to that question, but the experts figure it that way." She paused. "Your fire isn't big enough to cook the meat that high and far away."

Reubin laid more meat strips on the latticework above the fire. "It's not supposed to. The fire's just for keeping insects off the meat and any dampness away." Absently, he chewed on a strip of raw meat. "Generally, you make jerky by letting the sun and wind dry it. The brine helps harden and blacken the outside of the stuff better."

"Oh. It preserves better."

"Yep."

"Back to the wormwood saga, which is becoming longer than it takes to grow a forest of 'em. We've got sanderlings and other animals carrying pollen here and there. The next phase is that fruit develops and falls, which feeds more animals who've come to depend on it for survival. Okay, we've got sap rising and leaves developing and fruit developing and falling off. The fruit's called 'clumps,' a big pod full of cottonlike stuff and seeds."

"Here, let me do the back," Reubin said, and took the brush from her. He knelt behind her and began stroking her hair and fashioning it with his hand.

"Thanks. You're a man of many talents."

"Sure, kid. When do we get to the worm part of the wormwood."

"Right now. The worms feed on these seeds. The worm breeding season is nature-timed to coincide with the fallen fruit. Now I don't understand all I know about it, because I skipped biology class a lot—"

"Me, too." He continued brushing, moving to the sides of her head.

"I don't understand if worms do it by themselves, with other worms, by twos, threes, or whatever. But they do it. At that point, they head for the nearest safe-haven: the tree itself. After a sufficient number of years of this, a nice little worm colony has developed. The individual worms go about their individual business, and have little baby worms. Many of which grow up to travel out on their own, those who haven't bred and, after the fires have hit the area causing some kind of interaction between the falling sap and the actual physical contraction of the bark, manage to crawl down the trunk of the tree and begin the process again, but leaving their parents and some of their fellow siblings to keep up their work inside the tree, thus to—"

"You can stop and breathe anytime now," Reubin said.

"Thanks. Did I forget to say some seeds survive to germinate and grow—"

"No, you didn't get to that. But I kind of figured it."

"Ow!"

"Oops, sorry. I'll be more careful. This isn't something I'm very proficient at."

She turned partially, cocked her head and looked at him as if to question the juxtaposition of the notorious Habu working domestically on a woman's hair.

He made a face and shrugged.

"Where was I? Oh, yes, the monsoons—"

"You weren't there, but it sounds like a fine place to get on with the story—"

"As I was saying, come the monsoons and this whole place changes. Rivers become lakes, bulging and roaring. Streams become rivers, bursting their banks. Trickles become—I'm doing it again, aren't I?"

Reubin pulled her hair back, stretching it tightly against the sides of her head. "It's almost long enough for this to work. But I think you've got to wait it out another eight or ten days."

"The floods refurb the nutrition of the floodplain so that the trees can grow during the other seasons. Typical nature in action. But the floods take their toll on some of the trees, feeding another ecosystem with their corpses, but that's not important."

"Tell me anyway." He brushed all of her hair forward. "This looks a little too tacky."

"Sure. Your fingers feel good. Um, to end the story,

after the floods, things go along quite as you'd expect and you've got the upswing to the dry season where everything repeats.''

"The dead trees," Reubin prompted.

"Right. The floods take their toll. Uprooted trees, crushed trees, damaged trees, so on. An animal called a mudcat—after floods, recall—''

"I got the connection," he said.

"This time of the cycle is their high point. They feed upon sanderlings who've made their homes high in the branches out of reach. Not any more. Sanderlings, at this time, protect their young, and if they live through the floods and monsoons, they stay in the downed trees— which are now within reach of the mudcats. Have you seen one?''

"I think so. But I didn't know what it was called. Chubby, furry, about as long as my arm, feral eyes, and a slinky manner of traveling?''

"That's them.''

"I suppose that explains why they can't climb the tree while it's living, healthy, and upright.''

She nodded, pulling hair out of his hand. "Though I still don't know why they didn't adapt through evolution to climbing—that's where the food is.''

"Apparently they aren't dying out without the climbing ability.''

She nodded again. "You've a point. Like I said, I skipped biology.''

"So that's what we have to work with.'' Reubin smoothed her hair down, gave her back her brush, and went to the fire, adding small sticks.

"That's it. Boy, that's the first time my hair's felt half-way decent in weeks.''

"My first impression," he said flippantly, "is to find some kudzu and turn it loose here.''

"What's kudzu?''

"A fast growing vine that almost ate Olde Earthe at one time. Listen, why haven't we encountered farmers, lumberjacks, timber collectors, whatever?''

Tique stood and stretched. "They selectively cut

wormwood trees in these forests. Farther down the plain, where the floods really hit and spread wide, they have man-grown wormwood stands, like giant orchards miles and miles and miles wide and long.'' She tightened her jaws. ''Those are the first of their Company-planted orchards to come to term. One day most of the world will be like that.''

Reubin turned meat strips to the sun. ''We'll resume our journey in that direction when the jerky's done.'' They'd agreed the place to start their activities was in the heart of wormwood country.

''What will we do when we get there?''

''I'm not sure,'' he said. ''But I haven't found a weak spot yet to take advantage of. I've been thinking in terms of sabotage—equipment, machines, processing facilities.''

''That sounds dangerous.''

''We aren't on a church picnic.'' Reubin pinched the bridge of his nose. It didn't help alleviate the pressure growing within his mind.

9: TIQUE

"**T**his is more like it," Reubin said.

They stood on a bluff overlooking cultivated wormwood plains. As far as Tique could see, wormwood trees stretched out to the horizon. In the center of all the acres of wormwood squatly sat the only signs of humanity. It seemed almost out of place there, the human settlement. A great river ran through the huge wormwood groves and snaked at a distance around the settlement. Buildings and bubbledomes at the settlement were the only interruptions of the solid green plain below.

"The Selby," Tique said, "named for one of the early pioneers on Snister. You wouldn't believe the volume of water the Selby carries."

"I believe anything," Reubin said.

Cryptic, but serious.

"Off the river are the irrigation channels, see them? Like little arteries."

"That settlement. It appears from here that most of the equipment is stored there."

"As I remember." She smelled rain in the air.

Reubin's hair had grown out and his beard was becoming full. No longer did he look like the man in the arena. Down deep, she still had questions. But their familiarity had removed her initial fear of him. She would even go so far as to call them good friends.

"They take the finished timber downriver, I'd guess," Reubin said.

"Yep. Except during the roughest part of the monsoons, when usually nothing is harvested. Tugs sort of herd great masses of the cut lumber downstream to the gulf. There it's treated and cut to size, stuff you'd expect.''

"A big bite to chew," he said.

Looking out over it all, she realized the scope of what they were doing. "Us against all that? Two people can make a difference?" She hoped so. Truly she'd love to strike a blow for nature.

He stepped back and squeezed her shoulder. "Individuals have always made the difference. Look at Tom Jefferson. Lincoln. Silas Swallow. It's all right there in history.''

"You didn't skip history," she accused.

"Hell, I lived it."

"Right. But. It's us, two lone people, Reubin. Jillions of hectares of wormwood. What can *we* do?"

"Plenty." He dropped his arm. "First we 'liberate' a mobile comm set. It would be nice to know their moves if they take out after us. That's called enemy avoidance or some such technical term. Second we reccy the area, deciding upon our targets. When we hit, we'll do it up big. I'm not certain now, but most likely we'll sabotage their air vehicle fleet first, a little self-preservation move. I want you to be thinking about logic bombs, because I'm going to get you to a terminal and I want you to create as much havoc as you can.''

"*That* would work." She nodded approvingly. Screw up a few selected programs. Access wormwood operations center, change the irrigation schedules—even, *that's it!* "Reubin, I can try to open all major irrigation channels full and flood the plains." And by so doing, help restore the proper face of the world.

"Or something like that. We've got planning to do. Also, can you get into the data system?"

"Planetwide?"

"Yes," he said. "I want you to find the work orders or whatever they call 'em at the hospital in Cuyas and delay surgery for a man named Grant. Can you do that?"

"Certainly. What's up?"

"An emergency backup I arranged."

How had he done that? But Tique could see the genius of the plan.

He was studying the river basin below. "You don't reckon that you could open all the channels, do you?"

"I might, but I don't know if the river is running high enough yet to give us an out-of-cycle flood big enough to do the job." She thought for a moment. "I *can* fix it so that water pours onto the land. Perhaps that will be sufficient to do the damage."

"Well, you can't have everything," Reubin said. "Let's go."

"Where to?"

"The settlement."

"Oh." She shrugged.

"That place got a name?"

"Nope. Everybody just calls it the settlement."

"It figgers," he said. "On the way you can tell me what you know of the layout and how many people live and work there and the like."

"I've only been here a few times."

"Do they have visitors' quarters?"

"They do."

"Now we're cookin' with gas."

It was past midnight and the two moons had chased each other across the night sky. Tique waited alone two kilometers from the settlement. She hadn't been able to convince Reubin to take her with him on his scouting trip.

She began to worry. Then she recalled Reubin as they'd wended their way through the wormwood groves. He'd changed subtly. No more light banter. He moved fluidly, eyes roving constantly. His entire body seemed somehow more angular, more alert, more—well, *coiled* in anticipation and readiness. She shook her shoulders as if to shrug off a bad thought. Reubin Flood had disappeared; a wary, alert, not-quite-right person had replaced him.

They'd come close to the settlement as dusk fell. She'd sketched in the dirt what she remembered of the general layout of the settlement and the location of offices, housing, motorpool. As night swept through the groves, he'd ghosted along with it, visible one minute, faded with the rushing shadows the next. She shivered at the memory. She was glad to be on his side.

Though the scope of the task before them overwhelmed her.

She cursed whatever it was that caused all this. Then she remembered that her mother had died—or been killed—for some reason which she did not understand, and resolve returned to her doubting mind.

She was no longer uncomfortable living off the land and in the wilds. No more did she create and shape fog; she drifted within it for protection.

One minute she was sitting alone, her back against a wormwood sapling, the next moment Reubin was squatting next to her.

"Awake?"

"Reubin! You startled me."

"Look what I found." A dull wide-beam of light spread out. He appeared to be back to normal—not that his "normal" was typical of any other person.

"Um. What's that wonderful smell?"

"Food."

"Wonderful. Where'd you get it?"

He chuckled. "Same place I got this bottle of sour mash. From the visiting quarters, VIP section. Those kinds of things are always well stocked with whatever you need. Including this emergency light. And these genuine Wormwood, Inc. coveralls—I mean jumpsuits."

She took the package and pulled the heat-tab, opened it and sniffed. "Ah, real food, not charred by some fire, not dead and dry, not jerked, not full of grit, not raw, not strange. My God, rice and gravy. Jeez, I died and went to heaven."

"They also had shampoo."

No man would even think of that. "Super."

"The best part is that comm set. Scanner and everything. I already tried it and it picks up the settlement Operations center, the Constabulary channels, and those specifically dedicated to the wormwood cultivation operation."

"Where'd you get it?" It occurred to her that someone might miss the comm set and give them away prematurely.

"Governments are all the same. Official vehicles are always broken down in great numbers, many awaiting parts. This comm set will never be missed. Or if it is, they'll think somebody in the motorpool cannibalized it for their broken one."

Tique was spooning food into her mouth. Fresh mushrooms in the gravy.

"Want a drink?"

She almost said yes. "No. I don't want to kill the flavor. Um, Reubin? I'm afraid to ask what we're going to do with official company uniforms."

He pulled the heat-tab on his meal. "Hope it's fried chicken and greens. Christ, it's been a long time."

It wasn't fried chicken and greens because he'd have read the label and thus wouldn't have said "hope." "You like fried chicken and greens?"

"Sure do. Grew up with 'em."

"When you were a kid?" she asked.

"Yes. A long time ago." She saw his shadow tip the bottle against the stars.

"On Olde Earthe itself?"

His head bobbed up and down once. "Westmoreland County, old Virginia."

"What's your name? I mean the one you started with?"

One baleful eye stared at her from the dark. He took another drink. "I don't suppose it matters anymore. Bob Ed Lee, that was me."

"Well, Robert, tell me—"

"Do not," he enunciated, "call me that. I'm Reubin Flood." He drank again.

"Does the liquor ease the pressure in your mind?"

He didn't answer, but drank again.

Tique smelled the strong odor of the drink. She hoped they weren't in danger of discovery here, for he was gulping the sour mash down like a man dying of thirst. "Eat something, it'll help absorb the alcohol."

"Yes, dear." The flash of a grin. He put the bottle down, sat back on his butt, no longer squatting. He began to eat.

"I didn't want to chance operating a terminal in an unoccupied room. I'd like to have a hardcopy map of the immediate area. Surely there's an update of operations we could call up on the screen and print out. What they're doing in what area and where they're planning to harvest next."

"I can do that." She finished. The salad in the meal wasn't as fresh as she was used to from living off the land. But certainly full of ingredients more familiar to her palate.

She watched insects play in the beam of light.

The bottle gurgled again, but she held her tongue. So far his judgment had been good. But his brain must be filled with pain brought on by the pressure. Tique didn't remember her orientation on the Long Life treatment that well, but there were some adverse side effects you would get if you waited too long to take the next treatment. The pressure and pain associated with the dying effects of the hormone compound. There was a cumulative effect, too, from taking treatments century after century. You took your chances with the Long Life treatment. Many people didn't want the treatment because of rumors of the side effects. Many people found the wearing-off stage unbearable and suicided when the pressure began mounting.

"I knew they couldn't do all this heavy work without mechanical advantage," Reubin said. "Electronics can't do everything."

They were standing in the shadows of giant machinery, equipment so large Tique couldn't see the entire unit from this close. It was late night and Reubin had led them to the current harvesting area.

They'd circled the area twice and found no workers or sentries. "They don't really need anyone to guard their equipment," Reubin said. "There's nobody to protect it from—"

"Until now," Tique said.

"Right. Now let me look around here. These things have to work on pneudraulics, it's the only way."

"What are you talking about?" Tique asked.

"Compressed air, hydraulics, fluid dynamics. When you use those, you've got reservoirs, actuators, accumulators, the like, all of which will grind to an immediate and terrible halt if, for instance, sand is added to the system. Watch."

Reubin was twirling a large wing nut. "The refill valve of a hydraulic reservoir. Dump a handful of sand in it, will you?"

She bent and cupped sand in her hands.

"Just right. It'll clog the filters and go through the system before the machine stops and breaks. It'll cost them plenty, not to mention downtime."

Rain threatened, as usual.

Tique looked up again at the giant machines. They'd have to be mammoth, she thought, to clip branches off hundred-meter tall trees, top the trees, cut down the tree, and maintain a hold on the tree when the cutting is done.

Reubin was walking off, figure indistinct against the gloomy skies.

Tique caught up with him. She was thankful that the ecosystem kept a great deal of brush from growing around the wormwood trees, giving the groves a parklike appearance. Thus it was easy for them to move through the trees, even at night.

"I had visions," Reubin said quietly, "of us spiking trees and sabotaging equipment—"

"Spiking?"

"Like inserting a metal or ceramic spike which in turn ruins the saws at the processing plant. But likely they use laser cutters. And this plain probably holds hundreds of thousands of trees in various stages of growth. No matter what we do, it would be like a gnat buzzing around a herd of sheepaloe."

Tique had initially thought that their effort would be futile. She said as much.

"You never know until you get on the scene and can evaluate the situation," he replied.

Tique thought about their problem. "I'm not altogether certain I'm going to like our next step a lot."

"Like my old sergeant used to tell the troops: you should of thought of that before you reenlisted."

"I knew it," she said, already trying to resign herself. She didn't know if she was up to skulking around the settlement at night, finding an unoccupied and safe terminal, and spending the time it would take to figure out and do what was necessary.

Reubin reached into his pack and pulled out a bottle. He'd brought out two bottles of sour mash on his trip into the settlement. He was halfway through the second bottle.

"Perhaps we can scrounge up some painkillers when we sneak in," she said.

He drank again. "Booze does the trick. Besides, it tastes good, too."

Two nights later they approached the settlement dressed in the Wormwood, Inc. jumpsuits. Tique was nervous. The humid atmosphere didn't help, either. Sweat ran down her body. They'd cached their packs and the mobile comm unit. They didn't want to appear out of place.

Reubin walked casually as if he belonged there and had entered and left the settlement a thousand times.

They'd spent last night rehearsing and planning—though much would depend upon her ability to access the right systems.

Tique estimated the population of the settlement at perhaps a couple of thousand. Enough, she hoped, so that everyone didn't know everyone else. The settlement itself was laid out on a north-south, east-west basis, designed by industrial engineers for the greatest efficiency. Major roads led into the place at the center of the four cardinal points. Auxiliary roads, trails, tracks ran into the mass of buildings from wherever there was room between those buildings.

Some parts of the settlement were covered by bubble-domes, but far fewer than she would expect given the rainy climate. One of those enclosed areas contained the living quarters.

"Come on," Reubin urged.

They'd waited until rain was imminent and sweeping across the plain. The dark and the sheets of rain would help cover their activities—not to mention fewer people would be out and about. Though they had selected the time so that it wasn't too late, when their presence might not be too obvious.

From the major entrance of East Avenue, they walked between warehouses, cut across to North Avenue, and headed for the personnel bubble. A solitary maintenance cart passed them, its driver bored and sleepy. As they came closer to the bubble, the area was more brightly lighted than the storage and maintenance district they'd just traveled.

Reubin glanced over his shoulder. "Here it comes."

Tique looked, too. A curtain of rain was sliding across the settlement, obscuring vision, dimming lights behind it.

"Race you to the bubble," Reubin said and took off running.

"Reubin!" she whispered harshly, but he was no longer there to hear her. She loped after him. Of course, be natural, she thought. God, Reubin had guts.

Tique put on a burst of speed and caught Reubin at the entry. The entrance slid open and they charged in.

The first thing Tique saw was a woman donning rain gear, preparing to go out.

"You cheated," Reubin accused. He was waving his hands in the air and turned toward her, his body interposed between the woman and Tique.

Tique laughed and thought it sounded like she was strangling. It was one of the hardest things she'd ever had to do. Not the hardest, she amended. That was facing and reconciling her mother's death. Her determination renewed, she continued walking and glanced surreptitiously behind them. The woman was turning her head and moving on outside. Tique did not sigh her relief, for, superstitiously, she thought that very act might insure discovery.

She followed Reubin through a barracks area into a section adjacent to the bubble wall at the edge of the settlement. There was an entrance on this far side, too, where less foot traffic was likely, but Reubin had decided it would be safer to use East Avenue. Tique admitted that the time spent walking through the settlement had helped her control her nerves.

Here were one- and two-story individual units, nothing architecturally innovative, just prefab buildings put out in the wilds to house people. The individual units were for company officers and high ranking visitors.

Reubin led her to the farthest of the squat, cabinlike units, a rock-gray structure which had VIP #8 inscribed on the door. He'd explained that since it was the most distant from the housing office where visitors would be assigned quarters that it would be the least likely to have occupants.

As he thumbed the chime in case someone was there, Tique watched the rain beat on the bubble just past the cabin. She could feel it drumming into her mind, her blood pumping swiftly now, throbbing in conjunction with the rainbeat. No one answered so Reubin merely opened the door and walked in.

Reubin motioned her to stay there. He moved out of sight, gliding silently, his bearing somehow deadly in this innocuous surrounding. He returned and gave her the all clear signal and turned back inside.

Tique followed.

Reubin closed the door, went to the windows and changed them to the "full dark" position. No light would escape. When the place was so dark Tique could see absolutely nothing, she heard Reubin moving confidently and recessed lighting came on.

Two bedrooms, a kitchen-dining area, and a living

room. While not spartan, it certainly wasn't the height of luxury.

On a side wall was the console. Tique walked over to it, already running her actions through her mind.

Reubin had gone into the kitchen and now returned with a bottle of liquor. "Employee pilferage," he said and upended the bottle.

"Find pain pills," Tique said, and put emphasis in her voice.

It stopped him momentarily, but she ignored him, sitting at the console.

She obviously couldn't use her own code. That would wave flags all over the system.

She thumbed a keypad and the unit jumped to life. Immediately, she punched in NEFF 69696 FFEN. Another reason for coming in late like this was that the probability of Josephine Neff using the system at this time of night was very low. Tique didn't know what the system would do if the same code and thus person was doing business in two different geographical locations simultaneously. It just wasn't something she'd ever thought to wonder about.

She selected SCREEN ONLY, thinking that verbal would be distracting.

GO AHEAD COMMAND 2.

Good, access gained.

DO NOT LOG THIS TRANSACTION. DO NOT ALLOW OTHER ACCESS. DO NOT ALLOW ANY MONITORING. Safety first, Tique thought.

CONFIRMED, the machine answered. NO LOG REQUIRES COMMAND OVERRIDE.

COMMAND OVERRIDE. NO LOG.

CONFIRMED. GO AHEAD COMMAND 2.

Here goes, Tique crossed her mental fingers. SEND FOLLOWING CODED MSSGS WITH ROUTINE LIBRARY/INFO REQUESTS TO WEBSTER'S CENTRAL. She typed in the long series of numbers Reubin had given her. FUNDING CODES AS NECESSARY. She punched in the proper numbers Josephine Neff had when the Interior Minister had authorized the Webster's inquiry about Reubin's snake drawings from her aircar.

Reubin refused to tell her what the code was, what the messages contained. She included his messages with the routine requests to bury them in case someone or some watchdog program might catch on. If so, it would take weeks to work through the bureaucracy. Then, and only then, they'd have to decode his messages. Reubin had assured her this was impossible.

MESSAGES INSERTED, the system told her.

REQUEST STATUS OF SEARCH FOR TEQUILLA SOVEREIGN AND/OR REUBIN FLOOD.

PRIORITY 1 ALERT AND APPREHEND. SUSPECTS LAST REPORTED MAIN PARKING LOT SECTION 67 DOWNTOWN CUYAS.

Reubin was now leaning over her shoulder and grunted. His misdirection had worked.

She typed. SCROLL INFO RE ALEXANDRA SOVEREIGN, PREVIOUS MINISTER OF WORMWOOD.

Personnel files began to fill the screen and scroll off.

Reubin touched her shoulder. He smelled of sour mash. "I'm going to scout around outside."

"Okay." She swallowed. When he'd told her he'd probably do this, she'd been worried.

"I'll be outside in case somebody comes along to see who's illegally operating equipment or broken into a cabin," he said. "Like a sentry."

Then he was gone, lights doused one moment, and the door softly opening and closing. She touched the keypad on her console and lights came back on. She trusted him. In fact, a hazy scheme was forming in her mind.

She keyed "speed scroll" until the data was flying on the screen and she could barely monitor it.

The info on her mother ended with the autopsy. Nothing else.

On a hunch, she typed in REPORT RE INTERROGATION OF ALEXANDRA SOVEREIGN.

INTERROGATION FILES DELETED came the immediate reply.

Tique sank back in the chair and it scooted a little.

She knew exactly what had happened. Someone unfamiliar with the details of compsystems had ham-handedly tried to erase a file. Tique had seen it before. They delete a file, but forget to delete the file name entry references in indexes, contents lists, whatever. All of which pointed to the upper echelon of Wormwood, Inc. Nothing she and Reubin hadn't already deduced. A lower level official would have the technical expertise to erase and delete thoroughly.

ADJUST HOSPITAL RESERVATIONS CUYAS.

INSERT NAME/DATE.

She did so and changed "Grant's" reservations for "minor elective surgery."

REQUEST COMPLIED WITH.

Tique wondered who'd determined how the system would respond with appropriate statements for the activity. Some befuddled bureaucrat, obviously.

She found herself sweating and adjusted environmental control to cut the humidity in half and drop the temperature. Why not be comfortable? She hoped Reubin was alert outside. Of course he would be. Had he taken the bottle? She glanced toward the counter and saw it standing there, a perceptible amount of the liquor gone.

DISPLAY CURRENT WORMWOOD OPS THIS LOCATION, she keyed.

The screen filled, color coded with symbols sprinkling the map.

PRINT HARDCOPY AND LEGEND, she told the system.

The slot at the left of the console immediately spewed out a large sheet.

"Good enough," she said and looked around guiltily at talking to herself. "Get it together," she said louder and went back to work.

She split the screen, keeping the operations scheme. DISPLAY SELBY RIVER IRRIGATION LOCKS AND INDICATE PERCENT OPEN. She believed that terminology would get through the system.

On the right of the split screen, a close-up of the immediate vicinity of the river appeared. On it the locks and dams and irrigation channels showed. They were labeled numerically. Cross-referencing was easy. Determining which locks controlled the amount of water in which area was simple. She identified the areas where all the harvesting machinery was and began punching in numbers. She also decided to flood the locations where new wormwood trees were replacing recently harvested ones. She could destroy trees, too, not just expensive machinery. Finally, she was able to strike back at the Company for ravaging the world.

She told the system to activate her orders tomorrow night. She designed a sentry program to conceal what she'd done, one which would give monitors in Operations false readings on their monitor consoles. They'd notice it soon, though, because each lock had a mechanical water flow indicator in case of power failure. But nobody generally paid attention to fall back systems with electronics to do the monitoring for them.

Continuing to work, she planted logic bombs in many areas such as power requirements in Cuyas, decreasing allocation by twenty percent. She'd intended to get into the payroll records and wreak holy hell, but Reubin had cautioned, "In my experience, that's the one place you can most expect security programs designed by *real* experts. There is always somebody who thinks he can beat the system and embezzle a little here and there." Tique had thought about it and agreed with him.

She told the system to exchange every one thousand eight hundred and twenty-third number 9 with a 6 on the export orders.

The things she was thinking of were fun and worthwhile, but not of significant impact upon the growth and harvesting of wormwood. She was supposed to be affecting the very existence of Wormwood, Inc. Not playing tricks.

She got into the wormwood database and slightly changed the nutritional requirements of the trees so that when the engineers queried the system for the proper fertilizer and treatments, it would be based on altered data.

She found the database for controlling pests, and

switched treatments for several different insects and parasitic growths. She deleted the necessity for controlling certain others.

In an explanatory note, she found that one such treatment required low levels of a poison she couldn't pronounce because any more and it would prove fatal to the sanderlings. Hating herself for doing so, she changed all references she could find to double the dosage.

She leaned back again, realizing she'd been breathing hard and had been tense, leaning over the console with such concentration.

She shook her head. She still didn't want to cost innocent people their jobs, and that was what would happen.

Reubin had chided her, ''What you're going to do is *create* additional jobs. They'll have to hire more people to take care of the problems you invent. They aren't going to simply write this off, it's too lucrative.'' Maybe he had a point.

She worked hard for half an hour designing a rogue program which canceled every third large contract for wormwood. She insured it would repeat itself whenever the system was updated or changed. They'd have to do it all manually when they figured it out, until they could build a new system. It would cost the company considerable time and money.

She found the calibration specs for the cutting lasers and precision measuring equipment at the lumber processing centers, most of which clustered around the mouth of the Selby. She changed random numbers so that when wormwood was cut, it would be very slightly different than the buyer ordered.

Rolling now, she got into design specs of her own job. She changed the specifications for manufacture of water vanes, controlling valves, all kinds of mechanical devices, so that they would be prone to failure, structural damage, or malfunction. That might be the one place they'd never think to double-check—once they started searching the system for what she'd done.

Because they would figure it out eventually.

She felt like a traitor. Frustration built within her. She was destroying her own life's work. Sabotage. No, call it Habutage. Right, that's more like it.

She planted several "worms," programs designed to replicate themselves and eat up storage space and time in the system. She hoped these would help cover her other work.

Dawn would be here soon. She wondered where Reubin was. He should have come back to check on her.

Tique's eyes flitted across the console. The dataline with date, temp conditions and time caught her attention.

Suddenly, she realized it should be dawn. She killed the lights and changed the dawnside window from all-dark to clear.

Rain had gone, stars were visible. Except it was perceptibly brighter at the edge of the horizon. That she could tell for sure.

Where was Reubin?

She cleared the console and turned it off. She made sure all controls were set as they had been when she and Reubin first arrived. She put the bottle of sour mash back in the kitchen cabinet. She suspected that they only stocked full, unopened bottles so she added an inch of water, shook the bottle, and wet the torn label with her tongue, trying to make it look whole. Not very good, but it might pass a perfunctory examination.

She killed the lights and returned the windows to their normal clear-view.

Anxiously, she peered out the windows one at a time. She could see nothing, but the dawn sky was eating up darkness like some fantasy monster.

Hurry up, Reubin!

She slipped outside. She looked to see if people were up and about. No movement around the VIP cabins. She checked the nearby bubble exit. No hint of anything. She'd used it if she had to—though, because of its location, it might well show an indication light at Operations or Security, meaning it was being used. You never know.

Suddenly, Tique realized that it was no longer dark.

No sun yet, but she could see plainly, distinctly—not just outlines of buildings.

She hurried back to the cabin she'd used.

Tique was thoroughly alarmed now.

Reubin was supposed to be outside, guarding her from discovery. She'd been comfortable and not worried knowing he was out there. She'd felt safe.

Now she didn't.

She walked around the cabin, peering out each window. She went to the bathroom. She ate one of the prepackaged meals and couldn't recall what she'd eaten.

Maybe he was playing Habu and had gone off on some other business. Like killing.

It was totally light now, and the sun was coming up over the horizon.

Decision time. Another couple of minutes and her chances of discovery were too great. Should she continue to wait for Reubin? She could go out the side bubble exit and into the groves of wormwood trees to where they'd concealed their packs. Reubin would have no trouble finding her.

But suppose—suppose something had happened to him? He might need her help. He might count on her being there in the cabin.

What should she do?

Still looking through the window, Tique saw a couple of men departing one of the barracks.

If she was going to leave the settlement, she had to do it *now*.

What should she do?

10: REUBIN

Reubin left Tique in the cabin. He prowled around the immediate area insuring they were still safe. The cabin gave off no light.

No one was outside. Occasional light showed from barracks and what he remembered was a cafeteria. The rainy skies increased the darkness. As always, he felt strange being exposed to the elements and protected by the bubble. He felt the rain ought to hit him, and his body was waiting and anticipating it, but the rain merely poured off the bubble.

Habu came a level closer to the surface.

He moved away. Sure, he'd told Tique he would act the sentry. But there was no need. She'd been at work long enough so that Central Operations would have dispatched Security to check *if* they'd noticed unauthorized use of the cabin or the console. So that must not be one of the items they monitored.

Tique was safe for the moment. He had other plans anyway.

A shadow within other shadows, Reubin flitted along. When he came to the main entrance/exit of the personnel bubble, he donned the hood of the Wormwood jumpsuit. The material of the clothing itself was waterproof. With the hood up, in the dark, he did not worry about discovery.

Nonchalantly he walked out of the bubble and into the rain. He made his way to the motorpool. Every army, every organization he'd ever been in, or had anything to do with that was large enough to have its own vehicle fleet, named the dispatch and maintenance function "the motorpool"—even though the term "motor" was no longer accurate. Reubin thought of the archaic term as part of the human condition. Just like some religions: adjust to current conditions but maintain the bridge to the past and keep the same old faith.

Of course no one was working the graveyard shift—at least not out in the rain.

"Damn," Reubin said softly. The pressure was mounting again. He shook his head to clear it and wished for a slug of sour mash.

He'd originally planned to disable most or all of the aircars in the motorpool. But just as he and Tique had decided not to do anything outlandish here or near the settlement so they wouldn't be identified and thus hunted, he'd decided not to sabotage the aircar fleet. If every vehicle turned up sabotaged, it would take no genius to guess which one or two people of the entire population on Snister would have a motive to do such a deed. Which would point a finger right to Reubin and Tique. Which would mobilize the Constabulary with enough high-tech gear to pick them out of the forests with little trouble. He thought that alone he could evade detection—or outrun and evade pursuit; but not the two of them. Tique wasn't as mobile, nor as able to take the physical hardships. It occurred to him that he could be underestimating her.

Therefore, for personal safety, he would not sabotage the aircar fleet. He'd disable just one.

He crossed North Avenue and walked along toward the south as if he belonged. He turned right into the motorpool.

As he went onto the motorpool grounds, the rain slowed and stopped. He had to be more careful now, for he no longer had the rain as an effective mask.

It took him no time to reacquaint himself with the motorpool. One side of the motorpool was dedicated to maintenance and the other side to what had to be called the "ready line."

It was to the latter he went.

In shadows, he ghosted down the ready line. There were sleek, obviously fast aircars, designed specifically for personnel transport. Intermediate vehicles could carry small cargoes. Great, large airtrucks and barges for major freight which couldn't wait for cheaper and stronger ground transportation sat far back, making their own skyline. Looking at the barges, a twinge of sorrow hit him. He thought of the first time he'd seen Alex. What a wonderful thing had been between them; and the future had promised to be even better.

Reubin wished he knew more about the different models. Function is universal, he thought, but style and form are a matter of local design and manufacture. He remembered the far past when form was supposed to follow function; that was not necessarily true these days.

He selected one of the intermediate vehicles because he thought it might have the greatest range.

Reubin climbed into the cockpit and a light went on. He cursed himself for forgetting the basics. Swiftly he closed the door and thumbed the light out. He sat there watching through the bubble for evidence that someone had seen the light.

Nothing.

He adjusted his flashlight for the narrowest beam and dimmed it to where he could barely see. He popped open the front panel and studied the circuits. Let's see—what item could he disable for which they would not have parts on hand? A zero or low failure item. He thought for a minute and checked the circuit diagram on the back of the panel. As many aircars as he'd ever driven, never had he encountered a speed control problem. He found the appropriate printed wiring board and removed it.

If anyone tried to use this vehicle, the automatic systems self-diagnosis would indicate that the speed control function was inop and they'd give it to maintenance. Who'd order the part, Reubin hoped. Then it occurred to him that all they had to do was cannibalize a board from another vehicle which was already down. So he had to select a backup.

He lifted the front seat and hid the speed control printed wiring board in some seating foam.

It was his intention to have one vehicle he knew he could get in, start almost immediately, take off, and fly. He always liked to have one or more backup plans. This aircar would be available to him in case all the other aircars were in use—whether for what they were intended or involved in a massive air search for two outlaws.

Finally, he decided to ruin the self-diagnostic system. That would keep the aircar grounded for a long time and a technician would have to actually perform repairs instead of removing and replacing parts or PWBs.

He traced the circuit diagram on the inside of the panel cover with his finger, double-checking so that he did not destroy some essential function of the vehicle. He found the tiny computer which controlled the self-diagnosis. With his knife he cut into the circuits leading to the unit. The aircar would work, but the self-test wouldn't, nor would the machine be able to tell a repair tech what was wrong. If they discovered a speed control circuit missing, they'd simply be unable to explain it. It wasn't something you'd think of in terms of sabotage.

Reubin was confident that *this* aircar would be available. If they needed it.

He wondered how Tique was doing.

Attached to the inside of the panel was a small pouch of tools a technician would use to work on the electronics systems. Reubin pocketed this.

Silently he stole out of the motorpool.

It was his intention now to do the more dangerous task he'd assigned himself.

Steal a weapon.

A dicey job. Lasers and other weapons were not speed control PWBs. Suspicion would be automatic. Reubin hadn't decided if he'd disable some Constabulary member and take his weapon or try to get one from the Security Office. It would depend on the circumstances. Additionally, a company like Wormwood, Inc. which was in total control of an entire world and all the people on it would not be free and easy with weaponry.

He wished for rain.

He cut through the warehouse district toward headquarters and the Security Office. His earlier reconnoitering had given him a good mental layout of the settlement.

He recalled that Security and Central Operations were on the far side of the office district. He crossed West Avenue and paralleled South Avenue until he judged he'd gone far enough. Just as he was ready to cross South Avenue, a groundcar sped by, blowers creating a fine mist.

Skirting two large puddles, Reubin made it across. He dodged behind a small building labeled QUALITY CONTROL.

On the other side of SCHEDULING OFFICE was CENTRAL OPERATIONS. Just past there with a large expanse of pavement surrounding it was SECURITY. Company vehicles, some painted emergency yellow, sat outside.

Reubin circled the building. Who'd guard a Security Office? But best to make sure. He took a chance and checked each vehicle for weapons. Nothing. Wormwood, Inc. Security and Constabulary followed proper discipline.

He returned to the rear of the building and the door he'd seen there.

Most likely it would open to his touch. There was no reason for locked doors in a building of high frequency entering and exiting. Except for maybe the weapons locker.

Wishing he knew the internal layout of the Security Office, he touched the panel and watched the door slide aside.

He walked in as if he belonged there. To face a long, empty corridor.

Where was the control room? That would be the most dangerous part of the building, more people coming and going.

Down the corridor he ghosted, slowly, noiselessly. Doors were marked as military and security offices were wont to do: LATRINE, MEN'S. LOCKER, SUPPLY.

STAIRS, EMERGENCY. PERSONNEL. Of course, no LOCKER, WEAPONS. It could be elsewhere on this floor, in a basement or subbasement which would offer more security. Perhaps it was above on the second floor— the building could house no more than two floors. Or maybe they didn't even have one. Human nature, Reubin knew, would require a minimum of armament.

The corridor doglegged to the left and he peered around the corner.

It figgered.

A big, open room. Monitoring consoles, electronics comm gear. Two men at one console playing some sort of game on their unit to kill the boring night hours.

Reubin pulled back and thought. This would dictate the building's layout. He chastised himself for not having Tique sniff it out at the cabin before he left. But then she might have objected had she known his plans. At any rate, it was too late now.

Since the central control room was high-ceilinged, that would mean the first and second floors would be laid out around the central section. There should be corridors circling the building at an outer ring—or at least a hall or two leading elsewhere which would avoid the Operations room.

He risked another quick look. The two men were still engaged in their game. His eyes cataloged swiftly. Nothing which could be construed as a facility for storing weapons. There could be so few weapons here at the settlement that it might amount to a small box inset into the floor in the control room.

He retreated until he found the door to the stairs. STAIRS, EMERGENCY. Inside, he paused. No noise. Steps going up, none down. Which made sense. The settlement was designed as a base camp for wormwood growth and harvesting operations; they'd have little interest in digging into the ground—these prefab buildings could be put together in any number of ways, but underground wasn't one of them.

Silently he climbed the stairs. The door at the top

opened with little sound. He glanced out into another corridor. No one present.

Right across the corridor from him was a door marked WEAPONS. DANGER EXPLOSIVES.

Interested now, Habu stirred.

It was about time something went right for him. He scouted the corridor, listening at doors. Obviously this area was for officers of the Security section. Reubin guessed that "Security" encompassed more than just the police function, so there would be Security personnel in addition to the few Constabulary assigned.

At the inner end, the corridor terminated at a bubble overlooking the Central Ops room below. Other halls branched off this one, so that the upstairs was all connected.

Reubin returned to the weapons locker. It was natural that it be colocated with the officer or command function.

He studied the door. Metal. A mechanical lock, either as a fail-safe in case of power outage or just a double precaution. The electronic lock appeared innocuous enough.

Reubin decided that he'd been out of practice too long and that he might need an emergency exit. He checked the adjoining corridors. No stairs. Probably one more set opposite him on the far side of the central room. Too distant for him to take the chance. He didn't want to try the office doors to see if they would open because the two men below might have a monitor for going and coming in the offices—if for no reason other than to let them know when brass were present. A smart noncom would do that, especially on the night shift when nothing was happening and you could grab some sleep on your duty shift.

A small lift on the far side of the command room wouldn't help him. The stairs he'd used had a flap door.

Nothing else.

Reubin returned to the weapons door and looked it over carefully. He checked for hidden contacts, points which were not part of the locking system, but transmitted indications to warning devices and instrumentation.

Again, he cursed himself for not thinking clearly. Camera monitors. He went back down the corridor in both directions. Good. No monitors.

From the aircar repair kit, he selected a tool that was more wire than anything. He opened the mechanical lock in just minutes. He went down the corridor and looked through the bubble: no alarm. That overlook was convenient.

He returned to the weapons room. With his knife, he cut the insulation off the incoming power lead and clamped a clip to bypass it to ground. Again he hurried to the bubble. Still no alarm.

Back at the lock, he took a deep breath and pried the cover off the mechanism. The mechanism powered a small gear which went into the door. Not so good.

Reubin was tracing wiring with his finger when the writhing hit his mind again, this time worse than a migraine. His hand flinched.

At the wrong place.

He knew it when it happened.

He stumbled to the bubble.

The two men were moving from the one console to another. A flashing red light pulsed.

Seconds only.

If there were indications someone had tried to break into the weapons locker, they'd search the settlement and find Tique. Should he allow himself to be captured?

Working feverishly, he snapped the cap back onto the electronic lock, and removed his bypass. His head throbbed as he relocked the mechanical outer lock.

Adrenaline had Habu fully aware and alert now.

He didn't waste time going to the bubble again. He tried a few office doors to test his theory.

Locked.

The first procedure must be a lockdown—outside doors and internal doors all locked at the push of a button.

Fortunately, safety concerns overrode security and the door to the emergency exit stairs opened.

Reubin could almost feel feet pounding down the corridor from some other part of the building.

Inside the stairwell, he leaped for the handle to the roof access door. He missed and his head hurt worse. He couldn't take the time to dampen the pain. He jumped again and caught the handle. It creaked and gave way. As it did, Reubin shifted his grasp to an anchor handle next to it. He pushed the door up, and scrambled up behind it. He turned and closed the panel.

It stood to reason that particular roof access was supposed to be locked all the time and thus not connected to the electrical lockdown system of the rest of the building.

Cool air washed over him and he gulped it even as he moved.

Like most prefab buildings designed to be located either inside or outside of a bubble, this one was flat, allowing access to environmental and plumbing systems for maintenance and upkeep.

Reubin again wished it would rain. Damned planet, it rained when you didn't want it to, and when you did—

He jerked himself into action. Swiftly he moved to the edge of the building and peered over. Pavement, and facing the Operations Building.

Moving to the other side of the building, he estimated it had been only a minute or so since he'd set off the alarm. Though with his mind going off on tangents, it was difficult to be certain.

The back of the Security Building, while lighted, was not as dangerous as the front. An urgency chased him. Tique might pay for his mistake.

No rope, no visible external bars which would act as a ladder.

Well, hell. He slid over the edge, hung down as far as he could, pushed off with a heavy shove and let go.

The momentum of the push allowed him time to turn in midair. He hit the ground as he often had with a bubble-chute: knees bent and ducking his shoulder in the classic position. He rolled and came up running, no injury from the jump. He heard some sort of commotion in front of the building, so he kept the Security Building directly behind him. He dodged past a couple other prefabs and cut north on South Avenue.

Lights appeared coming this way, so he dived behind QUALITY CONTROL, almost retracing his original path to the security office.

He condemned himself for a fool. He hadn't needed a weapon badly enough to chance discovery—and that's exactly what he'd done.

Lights erupted everywhere and he felt trapped. They must either have a quick response team—or a tough commander who demanded discipline and instant response to alarms.

Give me control. I can evade the enemy.

–*No. Not yet.* Reubin wanted to slip through the security net quietly; Habu would battle or slaughter his way through. Though his Habu-aided running was fast, he still might be spotted. They might have mobile detection gear—although MDG wasn't standard equipment and an outpost like the settlement wouldn't necessarily require it.

His instincts took him around SCHEDULING and there was OPERATIONS. He felt herded. They'd thrown up a net and were closing it.

One of the reasons he'd survived for so long was that he'd done the unexpected at the right time. He fought the burning in his brain and sprinted for OPERATIONS. The least likely place for an intruder to hide would be the highest traveled area: OPS. People coming and going.

He ran around the back of OPS.

Now you're here, where next?

No time.

In, too dangerous. All the outside area under search, too high a possibility they'd intercept him. No down. Which left up.

OPS was a two-story prefab identical, as far as he could tell, to SECURITY. At the far end leaning against the building were some wall segments, meaning they were going to expand the building.

Reubin ran up these segments and jumped for the top of the building. He chinned himself over.

Same as the other building. Plumbing and environmental housing. While there was room between some plumbing and the cooler to hide, it was an obvious place to look. So he squatted next to the big machine and watched the roof access panel.

His line of sight was hindered, but occasionally he saw people going and coming hurriedly in the lighted area between OPERATIONS and SECURITY. He heard vehicles in front of the Security Building. Once, an aircar lifted off and he ducked between the housing and the plumbing. The aircar circled the area with a spotlight, then swung off into the night.

He'd really done it. He knew he could blame his mistake on the growing pain, pressure, and disorientation. But that didn't change matters. He'd made the mistake. Himself. Never mind the mitigating circumstances. The likely price to be paid was in lives, his and Tique's.

He returned to his waiting position.

Just in time, for the access panel cracked and then slapped open.

Reubin moved behind the metal housing.

A man with a beard climbed up. "I'll check it," he told someone behind him.

The man moved around the roof clockwise.

So did Reubin, keeping the housing and the plumbing between them, and all the time trying to watch the access panel in case another man came through it.

The man kept circling and flashed a light into the cubbyhole between the housing and the plumbing. "Nada." He moved on around and Reubin did, too. Soon he was back with the housing between him and the man and the access panel. The man sat on the roof and dropped his legs through the access. "Them guys in Security are seeing things again." He disappeared and the panel closed.

Reubin sank into the protected position and fought off the pain. The constant ache damped Habu's presence. He wished he'd gotten the pain pills in the medicine cabinet at the VIP cabin. He could use one now. Tique was in danger, though, and he'd caused it.

After a while, the activity died down a great deal. Perhaps he'd covered his tracks well enough. Maybe they thought the alarm was an electronic glitch. Even if he'd left a minor mark or two on the door or the mechanisms, nobody would be able to say that an intruder had done it. It was something that could happen any time, during normal operations or maintenance of the system.

If they found no hard evidence, then, he hoped fervently, they just might discount the possibility of someone doing what he'd been doing. On the other hand, if Wormwood, Inc. treated its employees the way it had treated him, then it would have a number of enemies, and Security and the Constabulary would be tough, well-prepared, and alert. Which is what it felt like to Reubin.

He commanded the pain into the background and assessed his position.

Dawn wasn't far off. He had no wristcomp to tell. He should have taken one at the arena when he'd taken the clothes and money. But he'd been mostly Habu, and drugged, and wasn't thinking clearly. Another error he suddenly realized: the stolen comm set. Still in his pack, cached out in the wormwood groves. Right now he or Tique could be using it to tell what trouble they were in. He cursed himself. That comm set would have solved his current problem of not knowing what Security thought *and* what they were doing about the alarm. The mental troubles associated with needing a Long Life treatment were causing him to make great errors in judgment.

And it would only get worse.

He lay back to fight the writhing in his mind. It came and went. He could relate it to no other experience as he'd never come this close to his limits for taking the Long Life treatment. Usually he gave himself what he guessed was a couple of years leeway—if not more.

He wondered if the more he aged, the more frequently he needed the treatment. It was not something scientists could tell, since Reubin was one of the originals and thus on the leading edge of the Long Life treatment program.

His mind shifted gears again. If the search turned up nothing, then hopefully it would peter out, losing its momentum before it reached the outer perimeter and the VIP visiting quarters.

The rest did him good.

When he decided the time was as good as any, he rose wearily and scouted the area from all four sides of the top of the Operations Building.

Extra lights. A man standing outside the front door of the Security Building, doubtless acting as sentry. Offset to one side, the Scheduling Building was lighted so much that Reubin could see a team of men threading their way between buildings.

Damn. They were thorough, looking for some evidence. He projected their path as concentric circles. Too much risk to climb down now.

But he was ready to chance it when he spotted roving patrols. Constabulary uniforms.

Uh-oh.

Dawn peeked over the horizon.

Reubin lay flat and began watching the entrance and parking area of the Security Building, for if they caught Tique, surely they'd bring her to Security.

Before he found a decent opportunity to climb down and make it to the cabin, it was full light. Still, he thought he'd try it, but people came and went around these two buildings too much. They were the hub of activity.

And because of the state of increased alert, Reubin didn't want to try to merge with other Wormwood, Inc. personnel. That might work, but the odds were against it.

He wondered about Tique. Would she stay at the VIP cabin? If she had any sense, she'd already have gone the

quickest way she could and wait for him where they hid
their packs.

As the business of the day commenced, Reubin returned to hide in the cubby between the housing and the
plumbing. Too many aircars.

He'd have to wait until tonight.

Unless a severe storm hit, rain and wind allowing him
to run with his head covered by the hood, effectively dis-
guising him.

As Snister rotated and the sun inched higher, the heat
of the day began to beat down. No clouds grew in the
immediate area.

His worry about Tique increased. Alone, he could
probably escape. Steal an aircar, outrun pursuit through
the cover of the giant wormwood trees. Swim downriver.
Something.

But he doubted Tique had the endurance or the natural
cunning he possessed. To say nothing of centuries of escape and evasion experience.

Was he becoming too protective of her? He did not
deny that he felt a growing attraction to her. A simple
explanation could well be that she was her mother's
daughter. Bright, alert, wise, attractive. And more important: good judgment, humor, the right values, and a
unique personal outlook on life.

Godamighty damn. He didn't need these complica-
tions. He needed to find the nearest LLI branch, get the
treatment, and ship out for the farthest frontier.

Pressure again built in his mind, but it didn't dim the
thought that what he really needed was to find Alexandra's murderer. To do that, he'd wreck the economy of
Snister. It wasn't just for his loss that he would take vengeance. It was also for Alex, who deserved better. And
for humanity which was poorer without her. Jesus, he
thought, the mush of my mind turns my thoughts maudlin
and soppy.

About noon, a brief rainshower gave him hope and
quenched his thirst, but wasn't sufficient for him to escape.

He wished he could still see the entrance to the Security Building.

Because he knew that if they captured Tique at the VIP cabin, then they would set a trap for him, her accomplice. It would be the first thing he'd do.

At dusk, his bladder was bursting, but he wouldn't go on the roof because it would be a trace of him, solid evidence even though the chances of discovery during the night were minimal.

At full dark, he'd been watching from the lip of the roof for a while. Nothing irregular that he could tell. No inordinate Security patrols. Had they decided the alarm wasn't really a legitimate break-in? He hoped so.

Then came the rain, thankfully, and Reubin wasted no time climbing down. He hurried over to South Avenue and headed for the personnel bubble.

Should he go off into the wormwood groves and look for Tique at their rendezvous point first?

No, the rain offered his best opportunity for checking out the cabin. If necessary, he could go around the bubbledome and enter the outside access near Visitors' cabin #8.

He walked swiftly, thinking that he'd had about enough of the settlement. He liked this place less than he'd liked a lot of other places. His mind was working at odd angles.

Closely, he circled the personnel bubble in the rain, checking the cabin from the outside. He returned to the main entrance with no indications of watchers. He'd engaged the beast within him so that the animal might detect ambush before his human senses could.

Following a different, longer route, he came upon the cabin. Inside the bubble he no longer needed the hood and therefore had to do without its protection. His hair was growing out well, as was his beard. For this reason if none other, he didn't want to be seen. But if they were waiting to trap him, so be it.

His knife along his wrist and in his fingers ready to

flip out in a twitch, he circled the cabin labeled VIP #8. Nothing.

But these people had proved to him they were efficient. Of course, no light escaped from the windows.

He stepped to the door.

Pain hit his brain like a torpedo. He almost fell. Disorientation made him nauseous. His eyes couldn't focus. The ground about him swayed.

He slumped against the door.

It slid open.

Somewhere deep within him, he wondered if this could be a trap.

He stumbled in.

11: TIQUE

Tique arranged the bed and a portadesk in the small bedroom so that she could lie on the floor and be concealed from a casual glance into the room. She remained in the front room, moving from window to window, constantly checking. She had adjusted them for one-way vision.

She decided that since something must have happened, she would not go back to the console. It wouldn't be worth taking the chance—though it was quite tempting to sneak into the security net and find out what was going on.

But she couldn't risk discovery.

Reubin might need her. He might be hurt. She worried about him, regardless of his extraordinary prowess.

Finally, after a day that would never end, night came. She robbed the medicine chest of first aid supplies—including pain pills. She put that in the package she'd made with all the prepacked meals she'd robbed from the pantry. She pocketed the pills to give him one—if he returned.

She decided to give Reubin one more hour and then leave.

That hour lasted almost as long as the whole tedious day. She cursed them both for the nine millionth time. For leaving the comm set out in the groves. She could be monitoring airways now and *know* if something were amiss.

"Well, hell," she said aloud and slung her makeshift

pack over her shoulders—a pillowcase with WORM-WOOD, INC. and the logo on it.

She checked the windows one more time to be certain there was no one in the immediate area.

Determined, she reached out and opened the door.

Reubin Flood stumbled in, still dripping, with pain etched across his face.

As he staggered past her, she slid the door closed behind him.

He went straight to the liquor cabinet in the kitchen and was soon gurgling from an upended bottle.

When he came up for air, he said, "You get everything done?"

"As much as I could. Here." She got out the pain pills. She handed him one. "For your pain."

He took it and downed it with a slug of whiskey. Then he went to the fountain and drank long. "See any movement around here?"

"Recently, no." A couple of people had approached the area, but veered off before reaching the cabin.

"Why are you here?" His voice was rough.

"Why weren't *you* here?" She didn't like her judgment questioned. "I thought you might be hurt and in need of my help."

"Oh." He drank again. Then he drank some more from the whiskey bottle. "Any food left?"

She produced a meal and pulled the heat-tab for him. "What happened?"

"I got hung up."

"Where? You were supposed to be outside guarding this cabin. At least that's what you led me to believe."

"Ah." Steam rose from his meal as he ate hungrily. "I, er, had a few things to take care of."

"Like what?"

"I was reconnoitering the motorpool and the Security area."

"Which took you more than eighteen hours?"

"Like I said, I got hung up." Briefly he told her what had happened. "Foolish of me, really. I know better than to take those high-risk for low-payoff chances."

"Not too much harm done." She felt guilty for her accusations.

"I'm not sure," he said, stuffing the remains of his meal into the slot in the wall. "But I've had this feeling . . ."

Tique waited, but he failed to continue.

"Let's go," he said. He went to the liquor cabinet and took the remaining bottle—this one, vodka. He added that to the one from which he'd been drinking and handed them to Tique. She pocketed the pain pills and silently put the liquor into her Wormwood, Inc. pillowcase. "The height of outdoor fashion, no?"

For a few moments Reubin scanned the map she'd printed. "Good work."

They removed all traces of their presence. They couldn't conceal the missing food and liquor, but it was possible that the custodial service people would think some lower echelon personnel had partied in the cabin.

As they stepped outside, Reubin said in a voice that couldn't be heard far. "It's my intention to leave by this outer exit as opposed to the East Avenue entrance we came in. It's still early and people are about."

Tique nodded, fear creeping upon her.

Reubin linked his arm in hers and set off with a long stride. Some of her confidence returned.

A big rain squall hit as they neared the bubble. Since this wasn't a personnel-sensor operated panel, Reubin hit the "open" control. They donned their hoods and went out.

A blast of rain hit and Tique wondered if the monsoon season weren't a little early this year. It would certainly accelerate the flooding she'd programmed. Uh-oh—

Reubin still held her arm and she leaned over and spoke in his ear. "The locks are supposed to open—within the hour. I had the ones around the settlement malfunction also, hoping it would cut this place off and hinder their recovery operations." Back from the river, the settlement rested sort of in a big crook of the river. A large grove of wormwood lay between the settlement and the river, located perfectly for the annual flooding.

Twenty meters out, Tique felt a low tingling sensation. Another step and the feeling was gone.

"Damn," Reubin said. "Hurry!" He was running.

She sprinted to catch up and the rain swept away. "What is it?"

"Intruder detector field. Somebody wasn't certain that the alarm last night was an electronic accident. They rigged that field just in case."

She puffed. "Could we go back?"

"Too late."

In a few moments, they reached the wormwood grove. Tique realized they were going to be hemmed in by the river.

Which was going to flood.

But Reubin knew that, too. It wasn't as if they had any choice.

She was surprised by her running ability. All these weeks in the wilds, using her own feet and legs had strengthened her, given her more endurance and strength than she'd ever thought she'd need.

Relief came over her. The trees would protect them.

But if anything, Reubin was running faster now.

In a moment, she found out why.

Two skycycles came through the air, under the lower branches of the wormwood trees. She could see their lights and strobes weave toward them.

Reubin stopped. "We ain't gonna outrun them. We're on a picnic." He took the pillowcase. "With the Wormwood jumpsuits, maybe we can fool them."

No way, she thought. Reubin wasn't that naive, was he?

They turned and waited for the approaching skycycles. The machines reached the two, circled, and locked on their spotlights.

Bathed in light, they stood there. Reubin waved, then gestured angrily. "Turn those damned lights *off*, will you? You're blinding us."

One of the skycycles settled to the ground next to them. The other hovered just above them, spotlight dimmed somewhat.

Way off, another light became apparent, heading in their direction. A groundcar.

Reubin turned to her. "They've already radioed in. That'll be backup heading this way. Good procedures." He turned to the man climbing off the skycycle. "Hey. Can't a guy and a girl take a walk at night?"

"Yessir," came the reply. Yellow chevrons meant Constabulary. The young man's voice was higher pitched than Tique would have expected from that muscular body. "But we want to see some identification."

"Sure, sure," Reubin said, slurring his words and waving the whiskey bottle. "Have a drink first?"

"Nossir. ID please."

Reubin lurched over toward the man.

Tique was scared. She didn't know what her face looked like in the artificial light, but she was certain that her eyes were big, her nose flared, and her mouth gulped air. Yet she stood there, forcing herself to look relaxed.

Reubin whirled and threw the liquor bottle at the stationary skycycle above them. It crashed into the driver's helmet. He lurched and the machine slid sideways in the night air. Tique couldn't tell whether the hit was sufficient to take the man out of action or not.

She turned her attention back to the ground and began moving toward Reubin and the Constabulary officer.

But she was too late to help.

Reubin's knife was out and bloody and the muscular young man was slumping to the ground.

"Come on," Reubin said, voice commanding. He sat upon the saddle of the skycycle.

Tique moved to join him when a laser beamed across the night from above, glanced off the skycycle and seared the saddle where Reubin had just been sitting. He was tumbling toward the body of the Constabulary officer. "Down," he shouted.

Tique dived for the ground and rolled out of the way.

Reubin flipped the Constabulary officer over and fumbled around his body. He came up firing a laser even as another swath of death cut across the ground toward him. The beam fused the controls of the grounded skycycle instantly and kept heading straight for Reubin. He rolled, firing continuously, death trailing right behind him.

Sparks and burning paint sizzled off the now-useless skycycle.

The groundcar was almost upon them.

The remaining skycycle was coming in for the kill now, obviously with no intentions of taking prisoners. Tique guessed the operator had seen what happened to his partner.

Reubin scored a hit on the man, Tique couldn't tell where. But the path of the laser wobbled and diverted and Tique thought with relief that it would miss Reubin. He was already rolling out of the way—of the original path of the death ray.

Into the new path.

Tique watched with horror.

Reubin rolled and the long line of light seemed to crease the bridge of his nose sideways, a black line appearing laterally across the bridge of his nose and one upper cheek bone.

The skycycle above kept him going and crashed into a tree, and began bouncing into it.

Reubin was on his knees, facing her. "Tique?" He held out the laser to her.

She scrambled to her feet and took it.

"When that groundcar is close enough, fire at it."

"Right now," she said, surprised at her own voice. It was calm and under control. She ignored the smell of burned flesh. Reubin must be in pain, too.

She lifted the weapon, aimed it, and pressed the firing stud. At least it was one of the small, personal weapons, not one with the supersighting mechanism and electronic eyes and all that other stuff she didn't understand.

She raked the groundcar with a withering fire. As she held the stud down, traversing the weapon along the vehicle, she wondered what Reubin was doing. Obviously, the first skycycle was destroyed.

The groundcar veered and dodged through and past a number of wormwood trees, and pulled up, far out of range. She didn't know if she'd connected or not. But at least she'd gotten their attention.

She turned to see what Reubin was up to, elated that she'd contributed significantly, and in an active role. Combat role, she amended.

Her elation crashed.

Reubin was standing there, doing nothing. Looking off in the distance, not at the groundcar, nor her, nor the ruined skycycle, nor the airborne skycycle which had caromed off deeper into the grove with its headlight and spotlight and strobe waggling all over the terrain.

Her intestines turned to water. "Reubin?"

"Tell me what happened," he demanded. His voice was rough but still maintained that element of command.

"They went off into the trees out of range, and they're stopped now. I see no activity in the backwash from the headlights." She paused. "Are you all right?" Then she saw movement. "Somebody—two, no, three men, are getting out of the groundcar." A spotlight shot out from the top of the vehicle and stabbed them both. Tique turned her head to avoid being blinded.

Reubin was standing there, eyes wide open, staring into the spotlight, not even blinking.

'Oh, no," she whispered.

"No time, girl. Let's get moving."

She swallowed the lump in her throat and said, "Where?" Her voice had gained about a million decibels on the high range.

"Away from the settlement. No safety there for us now."

"Reubin, how. . . ?"

"Do it," he said, his voice compelling.

She stepped off and he grabbed her elbow. "The men are fanning out," she told him.

"Go straight away from them. Jog, for we've a long way to go and need to save our strength. Panic kills more people than pursuit."

She settled into a long, rhythmic stride, trying to accommodate him. "Can you see at all?"

"No."

For the first time she was really, really scared.

"Are we near the river yet?"

"Not that I can see. The clouds have gone along with the rain, but I still can't see very far."

"Then we're running through water," he said, "that's not supposed to be here."

Reubin was right. They were sloshing ankle-deep in water right in the wormwood grove.

The locks had opened and tons of water per minute were pouring in from the Selby River. Not to mention all the rain lately.

"Check behind us," he said and pulled them to a halt.

She looked and saw nothing. "Not a sign."

"They've stopped to help the others back there," Reubin said. "They're confident with infrared and aircars they can track us and direct a ground party to our position. Let's go."

"We can't outrun that," Tique said. She marveled at his calm reasoning. He had adapted to no sight. No self-pity, nothing. Just business. And she was scared and worrying. Things couldn't get much worse.

"No, we can't." He took her arm and they moved off, walking fast. "So we've got to find something faster than we are."

What was he talking about? He sounded as if he had a plan—

Then she heard the river. "Oh, no."

"Yep," he said. "Can you swim?"

'Not very well," she said. Just a moment ago she was thinking things couldn't get much worse.

Right past a giant wormwood tree and there was the river, a sloping bank into the swift water.

"The rains have swollen the river," she said. "The monsoons must be early this year."

"It should be ameliorated by the open locks stealing volume and power from the river," he said.

"Makes sense to me," she said apprehensively. Whatever, that damn river was going *fast*. She said as much.

"The faster the better."

They stopped.

"Go downstream," he directed, "until we find a large branch or something to hold in the water, something that'll float." His grip on her upper arm tightened and she stepped off, heading downstream.

"The footing looks tricky here," she said. "Watch that root." She slowed.

He stepped high, and then down too soon. He tripped over the root. Instead of dragging on her, he let go and caught himself with his hands on the wet ground. He was wrist-deep in water.

The feeble light showed pain on his face.

"Another pill?" she asked.

"Not now."

The first one had worn off quickly. She had to admit, though, they'd gone through a great deal of physical activity, probably causing his metabolism to consume the medicine quicker.

Suddenly she realized how weary she was. With no respite in sight.

They resumed walking. Almost immediately they came upon some debris which had lodged into the elbow of a tiny bend in the river.

"Driftwood," she explained. "Some dead, some with leaves and stuff."

"Let's push it all out and see what floats the best. By my judgment, we're almost out of time."

She shuddered. "Translated, that means we were just about to hop in the water and swim on our own?"

"Right. Float, anyway."

"Here," she said and led him down a crumbling bank. "A fat bole of some kind of tree. A couple of big, dead branches—"

"Pick something that would cover us from visual if we need it."

"Sure. This one." She led his hands to the giant branch. Its diameter was as large as a regular tree.

He strained against it, and she moved to help. They were knee-deep when the thing slid out into the current.

"Wait," she said, trying to hold it and not altogether certain she wanted to go through with this.

"Is it floating all right?"

"It appears to," she said.

"Then push hard and hang on."

Together they shoved the great limb out into the current. The force grabbed it and dragged them along.

Tique whistled at the cold. At least it wasn't life threatening. She hoped. While the jumpsuit was waterproof, water still poured into it and soaked her body inside the suit.

"Kick until we reach midstream," Reubin said. "We don't want it to get hung up."

They kicked for a long time, Tique didn't know how long. At this point, the Selby was perhaps a kilometer wide, maybe more. She knew it was much broader upstream and at least tripled in width downstream. Since this was a narrow part, they were traveling faster than the ordinary speed of the current. She explained it to Reubin. "The venturi effect," she finished.

"I don't care what the hell you call it," he said. "The faster, the better."

"Do you think we will escape?"

She sensed his shrug more than saw it. "I hope. But don't forget that someone at the settlement took the precaution of setting up that intruder alert field. So it's not going to take an aquadynamist to—"

"Aquadynamacist."

"Whatever. It isn't going to take one of you-all to figure out which way we went when they don't find us in a saturation search."

"You're telling me there are categories of searches?"

"Everything has categories," he said. "There are survey searches, tracking, cordon, aerial grid—"

"That's okay, Reubin, really. I think we're far enough out. There's a small branch to your right. Straddle our, um, vessel, and lean against it."

He climbed up.

So did she, sinking back against a smaller branch, energy leaching out of her. She was so weary.

"Describe the sky to me," he said.

"Dark."

"More, smarty."

"Occasional clouds. Stars peeking out here and there. Moons still covered over to the west and south."

"Any sign of airborne pursuit from the direction we came or the settlement?"

She searched the sky. "Way back, a couple of lights appear and disappear. They don't seem to be heading this way."

He nodded. "They're searching where we were."

Water lapped over her right knee. "What are we going to do?" She couldn't keep the worry from her voice.

"You didn't happen to bring that pillowcase full of booze along with us, did you?"

"No."

"I guess that rules out having a party."

"How are your eyes?"

"Inop."

"Do they hurt?"

"No, but the bridge of my nose does. The beam just grazed my face, but close enough to kill my vision."

"Want a pain pill?"

"Yes."

She put one to his mouth and felt his tongue flick against her fingers.

"Thank you very much," he said.

"Oh, Reubin—" she began.

"Hang in there, girl. We'll win out."

"Are you taking bets?" She breathed deeply and tried to relax. "What's next?"

"We cruise down the river as far as we can until, well, I'll know when. They'll figure it out and send an aircar downstream, IR gear going every minute. We'll never be able to outrun it. Make that outfloat. So we gotta get off soon. For now, we rest and float, like Huck and Jim."

"Who?"

"Some river rats I read about."

She glanced behind them. Nothing yet. God, she was tired. How was Reubin holding up? Blinded, exhausted, in pain. She doubted he'd had any sleep, either.

A thought hit her. She snaked her hand into her pocket.

Her water-filled pocket. The printout of the wormwood operations, everything she had, was pulp. As she let the mess fall into the river, she told Reubin.

"Well, we've struck a blow for the good guys," he said. "We've caused them considerable problems."

She nodded and then felt uncomfortable for doing so. "It'll cost them a ton of money, too."

"Good. I've been thinking of another approach, anyway."

With no vision? He wasn't giving up. "Is your sight gone for good?"

"I hope not."

"Maybe we could concentrate on escape now. We've given it a good shot. You need to get to the nearest Long Life Institute center. They can give you new eyes if yours can't be repaired."

He splashed water on his face.

"It's bad, isn't it?" she asked.

"I've been wounded before."

"That's not what I'm talking about. The pressure. The pain."

"Look, Tequilla Sovereign. I've got a job to do and by God I'm going to do it come hell or—" He splashed water with his hand. "They extinguished a life from this universe. A fine life. A life which held no animosity toward those who caused her death."

"A position could be made for forgiveness."

"But they could do the same to other people they may have tracked down who had some significant part in the creation of the LLI."

She shrugged. "There's more to it than that, isn't there?"

With vacant, blinking eyes, he stared at her mouth for a long time. "Yess." His voice was low. "The beast within me will not let me quit."

She thought she saw life in his eyes, but he still had no vision. Even in the night, she was close enough to watch his eyes. She shivered and it wasn't all from the cold water.

* * *

"I believe dawn is coming," Tique said.

"It's time, too. Into the water and kick for shore."

They slid into the water, Tique on the east, Reubin on the west side. "Reubin?"

"Over here, we want to kick toward the shore the settlement's on."

It made sense to her. They might have had to cross the raging, flooding river for some later reason. Returning to that shore would be better now than a full crossing later.

She climbed over the great branch and they began kicking side by side.

"The river feels slower here," Reubin said.

"That's because it's wider, much wider. A couple of kilometers."

"We've got a long kick."

"We weren't in the center. We've perhaps half a klick to kick."

"Poetry," he said. "Keep your eyes to the north. If an aircar comes speeding down, just above the river, we're dead—if we haven't reached the shore. They're due."

Tique kicked harder. "What's the range of their infra-red gear?"

"I don't know. It depends on the model. I doubt they have much use for it here so they don't have very sophisticated models. Say a kilometer, depending on the altitude of their search. Half a klick on each side, maybe more, maybe less. The farther from the centerline, the less reliable and precise the readings. Maybe double that."

"So we've got to be at least one kilometer out of their line of travel."

"Yes, if they aren't very high. We might register, but vaguely; perhaps our IR signature would be mistaken for an animal."

Tique realized she was famished. Surely their packs were gone with the flood, too far upriver anyway. It struck her that Reubin could no longer seemingly conjure up food from nowhere. *She* was the one with eyes.

Predawn light gave an eerie cast to the surface of the river. As she kicked, Tique kept her eyes moving.

Suddenly, looming up behind them came great behemoths. They seemed to swirl in the mist rising from the river, swinging around behind Tique and Reubin and their tree-vessel.

"Reubin." Her voice reflected her alarm.

"What's wrong?"

"Something. Something's charging down at us, chasing us fast."

"Men?" he asked. "Slide down in the water, cover your head and leave your eyes and nose out. Let the branch drift of its own accord." He ducked down himself.

She studied the situation once more, taking her time. Finally, she figured it out.

She shook Reubin's shoulder. He cascaded water and his face asked the question.

"It's logs," she said. "Wormwood logs." They were coming out of the night into the dull gloom of the predawn morning, attacking the two on their makeshift raft. "Somewhere upriver, I'll bet. The rising river and the monsoons. All increased the speed of the river and broke loose a pen of logs. Hundreds of them." She thought that they were likely the last bunch harvested before the monsoons and not yet finished to float downriver, herded by tugs.

Reubin climbed onto their craft. "Well, we are ahead of them. We're safe. They should provide us extra camouflage from a visual search."

"You don't understand," she said. "They're cut from the giant wormwood trees. They're tons heavier than us. They're longer and more dangerous. They're *trimmed* logs. Their CD is less than ours—"

"Cee dee? What are you trying to say?"

"Coefficient of drag," she explained. "We've got limbs and even our legs trailing in the river, slowing us down. Like a sea anchor. These have nothing trailing in the river. They're outrunning us." A great log slashed into the very tip of their vessel, spinning it around and causing Tique to momentarily lose her grip. She tumbled in the water. Clumsily, she paddled back.

"Can we grab one of them?" Reubin asked. "It would be safer to run with the big boys."

"No. They spin in the water. Nothing holds them one side up."

Reubin said nothing.

Tique detected two logs caroming off a third. "Reubin. Get off on the downriver side. Quickly now." She was scrambling over the branch even as she spoke. Reubin snaked across even more swiftly.

One of the logs slammed into their craft. The trunk rolled in the water, pushing Tique and Reubin under.

Tique coughed underwater and felt a strong hand on her arm guiding her back to the surface. She broke free of water, coughing, spitting, and choking.

"Use your eyes," Reubin demanded.

The urgency in his voice dragged her to her senses. She wiped water from her eyes.

"What do you see?"

She scanned the surface. Around them, giant logs rode the river, some smoothly, some swinging, some crashing into each other.

"It sounds interesting," he said conversationally.

"We're clear for the moment."

"Let's sort of guide this raft toward the shore and out of the mess," Reubin said.

Their branch swung off-angle to shore, but they managed to kick and inch themselves in that direction.

Tique looked upriver. Jeez. "Reubin? About a million logs are heading right for us. Right now."

"Just what we needed. Time to bail out." Their tree limb swung in the water. "Grab the fabric of my jumpsuit. Not there. The shoulder. Stream out behind me and kick like hell." He pushed off from the safety of the branch. "Guide me toward shore—and around any logs in our way." He began to stroke in the general direction of the river's bank.

"Reubin—"

He turned his head. "Our coefficient of drag has to be less than wormwood logs, no?"

He was right. Guiding him, she was able to steer them around logs and out of harm's way. But it took time, valuable time, and increased the possibility of being caught out on the river.

Finally, they struggled ashore.

Reubin lay in the water, holding onto a wormwood root for several minutes. Then he rose wearily. "We've got to go. We're out of time."

They scrambled up on the bank. With the flooding, it wasn't a climb. The river was already pouring over the lower banks. As far as she could see, water lay below wormwood trees.

Standing there, Reubin said, "I can almost feel it rise up my legs. We'd best get clear of the river, for the flood will grow."

She nodded unconsciously. He took her arm and she sloshed off.

Tique noticed a lack of small animal life, including birds. Insects were thick in the air, and buzzed as if driven mad.

"The flooding's driven all the animals inland," she said.

"That might mean it'll get a lot worse before it gets better. How long do you reckon before they fix the locks you jammed open?"

"If they can get past some fancy tricks I put in the programs, early today. If not, they have to get people out there and manually close each one."

"Command override wouldn't work?"

"Nope." Tique grinned at the memory. "Command Two, Josephine Neff, was the one who did all that. You don't command override a command command."

"Are you all right?" he asked.

"Just giddy from hunger and exhaustion."

She sensed him tense his body. "Do I hear something?"

She stopped and searched the sky through the trees toward the river. "Maybe. I don't see anything."

"It's past time for them to have sent someone down river. That was the most obvious course for us to take."

"There," she said, pointing unnecessarily. "Over the river, to the north. Moving slowly."

"Quickly now," he said. "Run, run like the wind. Take the most open route. In one minute stop. Our combined body heats in the same location might be strong enough to give us away. If we aren't moving, we could be mistaken for sleeping animals. Go."

She was running before she realized she'd left him blind and alone. But she acknowledged his logic.

Shortly she stopped and threw herself down behind a tree—and cursed. Water was all over the ground and she had almost dried. She peered around the tree and tried to spot Reubin. He was nowhere to be seen.

Turning her attention to the skies, she tried to locate the searching aircar. There. Almost level with them. Appearing and disappearing through the tops of wormwood trees.

Soon she detected the machine far south of them, journeying the same speed at the same altitude. That fact told her they hadn't been detected.

She climbed to her feet and slaked water off her jumpsuit.

When she returned to where they'd split up, she couldn't find him.

She looked around. Nothing.

"Reubin?"

"Here," he said.

There he was. Five or six meters up a wormwood tree, clinging to the bole like a spider. Slowly he climbed down. You'd never guess he was blind, Tique thought.

When he was down and next to her, he rubbed his hands on his thighs. "I thought that if a heat blob appeared on their screen well off the ground, they'd think it was an animal more than a human."

They moved off, trudging inland.

Time moved slower than they did. Or so it seemed to Tique.

She was weak from hunger and exhaustion. She even wished for some of Reubin's gnurl jerky. But she didn't complain. It wasn't yet sunset.

It had rained, cleared, and rained again. Definitely monsoons. Now it was dreary with dusk coming on.

Reubin had estimated they'd traveled ten or twelve kilometers. "It would have been more without having to wade most of the way."

Now they were on "dry" land, more of the eternal wormwood grove, which had been soaked by the torrential rains.

"How long shall we keep going?" Tique asked.

"As long as we can. Their search will expand past the river banks in broad sweeps. We need a bunch of Ks between us and the river."

"That translates to all night."

"If we can," he said. "They'll use more than just that first aircar. That smart guy up at the settlement will figure the speed of the Selby and estimate an approximate dawn location for us. They'll fan out from there."

"That's why we're heading north, too?"

"Right."

Reubin had explained earlier that they wouldn't expect him and her to head back toward the settlement.

"We need food for energy," he said. "Do you see anything edible?"

Reubin stood silently, his flashlight held steadily in front of him.

It was completely dark, clouds obscuring the stars. Tique thought that she might actually be dry for the first time since she'd stepped out of VIP cabin #8.

Against her better judgment, she was walking silently alongside a rock-strewn stream.

The mudcat was sitting on its haunches, totally absorbed by the light, almost as if it were locked in place. "Jacking," Reubin had called the technique. The beam holds the animal's attention as if hypnotized. He hadn't been certain the idea would work, but it was worth a try.

Tique spotted the animal, and Reubin took the light under her direction and held it in position.

Now she grasped a rock high over her head, closed her eyes, and smashed down on the mudcat's head. A sickening thud came, and she felt the vibration through the ground to her feet in addition to hearing the noise. "Got him," she said quietly.

She carried the fat, furry animal back to Reubin. It was surprisingly heavy. "Now what?"

He held out his knife. "Gut him and we'll eat."

"Do what?"

"Clean out his innards, his entrails."

"How about if I just cut off some meat?"

"Tique, you're not squeamish after all this time?" She could feel his grin, and not see it above the glow of the light. "Besides," he went on, "in the history of eating animals, the most sought after delicacy of any animal is his liver. It's generally the most nutritious."

He held the light while she began to saw at the mudcat.

"Feel for the meat under the fat," he directed.

"Ugh." Then she had an idea. She put the knife down and took out her pencil laser. It worked well for the same purpose.

Reubin said nothing, obviously following what she'd done. In a moment he said, "Good thinking. We'll make a woodswoman of you yet. But I hope they haven't got energy detectors in operation."

"Would they?"

"Not necessarily," he said, "except for that wise guy. He knows we have the laser from the Constabulary officer."

"But this pencil laser isn't that strong."

"Right. That's why I think it's okay. Besides, it's helping to cook the meat."

They sat on what Tique had described to Reubin as a stone orchard: a field of smooth boulders alongside the stream. They'd just finished eating.

"Greasy," she said, "but it assuages the hunger."

"In the morning, we'll find something green."

Tique leaned back against her rock. Automatically now, she scanned the sky.

And saw what she didn't want to see.

Running lights of aircars.

"They're coming," she said wearily. She'd thought things couldn't get worse. Now despair set in.

"How far?"

"Two of them, perhaps half a kilometer apart. Not far at all, but heading away."

"They missed us on their pass. But they'll be back soon." Reubin's voice took on a note of excitement and command. The exhaustion had gone from him like a shed cloak. "Were they running spotlights?"

"No."

"Look, here's what we'll do. Heat about six of these boulders with your laser. Not real hot, but good and warm. Then heat up a couple of them in the stream hotter than the first bunch."

She hurried to follow his directions. "Finished." A glance to the south. "The aircars are coming back this way."

"Curl yourself around one of these rocks," he said, feeling his way to a boulder. "First cover us with brush or a fallen limb or something. Quickly now."

She did so. They were hidden with leaves and branches and wrapped around warm boulders. Those she'd heated in the edge of the stream were hotter and burning off dampness.

"Got it," she whispered unnecessarily. "A hot springs. Maybe gnurls sleeping near it. Or simply hot boulders from the underground springs. Which mask our IR signature."

"Right," Reubin said, "not to mention the steam from the river will interfere, too. Their scope will be a mess of various shades of red."

"Gee, here I was worried," Tique said.

"Unless it's so strange they stop to get out and check."

"Oh. Here they are. One's almost overhead."

The aircar swished through the air far above them.

Tique watched as it passed, feeling safer each moment until it swung around and returned.

A spotlight shot out and crisscrossed the stone orchard. It lingered on the immediate area, darting about. Tique held her breath.

After about a century, the aircar slowly moved on, then sped off to catch up with its mate.

Reubin was on his feet. "Time to go."

"We're safe here, now," she said.

"Suppose on the next pass the onboard computer matches the first with the second. The patterns will be different, inordinately so. We can't insure the same intensity of heat. And the configurations of heat emanations will be significantly changed if you and I move an inch and we've already moved a lot."

"Let's go," she said.

"It's green," she said, two days later. They were walking along, paralleling a ridge.

"It tastes green," Reubin said. "Like seaweed. But the only thing I can see is dark and light."

"That's something."

They'd been discussing their plans. The main thing they had to do was avoid capture. Then wait for his eyes to get better—if they would. Then, finally, head for Cuyas. Reubin had said that they could decide what to do by then. There was nothing for them anywhere else on Snister, except Cuyas. Reubin staunchly refused to consider escape until he settled the score and found out who, what and why.

"I'm not certain of our location," Reubin said, "but I think we ought to swing our course farther from the river. Just a feeling, you understand."

She'd learned that his feelings, judgments, and hunches were seldom wrong.

"It'll cost us more time," she pointed out.

"We've got plenty of that," he said.

"I do. You don't. Try to relax. Take this pill."

"Thanks."

His spells lasted longer and now there was disorientation.

And she was running out of pain pills.

They slept the night through.

But when Tique woke, Reubin, for once, was not already awake and waiting for her.

He lay where he had slept, in the bed they'd made between some raised wormwood tree roots. They'd stuffed the depression with soft vegetation and clumps, the cottonlike fruit of the tree. The night's rain had been soft and for a change the tree itself had offered protection.

Reubin was tossing and turning. Tique thought about waking him but decided to let him sleep—though his sleep reminded her of a person in a tortured coma.

After two hours, she became alarmed. She checked him, then decided to wake him.

She couldn't. She tried, but he would not wake.

He was feverish. He must be unconscious, not asleep. She bathed his forehead.

In his stupor, he muttered, "Lemme alone." His head rolled back and forth. "No. *I* have control. Not you."

He seemed to freeze in position. "It *isss* my job." His voice was so different from Reubin's that Tique flinched away involuntarily. Habu? There was some internal battle raging and Tique wanted to wade in there and help Reubin. She'd seldom felt so strange and helpless.

Was Reubin dying? Was he in the last mind-wrenching coma which comes before death? She was amazed he was this close to the end and had still been able to function. He'd been way overdue for a long life treatment.

If she didn't do something, he was going to die.

What in the *hell* could she do?

She went into a nearby stream and collected some green river plants they'd eaten before. She didn't want to leave Reubin to hunt food. She found a few berries alongside the stream and went back to Reubin.

No change.

She ate a little and bathed his brow again. She put several of the pain pills into his mouth and forced them down his throat with water and two pieces of the river plant.

He gagged and choked. But she held his mouth closed and he swallowed the mess. When she let go of his mouth, his tongue lashed out and flickered at her as if an entity itself, darting here and there for a moment.

Was this thing Habu?

She thought of her mother.

No, she would not accept this.

She continued to bathe his head and began talking to him. "Reubin? It's me. Tique. Tequilla Sovereign."

No answer.

"Mister . . . Habu? I don't know what's going on with you two, but I'd sure like to." She thought for a moment. "I'd like to believe that Habu is helping ward off the madness crushing Reubin." Why couldn't they have designed better, more efficient Long Life treatments?

His face showed no change.

"I'd like to think that." She felt awkward.

He was going to die and Mother would not be avenged. The hazy plan she'd been turning over in her mind finally solidified. A scheme worthy of Mother herself.

"If you're going to die," she said slowly, "it would be a terrible thing. You have a legacy of the dead left behind you; but you have nothing to carry you into the future. The future you've helped insure, you and all the Original Earthers." She tried not to become maudlin.

"Robert Edward Lee, think of Olde Earthe. Can you hear me in there?" Her palm told her the fever had reduced. The pain pills must have contained an antipyretic to reduce fever in addition to the analgesic for pain. "Think of Virginia. Mother was from Vancouver and she used to rave at the beauty of it all. Hell, think of Mother. Alexandra. Your wife. You have a mission."

Would she never get through to him?

His eyes flickered open and immediately riveted on her face. Could he see? Whether or not, those eyes were not human.

Tique swallowed her fear. "Give me back Reubin." She knew she could never finish without him. "Reubin?"

His body twisted and tensed oddly.

She thought, given the chance, her scheme would work. She would do it for Mother, if not for herself or Reubin or any other reason. He couldn't die.

She shook his shoulders. "Reubin! Wake up. It's time. You can't sleep anymore."

Nothing.

"It's me. Tique. Short for Tequilla. Mother named me that because it was that or get a tattoo, she always said. She inflicted *me* instead of herself. She must've been a hellraiser at one time. Is that why you liked her so much? Because she was so different? You know what I've gone through with this goddamn name? I doubt you do. I've paid for Mother's wild streak and if you think I didn't hold it against her, you're wrong. I fought my whole life for Tique, one syllable please. But I loved her. Come on, Reubin, live. We've got work to do. You Original Earthers must be something different to have the gall to name your offspring like that. Would you and Mother have selected such a funky name for your child? Did you have offspring already, Reubin?" She bit her tongue. He'd told her that he'd had a child who was killed along with his wife on Tsuruga. Had he any other children? It was important to know.

"Come on, damn you! Grab your intellect and rise through that mire."

The riveting eyes clouded over and closed. His body relaxed.

"Reubin. Use your resentment. They killed Alex. Revenge. Hatred. Use any goddamn thing you can think of. Just come back to consciousness."

She shook his shoulders again, this time with more strength. "Don't give in. You're strong enough to rise above this; you've been doing so the entire time you've been here. Don't stop now."

She slapped him lightly.

He moaned.

"Don't give up. Fight, Robert Edward Lee, Reubin Flood, whoever the hell you are."

Out of the cycle of his shallow breathing, he took a deep breath.

Tique held her own.

She unsealed the top of his jumpsuit and bathed his chest with the wet cloth.

When she finished, he was awake and watching her.

She moved her hand behind her. His eyes didn't move, didn't follow the motion. He was still partially blind. Was he conscious? If so, was he Reubin Flood? Habu? Or, more likely, a brain-dead babbling fool?

"Reubin?" Her voice was a hopeful whisper.

He grimaced in pain and settled back. "Yes."

"Is it you?"

"Yess. Yes."

"Reubin Flood? Robert Lee? Habu? Who?"

"Me."

"Habu?"

His eyes blinked and he closed them. "No." His voice turned into a whisper. "Not anymore." He fell into a natural sleep.

After an hour, he was awake, eating berries one by one.

"Do you know what happened?" she asked quietly.

He nodded and cleared his throat. "I waited too long for the Long Life treatment. My mind is under constant attack from itself, from time, from within, from nature not wanting it to continue under this altered existence." He sank his head back, finished eating for now.

"You were fighting with Habu, weren't you?"

His eyes remained closed. "I don't remember. Habu survives. I'm certain he cut through the miasma of pain and dying mind and somehow dragged us back."

Tique knew instinctively that it could happen to him again, and soon. He was going to die. To die in the middle of their attack on Wormwood, Inc. He'd never live to see the end of it. But she knew also that no matter about the revenge, she cared whether he lived or died. She wanted him to live, for his own sake. For hers. For Mother. "So Habu isn't all bad." He'd misled her before.

"Not terminology I use."

"*What* is Habu?" she asked, gathering courage. At times, Habu had truly frightened her.

He propped himself up against the root. His eyes moved but didn't appear to see anything. "I'm not certain. He could be a figment of me brought on by psychosis. Sometimes I think of him as an alter ego who runs things when I cannot; but that's rather simplistic. Other times, he cries out in a primordial, primitive way and I think he is a strange alien creature who's taken up refuge inside my mind. Such is his strength and response. He could be a being stranded in this universe since its creation. Or the essence of that being. He found me and I unlocked something, or something in me snapped, and he moved in."

"On Tsuruga?"

"Right."

"And you have no memory of how or when he appeared?"

Reubin's face fell and Tique felt guilt at putting him through this. She needed to know the answers, though. In case she had to relay it someday.

"No. I don't remember the time or circumstances. All I know is that I went mad, stark raving berserker insane crazy for a long, long, long time. A year. Three years, Tsuruga time. Gradually, I became *sanely* aware and slowed down killing . . ."

She waited. When he didn't finish the thought, she said, "So you were not necessarily in control of your senses when you did all the killing."

He shifted position and then rested his head against the root again. "No. Yes. They . . . Well, the thing happened and I went berserk. For a long time I killed them. By hand. By guerrilla tactics, in and out of the jungles. Living like an animal myself. I have flashes of memory about snakes. Fiendish laughter and it was coming from me. More snakes. All the while I was killing people. I attacked them. I sabotaged power relays. Public utilities. Public transportation. Communications facilities. Poisoned water sources. I—I wanted to do it only to those who had been responsible. That's what I wanted. The snakes multiplied. I think I remember not fearing them. I was obsessed with them. I survived many a bite of the habu, became immune . . .''

''Could that possibly be—?''

He nodded. ''It doesn't make biological sense, not that I know of. But the inordinate amount of habu venom could well have affected my mind in some organic fashion. Hence Habu. There are many possible explanations.''

A silence stretched between them.

Finally, she said, ''At least you did not intentionally commit genocide.''

His face took on a grim smile. ''To date, no one in history, no human being we know of, has killed off an entire planet, a goodly portion of its population, and wrecked its natural ecosystem. Except me.''

''Hah,'' she said. ''The bastards deserved it.''

''Many of them did.'' His words were quiet. ''The snakes multiplied fantastically. I didn't really mean to kill everyone who died. I was simply reacting and killing was a way of life. An obsession. The only thing I knew. Attack. Attack.''

She recoiled at the violence in his voice. Calm him down. ''But you recovered your sanity and escaped yourself.''

He nodded tiredly. ''Other than the initial trauma of seeing . . . well, at any rate, it was the most difficult thing I'd ever done myself. Dragging myself out of the sea of madness.'' He blew out his cheeks through a pursed mouth. ''I stole a scientific expedition's ship. I'm a good pilot. I ditched it into a forgotten sun, and took the lifecapsule to the surface of another planet. I've been on the run ever since. I've taken many treatments from the LLI, paid my time to them—or went my own way, wandering the galaxy—''

He was lost in thought so Tique took the opportunity. ''So you became sane and went about life. Did you, um, marry again?''

His sightless eyes tried unsuccessfully to search for

hers. As they rolled back and forth, Tique again felt his strangeness. "No. Not since Tsuruga—except, of course, for Alex."

"Oh." Slip it in now. "But surely you weren't, um, celibate for centuries."

He actually laughed with mirth. He shook his head. "Not hardly. For a couple of centuries, I was a wild one. Chased all the women I could. Partied a great deal. Ran with the big dogs, but never got some of them big fleas."

She thought she understood what he meant. She hoped he was thinking of her and her questions as just another nosy female, always wanting to know about a man's past and the possible competition from fond memories. "Any children?" she asked as if in afterthought.

"Nope. The LLI fixed that at my first Change after Tsuruga. And every Change since. I need no children. Though it was close once or twice. The way I understand it, when you reach the tail end of your current life, the treatments wear off. Evidence my mind rotting away as we speak." He grimaced at what Tique thought was returning pain. "Along with everything else, the sterilization treatments wear off."

And he was far removed from his last Change. Anyone could tell from the way his mind was being constantly assaulted by itself. The probability that he was fertile right now was high. Many women took the nonfertility treatments. Tique simply took a monthly pill. For which she knew she was long overdue.

He laughed again. "Because of my, er, notorious behavior which lasted a century or two, Habu's reputation became enhanced as a womanizer, too. One who could and did charm the most beautiful women. Often I've wondered if the serpent within me didn't somehow direct that activity for his own knowledge or gratification." He crossed his arms. "Perhaps I was still insane, still striking out but in a different direction. Maybe it was a manifestation of some obscure death wish—high profile existences ending with intentional unmasking of Habu." He shuddered.

What a mess of a life he'd had.

He continued. "Gradually, I calmed down, changed my ways. But it seems that I do court danger, whether physical or otherwise . . . It's been occurring more and more frequently this particular life, not just at the end when I'm due a Change. Perhaps I'm undergoing some other metamorphosis. . . ."

Tique shivered at the possibility. Jeez, what else could happen to him? But her spirits were rising. She'd found out what she'd needed to know. Her scheme might work.

She fed him and gave him water.

They stayed there for the entire day while he rested and got over his exhaustion. He had enormous stamina. Of course, he was a man accustomed to the hard life of the mercenary. Hardship had been his constant companion.

His strength returned slowly.

Tique schemed and planned. It was obvious he would not live much longer—at least as a sane human being. If he did sink into the mental oblivion before death, would Habu come through and take over? Would she be traveling with an alien monster? She shivered again. While she'd seen different facets of Reubin, and even Habu, she knew she'd never seen Habu in absolute control. Not from what Reubin had said. She thought of him on Tsuruga, someone who bore little or no resemblance to this Reubin Flood.

The next morning, they resumed their journey.

Three days later they were camped near a small stream.

Tique had checked Reubin's wounds: the one from the slaybot was healed. The burn on the bridge of his nose was now a mere shadow. He had amazing powers of recuperation. She hoped his eyes responded as well. She hoped more that these recuperative powers would hold off the madness and death hovering over him. While he still suffered mentally, he showed no signs of sinking back into that final coma.

She was tired of setting snares, sneaking up and killing animals, and fishing with her hands. Rarely she used the laser, in case someone could pick up the energy expenditure.

But they weren't starving and, except for his eyes, they were healthy.

At this point they were waiting for soup to cook. She'd lined a hole in the ground with a mudcat skin. Inside she'd put water and greens and mudcat and sanderling meat.

She placed another hot rock into the mixture and took the cooled one out. "It sounds awful," she said, "but smells divine." She dropped the cool stone into the fire and leaned back again.

Reubin squatted, the hood over his head covering his eyes to help them heal faster. "Right domestic, no? Soon, we'll be fixing biscuits and everything."

After starting the soup, she'd stripped and gone into the stream to bathe. Now she sat with her arms around her legs, still unclothed, her garments drying upon a rock. It felt comfortable in the warm, setting sun—no rain yet. "How are your eyes today?" she asked.

"I guess they're all right."

"Still seeing shadows only?"

He took the hood off and slowly opened his eyes. He blinked for a minute. "Not quite twenty-twenty—yet. For instance, I can't count the freckles on your left shoulder."

Casually, she glanced at her shoulder, then she realized what he'd said.

She squawked and scrambled for her clothing, much to his obvious amusement.

Two hours later and still piqued, Tique was sipping warm soup from a spoon she'd carved with Reubin's knife. They simply dipped their spoons into the "soup skin" right there in the ground and ate out of the pot.

Against Reubin's better judgment they kept the fire going. She tightened her collar. It was nice to be dry and the fire kept the damp away.

She ate her fill and settled back against a tree. Reubin was still eating. He kept glancing at the fire. Night had fallen and a strong breeze came out of the southwest.

"At night," he said, "you can see a fire like this from miles away—if it's clear. Hell, a satellite programmed for it can pick it up. How many campfires you reckon are burning out here right now?"

"Beats me, but they have to see through the foliage of those wormwood trees."

"Which they can easily do, girl. I'm telling you somebody smart is planning their moves."

But he didn't move to douse the fire. He needed comfort and dryness as much as she did.

He took his knife out and tried to spear a hunk of meat in the soup. He still couldn't see that well—and this was night with only flickering firelight to aid him.

She'd never forget that tranquil setting. She was full, pleasantly so for the first time in a long time, and the food had been of at least more than one basic food group. The walk that day hadn't been difficult. She was sleepy, though. It was hard to believe that anything else existed in the universe outside of them and the wormwood groves. Civilization and murder were so far removed that they seemed fantasy. She'd changed a lot, and for the better. She could handle herself physically now, against nature. Her weight had shifted to muscle and sinew. She was flat out amazed at herself.

She thought tonight would be the perfect time to seduce Reubin. Yes, soon.

Tique was watching him clean and put away his knife when the skycycles swooped in low, from downwind, in a virtual horde. Well, six anyway. Immediately following came several aircars, black against the night and showing no lights.

Light shot out and Tique felt a tingling sensation all over her body. A stunner! She breathed shallowly and tried to move, but she couldn't. It was as if she was frozen to the tree with the tableau of action occurring right there in front of her.

Reubin was rolling, actually rolling, in a zigzag pattern. Men were tumbling off their skycycles. Two great searchlights illuminated the area from aircars above, giving an eerie shadow-relief as the light was interrupted by the wormwood trees and their branches and foliage.

Reubin was scrambling on all fours now, dodging lances of light from the men. Deadly light. No stunners, those.

Animals and birds chirped and grunted and croaked and screamed at the interlopers.

Reubin rolled again, behind a skycycle, and came up leaping over the machine with his knife in hand. His arm pumped and blood spurted from a slashed neck. He snatched the weapon from the dead man's hand before the corpse relaxed and fell.

Tique couldn't believe the speed with which Reubin moved.

For they all were firing at him now, lasers too, not just stunners. He'd been slated for death before, at the Corona arena, so do it now, they would figure, and kill him escaping and assaulting law enforcement officers.

But she was to be captured, that much was easy to see.

Reubin flipped back over the skycycle and rolled out from under the front of the machine, firing steadily, pulses of light springing out, dying, lancing elsewhere, seeking targets. Three other men were down by now.

She watched Reubin dodge around the bole of a wormwood tree into the dark. He collided with a large root, telling Tique that Reubin still couldn't see all that well. Had he been jesting with her about the freckles and her shoulder? It would be like him to do that.

Two men moved quickly toward her. She fought against her invisible bonds. Damn it, body, work for me, just this one time. Come on!

Nothing.

One of the aircars had forced its way through branches and an open segment free of growth and was settling to the ground, men scrambling out even before it touched down. Armed men.

Light burst from the aircar and the area was no longer shadows. Tique wanted to cry out in frustration, but couldn't.

The two men were upon her.

Reubin stepped around the tree against which she leaned, cut them down with his laser, and reached for her.

The new force saw him, shouts rang out, but one cautioned, and no lasers came their way. Stunner beams did, though.

Tique found herself thrown lightly on Reubin's shoulder and banged her elbow on the tree as he pivoted.

Reubin started running.

"Get them!"

Tique felt another stunner beam strike her in the shoulder as she bounced on Reubin's back.

Out of the intense pool of light, Reubin ran right into a small tree, causing him to grunt. He expelled air and staggered. The collision had stunned him.

He took a deep breath and began running again. This time he tripped over something Tique couldn't see and they sprawled together.

"Goddamnit," Reubin said, voice almost casual.

He moved Tique off him and rose quickly to his feet. He picked her up again.

"There they are!"

Lights and stunner beams sought them.

Reubin tossed her on his shoulder and began running for the dark again. He brushed a tree with his free shoulder.

Tique guessed he couldn't see worth a damn.

He tripped on something again, staggering, catching his balance.

Tique performed what she considered a superhuman feat. She forced air through her throat and worked her tongue.

"Leave me."

He kept going, a stunner grazing his left leg right below where Tique's head hung near his hip.

Again. "Leave me."

"No."

He collided with a tree, bounced off, tripped over a rock, and fell.

Tique hit hard.

They were out of sight momentarily behind the rock.

Light shot over them and about the trees.

Reubin's face loomed above hers.

In the backwash of light she saw his eyes. Serpentine cool. Dangerous. Fire sparkling. They were the doorway into his soul, not indicative whether he could see well enough or not.

His mouth worked, but no words came out. He tried again. "Do not worry." He enunciated each word slowly. The next words were slower even. "I . . . will . . . ssss . . ." Then nothing.

His eyes softened and he smoothed hair off her forehead.

His eyes hardened again and he was gone.

Tique's vision was at about eighty degrees, taking in the top of the rock and the corner of a tree. Lights caught her and heads peered over the rock.

"Where is he?"

"Gone. They warned us—"

"Never mind. Get her." The man snapped into a handset. "He's not here."

Tique was again lifted and carried between the two men.

Before they reached the campsite, screams erupted from out in the dark.

Then silence.

A curse, "He's slittin' throats! Get—" Whoever it was, his voice trailed off into a gurgled shout and died.

As they reached the area of activity, men were running into the dark, lights in one hand and lasers in the other.

"Shoot to kill!"

"I'll get the bastard!"

Another scream. And another.

"He moves so fast I can't line up a shot."

They carried Tique to the aircar. As they were handing her in, she saw a shadow detach itself from other shadows.

She saw it because there was a constant crisscrossing of laser fire behind him, contrasting a weird hue with the background.

The shadow moved more quickly than a human had a right to. It settled on the farthest skycycle and the machine rose swiftly.

"He's stolen a 'chine!"

Reubin was guiding the skycycle with his knees while firing a laser in each hand. Snaps of light created chaos, screams, panic. And death.

As the skycycle broke through the wormwood tree's topknot, they dumped Tique on the floor of the aircar.

Her plan, her scheme, would never reach fruition. And that she regretted most of all.

12: CAD

"**H**e might be the most dangerous man alive," Cad said. He was leaning on the back of a couch, dividing his attention between the scene on the wall and the startling woman who seemed hypnotized.

Josephine Neff fascinated him. Her low voice, it seemed to him, was pitched thus to make her more sensuous—if that were possible.

His attention was dragged back to the wall. Fels Nodivving was standing there, staring at the scene depicted. The Prime Minister gave the impression of brutishness, but Cad thought that an affectation. Nodivving was wide and muscled, but Cad was well aware that he had a sharp mind. Why the PM of Snister and the CEO of Wormwood, Inc. were doing this, Cad couldn't guess. Though he had to admit, normal people might not notice; good reporters caught on to that kind of behavior right away.

On the screen was a frozen panorama shot of Reubin Flood standing in an arena they called the Corona, challenging the hundreds of thousands of people present and, by televideo, the entire planet.

Typical Habu, Cad thought. They had to have pushed him to the limit for Habu to emerge so quickly and triumph. But at last, a current picture of the man. He didn't look as odd as you'd think an Original Earther would.

"You've seen the replay twice," Fels said, turning, determination on his face. "Now tell us about this so-called 'Habu,' will you?" Nodivving's voice took on a wistful tone. "He doesn't look so tough to me; I could take him."

"Also, you might tell us what's in it for you." added Josephine.

Cad wondered if there was anything between Nodivving and his exec. The signals weren't there; but the relationship could have been done and gone by now. Josephine Neff did not appear one to suffer a single man for long.

He turned to face her directly. "Me? I, madam, am a journalist. I've made Habu the centerpiece of my work. I've tracked him across the galaxy. I'm *the* expert on Habu." He gave her his practiced smile. "Habu supports me, if you will. I live off of him."

Neff saw something in him. His eyes? His bearing? He could tell. Perhaps he was getting too complacent.

"Suppose," she said slowly, "this Habu is captured. Suppose he is killed. Where does that leave you?"

He shrugged. "Compiling a biography, I suspect."

"And?" she prompted. She was perceptive. She reminded him of himself. And he liked that trait.

Nodivving was watching the interplay, interest on his face. "Tell us, Abbot, tell us. If this man is the most wanted person in the galaxy, why isn't there a reward?"

Cad coughed. He shrugged again.

Nodivving turned his face hard. Tough intelligence gleamed in his eyes. "Could it be that there *is*, in fact, a reward? Could it be that you intend to collect that reward?"

Cad coughed again. His sponsors wouldn't like him using their names—but he could talk generally about it. "Well, a couple of the Federation Council members are interested, and have posted, um, additional sums for the capture of Habu."

"Politics," Nodivving said derisively.

"So?" Josephine's voice became louder. "You'd do the same. Have done the same."

Nodivving shot a grin of acknowledgment. He turned back to Cad. "The Fed itself is officially looking for Habu, am I correct?"

Cad nodded. He'd successfully diverted the original line of questioning. No need for them to know of his personal interest in the case.

Nodivving grinned a knowing grin again. "Perhaps it is that you have a commission to apprehend Habu. Dead or alive?"

Cad tried not to react. Wormwood, Inc. had its sources. Perhaps the parent megacorp, Omend Galactic Operations, was also interested—and assisting its offspring.

He wondered what had really happened to Flood to trigger Habu. Doubtless, he'd never get the straight story from Nodivving or Neff. But Nodivving had let his mask slip. He'd extrapolated correctly, surely figuring that Cad wouldn't come this far this quickly without good and financial reasons. He didn't answer the Prime Minister.

Josephine said, "Let him tell it his own way, Fels. Surely he wouldn't admit to some secret commission?" Her eyes appraised Cad.

"We've all secrets we don't wish to discuss," Cad said pointedly, referring to whatever had caused Habu to come forth.

"Background, please," Nodivving said in an even voice.

"Your Reubin Flood is a legendary man," Cad began. "He is an *actual* legend, not a myth as the story has evolved. Upon odd occasions, Habu emerges from the man, wreaks havoc, death, destruction." He smiled grimly. "Tissue samples and blood analysis confirm his identity." He was fortunate they had saved those so that he could match it with his data.

Josephine rose and walked to the frozen scene on the wall screen.

"Nobody knows him," Cad continued. "He changes his name often. He disappears. Some say he is a legend from even farther in the past, others say he has some access to the Long Life Institute. Nobody knows. Suffice it to say that the legend known as Habu was born centuries past, but may have its roots in obscurity—

which I'll talk about shortly. But the circumstances were unique, the thing happened, and the legend grows with time.''

''What happened?'' Nodivving asked, surprisingly showing no impatience. ''I've heard of Habu. I always thought it a myth. Until we received your message and researched Habu here. There is very little information available.''

''It was the planet Tsuruga, the Ryukyu Retto group in the Fukui Prefecture. A group populated by Orientals of Olde Earthe—long before the eventual assimilation the Long Life treatments have helped cause. Tsuruga was settled by Japanese and Okinawans—who are Japanese, too, but of a slightly different ethnic background.'' Like me, he thought.

''Get on with it.'' Nodivving's patience was running short.

''A man named Robert Edward Lee was an assistant military attaché with the Embassy of Earth. The Rollback came along and the resultant cataclysm. Racial and religious hatred exploded among the inhabitants of Tsuruga. Pogroms, lynching, killing, everything. Hatred of Earth spilled over and all people from Earth were hunted and killed. First they went after Jews, then blacks, then all Caucasians. It was a crazy time. As every kid learns in history, the Rollback caused the face of humanity to change, planets everywhere dumped the yoke of Earth. After it was all over, some planets regrouped, others are still being rediscovered. Earth became Olde Earthe, and gradually the Federation grew into what it is today—''

''Skip the history, Abbot, get on with the Habu business.''

''This man,'' Cad said, ''was bringing his wife to a hospital. She was pregnant and contractions had begun. A mob tore them from their transport. The mob ripped the clothes from Lee and his wife. As the story has it, right there in some public park on Tsuruga, the woman began giving birth.

''Somehow the baby became the symbol of the great satan, Earth, and thus became the focus of the mob.''

Cad was breathing fast now. ''In front of Robert Lee, they strangled his wife with the umbilical. The tiny infant, only moments old, they smashed to death against its father's body, this man they now call Habu.'' He paused. ''There are tales on Tsuruga—tales mothers use to frighten their children into behaving—of just how it happened, the details seem to get more gruesome with every new generation.''

There was a long silence. Then slowly Josephine nodded. ''Undoubtedly, the way they killed the child was the genesis for the implantation of two beings within one being.''

This woman was as quick as they come, Cad thought. ''That is the moment most experts agree that drove the man insane, put him over the edge if you will.'' Cad sighed. ''They beat Lee until he was unrecognizable. They thought him dead and left him there with the torn and bloody remnants of his family.'' Cad had to reconfirm his own commitment. Every time he told the story, the horror and drama and human tragedy affected him. But this incident, no matter how terrible, couldn't excuse Lee/Habu from murdering millions of residents of Tsuruga.

Including all of Cadmington Abbot-Pubal's family, relatives, friends. Not all at once. But over the years, all were dead from Lee's actions. Cad's heritage gone, wiped out by one man and the temporary madness of a mob. His mother had been the first to go— Stop! Back to business. He cursed himself for a fool. He hardened his mind.

Cad walked around the couch to the frozen scene on the wall and studied it.

''If we're finished with the drama, perhaps we can proceed?'' Nodivving was oblivious to the human tragedy. At least I've still got my humanity, Cad thought, seeing the Prime Minister with new eyes.

Cad turned back to Nodivving and Neff. ''Lee returned to consciousness and crawled off, terribly injured. Something had snapped inside him. He recovered in the wilderness. He began killing residents of Tsuruga. For years he hid out, destroying crops, power stations, killing people. Classic and new guerrilla tactics. An animal, that's all he was. He lived like one. Some say the essence of the slaughtered child drove him. He was hunted and hunted by experts, but he seemed to have some sixth sense which alerted him, which allowed him to escape each time. Documented cases of berserk behavior show a duration of hours mostly, a day or two at the upper limit. But his berserk behavior lasted years."

"To the snake part," Nodivving said.

Cad began to pace. "*Trimeresurus flavoivurudus*. A snake from Okinawa on Olde Earthe. Okinawans called it the habu. Of the viper family. In a zoological garden, not many of the species. But one which was shown to reproduce swiftly on Tsuruga. And the venom became much more deadly. Instant death. There was no natural enemy for the snake. Lee stole the snakes from the exhibit and allowed them to reproduce. He turned them loose far away from towns and cities and discovery. They multiplied at a phenomonal rate."

"How'd Lee know to use this?" Nodivving asked.

Right to the quick of matters. That had been one of Cad's favorite speculations. "No one knows for certain. But recall he was a military attaché. He was from farm country on Olde Earthe. I think he'd run across something similar, I don't know. But I do know that something similar occurred on Olde Earthe. An island called Guam. Lee studied the place as part of his dissertation for War College. *Boiga irregularis* otherwise known as the brown tree snake. It was said to have arrived on Guam from Australia, the Solomon Islands, New Guinea. Maybe with American soldiers in World War II. No natural predators. They mated and a snake population explosion occurred. They ruined the island. Got into the power grids and shorted things out. The brown tree snake ate all the birds and their eggs; thus the island became birdless. It thrived in the tropical jungle. Invaded homes and businesses." He shuddered at the memory of the writhing mass on

Tsuruga. "Lee knew the history—and the devastating effects—of the brown tree snake on Guam. He applied his learning to Tsuruga. Accident on Guam; lethal intention on Tsuruga."

Nodivving was nodding. "I've a new appreciation for this man. I knew there was something different about him. He was an even match for me—"

"Fels," Josephine said.

Cad picked up on it. "You met Reubin Flood?"

Nodivving nodded and waved a dismissing hand.

Josephine filled the gap quickly. "The research we've done shows that Habu is a legend along with the likes of Audie Murphy, Davy Crockett, Harold G. Eggerholm. Warriors all, but historians are unable now to pinpoint the accuracy or reality of those legends."

"He is real, all right." Cad looked at the woman looking at him.

"We know that." Her voice was dry. "I was at the Corona that night."

Now Cad understood. This woman had been fascinated by the spectacle, the one he'd just seen replayed. She was obsessed by the power and violence of Habu.

Cad eyed Josephine Neff with a new understanding. Try something and see what happens, he told himself, attracted to this woman as no other had attracted him, ever. "The Habu legend has grown so much and changed with the telling over the years and centuries, it has been said that Habu is the first being, the only man who has lived since the beginning. That he crawled from the primordial soup a serpent and changed into a man. That he was the original womanizer, the one who tempted the First Woman out of another man's bed, and thus destroyed Eden. It is said he searches for that First Woman still, that she exists as he exists. That in search of her, he's made love to Cleopatra, Monroe, the Great Catherines—both of them, the Czarina and the third Empress of the Second Galactic Empire."

Josephine's face was slack, her eyes glazed yet staring at Flood's figure on the wall.

Cad went on. "Habu is said to be untamable, and only

simmers beneath his current human persona, waiting to explode from beneath the surface.''

The room was quiet. Cad couldn't help but notice Nodivving studying his executive officer closely, a curious look on his face. Not swayed by romanticism this man, Cad knew. Josephine operated under different conditions, for different reasons. Nodivving was a realist, a materialist. A man with a lust for power. A man who loved to best other men.

Cad decided to flesh it out a little more. He was winning Josephine and knew right then he'd need an ally. ''Other stories say Habu goes through life drunk and wandering because of his eternal sorrow and grief, until he undergoes some unexplainable periodic metamorphosis into his Habu persona. This particular myth has it that Habu originated before or concurrent with the first man and first woman, and went out into the galaxy among the first explorers, with Silas Swallow and his people. Always in the lead echelon of expanding humanity, always seeking new places, new adventures to help him forget. A continuous catharsis, if you will.''

''That would explain his long life,'' Josephine said, already finding connections.

''Lonely, ever lonely,'' Cad said softly. ''Women ofttimes invoke his name: Habu. He knows how to keep out of your sight. He's like a soft wind. He's part shadow, part morning mist, and part of the falling dusk.''

''Let's cut the crap, shall we?'' Nodivving snorted his displeasure. ''How in hell can a man, a man born of woman, be what you claim him to be?''

Cad stretched. ''I claim nothing. I'm merely repeating what has been said and written.'' He shrugged. ''My educated guess is that after he'd been berserk so long, and keeping in mind the slaughter of his family, his mind warped. The snakes gave him ideas about serpents, and were with him as he came out of his years-long berserker rage. Psychologists have fancy technical terms for all this. Robert Lee, or Reubin Flood, probably doesn't know the answer himself. Experts have speculated that his own serpent persona has settled into his mind permanently as a result of a combination of things—a unique combination." He paused and thought.

"That combination is?" Nodivving said.

"His age. He is ancient, even among those who take the Long Life treatment. Another factor is his madness. Insanity is the prime cause for abnormal and bizarre behavior. Perhaps he took a Long Life treatment while he was still insane from Tsuruga and it cemented the dual persona. This latter would account for something I've been able to determine through research and good guesswork: I believe that Robert Lee *always* waits until it is almost too late to take the Long Life treatments. So that he is partially mad naturally, as it were. To this I attribute his Habu persona. Habu gains control through the waiting and increasing madness, subconsciously keeping him/it/them from the Long Life treatment until the human half overcomes the urge. I think Habu will become prime, the controlling persona, if Robert Lee goes mad as a result of failing to obtain the Long Life treatments. Always, toward the end of his current lives, Habu forces Robert Lee into dangerous situations. As a point, note where he was before here: a mercenary on a warring planet." Cad thought of the constant mental battle for control which must occur between Lee and Habu. Cad also wondered what the connection was. How had Reubin Flood gotten from Karg to Snister? And, more importantly, why?

That, Cad decided, was the piece of the puzzle he was missing. That was the reason for Number One and Number Two on Snister showing so much interest. That was how Flood had wound up in an arena.

He finished up. "So all these factors make up the composition that is Reubin Flood—now—and Habu. Madness. Science. The brutal nature of his wife and child's murder. Frustration at the time that he couldn't prevent the atrocities. Rage. Sorrow. You can probably add to the list."

Josephine nodded and turned from the wall scene. Her voice began low and grew in octaves and intensity. "Mythology has it that only woman can stand between the serpent and man. The stag, the eagle, the lion are the secular enemies of the serpent. We've sent a stag called the gnurl against him unsuccessfully, we've sent a lion called a snarv to kill him unsuccessfully. The eagle remains. From the heights. From above. Take him from above, it is plain.''

Cad shivered. He saw Nodivving watching Josephine with a disbelieving look on his face.

She continued. ''Myth has it that the serpent is the guardian of immortality, the spring of life. Thus Habu and his legend grows and does not die. Why he is ready to erupt to the surface of the double being. Myth also has it that the serpent is immortal, living differently but alongside man—just as you, Cadmington, speculated earlier—waiting to strike out, to offset man's existence.''

Cad couldn't resist. ''Legend also has it that when Habu sheds his skin, he then sheds his old age. A metaphor for resurrection?''

Josephine still had that faraway look in her eyes. Cad felt himself inexorably drawn to her.

''Goddamn, Josephine,'' Nodivving said, ''you're really weird when you get mystic like this.''

Her eyes blinked rapidly, lingered on Cad, and closed. She breathed deeply. She opened her eyes and spoke, her voice back to its customary whisper. ''So this man goes through some kind of deterioration leading to the merger of two personas and eventually into the ascendancy of Habu. Perhaps each time he has a Long Life treatment, it brings out Habu more and more. That's the man who is running about out there in our world, loose. That's our enemy?''

Cad didn't know what to answer. But at least she was back to normal. He regretted not having time to get the Fed to do a full brief on these two for him. But how was he to know they'd be center-stage players in this game? The Fed shrinks would have had a field day analyzing Fels and Josephine.

One thing Cad did realize. No matter the cause of the current ''Habu Breakout,'' Habu was in trouble. Habu had erred, and Cad had found a gold mine. Cad now had analyses of blood and tissue; personal identifications which would never change, even after Long Life treatments. Additionally, he had a fresh IR signature—though Habu might accomplish the impossible and *change* his infrared configuration significantly.

Another unexpected present: current voice-print and photos—which a Change might affect. Actual videos, really. Cad found himself with more new facts and details than he'd managed to dig up in the last few centuries.

"You *what?!*" The strident, shocked tone awakened Cad. He rolled over.

Josephine was sitting up, dressed again in that gossamer thing and smelling of female musk. She spoke into a bedside unit.

"I ordered no such thing."

Cad studied her stiff back. Something was amiss. He could read body language well enough to know some major crisis had erupted.

"Find out more and call me back." She snapped the disconnect and turned to Cad. "Fools."

"What's up?"

She sank back against her pillows. "Some problem with irrigation or some damn thing—they don't know yet. They say I authorized—no, *I* made changes which have caused numerous glitches and groves are flooding and equipment is being ruined and—"

Cad rolled over and began massaging her shoulder. "Slow down. Why would you do all those things."

"It's perfectly logical. Someone is using my name and code. I'm Interior Minister. That stuff comes under my job function."

"Surely they have experts digging into it right now."

She nodded. "But there are safeguards the experts can't break—yet. Not to mention the system thinks that Command Two initiated the whole thing and thus will not respond to lower ranking queries and tracing attempts. And finally, there is a berserk program replicating itself,

duplicating files again and again, eating up system time
and space, interfering with the programmers trying to
straighten the mess out."

"What's the outcome?"

She shrugged his hands off and sat up. "Economic
chaos. Administrative turmoil until it's straightened out.
One hell of a lot of lost man-hours, equipment, property,
and product."

His curiosity began burning. "Would you say a severe
economic setback?"

She nodded curtly. "It'll kill the profits for years, unless somehow we recoup miraculously. They've found
only the tip of the iceberg. Other things must be going
wrong at this moment we don't even know about."

"Industrial sabotage," Cad said. "Anything else unusual?"

She sank back down and turned toward him. "An intruder alert. At the same place, a settlement way out
which is the hub of the wormwood business at the present
time."

"Are intruders unusual?"

"Yes," she said, "but nothing compared to what I'm
thinking of right now." Her arms stretched to him.

Ignoring her, he stepped out of bed. "That's it. Don't
you see the connection?"

"What are you talking about?"

He began pulling on his clothes. "Don't you see?"

"No." Her voice caught his excitement, her whisper
higher.

"Flood. Lee. Habu. It's him. He's supposed to be a
computer genius. Sometimes I believe he has access to
the Long Life Institute and its galaxy-wide network. That
would answer how he escapes so often leaving so little
trace."

"You're saying that Reubin Flood is out there in the
wormwood groves skulking around, sneaking about, and
disrupting things?"

"Yes. Damn it, Josephine. This is our break. He's
waging economic warfare. It's so obvious." He thought

for a moment. "The fake trail he laid to some apartment here in Cuyas. The Constabulary tore the city apart with no results. It all adds up." It was time for Josephine to level with him about this woman Tequilla Sovereign and what had caused this "Habu Breakout." He'd get the information out of her soon.

She nodded, understanding lighting her face. "Let's get down to Operations."

"He's a brilliant tactician," Cad told the constabulary face on the screen, "and he ties his tactics in with his long-range strategy."

"Understood, sir." Uncomfortable eyes from taking orders from an unknown, noncompany civilian. Captain Mcdemman was very military.

Cad didn't know whether it was night or day. He'd gone to bed with Josephine after lunch and just now quit because of this crisis.

"It just happened," the Constabulary captain said. "They exchanged fire and the male and female escaped. I haven't gotten the complete story yet, but I understand there is at least one fatality. We suspect it is tied in with the attempted break-in at Security headquarters—"

"The weapon storage area?"

"Yes, sir."

"It is, no doubt about it." Cad considered for a moment. "You're running a search now?"

"It is being organized."

"I'll get back with you. We will maintain this comm channel." Cad had to think more. He had to know more. "Out for now." He rose from the console and went over to another. Josephine was there with a senior programmer running tests. She looked up. "Anything?"

"I'll confirm it was him. Habu. We need to talk."

She nodded. "Stay with it," she told the woman beside her. She led Cad to a coffee dispenser on the wall. "Well?"

"Who is the woman with him?"

Josephine shrugged and avoided his eyes.

"Josephine, I need to know these things if I'm to help."

"Her name is Tequilla Sovereign. She's the one who killed the power at the Corona and aided his escape." Josephine looked angry at having to discuss another woman. She tossed her hair. "Tequilla Sovereign is a no-account; a conservationist who plays with fog-shaping. Her mother had all the guts and strength in the family."

"What's her connection?"

Josephine paused for half a minute, then poured herself coffee.

Cad poured his own. "Tell me."

"In a nutshell, your Mr. Flood married a woman named Alexandra Sovereign. They were to take the Long Life treatment together and go off wherever it is the LLI sends people like that. Sovereign returned to Snister, died of a heart attack. Flood showed up accusing murder, went berserk—which we now understand—and was captured and sentenced. The young woman is Alexandra's daughter. There, does that explain it all?"

"For now," he said. There is a lot missing from your account, he thought. And some of it rings false. But I don't care. It's part of the back trail. "It explains his actions, though. He thinks Wormwood, Inc. is in some fashion responsible for Sovereign's death. That and the closeness of the Change and his treatment set him off. Remember it was the death of his wife, among other things, which triggered the carnage on Tsuruga. Habu is running things, lurking there to explode into action."

Her jaw became slack while she must have followed his words with her own mental pictures.

Hours later, Cad was back with the Constabulary captain at "the settlement." On one screen a duplicate of Mcdemman's search pattern map sat staring at Cad trying to tell him something.

"—the storm winds and rain, of course, hinder our search. Now—"

Cad interrupted the man. "Look, Captain. If they're on foot and you're running IR scans, that leaves only one, I say again, one, method of travel to get them out of your expanding range.''

The captain's eyes studied his own console. He nodded slowly, keyed another comm link and spoke. ''Have them run an aircar downstream. Have somebody figure the speed of the river and the approximate location somebody floating along would be now if they went into the water almost immediately after the confrontation.''

Cad nodded his approval. ''Then run your search patterns from that location.''

''That was my intention,'' Mcdemman said.

The guy was good, Cad thought, but jealous of his position, and unhappy at some civilian thinking as fast as he did.

Days later, Cad was still in Operations. Josephine had long since lost interest. Cad thought that she wasn't there because the smell of blood was gone; no longer did the sense of urgency loom over the place and the immediacy of capturing the fugitives had receded.

He spoke to the captain. ''Give me an overlay of the position of your work crews now.''

Mcdemman's fingers flew. ''Most of 'em are coming in from their outlying locations for nightfall.''

''Skip those.''

''Right.'' The captain no longer ''sirred'' him. ''There.''

''Not many outposts,'' Cad noted.

''Right. Not with unpredictable monsoons and natural and *unnatural* flooding.''

Cad turned to the Operations officer next to him. The man smelled of stale coffee. ''Superimpose the heat-source images from the satellite.''

The screen fuzzed for a second. It was the same procedure they'd done all night for the last few nights.

Time stretched out. The geosynchronous satellite showed its own number of heat-sources.

The computer deleted the sites provided by the Constabulary captain. The few they checked out this night and the previous nights had been false alarms. But they had to investigate each one.

"A new one just popped up," said the Ops officer.

"Do you pick up the new one?" Cad asked Mcdemman at the settlement.

"Got it. Dispatch troops in one minute."

"We've got *her*," the captain's excited voice shouted.

"Never mind her. *Him*. What about *him?*" Cad demanded.

"Hold it. Casualties. Fatalities." The captain's face turned dark. He spoke aside. "Send out more men! Hunt him down. I don't care—" He glanced at Cad on his screen. "Orders are orders" He turned back to address Cad. "The man escaped, that's what happened, Mr. Abbot. But we're still looking."

"Captain, be advised he is a killer with no moral compunctions against killing humans."

"I damn well know it. I've lost men—"

"Look. I don't know how rational he is." Cad was thinking quickly. "But it's possible he's developed a relationship with the woman. Could you take her back to the settlement and use her as bait?"

"This man Flood would walk into the lion's den?" Mcdemman was incredulous.

"He did at least one time previously, did he not?"

"But we weren't expecting him."

"Believe me, Captain. That won't matter one bit."

"If you say so, *Mister* Abbot."

The damn fool didn't believe him. Was it worth putting his prestige and hard-earned goodwill on the line now? He could ask Josephine to issue the orders; and she would. She trusted him and he could use that political capital.

Maybe he'd wait. Just a bit. See what happened. Because it was obvious that they wanted Flood dead and the woman alive. Nodivving and maybe Neff were working at cross-purposes with him. He needed to solidify his position by being right all the time. He needed to figure out just exactly what the hell was going on.

Well, my old friend Habu, test their mettle. Some people need convincing before they'll believe.

Cad decided to wait. If he knew Habu, something would certainly happen.

Something fatal.

No... never... uncontrollable... come... Really... He had remembered before they had left.

Cal looked to wajd. It is now, Hayo, remains Lookinroute... barroom...

13: HABU

His nostrils flared.

The blood smelled good.

Blood on his body was natural. As it should be.

Branches whipped at him. Foliage lashed him.

The men below fired at him.

He fired back, instinctively guiding the skycycle with his knees. His body had done it before, many times, so he knew how. Battle came natural.

Popping out of the wormwood tree cover, he encountered aircars. They hovered near, clogging the sky.

Pinpoints of light flashed at him.

A wide-beam spotlighted him and wouldn't go away.

He raked the decks of those aircars with his lasers. He preferred a knife or his hands and feet and teeth to rip into his enemy. But he could use these tools.

The spotlight bothered him and he threw one of the weapons at it and burst the worrisome thing.

He looped his skycycle and came down among the aircars. He jumped from his machine onto the open deck of an aircar.

With a snarl he attacked a man standing there, gutting him with the knife he now held.

As if in afterthought, he stepped into the cockpit and fired and fired and fired the remaining puny weapon. Men fell and died.

He backed out. The glare of lights had lessened. Good. He operated better at night. His vision was oddly blurred, focus coming and going.

Other aircars were edging closer now, curious to find out what had happened.

He jumped lightly and surely onto another aircar. This one had no deck. He ripped the door open and dragged the occupant out and tossed him free.

The scream which followed was satisfying.

The man within him struggled for ascendancy, and managed to help him guide the aircar. It nosed into another and in an instant he was out of the cockpit leaping onto the rear of that aircar. Two men within emanated fear. They fired weapons through the bubble which was strong enough to contain the energy. Else why install them? Fools.

He leaped to another aircar, this one with a rear deck for carrying heavy items. The jump over dizzying heights thrilled him. He was free and doing what his sole purpose was: kill.

A man jumped off the aircar and did not scream. Fright had burst from his face and given up his man-soul.

Pings on metal and caroming light from the bubble showed him other aircars firing upon him now. He raised his fist with the bloody, dripping knife and challenged them with a scream.

All action stopped for a space.

Then it resumed, the other aircars backing away, some slowly, some swiftly.

He reached for the deck hatch.

Locked.

The man within him told him to fire at the locking mechanism. He did so.

Suddenly, the aircar flipped over.

Without a grip, he fell.

He dropped the weapon and reached for the upper branch of a wormwood tree. He dragged it down and dangled, whipping up and down for a moment, hanging by one hand.

He put the knife in his mouth. The blood upon it tasted salty and thick and satisfying.

Two aircars edged his way and men began firing at him again.

He dropped to a lower branch and scrambled to the trunk of the tree. Swiftly he worked his way down, circling the great bole. When he ran out of branches, he used small limbs. When the limbs were no longer there, he used cracks, crevices, and holes he should know the purpose of.

He snaked his way down the tree by feel more than by sight. It was night, but his vision came and went.

When he reached the ground, he hunkered there, looking for enemy.

Somewhere came the storm. He sensed it. Off in the distance lightning cleft the skies. Clouds boiled. Skies and stars disappeared. It was heading this way.

The man within was trying to tell him something, trying to get him to do something.

The woman.

Tique.

What—

Pain struck within his head, pain he'd shared before.

He rose and took a step.

A disorientation sprang from the pain. He fell back against the tree. His vision became darkened as if covered by blood.

He slumped down, the bark of the tree upon his back somehow comforting.

The pain rushed over him in waves. He pawed at his head. He screamed. He rolled on the ground. He slid on his belly. Nothing helped. Another primal scream tore angrily from his throat.

After awhile, the storm arrived. Wind lashed the trees. Debris fell from the world above. Cold rain cooled his fevered brow. He drank and drank again from a rivulet running off the tree.

Down deep within himself, both he and the man understood the tree. It was the lifeblood of this world. Without it, this place would not survive. He felt a strange remorse at what he—the man, that is—had done to the trees here. Never before had they struck against the root of life of an entire world. But it was not the trees they fought, it was men. His animal nature sensed this world's anger at the invading men. This world, this land damned these new and foreign trees men had planted. It cried out that this plain was not as it had always been. This part of the world wept for itself, manifested by the inordinate rains.

He tried to coil, but couldn't. So he curled up into a ball at the foot of the tree, right under the rivulet of rain pouring from the boughs above. The cold water cooled his burning body. His metabolism attempted to deal with it, but he managed to allow himself to cool several . . . degrees? He bared his teeth to force the man back and fell asleep.

When he awoke, the pain had receded. His vision was good. He knew which way was up and which down.

His first tentative steps told him that within him, he and the man had reached the old accommodation. The man would wait within; they would not do combat between themselves.

He knew that he would not exist if not for the man—the basis for his existence lay in the man's powerful mind and his creator directed him on a primal level. The imperatives which guided him were buried deep within the man, and these he could not ignore. But he would not do the man's bidding.

As long as survival was at stake. Vengeance. Killing. Those were his duties.

He looked out through cunning, intelligent eyes.

Habu.

Not the man.

Not the serpent.

Both.

Together.

Habu.

Habu exulted in his freedom. The man-half was proud of their power.

Habu breathed deeply of the rain-cleansed air.

He tuned his senses.

Nothing. Normal woodland activity. Animals. Birds. All avoiding him and his location. Perhaps he exuded the killing smell.

He moved for awhile, searching for the location of last night's battle.

Shortly, he found it.

Nothing remained. Blood had seeped into the ground to be leached into the soil by the deluge. He found the ruins of their fire.

Limbs above had been destroyed. Scorch marks and bleeding sap showed where lasers had fired and struck the trees. Scraped ground. Indentations. Men had been here and hastily departed.

Tique?

No sign.

They would have captured her. They needed her for information. They needed her to catch him.

Tique became his imperative. Get to her before they had time to disassemble her. Time to pry into her mind and turn it to fodder.

That is what they'd thought they'd done to him. But his mind had persevered. Something within had spoken strange things, and they had believed.

Habu had lurked just beneath, corralling the man's mental quickness and intelligence, protecting it, while that strange thing within had interceded. Idly, he wondered if that strange mechanism within his mind was the bridge between the man and the serpent-beast.

He kicked over a log and grabbed a handful of insects and larvae. He jammed them into his mouth. Acid. He pulled a few berries he knew to be edible off a bush and ate them to sweeten the insects.

A bird flew by.

Swiftly, he snatched it from its flight. The reaction hurt his arm. He'd moved too quickly for this body.

He bit the bird's head off and spat it out. Walking along, he ate the bird meat and sucked the bones.

He judged his position and began running. He ran easily. The man knew that he had to reach the settlement by nightfall, though perhaps that would be too late.

They might take Tique away before then.

Unless they made a mistake.

It was also possible that they would use Tique to lure him.

So be it.

He ran faster.

His vision was much improved this day. The animal response within him had helped repair the damage and use what he saw to better advantage.

The running pleased him. Because of his heightened awareness, he knew that the running served to hold back the disorientation and the mind-pain. In fact, the increased speed of the blood pumping through his body, gathering sustenance and clearing out impurities, caused the mind-attacks to retreat.

But they still lurked there, ready to strike when his guard fell. The man was trying to install programs within their mind to hold back these attacks.

The man slithered back into the joint control. But when it came to this type of activity, Habu was best.

Habu *must* be both of them. Alone, they were each. Together they were Habu. The ultimate Habu.

He ran on.

He thought.

At the settlement. That thing which had told the men about him and Tique. That . . . detector field? Intruder detector field, that was it.

They'd still have it in operation.

Have to bypass it.

How.

Enter the settlement with men.

Right. Find men.

He searched his memory for the Wormwood, Inc. current operations areas Tique had called up on the screen and printed out and lost in the river.

There.

Just follow the terrain. They'd be working furiously to wrap up that phase of harvest before the monsoons prevented work in the groves.

Altering his direction slightly, he increased his pace. He ran with long, sure strides bearing around great trees when his path was blocked.

Fortunately, they'd already been heading back toward the settlement.

Which reminded him. Some intelligent man had figured they would do that very thing. Which in turn called for further caution. So if Tique was still at the settlement, then that smart man would use her as bait for him.

They wanted Habu dead. Not just for what he'd done in the arena, but for what he knew and surmised.

Yes, Tique would still be at the settlement. At the security building.

The only reason he could think that they would keep her there this night without intentions of trapping him, would be bad weather making travel dangerous. It also occurred to him that he had decimated their ranks last night, and that they might not have the men to spare to take her away. They might be using all their men searching for him right now.

Let them come.

The people at Cuyas could also be dispatching reinforcements. They'd have time. Unless they expected those at the settlement to send Tique to them immediately.

Too many variables.

He concentrated on his senses, running well, dodging great wormwood trees. Grabbing big, pulpy insects from the air and eating them.

At midday he reached the location he remembered from Tique's map.

Gone. Nobody here.

New saplings planted.

He tried to remember whether Tique had said they grew from seeds, roots, or what. It didn't matter anyway. Seeds, that was it.

He turned and ran toward the settlement. There was only one way left—without alerting them that he was there.

Wait outside and enter the settlement with other men so that the machine running the intruder alert system wouldn't be able to distinguish him from another. His IR signature had changed, so that might not be a consideration.

Habu was either colder or hotter than a human, depending on his activity. So his IR signature was different than the one they had in their computer systems. He'd used that technique before to escape or avoid capture. One day someone was going to figure him out.

Not only his Habu identity.

But his ingress into the computer system of the Long Life Institute. He'd buried identities—

Disregard.

Back to the present.

Maintain Habu.

Concentrate on the task before you.

The lay of the land, since the new saplings had been planted, was more open, more veldtlike. His pace was smooth with fewer obstacles such as grown wormwood trees in his path.

He was invigorated. He ran well. His blood flowed. His heart pumped rythmically.

He was fortunate, too, that he'd had weeks and weeks in the wild, honing his muscles and nerves and reactions. He was more attuned with the land. He was physically capable of running all day with little or no food.

And the running exhilarated him.

Habu was free and doing what he did best. Kill. Survive.

The running pleased him, helped cleanse his mind.

He wished he could remove his clothing. His boots. But he knew he'd need them, and it was easier to wear them than carry them awkwardly while at a full run.

This was life.

Hunting. Killing. Surviving.

Living.

He had no need of computer access, no need of hormone treatments, long life processes, no need of human accoutrements.

He screamed his pleasure wordlessly and the groves silenced immediately.

The alien noise had interrupted the natural flow of things.

He would not exult again. Not aloud anyway.

He found a rough roadway leading directly toward the settlement.

He increased his pace.

He saw no one.

Was it because this was a little-used way? Or because all men were forted up in the settlement?

He'd find out.

He continued running, the way easier for him now.

He was squatting on a lower limb of an ancient wormwood tree studying the settlement in the dusk.

Before he'd climbed the tree, he'd circled the settlement. Nothing unusual that he could tell, though he certainly was no expert in the human configuration.

One change was evident. Only one ground access was being used. Airbarges, three of them, had come in from random directions.

But all the ground traffic had used the East Avenue access. He attributed this to the intruder detector field and heightened security.

He sucked on eggs he'd found in a hole in the tree.

He surveyed what he could see of the settlement. The only unusual activity seemed to be in the motorpool. He could only see a section of the maintenance area, and there was much coming and going. Perhaps repairing damage which had occurred during last night's battle.

One egg wouldn't flow out, so he broke it open and ate the embryo. Tiny, not-yet formed bones crunched between his teeth.

Very little traffic had gone into the settlement, and none had come out. They were battening down the hatches for night.

Clearly, they were expecting an assault. They had much to fear, for Habu was about.

He stifled a challenging scream.

Habu finished his meal and his surveillance. He slunk down the far side of the tree, his hands and feet seeming to stick of their own accord for the briefest part of the second the hold required.

Back through the grove he moved, until the road angled out of the direct line of sight of the settlement.

Here he'd wait for his transportation. He hoped somebody was out late and wouldn't be returning to the settlement until after dark. Though with the lights at the entry point, it might not matter.

He looked at the swiftly darkening sky. A good, hard rainstorm would fit his purposes.

Not to be. Not now. Clear skies.

A groundcar sped past, too fast for him to catch—though the driver did slow for the curve.

He hid behind a medium-sized wormwood tree, so that he could rush out onto the roadway or climb the tree and scurry out that one low branch which overhung the roadway a little.

Time passed.

The sun was down, but light still abounded.

Habu wondered idly what they'd done with Tique.

He heard something coming. He readied himself. The noise continued as if from a long way off. It was moving slowly.

He waited.

He wondered how different his life would have been if he'd never met Alexandra Sovereign. If he'd met her and never married her, just gone his own way. He didn't know. Habu was able to divorce his emotions from those of the man. If he wanted. But the same things drove both. However, he was Habu now and things were as they were. As the man, he hadn't expected to live through the experience here on Snister. Habu didn't care. He had his function to accomplish.

He would do so or die trying. Perhaps he would accomplish his function and die in the doing. So be it.

A great machine appeared in the distance. Habu studied it. With pneudraulic lifts and arms and a large freight deck, it must be one of the wormwood transports, possibly coming in for repair or periodic maintenance which couldn't be performed in the field. Eventually, the machine trundled to Habu's position. Dusk was leaving and night falling.

From his vantage point, Habu inspected the vehicle. Way above on the front at top left position was a driver's control bubble. Two men sat inside, feet up and talking. One man touched a joystick and the machine began turning to accommodate the curve.

As it passed, Habu checked the rest of the machine. Nothing. Not even a safety man at the rear.

To avoid monitors they could watch in the control bubble. Habu slunk through the falling night to the rear of the great machine. He could walk upright under it between the great treads. He could walk as fast as the machine was traveling.

He let the machine go past him and grasped a rung above on the rear of the vehicle. He swung himself up more rungs, hand by hand. He scouted the entire vehicle, dodging monitors.

Finding a rodent which must have come aboard on a processed tree, he drank its blood. He might have need of such sustenance.

The giant platform contained several maintenance access covers he could remove to hide in the inner workings of the machine. He decided against that plan.

It would be best if he merged his IR shadow with some other heat source.

Just in case.

Forward, he found a great reservoir of an oillike fluid, obviously circulating through the mechanism somewhere for coolant purposes. He traced the bubble-derived tubing and found the return lines, as big as his arms, hot fluid pumping back into the reservoir for cooling. He wedged himself among these lines to see if the fit was right. He was able to stand between two of the lines which came up from below. The bubble material wasn't treated to hold the heat in for obvious reasons. He went to an outside viewport and watched until they approached the settlement.

When he judged they were near the location the intruder detection system would most likely be working, he wiggled in between the hot lines.

Let them try to identify him.

His only worry was if someone searched the machine specifically for him. It would take them a long time, for this was a large vehicle with many possible hiding places.

The machine ground on, coming in East Avenue.

Nobody came through searching. The machine did not stop.

He was in the settlement.

He thought about dropping off now, but decided it would be wise to check the motorpool.

The machine was quite slow, but eventually it cranked into the motorpool.

Habu stood in the dark, staring out the viewport.

The entire motorpool was lighted. Men were everywhere. The platform machine he was in continued through the main area and went into the back where the larger vehicles were parked along the outer edge of the settlement, near West Avenue.

Habu waited for the men to shut down the machine and leave. Luckily—for them, perhaps—they did not have to go into the lower sections to shut down systems; it must be all centrally controlled.

He waited to insure no maintenance technicians were about to climb on and get to work.

Habu dropped off and melted into the shadows.

He scouted the entire motorpool. His first interest was if there appeared to be an inordinate number of official personnel transport vehicles. Aircars which had carried fresh troops here.

He saw no more than he remembered upon his/Reubin's initial survey. Though security vehicles could well be stacked up all over the command area near Ops and Security.

But there was a lot of repair going on. Aircars, primarily. Perhaps he'd taken his toll upon them as well as the men last night.

He looked to see that the aircar he'd sabotaged was still there. It wasn't. It was on the red line, awaiting parts.

Good. He replaced the printed wiring board. The machine was ready—except for the auto-diagnostic system he'd destroyed.

He ghosted out of the motorpool, reveling in the cool shadows with which he felt so familiar.

Silently, he retraced his path of so many nights ago, in and out of alleys and side streets, moving even with South Avenue.

He crossed South Avenue by walking out in the open, as if he had a purpose.

He cut down past QUALITY CONTROL and SCHEDULING as he had before. He stopped there, in the shadows, and took account.

In front of him was the well lighted area of OPERATIONS and SECURITY.

Security abounded. He counted two roving patrols. Sentries stood at the entrances of both buildings.

So they were using their manpower.

He sniffed the air as if he could find a hint of Tique. None.

Too many alien smells here clouding the spectrum.

He ran his hand through his hair and beard, trying to make it look more normal. His hair was still not so long that one couldn't tell from a distance that it was unkempt. And his beard was half-full, not yet needing trimming.

But they knew what he looked like from last night.

So be it.

He explored his mind. The man and the beast were intertwined back there, Habu the result. The pain and disorientation were held at bay by force of will.

He moved around the area, circling until he came closest to the Security Building. It was the only logical place to hold Tique against her will.

He would have to move quickly, so quickly that patrols wouldn't have time to double-check readings on detection gear if they were carrying such.

He clung to shadows, watching the open area, mentally timing patterns and routes of patrols.

He charted his course up the side of the Security Building.

He moved around some more, counting. He didn't think that there were too many Constabulary vehicles parked there.

Of course, had it been him, he would have concealed the vehicles of the reinforcements to add to the element of surprise in the trap. If trap it were.

He waited a while. Early night was not the time to attack.

That's what they'd think, too. He decided to go in while this shift was on duty, for he'd learned their patterns.

Also, if he did find Tique and they did manage to escape, it would give them a great deal more darkness in which to flee.

He wished he'd had the presence of mind to search for the laser he'd dropped while falling from the aircar last night.

But he'd been undergoing his metamorphosis and not thinking straight.

His knife would do.

And his serpentine reflexes.

Now.

The patrols were momentarily out of sight and sentries were not facing the side of the building where there were no entrances.

Habu slid through the night, reflexes pushing the human body faster than that body was designed to function. He knew the body would pay for it later, in soreness, in depleted energy. He ran low, snaking side to side, using shadows. He went up the side of the Security Building, beginning with a leap. He barely touched protrusions such as antennae and was atop the Security Building scanning the ground to determine if he'd been seen and breathing deeply to catch up.

Nothing.

No one changed routines.

The patrols had turned and the area he'd crossed was under surveillance again. He thought it possible that he could have eluded detection anyway. These humans did not use their senses. They depended too much on electronics and machines.

Habu slunk around the circumference of the top of the building, studying the approaches, the aircars, the patrols. He needed to know positions, numbers of enemy, probable routes, everything, so that his instinct could make the correct decisions.

Finally, he went to the access panel which had saved him the time before. He lay atop it for a few minutes, listening, determining if the stairway was in use. Nothing. Gently, he lifted the panel and it didn't move.

Locked?

He moved the mechanical handle and it refused to budge.

Again he put his ear to the panel.

Judging the stairwell clear, he grasped the handle and strained against it.

Something snapped and clanked below.

In a blink he opened the panel and dropped down onto the landing. He checked for evidence that he'd aroused someone's curiosity. Still nothing. These soft men preferred lifts to carry them to the upper floor.

He leaped and hung by the anchor handle and closed the panel, rearranging the bent metal of the latching mechanism. It would pass a cursory examination.

Listening at the door, he heard nothing save air being pushed through the ill-fitting door. He opened the door and peered out.

The weapons locker had a new lock.

No one was in the hall.

Swiftly he moved to the end and looked through the bubble to the big, open room below. Several men. No lazy, inconsequential shift this. They were alert. Habu decided that the Security boss here had not gotten reinforcements, for whatever reason. He pulled back and placed everything in his mind. Six men monitoring consoles. Corridors leading into the control room.

Where would Tique be held?

The answer was simple. For a community of this size, there would be no reason for actual prison cells. Justice and incarceration would be accomplished elsewhere.

But there would be one or two holding cells. And the

most logical place was adjacent to the control room where Security personnel were on duty around the clock.

Habu replayed the scene in his mind and identified two doors against the far wall as possibles—no, probables, for view-ports were inset in the top halves of the doors.

None of the Security people were paying attention to the holding cells. But that meant nothing.

Habu glanced again and, since no one was looking this way, stayed at the bubble and looked. A Constabulary captain had entered from a corridor opposite this bubble and went to the comm console.

Seven men.

The captain would be the key. Likely he was the ranking Security officer on duty—if not in the settlement. Take him out and behead Security, at least long enough for confusion to reign and for Habu to take advantage of that confusion.

Habu pressed himself against the wall to appear as a shadow.

He'd wait until the captain completed his comm link. It would be foolish to do otherwise.

The captain finished whatever he was doing, stopped at several consoles overseeing the operation.

That was enough for Habu.

He slunk away from the bubble, took a cross-corridor, one he remembered from before which, by virtue of its design, must circle above the central control room.

He found a matching stairwell and hurried down. Carefully, he edged the ground floor door open and looked out. He could see a portion of the control room.

He waited.

The captain soon appeared, walking into the corridor. He held himself confidently, and wore his Constabulary uniform with military bearing. The captain was a veteran. Could he be the one who'd anticipated Reubin's movements so well?

Whether or not he was, it would not do to underestimate the man.

The captain stopped and opened a door in the corridor. He began to go inside.

Habu stepped out into the corridor and moved quickly.

"Captain?" he said, his voice sounding strange and thick even to him. Perhaps it was a voice Reubin's ears were not used to hearing. Perhaps he hadn't spoken enough in the last day or so that his throat wasn't prepared. Perhaps it was the exultant screams he'd let out in the groves. Perhaps the screams had scoured his throat.

The captain stepped back out of the doorway and looked expectantly at Habu.

The Wormwood, Inc. jumpsuit fooled the captain for less than a second. Bright awareness erupted from the man's eyes.

But the time was sufficient for Habu to reach the captain and grab him, lining his knife up with the captain's throat.

Involuntary spittle drooled from the corner of the captain's mouth.

Habu had his left hand in the captain's hair, stretching his throat. "Your name," he hissed.

"Mcdemman," came out in an expulsion of breath. His black hair was slick, but Habu maintained his hold. "I didn't believe—"

"Ssilence. Where iss the woman?" Words came easier.

Mcdemman's eyes were lunging every way possible. Habu knew the man was dangerous, professional and, worst of all, proud. Habu was wounding him in the worst place of all: his pride.

Habu inched the knife point into the captain's throat. Blood seeped out and stained the knife.

Mcdemman got control of himself and held still.

To make his point, Habu showed the bloody knife point to Mcdemman and then put it into his own mouth. He cleansed the blade of blood.

Mcdemman's face underwent a change. Doubt echoed from his eyes.

"Tell me," Habu hissed.

"Temp dent," Mcdemman said.

Temporary detention. "Where?"

"Just around the corner." Mcdemman pointed down the corridor and into the control room.

Habu had been correct. "Do you have a key?"

"It's opened by the duty officer at the central console."

It sounded right. Habu removed the laser from Mcdemman's hip. "Cooperate and live." His voice still sounded strange to him. He doubted he could trust Mcdemman. Habu pushed the Constabulary officer down the corridor.

They emerged into the control room. Habu shot dead the man at the central console. The remaining five froze. The reek of burned flesh rose into the room.

"Tell them to line up against the wall." Habu indicated a position next to the two holding cells.

"Do as he says," Mcdemman said. "Now."

Slowly, the five threaded their way to the wall.

"Dissarm," Habu directed.

Nobody moved until Mcdemman made an angry gesture. Only two had weapons, and they put them on the floor.

"Push them away," Habu said.

With feet, they kicked their lasers away carefully, like men familiar with weapons would.

Habu urged Mcdemman out farther into the room. "To the central console."

When in front of the command position at the console, Habu said, "Key open the door."

Mcdemman leaned forward and thumbed a key. A door opened. For a moment, nothing happened.

Then Tequilla Sovereign stepped to the threshold and looked out curiously. Her eyes took in the situation and grew large. "Reubin!" She stepped out, straight, ignoring the men against the wall.

Habu started to warn her. But one of the men against the wall grabbed her.

Habu began to move to the side and Mcdemman launched himself at the console. His fist slammed into a red button.

Even as Habu was moving, alarms went off. A light pulsed red. Habu jerked Mcdemman from the console and fired the laser into his throat. Habu didn't wait for the body to fall. He stiff-armed himself over a console and bounded to the five men and one woman.

Two of the men were diving to the floor for weapons. Habu landed on one of them, and went to his knee. He heard and felt the snap of ribs and spine. The man made no sound, but simply went limp.

Meanwhile, Habu's knife was swinging and sliced into the side of the neck of the second man on the floor. The man had a hand on his laser, but Habu worked the knife farther into the throat and felt cartilage crush and break. Blood gushed over Habu's hand and sprayed the floor.

He rolled and upended another man who was rushing to help. With one hand, he snapped the man's neck and tossed the body aside.

Another man was trying to hold Tique; she, in turn, was grappling with the fifth man, trying to keep him off Habu.

Habu rose. The three expressions which greeted him, including Tique's, reflected his wicked and deadly visage.

One man cowered back, and the other released Tique.

Habu struck. One broken shoulder, probably not fatal. Again, his hand moved faster than the remaining man could follow. That man had initiated the slaughter by grabbing Tique. He died, bones from his crushed nose and cheek slicing into his brain.

Tique's hand went to her mouth, her body was slack, paralyzed with shock. Habu grabbed her. Wet, sticky blood from his hand stained her blue jumpsuit.

Her eyes were blank with horror. She had seen his killing lust. She had seen his wild eyes. She had seen him kill six men in less than half a minute. She had seen Habu when she was expecting Reubin Flood.

He had no time for reflection. Their time had expired. Even though it had been mere seconds since the alarm had been triggered, that was enough time for the mobile patrols outside to respond. And, Habu knew, all the doors would have gone to the lock-down position.

They were trapped.

14: TIQUE

Tique felt like her body was made of lead. The Operations room for Security and the Constabulary had been turned into a slaughterhouse.

Reubin stood before her, reaching for her, blood all over him, a weird, abnormal expression on his face, making sibilant breathing sounds from the exertion. She'd never seen a human being move so fast.

Her eyes locked on to the blood splattered man in front of her. His very bearing was not human. No *person* could move so fast and kill so quickly.

Instinctively, she flinched back from the alien visage reaching for her. Her thoughts were uncontrollable. He frightened her so much that she preferred the company of the dead.

He had her arm and she was acutely aware that his bloody hand was dripping on her jumpsuit.

"Come," he told her in that odd, hissing voice. The light in his eyes had gone. No longer was there an underlying humor. Not only that, she realized, but the humanity was gone from his eyes, too.

As he dragged her down the corridor, she wondered what had happened to him last night and today.

He'd been virtually sightless last night, unable to move without stumbling and colliding with obstacles. Now he moved with superhuman speed and precision.

She overcame her paralysis. "Wait," she whispered, hoarse from the horror of it. She wanted to say, "Don't touch me," but her mouth wouldn't articulate the words.

Quicker than she could follow, he ducked and his shoulder slammed into her middle and lifted her onto his back. Blood smeared her. She was petrified.

This was Habu.

She'd seen some last night; but this was so startlingly real.

Habu.

The legend. The one who'd supposedly killed more human beings than anyone in the history of humanity. All doubt was gone, she knew it was true.

He ran up a stairway, then along a curving corridor. She bounced on his shoulder and against his back. "Reubin," she said, but the word was crushed with her mouth slapping into the small of his back.

An armed man was coming down the corridor.

Reubin dropped her and sped ahead, launching himself at the man who stood there with a stunned expression on his face. He grabbed for his weapon too late and Reubin smashed into him.

Reubin rose and the other man remained limp on the floor.

Reubin picked her up again. Her left hip was a flame of pain where she'd struck the floor.

Soon he turned right on an intersecting corridor, then right again into a stairwell. This time he set her down gently. He jumped without effort, held onto a support, and opened the panel. Then he was on the roof reaching back for her.

Momentarily she hesitated.

Blood dripped on her.

Besides this creature, he was also Reubin, her mother's husband, the man who'd rescued her. The man whose judgment and values she'd believed in and trusted. Now was no time to quit. He wasn't trying to kill her, that much was obvious. It didn't make him any less frightening, but she recalled the underlying trust in him she'd developed. His eyes gave her a compulsion to leave the stifling confines of the settlement. The events of the last few minutes had a starkly unreal quality.

"Hurry." His voice was a rasp.

She said a quick prayer and grasped his extended hand. She was lifted without effort onto the roof.

Reubin closed the panel and moved around the rim of the building. His movements were fluid and swift, showing an incredible energy.

He motioned her to the side of the building. She looked over the edge. No one was there. Why not? She'd heard the alarms.

He gathered her under one arm, hung from the lip of the roof, and dropped, landing lightly, her extra weight causing him to sink into a squat. He put her back on her feet.

He *smelled* different. And it wasn't all stale sweat and filth, either. Or was it her imagination?

She followed him to the corner of the building.

The front of the Security Building was ablaze with light. Several men knelt there, weapons drawn, facing the main entrance. Tique guessed that a similar team would be waiting in the back.

A new thought struck her: she would be judged as guilty as he for the crimes in what had been the Security control room but was now a charnel house.

Reubin took her hand, led her back into the dark, and circled outward. She jerked her hand free from his, aided by the slick, thickening blood. She wanted to ask questions, but she held her tongue.

He moved toward shadows, but toward the Operations Building, too. She didn't understand.

When they reached a location in which the parking area between the two buildings was in the direct line of sight from the front entrance to the security building, Reubin cut back that way.

What was he doing? They were heading back toward the Security Building. At any moment someone would discover them.

He urged her to move faster, no longer snaking in and out of shadows. He must have sensed her reluctance. He lifted her again and ran.

He tossed her into the back of a Constabulary aircar and climbed into the front.

She was breathing hard, more from apprehension than from the physical activity. She crawled over the front bench to sit beside him—why, she didn't know, except she did want to follow what he was doing. He had the electronics panel open and had done something inside. He closed the panel and hit switches. The machine started immediately and surged ahead. He drove it on the ground to the north, as if seeking a ground access to East Avenue and escape.

She heard nothing, but laser fire glanced off the bubble just as Reubin guided the aircar around the corner of a building.

They intersected East Avenue and, to Tique's surprise, turned *west*. Reubin kept the vehicle on the ground. Soon they sped through the central intersection, crossing North-South, and were traveling on West Avenue. Tique saw one groundcar moving up North Avenue, but nothing else. Back to the southeast, she saw flashing lights.

It wouldn't be long before other aircars were scrambled to follow them. Was Habu driving Reubin so hard that he couldn't plan ahead to try and outfly pursuit?

Reubin pulled the aircar to a stop, his fingers thrumming the control panel quicker than rain. "Out," he said. His eyes were afire and intelligence peeked out.

She obeyed instinctively, knowing their only chance for survival rested in his cunning. Her picture of Habu was filling in. In addition to what she'd already observed, an animallike aura hung over him, from his breathing and now-tight jaw to the quickness of his reflexes.

As she climbed out, she saw him hit the "execute commands" pad and dive out his side. Hatches slammed automatically, and the aircar lifted off, climbing for altitude and heading west.

Reubin was up gesturing her to follow him before she'd stopped rolling.

He passed her and faded into the shadows, his movements side to side, as if flickering like the shadows from a fire.

With no real choice, she hurried to catch up and finally found him at the corner of a warehouse. They went si-

lently along the wall until they emerged on the far side
in what had to be the motorpool.

Tique followed Reubin around the perimeter of the motorpool, past the great machines at the back to a more
obvious maintenance area. He was difficult to follow. He
merged with every shadow and moved too fast.

Until then, she'd seen no other people. But once they
reached the maintenance area, she saw several, surpris-
ing at this time of night.

They stood atop vehicles and were all looking to the
southeast where the action centered around the Ops and
Security Buildings. Tique glanced that way herself. Reflected off of buildings and into the night skies, she could
see laser fire. Red lights rotated. She thought of the time-
worn expression: all hell was breaking loose. After the
slaughter back at the Security Building, she almost felt
she could enjoy the prospect of being captured. She'd be
killed and this nightmare would be over. But for now,
she had to go along with Reubin.

Aircars were rising, strobes throbbing angrily. They
circled momentarily, some moving east. Then one and
another and then all of them sped off to the west, gaining
altitude and increasing speed.

Tique tried to think. What did she know of aircars?
The same as anybody else. But it stood to reason that the
Constabulary vehicle would be the fastest of them all.
Reubin had probably chosen that specific aircar for the
same reason. Hopefully, that abandoned aircar would
maintain a lead over the pursuit long enough for them to
escape.

They were hidden behind an old airbarge. Reubin was
simply waiting. Soon the activity died down and men
went back to work.

Tique estimated it was about midnight. Did Reubin
think these workers would quit then, their shift finished?
It was worth hoping for, whatever his plan.

Tique watched the skies. The moon which looked like
a crushed helmet was up and disappeared behind heavy
clouds. Strong winds ushered those clouds from the
mountain range toward the settlement. Tique watched

them charge this way. Monsoons washed over the settlement. What was she doing here? When had the universe moved 180 degrees out of phase? Here she was crouching, trembling in the middle of the night during a growing storm a million kilometers from anywhere alongside the most notorious killer in history, alternately scared to goddamn death and angry as hell at those who'd caused all this.

She was slowly becoming more used to Habu's presence. If Reubin Flood was still occupying space in his body, she was beginning to feel reassured he wouldn't let Habu harm her.

Or so she hoped.

Reubin stayed put.

Tique watched men hurry in out of the storm. She hoped their shift was over anyway, and also fervently wished that there was no midnight to dawn shift.

She still didn't know how she felt. Relief mingled with horror? Deep inside, she'd known Reubin would return for her.

And, boy, had he ever! He'd brought minions from hell, too. *Now* she understood about Habu. Her mental picture of what Reubin had gone through was becoming more complete. The myths and legends. How he had been able to outfight an entire planet—or two. Until last night, when she'd seen him in action, she hadn't known whether she believed or not. Though she had to admit, Reubin Flood himself was quite competent at survival and fighting. He was quite an antagonist, she thought, recalling the Corona. His fighting at the Corona paled in contrast to what she'd seen him accomplish last night and tonight. The Corona had been structured; this was pure animal reaction.

She'd listened to the Security personnel last night on the way back to the settlement. They thought they'd encountered the very devil himself. They spoke chillingly of the many deaths, even though they were professionals themselves. All were subdued. Except Captain Mcdemman and his shouted questions and demands over the comm system. Until one man had reached over and turned off the comm set.

Reubin's sticky, wet hand took her wrist and led her along the rear of the line of vehicles.

He urged her into one, a medium sized aircar with a small, open deck in the back. She got in.

He went around and climbed in the other side.

This was the first aircar she'd ever seen in which the interior light didn't work. It figured, though. This was the maintenance section, not the side where all the vehicles were in working order ready for dispatch.

While she slaked water off herself, Reubin shook it off him. The water slinging off of him was pink. His hands moved knowingly over the controls. She felt the vehicle coming to life. A blinking red light showed ''AUTO-DIAGNOSIS INOP.'' Reubin's hand moved again and the light dimmed.

He started the blower so they could see out the bubble. Rain pelted against them fiercely. As the car rose, the wind and the rain blew it so that it felt very unstable.

Tique watched Reubin navigate the vehicle out of its slot. Slowly they rose, fighting the wind and rain. Another wave of doubt overwhelmed her. Here she was, going off into the wilderness with a homicidal maniac. No, a genocidal maniac. Alone. In a broken aircar in one hellacious storm. She wouldn't have dared to go out in a groundcar, much less an aircar. She closed her eyes and swallowed her heart back down her throat.

In a few seconds, they were outside of the settlement spiraling up into the core of the storm above them. She felt as if she were riding a berserk bubblevator. Now out of discovery's way, Reubin increased the instrument lighting.

For the first time, Tique was able to concentrate on him.

His face was hard, the beard streaked with water. His hair was plastered down. His eyes moved constantly, watching the control panel and staring out the bubble.

Lightning streaked nearby, highlighting his face in relief. The profile seemed strange to Tique, as if he'd changed somehow. His whole body gave the impression that he was coiled, ready to lash out, to fight. She couldn't bring herself to even *think* of what she'd dubbed as her "scheme." Her idea had sounded noble and wonderful and appealed to her. But now?

They stopped gaining altitude and went forward slowly. He had some specific maneuver he was intent upon completing.

After a few moments, he brought the vehicle down, almost all the way, until Tique could see the tops of trees whipped by the storm in the backwash of lightning. Her stomach felt as if the bottom of the world had dropped out. Never had she ridden in an aircar flown this far out of its performance envelope.

Then she understood. Reubin was trying to avoid radar. The storm might hinder visual sighting, but radar didn't care. He'd moved to escape the initial detection by spiraling up, then moving slightly enough so that they were no longer directly over the settlement and appearing to follow the other aircars in pursuit of the stolen Constabulary vehicle. Immediately, he'd dropped all the altitude to get out of the line of sight of the radar.

Unless they had a satellite relay, she thought. If so, there was nothing she and Reubin could do to avoid it.

Reubin stroked the control panel. "I have sset the terrain-following gear," he said, voice rasping and stressing the "s" in set. An odd sound. "You drive."

He leaned back and she keyed the controls to respond to her side. The vehicle surged forward. She decreased the speed. Too much speed in a storm was dangerous. Her hands were sweating. Violent winds buffeted her. Her terror returned; but this time it wasn't fear of the unknown, but fear for her very life.

Reubin climbed into the back and scrounged around. She activated a light for him and watched in the mirror while flying by instruments which she didn't think she could trust.

He found the emergency provisions.

She thought he was looking for the first aid kit. "How's

your head?'' she asked. Was he coherent? Would he respond?

"Head?"

"Yes. Your pains. The pressure from not taking the Change yet.''

"Oh. S'all right.''

He'd torn the package open and found the rations. He popped lids and tops, not waiting for heat-tabs. Without offering her any, he dumped the contents into his mouth and, mostly without chewing, swallowed rapidly. It was like he was feeding a famished machine.

She concentrated on flying. The physical challenge helped release some of her tension. She was actually glad she had something constructive to do and that she could contribute.

Occasionally, he released air through his throat, a sibilant noise.

She checked the instruments, mad at herself for what she thought. She'd had a growing attraction for Reubin and his rough, casual manner. Hence her scheme. But now she was reassessing her feelings.

This man was not the same *person* with which she was becoming so familiar. Not the same emotionally vulnerable man who had gone blind and made jokes. There was no vulnerability about Reubin now.

He was Habu. He was possessed.

She remembered him fighting the attackers the night before at their camp in the groves. He'd undergone some trauma even before her eyes. He'd gone sort of berserk, killing, running, carrying her. His mind must have been full of pain and bursting from the pressure. His intermittent sight had added to the trauma. He hadn't been able to articulate himself well to her at the end. And from what she'd seen and heard afterward, he'd killed many men, some horribly.

Had Reubin Flood gone mad? Was that the answer? Had the pressure finally burst within his mind? Was it now too late for the Long Life Institute to save him?

Tequilla Sovereign feared the worst. Something inside

her refused to let pity out. She did not pity him. She knew that was the last thing he'd want.

Could it be that he was schizophrenic? Perhaps the trauma and mental pain and pressure had caused his alter ego, this Habu, to emerge. It occurred to her that she'd never know.

He drank from a thermos.

"The course is set for Cuyas. Is that correct?" She watched him in the mirror rear-seat monitor.

He exhaled. "Yess." The thermos was empty and he opened a patch in the bubble. He pushed his head through the opening and rain drenched him, running down his neck into the cabin. Wind and rain lashed his face.

Finally, he pulled his head in and sealed the patch.

He curled up on the back seat. "Sstop before reaching populated areass. Drive sslowly sso as not to attract attention."

He laid his head on his arms and closed his eyes.

"Who *are* you?" Tique whispered.

He opened his eyes, still wet yet unblinking. "Habu."

She landed alongside a stream in a ravine a couple of hours outside Cuyas. She piloted the aircar down gently, not wanting to wake up . . . Reubin. She didn't understand the metamorphosis Reubin underwent if in fact it was such, and she guessed it was. What she didn't want was to face Habu now. She needed to reconcile some things in her own mind.

Tique slid the vehicle under some trees and shut down the systems. It had been difficult operating the aircar without the auto-diagnosis system, but gradually she'd mastered her fear of the machine falling from the sky.

She was apprehensive about which persona Reubin would be upon waking.

She sank back in her seat and opaqued the bubble. She turned her head and saw Reubin resting easy now. Her eyes closed and she fell asleep wondering.

When she woke, he was gone.

The morning was cloudy, but not yet raining.

Momentarily disconcerted because of his absence, she gathered control of herself. She climbed out of the aircar and stretched. An ache in her thigh reminded her of Reubin dropping her to the floor in the Security Building.

A strong breeze blew from the south.

But something smelled good. Her mouth watered.

On the other side of the machine, Reubin sat near a fire and waved her over.

He stood when she came up.

He was roasting food over the fire.

"Fish and sanderling," he said, "just like the good old days." His voice was clearer.

Tique hesitated. There was something different about him now. Got it. He'd shaved. His smooth face was not nearly as pensive nor foreboding as last night.

He saw her hesitation. "Tique? It's okay. It's me. I'm back."

His body was relaxed, almost languid.

She believed him. "Hello, Reubin, I've missed you."

She ducked her head to avoid the searching look he shot her. Relief flooded through her.

They ate and drank clear stream water, evoking the memory of the recent past. Yet Tique was still nervous—until, toward the end of the meal, his face tightened in a grimace.

"The pain again?" she asked.

He nodded.

She went to the aircar and found the first aid kit. The pain pills were there, a few of them, and she brought the container to him. She shook out two and he swallowed them.

"Thanks."

Her heart went out to him again. He needed someone to care for him. Her own feelings were a jumble of confusion.

Chewing on a charred piece of sanderling, Reubin said, "Sometimes, when I change, it's not so distinct. When I was in the arena, Habu was there with me, helping. But the other night he took complete control. I saw some abhorrence in your eyes—"

"Not abhorrence," she lied. "Not that. Apprehension maybe."

"Thanks. It happens. The more he possesses me, the more nonhuman I become."

His terminology was interesting. He had said "nonhuman"as opposed to "unhuman." There had been an alienness to him.

"It must play havoc with your psyche," she said.

He nodded and handed her the thermos. "When I get like that, it's as if Habu has burst through to the surface to perform some specific function. Maybe it's survival, I don't know."

"Has it always been thus?"

He looked at her. Her empathy must have shone through her question. "Yes, sometimes. In my other lives, since this Habu creature has taken up cohabitation in my mind, I've wished to avoid situations which bring Habu on. But I don't generally get away with it. Subconsciously I seem to court danger. Hell, I don't know." He paused and shot her a grin. "It ain't something I can very well take to a shrink, is it?"

He must lead an awfully lonely existence, she thought. Empathy surged through her. Then understanding came over her. Knowing her mother, she could see how Alex and Reubin would have struck it off just right. How the promise of long term companionship was one of the key factors attracting them to each other. In addition to being fellow Original Earthers.

Her understanding led her to sort out her own feelings for Reubin.

What hell had he gone through, century after century, with that terrible thing locked up inside of him?

"Will you tell me again, Reubin? Of Habu? Of the legends about you?"

Reubin sighed deeply. "You see, the legends grow because, as I mentioned, I gravitate toward dangerous situations. I don't want to, but I do. And occasionally, Habu emerges. If we live through this, in years to come, tales of slaughter in the backwoods of a planet named Snister will permeate the fabric of our civilization."

She could see how that would happen. "How did it all start?" She knew his family had been killed. "I mean what did you go through?" She needed to hear it again, to reinforce her determination to go through with her scheme.

Reubin lay down on the soft turf and closed his eyes. "The world called Tsuruga." He told her of his wife and their child. He told her again of uncontrollable, berserk madness which gripped him and carried on for years. He had suspicions, but no real clear proof, of how Habu had lodged inside of him. "Before, I speculated about possible psychological genesis of Habu. Maybe it was a combination of all the circumstances, including living with habu snakes instead of people. I am afraid that what it amounts to is a pool of madness from Tsuruga which recedes and comes forward upon specific physical and emotional stress conditions and prompting." He sighed. He seemed to drowse for a while.

Tique sat next to him while he slept, evaluating the pluses and minuses of her idea.

His eyes rolled and opened. "The speed of Habu's movements and reflexes are far more than a human body is designed for. Thus my metabolism burns at high speed. My muscles and joints aren't used to that kind of quickness. I'll have residual aches and pains for a long time."

"Unless you get to a Long Life Institute office," she said.

He looked at her sideways. "That's pretty well out of the question now." He closed his eyes.

She understood. He was telling her it was too late. The pain was too much too often. The pressure was too great. He'd never live, at least as a sane man, long enough to travel to Webster's.

She rubbed his brow. It was hot. She poured water from the thermos on her fingers and massaged it into his forehead.

He seemed to relax.

"You've been a mercenary," Tique said. "A soldier. How is it you . . . well, you know, became a soldier? Is that what made you Habu?"

"On Olde Earthe?"

"Yes." Tique couldn't imagine anyone born so long ago still alive now.

Reubin was silent for a while. "It used to be a much-needed occupation, back in the old days." He smiled. "I remember doing my dissertation for War College. Do you know Olde Earthe geography?"

"No."

"Well, it doesn't matter. My dissertation was on the effects of war on Pacific Islands. Specifically, an island chain named the Marianas. Guam, Tinian, Saipan. Fifteen total. But those were prime. After World War II, those islands were bombed-out shells. A lot of Americans died reclaiming them. That was one fighting machine, the American military back then. They went from island to island, relentlessly. Names that still ring through history: Saipan, Iwo Jima, Okinawa.

"Well, one of the things I learned was that the American government had to get some vegetation on the islands quickly before they washed away into the sea. They brought in a South American plant called tangantangan— one which I've been thinking a lot about lately. Tangantangan grows superfast, especially with a lot of rain. It's as quick as kudzu—another Olde Earthe plant brought from Japan to the United States during something called the 'dust bowl.' Now—"

"And you told me *I* was long-winded when I briefed you on wormwood—"

"—during my study, I learned that Guam had almost been destroyed by a certain brown tree snake. As the story goes, the same American troops who liberated Guam from the Japanese inadvertently brought in this snake from the South Pacific. It had no natural enemies and proliferated. It ate small birds and all bird eggs. It literally destroyed the ecology of Guam. On Tsuruga, I remembered some vipers they called habu, and extrapolated something similar. The results were a shade more than I'd anticipated." He fell silent.

"Japanese?" she asked. "In the war? I've heard that . . ."

"Tsuruga was populated by them and their ethnic

cousins from another island named Okinawa. It's the home of the original habu. Interestingly enough, my study of military history about World War II enabled me to learn, um, the battle tactics of the Japanese. That stood me in good stead later on Tsuruga.''

"All of this stemmed from a dissertation?''

"Something like that. Even back then, military were concerned about the *effects* of war, not just how to wage it. Hence my dissertation on specific war-torn islands.''

She thought about it and knew what he said was true. It wasn't something she associated with any military.

He closed his eyes again. "I haven't talked so much in a long time. Thanks.''

"For what?''

"Listening. Empathizing.''

"Sure. Anytime.'' Tique didn't know what to think. Reubin Flood was a man of many levels, and not a few contradictions.

After a while, he rose and said, "I soaked in the stream earlier and it seemed to help my head.'' He stripped his jumpsuit and undergarments and walked into the stream. He sat and leaned against a boulder so that only his eyes and nose were out of the water.

Tique ate a small piece of fish and decided she was dirty and should bathe, too. She shed her jumpsuit and stepped into the water, conscious of his eyes on her. Could she go through with it? Hell, yes.

She swam and splashed for a while.

The threatening clouds burst and a light rain began to fall, as if pulling a curtain down over their world. The small fire hissed out and Tique shivered involuntarily. Mist rose from the stream.

She paddled over to Reubin. He was sitting up now, simply watching her. A streak of pain swept across his face. She reached over and touched his cheek. It was hot. Now was the time.

"Reubin? I've a suggestion for easing your pain.'' She moved closer, floating over his outstretched legs.

He was fragile and needed repair, she told herself. What she was doing was not being unfaithful to the memory of her mother, either, she realized. She was helping Reubin. And doing it for Mother, too. More than just a gesture.

And doing something that she would question herself forever for not doing.

She grasped his shoulders and pulled herself down.

"Time factor compressibility," he said. "A military term for 'We're out of time.' It is my intention to attempt to resolve this problem before I become, ah, well— At any rate, I'll try not to leave you holding the bag."

The rain had blown off and they were sitting next to the rekindled fire. Tique thought that her therapy had worked—at least temporarily.

She took a deep breath. "I'll be okay. I have friends. I can escape offworld and start somewhere else. For that matter, I can take the Change right now—I'm in the zone anyway. The important thing is to save your life. We need to get you off planet right away."

He sat up. "No." He rose. "Alex is dead—"

"We've made them pay dearly. They will pay, Reubin. Year after year until they debug the system. I done good."

"No doubt. Look, Tique, there is a compulsion within me. I do not think it is a moral imperative, but I believe that it is a personal imperative—to me and Habu—that we make Wormwood, Inc. and Fels Nodivving give us an accounting. There are good and logical reasons in addition to our personal ones. We don't know that they haven't already kidnapped and murdered others who were at the core of the Silas Swallow project. We don't know that they won't do it again in the future to some other poor souls."

Tique surprised herself. "Well, let us go and kill the bastards."

"Careful it must be, for I've come to the conclusion that Nodivving or someone close to him is a brilliant tactician and is able to anticipate what we're going to do before we do it. We have ample evidence of that."

"So what do we do?"

"The unexpected."

* * *

They concealed the aircar and walked into Cuyas at night during a rainstorm. Having lived in the wilderness for so long, Tique had come to be more sensitive to the frequent rains. If she didn't want, she wouldn't ever get wet—except for her nature hikes. The rain became a nagging bother.

"I've friends," she argued. "Let me comm one of them and we can hide out there."

Reubin shook his head. "No. The tactician will expect us to return here to Cuyas. It's our only logical move other than to turn into hermits surviving off the land and our psych profiles will negate that. No. We'll go to the hospital per my plan."

Tique raised her hands. "Whatever. You know, I swear I spent half the night on the computer at the settlement doing your chores. That one coded message was—"

"More than one."

"Whatever, it took me forever—"

"Look natural," he said, "here's the library."

"Goody," she said dryly. "They even have some real books."

They went into the library and Tique got on an info console and tapped into the hospital. She activated Reubin's previous reservations for vanity surgery. She didn't think the idea would work had not the medical requirements been light and needed only the mechanical nursing assistance available in each room. She put down Doctor Crowell, the pathologist, as the surgeon of record, "Don't call him, he'll call you." Doctors are all alike, she thought with a smile. Crowell might have been part of the conspiracy, but she doubted it.

The orders she gave the hospital were those of specific high-protein diets (a matter of selection from the hospital's food services lists) and no visitors. The patient would remain in his room until the doctor felt the patient was fully ready for surgery. Which gave them a few days.

Then she thought that she'd be hiding in his room and might cause the systems to cry foul, so she doubled the reservation, and programmed both Mr. and Mrs. Grant for similar regimens and eventual surgery.

They moved into an assigned family room at the hospital. Since the treatment was voluntary, no one questioned them coming and going.

Reubin kept his face shaved and styled his hair. He did not look anything like the original picture of himself in the arena. According to the newsvid, he was wanted now more than ever, having killed people in and around the settlement. The Constabulary had generated a computer drawn image of him with beard, unkempt hair, and wild eyes.

There was no mention of Tique. Though she did have her hair permed differently at the hospital's salon. She'd changed, too, from walking all over half the damn world in the rain. Someone who knew her would have to look twice to recognize her.

The tricky part was money. In accordance with Dr. Crowell's "wishes," the charges mounted and were not to be levied until the successful completion of the treatments.

Money for use in the city was a little more difficult. Tique had tried to get Reubin to let her become creative with the hospital's accounts or some other system ingress. He refused because, as he'd previously stated, finances were the one place where it was most likely to have hidden safeguards.

"Too risky," he said. One night he went out alone and came back with a large amount of cash.

Tique did not inquire.

They checked the university and zoological gardens for the items Reubin told her he'd ordered, somewhere in that lengthy coded message she'd sent.

Tique had built a new professor's identity and allotted that professor a mailing code. Anything received for him would trigger an alert to the hospital room. They'd arrange for it to be delivered to some other location, they'd decide where at the time.

Only then would they take action against Wormwood, Inc.

To kill time, they walked every day. One of the things Reubin did was to walk past her apartment building. He could detect no surveillance. "Probably mostly electronic," he said. "But we can't very well go up to your floor and find out."

So they walked past many of her friend's places and could tell nothing.

Until they checked on a friend with a house, not an apartment deep in a building.

"See that aircar?" Reubin asked.

She nodded.

"See the larger exhaust vents? Well, ordinary vehicles don't need that big and tough a machine. Let's get out of here."

The next day the hospital's system notified "Professor Grant" that a package had arrived.

"The ship was unscheduled," Reubin said. "Unless I've lost my sense of time."

"The government courier," Tique explained. "A way off planet for you?" she asked.

"Possibly." Though his look told her it was too late.

She checked the listings. "Departed this morning." She saw the hope die on his face. If only they'd known . . .

But the Fed mail system would send mail by the first available ship.

They returned to the library. Reubin had decided the library was a likely place to receive his order. "After all, it's logical for a professor to pick up his mail at the library."

Reubin reconnoitered the entire area first. He'd been getting jittery. Which wasn't helping as the pain and pressure in his brain was constant now. He'd drift off, losing his concentration. Tique tried to help as much as she could. She forced him to take pain relievers. At least he hadn't lapsed into another coma.

She waited outside. He went into the library to retrieve his package. He came out and walked quickly down the boulevard. As they'd agreed, Tique waited for a long time to insure no one was following him.

When they met later at a restaurant, Tique wondered what was in the small packet. She asked him.

"Seeds," he said. "I'm taking up farming. It's a good thing we had a professor and a university and a zoological garden to back us up, else these never would have cleared customs."

She didn't understand. "How did you get them?"

"Some of those coded instructions were to a firm of solicitors I keep on retainer. They control some funds for me and do my bidding, should I need it."

"Why didn't you ask for help?" Tique asked. "We're dealing with murder, or so you keep saying." Then she realized the futility of Robert Lee/Habu going public.

When they returned to the hospital, Reubin put his hand on her arm. "Hold on a minute. Let's just keep walking right on by."

When they were perhaps a kilometer away, Reubin went back alone.

Shortly, he returned and urged her on. "Constabulary. It appears we've been sniffed out."

"The package?"

He shrugged. "I don't know. I doubt it. That tactician knew we had to be here in Cuyas. He set up a program to query all places where lodgings could be had. Eventually, the hospital popped up and the computer sifted through databases and we appeared as an anomaly."

Tique thought. "We must have just missed them, because the hospital's computer is going to tell them about the package and the pickup at the library."

"You've got a point. But," he hesitated, "it may turn out for the best, because that will confirm to Nodivving that I actually received something from Webster's. And it's important for him to be able to authenticate that fact."

15: CAD

"We'll deliver her to you in the morning," Captain Mcdemman said. "My men are maxxed out right now. That is, the few I have left."

Fool, Cad thought. "Be advised, Mcdemman, you are in danger."

"From one man?" Mcdemman slicked his black hair with a hand.

"Tell me again what your men reported about their encounter out in the groves," Cad said.

Mcdemman looked down. "It was dark. There was some kind of animal—" He looked up at Cad on his screen. "Nah. I'm not going to lie. One man killed them all."

"Why didn't you report it sooner than this afternoon?" Cad asked.

Mcdemman pursed his lips. "For the same reason I'm not sending her to Cuyas until tomorrow. Bait."

I knew it, Cad thought. "You're playing with fire, Captain."

"I've got all the remaining men on duty, here and about the settlement," he said. His voice dropped. "I want him. I want him bad."

Cad shook his head. "Habu, man, it's Habu."

Mcdemman looked uncertain. "I've heard the myths. I don't believe them. Last night he was drug-crazed or something. Also, I've got IR set up to cover the entrances and the intruder alert system surrounding the settlement. We'll survive. And the woman won't talk."

Cad knew that Mcdemman didn't have enough rank to chance drugging her. "Very well, Captain." He disconnected the link.

He never saw or heard from Mcdemman again.

He rose wearily. He'd been living here, it seemed, most of his recent memory.

The others in Operations now took him for granted. But he wouldn't be here without the power of Josephine Neff.

He wondered if he'd ever see this Tequilla Sovereign. If Habu were alive and well, he'd come for her.

Cad had not insisted with Mcdemman. He could have had the woman shipped out to Cuyas right then, or reinforcements dispatched to the settlement. Didn't these people have the wherewithall to name their towns and cities?

A sixth sense kept Cad in Ops for an hour. Right on the money, one hour later, an emergency call came in from Wormwood Operations at the settlement.

When they told what had happened, Cad understood why the Constabulary hadn't been the ones to make the report.

Too many more deaths. Mcdemman had paid for his arrogance. But overriding it all was Habu, Habu breaking out of his human persona again. Habu on the loose. Cad was excited, able to witness a classic Habu operation. If Habu had completely shed his humanity, Snister was in for it. And Cad had a front row seat.

The few remaining Security people were airborne, chasing down the culprits.

"They're not in that aircar," Cad said, knowing it didn't matter for no one would believe him. Except Josephine. She was getting under his skin. Taking his time. Taking the edge off his thinking. He'd immersed himself in her. "Which way are they heading?" Cad asked to get his mind back on the problem.

"Toward the gulf," said the duty officer.

"Directly away from Cuyas," Cad said, checking a map. Millions of hectares of undeveloped wild land that way, too. The whole thing stank. He shook his head.

"Somehow, I don't know how, but I'll tell you this right now. Habu is not going away. He is coming here. His job at the settlement is finished, whatever that purpose was. That leaves only one location on this entire stinking world he will have anything to do with. Right here."

The Ops crew had learned to listen to him, but go about their business.

"Do whatever the hell you were going to do anyway," he said. "Inform me of any new developments." There wouldn't be any, he'd bet.

He left the underground Ops Center and took an outside bubblevator up the central structure of Government Center. He looked out on the rain-covered city of Cuyas. "What a depressing world," he said aloud.

He thought about the late Captain Mcdemman. Cad knew he could have prevented the deaths, but he hadn't interfered, hadn't called in Josephine to make them do what he wanted. He had wanted to see Mcdemman's arrogance destroyed. Now the man was dead and Cad regretted his own inaction. The damn fool!

Besides, Cad was beginning to sniff out what had really happened to set this whole thing off. Habu's motives were never very complicated. He was out for revenge. Or his goal was simple survival. Probably both. So Habu would make his way to Cuyas. He'd done all that rogue programming and terrorized the settlement. Decimated the settlement, now that Cad thought about it. He felt chilled. He thought about the deaths. Historically Habu had been a great deal more lethal.

When Cad entered Josephine's office, she spared him a smile. "We've found a couple more rogue programs."

"They're probably there for you to find and miss deeper traps," he said. "Robert Lee has some kind of in with the Long Life Institute, and it may be via the computer system. It would account for his ability to stay one step ahead of the Federation authorities—"

"And you?"

She was no fool herself. Just as he was figuring out what was really going on here, she was figuring him out.

Well, that was okay. "Yes. He's stayed out of my grasp,

too. I'll admit he's good." But I'm good, too, he told himself. I just need the right break.

"I've had time to check up on you," she said, her voice lower than ever.

Cad kept his face neutral. "I could say something about trust, but—"

"We understand each other," she finished for him. "You are a journalist. But buried somewhere in the Federation Council, you've gotten a commission to apprehend this Habu. Dead or alive. Over and above any Federation or local announced rewards."

He nodded. "I see no conflict in our two purposes." He could not tell her about the Council member who had suffered at Habu's hands and who would spare nothing to see Habu dead. A Fed member of Council with enormous power.

"I haven't told Fels," she said.

Think that one through, Cad old boy. He did. She was used to his silences. He sensed office politics here. "That could be to your advantage?"

She nodded. "Let us go bathe."

Cad found himself stripped and in a whirlpool.

Before Josephine got in with him, she waved an instrument around. Then she nodded to herself. "Good. No bugs."

"That thing won't detect directional spy devices," he pointed out.

She dropped her robe. "Nope. But these walls and this room were designed to do that very thing."

Soon they were sipping champagne, sitting arm and arm.

"You see," Josephine said, "it was all Fels' idea. I didn't count on so many deaths—rather, *any* deaths. Can you understand that?"

"Yes," he answered truthfully. This was the best champagne he'd ever tasted. Life with Josephine Neff had its perks.

"Now there are dead people all over the land, out there at the settlement."

"A terrible thing," he agreed. And more than likely

will be here, too, very shortly. "It would weigh on the conscience." An attempt to urge her in the direction she was already taking.

She looked up at him over her crystal glass. "Oh, come on."

He grinned weakly.

"Fels came from our parent company, Omend Galactic Operations—the federationwide megacorp—knowing something. He was some kind of biggie there and got himself assigned to Snister as Chief Executive Officer of Wormwood, Inc. Solely, I think now, to be near the woman. He'd discovered something. Behind the scenes he aided Alexandra Sovereign to climb the career ladder." Josephine stopped and considered her drink. "Now that I think about it, Alexandra would have made it on her own—although perhaps not as quickly. She didn't use her—well, never mind."

"Go on." Knowing the kind of woman Josephine was, he could guess what she was going to say. Alexandra Sovereign had not used her body and attractiveness as Josephine had.

"So, Alexandra knew something Fels wanted to know. She came back from a trade mission to some godawful planet or other, married, and ready to ship out through the Long Life Institute. New lease on life, new life, the whole thing."

Cad saw it now. "Nodivving panicked. His fish was leaving."

"Right. He'd tried everything. The romantic attention of the most powerful man in the world should have worked. But at first she was married, then her husband took the Change and Fels thought he had the in. She put him off and off and strung him along and finally told him, 'No way, Fels, I'm enjoying my freedom.' " Her laughter tinkled low. "You should have seen the frustration build in him. Christ, it was almost worth it to see him ready to explode. Anyway, unbeknownst to me," Josephine stopped to emphasize her point that she didn't know what had happened, "Fels grabbed her, drugged her, tried to get the info from her."

A long silence.

Cad could guess. "And?"

"Alexandra Sovereign up and died. Period. I wasn't there, I don't know the circumstances."

"Torture," he said. "An overdose of drugs."

Josephine nodded. "She had this thing in her head nobody knew about or guessed—"

"A biochip."

"Like that."

"You know what that means, Josephine? It's a sign. She was important, somewhere, sometime, probably in her past lives."

"That's what I guessed," Josephine said, her voice falling even lower.

So Josephine wanted it known she'd had no part in illegal activities. She'd merely take advantage of any situation which could benefit her. A thing she had been doing in joining Fels Nodivving in his quest. Until the deaths. Now she was disassociating herself with Nodivving and his plot. Was Josephine showing a little conscience? It was hard to believe. Most likely, she was playing her own hand to better her position. "Should Nodivving be brought to light as one who was responsible for Sovereign's death," Cad said thoughtfully, "that would probably leave you as CEO."

"Command One." Her voice was louder. Her anticipation hung there between them.

"Running Wormwood, Inc. and Snister."

"Right. Now listen here, Cadmington Abbot-whatever. It's in both of our interests to capture this Habu and the daughter. It's in Fels' interest for them to be killed. These two fugitives start talking in public and Fels is a goner. So he'll want them dead."

"That might explain a lot of Constabulary nonprocedural behavior at the settlement," Cad said, thinking aloud.

"Whatever. You, Cad, must capture the two."

"Me?" he said mildly.

"It's your job anyway," she retorted. "I'll fix it so

that Fels and I depend more and more on you. After all, you're the expert on Habu."

He thought long and hard. He finished his glass of champagne and poured them refills. He intertwined his leg with hers in the warm water.

"Done," he said finally. He knew he couldn't fully trust Josephine. After all, she was stabbing Fels Nodivving in the back. What the hell. Just be careful.

She snuggled closer to him.

He smelled her, even in the thick humidity of the wet room. "I'll tell you right now, Josephine. Habu is not hiding out in the wilderness. Nor in some gulf port. He's coming this way. This is the only place he can accomplish his purpose."

"Revenge?"

"Vengeance."

"What's the difference?" Josephine asked into his ear. "Tell me your real interest."

"What do you mean?" He put his glass down so that he could use his hands.

"You aren't chasing Habu for the Fed because they pay well. There's a passion in you when you talk about him. You've a personal interest. Tell me."

The Fed allowed Cad to take the Change and he had one of the few waivers to the Long Life Institute's mandatory pioneering policy. Government must insure continuity. Not to mention an enormous amount of political power from his Council sponsor. The LLI allowed exceptions for some in the Fed who wanted to remain on the job. It was the only way the LLI could absolutely assure its autonomy from hostile Federation politicos.

"Tell me," she prompted.

"Short and sweet," he said. "The planet Tsuruga? My folks, my fellow siblings. A lot of my relatives. Friends. Dead. Directly by Habu in person or as a consequence of his actions."

"Oh." Josephine considered him. "You don't seem all that torn up about it now."

He shrugged. "It's been centuries."

"You're a tough man," she said. "You got over it."

"I did."

"But you never, ever got over your compulsion, your obsession with killing Habu, did you?"

She'd figured him out quicker than he would have believed possible. "Now I know why I like you so much," he said and slid down deeper into the water.

"It is amazing to me," she said, "how one man, this Habu, can kill like that."

"I told you his history."

"I remember." She shivered next to him. "What kind of man is that?"

"Half man, half serpent they say."

"That idea is absolutely disgusting and I don't beleive it. He is a warrior. I saw him."

She'd been present at the Corona when Habu had triumphed and then escaped. "Whatever you think, Josephine." He remembered her attention on the replay of that combat when he'd first come to Snister. She'd watched it as if hypnotized. Cad put another piece of Josephine in place. He was beginning to understand what made her tick.

She turned to him, smiling. "We scheme together then."

"Let us cement our new relationship," he said.

"Done."

He spent most of his time in Ops. He had two programmers assigned to him. They ran thousands of routine, precautionary checks.

While doing so, the Constabulary finally tracked down the Constabulary aircar Habu had stolen.

No sign of them.

Then an aircar was discovered hidden in some brush alongside a stream outside Cuyas. The aircar had been stolen from the settlement. Prints showed the fugitives had been the occupants.

At that time, Cad came up with ideas for programming search patterns. You don't hide in a high-tech city like Cuyas without leaving a trace here or there. He'd already planted observers on all known friends and associates of

Tequilla Sovereign. Not to mention a plethora of electronics surveillance devices.

The computer turned up the odd couple and their requirements at the hospital.

"Grant," he told the duty officer. "Can you believe it? Grant and Lee?" The woman looked at him as if he were strange. "Guess you had to be there," he said. He dispatched the Constabulary surreptitiously since a quick check showed Professor and Mrs. Grant were not in their room now. The computer gave up the information that their package was ready and that they'd ordered it delivered to the library.

Nodivving appeared. His large frame seemed to dwarf the room. Business became more brisk and procedure followed exactly.

"I *want* them," Nodivving said. "But, and record this as an order," he told the duty officer, "I will have no more deaths. These people are extremely dangerous. My orders, therefore, are for them to be shot on sight."

"Recorded and logged," the duty officer said.

Cad shook his head. Nodivving was so transparent. Couldn't anybody else see it?

Nothing happened for two hours. The package had been picked up at the library before the Constabulary arrived.

"Nothing," Cad said. "He's sniffed out our trap."

Nodivving glared at him.

"Do not forget," Cad said, "that I am the one who found the trail and traced him to the hospital."

Nodivving nodded curtly and rose from the console. "My orders stand. Carry on."

Cad thought furiously. His archenemy was now loose in the city. He was cut off from his base. Cad did not know whether Habu had another safe location within the city or not. But for that matter, he could walk right out into the forests and eternal rain and be safe.

When would the carnage begin?

But the package bothered Cad. There had been no sign of the fugitives for days and days. Now he'd gotten a package. To Cad, it symbolized something, what he didn't know, but it was as if Habu had been waiting.

Was that waiting now over?

Cad liked to be the one to take the initiative. He knew enough about Robert Edward Lee/Reubin Flood/Habu that told him something was about to happen. A sense of disquiet came over him.

Habu will strike.

No doubt.

It was a matter of when and where.

Down deep within him, Cadmington Abbot-Pubal knew it.

Habu would strike.

16: REUBIN

As Reubin walked along next to Tique, he stumbled against her. Reality faded in and out as if his vision were telescoping. The very topmost point of his head felt as if it would explode upward. Pain filled his brain, from ear to ear to brow. He didn't know where he was.

Feeling somebody—Tique?—grab his arm and pull him, he followed.

Control, urged something deep within him, deeper even than the pain and disorientation.

His breathing was quick and shallow and he concentrated on that. Breathe, he told himself. Do not suffocate. Maybe killing himself would relieve the pain.

His legs moved of their own accord.

He felt Tique next to him dragging him off the walk. A few people looked at them oddly.

It had never, ever been this bad. He'd never pushed the Change so closely before. He had gone past the time. Now he knew why many people suicided.

But the docs and techs at the Long Life Institute had told him once that he was one of the first, the leading edge of the project, and thus an experiment in himself. He guessed that most of the other "firsters" were long dead as a matter of attrition. Legitimate death. Accident. Refusal to take the treatment. Suicide. Madness.

Control. Now. Do it. Do so now. The urging held an element of command Reubin couldn't ignore. He gathered his will.

His brow burned, but his balance improved. Pain and pressure receded.

Habu. That's right. He was Habu. We're not going to live much longer are we? His mind was slipping fast now. He was dying. *They* were dying.

Yes. But together we can survive a bit longer. Together. Assert your control. Now.

He found himself up against a wall of a building marked "Public Works" with Tique holding him tightly as if trying to protect him from outside attack.

He rolled his eyes. He adjusted his breathing. He pushed Tique away.

She looked at him through concerned eyes. "Are you better now?"

"Yess—yes. Yes, I am." He glanced around. Raining. How had he missed that? Good though. People inside or hurrying and not paying us attention. "Let's move."

They walked off slowly.

Tique had linked arms and was helping support him. "Reubin? Are you going—? I mean—" She held him from swaying. "You're not going to make it, are you?" Her voice was strange through the rain. Droplets scoured her cheeks.

Control. We will finish it now. Let me have the pain. Let me have the pressure. Control.

He acknowledged the imperative.

Done.

Reubin Flood shook loose from Tequilla Sovereign.

"Reubin?"

"I am all right." His voice felt clear.

"I know lots of people. Let me find us help. Come." She held out her hand. "Come on."

"No." The pain was gone, the pressure well down. Blessed relief. "No more running. We have what we need." He tapped his pocket. His words were precise and quick. Habu was defending the last bastion. When that went, he/they were dead. Habu's survival mechanism had reached its limits. The two were working together now without the metamorphosis. Two entities fighting the same battle for survival.

"Now?"

"Now. The showdown. Nodivving and Snister. It is time for them to pay."

"What happened to your pain?" she asked. "It couldn't have just disappeared."

He wiped rain off her brow and lifted her hood over her head. "It's okay now. Another couple of hours and it'll all be over."

"Reubin?" She jerked her hood back off. "I'm worried. I am scared to absolute death that you are dying. That you will die. I care, Reubin, I care. Forget this vengeance business. Let me get you help."

"Are you coming or not, girl?" He made his voice light and brusque. He turned and walked off.

"Wait." She caught up with him. "Go ahead and die, goddamnit. I'll even help you."

"Let's find a public booth."

Together they sat on the bench of the public booth. Outside the bubble a storm blew. Reubin had never seen a world with such bad weather. How the hell could the people of Snister stomach this stuff all the time? He knew that he was more of an outdoors person than most people and thus the discomfort of weather would strike him more than anyone else.

Following his instructions, Tique set the console up for taping the message and to delay-comm it in an hour.

"You're set." She adjusted the picture so that she was included.

Reubin massaged his temples. "This message is for Fels Nodivving." The CEO would receive it immediately. No underling would delay it—though no doubt they'd review it.

"Nodivving, look." Reubin opened the packet and spilled seeds in his hand. The tangantangan was small and black. He'd remembered it from his military history study of Guam. The same source from which he'd learned about the brown tree snake. "These seeds are from a variation of the *Leucaena*, this one called *leucocephala*. Tangantangan. My study of history showed about fifty varieties in South America of Olde Earthe. But after the

Second World War, they seeded bombed-out Pacific islands with it. It took over.'' He grinned mirthlessly for effect. ''Not only will it thrive on Snister, it will overrun the land. It will outgrow wormwood saplings and take over. The climate is perfect. You can feed goats on it, and make charcoal with it. You'll need a crop to replace your wormwood. Become a goat farmer, Nodivving, it suits you. But, and your experts will have to confirm this, if eaten, say by a mudcat, the mudcat's fur will fall out and he will die. The wormwood centered ecosystem will die, too.'' While he recalled tangantangan caused hair to fall off horses and cattle, it was a bluff about mudcats. Though his speculation on this point could conceivably be true.

He paused and sorted seeds. ''These are kudzu, a leguminous vine. *Pueraria thunbergiana.* It will take over the land where the tangantangan won't. It will hold soil, prevent erosion. Translated, that means that the flooding part of the wormwood cycle is finished. Wormwood production will cease. It doesn't kill other plants; it simply grows *over* anything and everything. Plants, trees, mountains, buildings. It kills vegetation by clogging it and keeping sunlight off it.'' Another Japanese connection, Reubin thought. Kudzu was originally from Japan on Olde Earthe and brought to his native United States for erosion control and fodder for animals. Little had they known then what would happen.

He shook his head to bring himself back. ''The seeds I hold here will destroy Snister and Wormwood, Inc. I will give you one hour to consult with experts to confirm what I've said. It's been proven time and again these plants cannot be totally eradicated.

''At that time, I want you to be in your aircar above the city awaiting another comm from me. You will have five minutes to arrive at a location I will give you.

''If you choose not to come, Tique Sovereign will be out in the wilds spreading and planting seeds. My guess would be two years before there is enough tangantangan and kudzu growth to impact your operations.''

He put the seeds back into the packet and pointedly handed them to Tique.

"This is the only communication you will receive. Be there when I contact you and respond within the five minutes. Come alone." He cut the taping.

Nodivving wouldn't come alone, but he'd come. Nodivving would welcome the opportunity to confront Reubin. That unspoken challenge had been there since Reubin had faced him in the PM's suite during the review of the autopsy. And Reubin had been attacking Wormwood, Inc. successfully. He was also counting on the fact that he had beaten Nodivving for Alexandra's affection. Nodivving would come.

A wave of madness and death broached the bastion. Habu fought it for a moment and it slowly ebbed back.

Tique was double-checking the "message-delay" commands. "One hour and it'll be sent."

"Good. That give us two hours to set up." If he lived that long. He plucked the package of seeds out of her hand.

She looked at him long. "You wouldn't."

"I would. And may."

"You'd ruin an entire world?"

He flashed her a grin without humor and snapped his fingers. "Like that."

"You take enormous responsibility upon yourself, Reubin." Her conservationist background was showing. Reubin knew how difficult it was to go against your own nature.

"Habu performs his function," Reubin said slowly. "I'm beginning to think he is some demon who has lived since time began, a demon who helps maintain the balance in the universe."

She was looking at him strangely. He still believed the pool of madness was the causal factor, and maybe the Long Life treatments. Whatever, the trauma had begun on Tsuruga.

Tique pushed out of the bubble, anger showing in her movements. He was threatening to destroy *her* world. Well, whatever she chose to think. He remembered Habu's communion with this world, the understanding of the wormwood trees and their relationship to the planet. He still needed to decide whether to sow the tangantangan and kudzu seeds or not.

Reubin stood at the bubble and looked out over the arena. "Why do they call it 'Corona'?" he asked.

"Beats me." She was at the command console. "Josephine's code still works." Her fingers danced over the console. Images, confirmations, schematics, and prescribed sequences sped across the screen. "Corona is now on its own power," she said. "And locked down. No entry or exit unless I allow it. No comm link in or out. Thus no computer system access from outside the facility."

Reubin had "subdued" two Security men and three animal handlers, the only people present at the arena this afternoon. They'd gone to the VIP suite and Tique had slaved Corona Ops to her console.

Now they waited.

"Let me try this," Tique said. On the schematic showing, she keyed three stations. "One, two, three," she said.

Reubin looked out the bubble and a panel opened on the wall to the far side. "You've got it."

"I can do what you want, Reubin. But I don't know if—"

"It is too late, Tique. We've got to win or we die." I die anyway, he thought. The plan he'd counted on had not happened, though he had sent the message in plenty of time. He decided if he escaped this arena today, he'd steal a ship and go into transpace. Perhaps the mathematics of that would hold back the madness. But he didn't really think so, for even now Habu was backing from the last bastion; madness and death spilled over and advanced with palpable anticipation. It did give him an idea, though. "Tique? Before we start, do one thing."

She saw the seriousness in his face. "Anything."

He smiled faintly. There was promise in this woman. She wasn't her mother, but . . .

He wrenched his thoughts back. He could tell his control was slipping. He and Habu were losing. The pressure was building again, greater than ever. Pain was coming like a storm rolling over wormwood groves toward him. He added some of his last remaining spiritual energy to Habu's arsenal.

"Reubin? What is it?"

"Use Neff's code. Tell the spaceport to ready the corporate spaceyacht."

Her face saddened. "You are going off to die. In space. Oh, Reubin—"

"Hush, girl! Do it. I'll probably die here this afternoon." He hoped he could live through this. He thought of Alex and determination surged through him. He *would* avenge Alex before he died.

In a moment, "It's all set up."

Reubin said, "It is not like I will die." Sure. "If I go off at a certain speed, I shouldn't age—"

"Almost frozen, year after year, century after century," she said, "on the verge of madness and death."

"It's all I have," he said. "There is no other way. Well, there *was* one possibility." He explained his call for help. "But that's obviously not going to work now."

"One of the coded messages?"

"Yes." He shook his head. "Too late now."

"Reubin, I can't accept you flying forever in pain and in madness—"

"Then I will explode the ship." And may do so, he thought, by impact on Government Center, capital city Cuyas, on the planet Snister.

"Reubin, I think—"

"Call Nodivving."

She hesitated then slumped her shoulders. "This is it, then." She rose and stepped over to him.

She smelled good. Concern, empathy, sympathy—all exuded from her. "Reubin? I can help again. It worked before." She circled his neck with her arms. "I care."

He pushed her away gently. Pain flushed his face. "I have no time," he whispered. "Call Nodivving." Waves of horror lapped through his mind. *Not yet. Fight.*

She gave him one last piercing look and went quickly back to the console. "Move over into the area of the pickup."

He did so, forcing back the pain. Not much longer.

"Got him. You're on, Reubin."

"Nodivving?"

The Prime Minister's face filled the screen. From the background, Reubin could tell that the man actually was in his aircar. "You're calling the shots, snake-man."

"You and me," Reubin said. "One on one."

Nodivving looked interested. "And?"

"Just you in your aircar. Come to the Corona. You'll be given entry instructions when you arrive."

The bait was tantalizing, Reubin could tell, to Nodivving. He'd had to listen to the reports of Habu's prowess and sit there doing so powerless. For a strong, physical man, this was agonizing.

"Do I trust you?" Nodivving's grin told Reubin they were both on the same track. Neither trusted the other and both knew that the other would stack circumstances in his own favor.

"You have no choice," Reubin said. "Tequilla Sovereign even at this moment is waiting in fertile fields to plant seeds. She has a sufficient quantity to spend a month in different locations throughout this world." He grinned at the PM. "You've no doubt confirmed what I've said about the seeds and their respective plants?"

Nodivving nodded. "Let's get this over with."

"You have only about three minutes. You'd best hurry."

Tique cut the connection. "He doesn't have much choice, does he? He's got to cover up Mother's murder, and do it himself."

Murderers don't remain CEOs and PMs, Reubin thought. "All systems go?"

She nodded. "Tape. Transmission. Everything."

Reubin sighed and pain struck. No blackness this time. Pure brain-piercing pain. He bent double, then straightened out. "I'm going," he said, voice hoarse.

"You can't do this," she said.

"I can do anything," he said, gathering his strength for the final act. "You insure the blast doors are up around this suite and it will work." If they couldn't get into the VIP suite, they couldn't access any controls or controlling systems. Since the VIP suite's landing ramp was outside the bubbledome, the VIP suite was vulnerable. Thus, obviously, the blast doors.

"You are going to your death," she said flatly.

He reached out and caressed her jawline with his fingers. He couldn't think of any final words, so he turned and went out.

Behind him he heard the swish and clink of the blast doors closing around Tequilla Sovereign and the VIP suite. She'd do her job.

Halfway down the ramp, Rubin paused and drank from the bottle he'd taken from the VIP bar. Whiskey didn't seem to help any more. Though it might well be the last thing he ever tasted—except, perhaps, bitter defeat.

But he kept the bottle. It was part of his plan. None of this would be worth the effort if he couldn't extract what he wanted from Nodivving.

In a minute he was striding across the arena floor. In the center of the arena he stopped. He looked up at the bubble and saw Tique's anxious face. He waved his reassurance.

The great double doors at the far end opened, and an aircar edged in. Reubin could see several other aircars and skycycles right behind Nodivving's vehicle. They rushed for the entrance, but the doors slammed shut on them.

Reubin didn't know if the Corona was a designated shelter in case of planetary attack, but thought it could serve as one.

The aircar swung against a side wall and Nodivving's wide figure stepped out.

Reubin thought that if it were him, he'd have tried to kill the other in the center of the arena with the aircar. But Nodivving was playing by the rules laid down, fearful of the biological cataclysm Reubin had promised.

And fearful of exposure as a murderer.

Nodivving walked confidently toward Reubin.

Reubin moved slowly toward Nodivving, tipping his bottle and drinking greedily. It did help a little. The pain abated as the liquor went down.

Reubin knew that the Prime Minister was alone, else Tique would not have let the man and his aircar enter the arena.

Reubin seemed to stagger and came up with his laser pointed right at Nodivving.

When he'd staggered, Reubin saw Nodivving's hand disappear into his jumpsuit.

They'd both decided to go for the upper hand at the same time. Only Reubin was quicker. Habu, anyway.

"Hold still," Reubin said.

"This is fair? You indicated it would be an even contest. If I win, I get the seeds."

"If I win?" Reubin asked softly, hoping Tique could pick up the conversation.

"You go free." Nodivving stood confidently.

"Your weapon," Reubin said, indicating with his own laser.

Nodivving slowly removed his hand and held out the weapon to Reubin.

"Toss it here, easy now." Reubin set his bottle down on the sand and snatched the laser from the air. "The other one," he told the PM.

Nodivving went into a rear pocket and came out with a similar laser. It was what Reubin would have done himself. Likely, the man had a third weapon.

Reubin moved over to the aircar and put Nodivving's two weapons and his own into the open hatch all the while watching Nodivving.

He went back to retrieve his bottle. He lifted it for a drink, watching his enemy out of the side of his eyes.

Nodivving was bending over slowly, hands reaching toward his boot.

Reubin produced his own hidden laser. "Perhaps you could give me that weapon, too." Fortunately, Corona Security had been armed.

Nodivving nodded agreeably and did so. When Reubin had put those weapons in the aircar, he was almost certain Nodivving possessed no more weapons.

Reubin climbed upon the aircar, his feet dangling, and waved to Tique. He drank from his bottle.

He tossed Nodivving a knife. "Your turn."

A side door opened and three gnurls charged out. While they were mean beasts, Reubin could tell they were not as agitated as those he'd fought in the arena.

Not drugged.

Nodivving swung to face them, moving fluidly, instantly alert.

Pain assaulted Reubin. He cursed himself for a fool. Habu would have simply killed Nodivving and made a run for it.

But no. He had to go through this elaborate charade, tailored to his assessment of Nodivving's psychological character.

A charade designed for one purpose: to get Nodivving to confess to the murder of Alexandra Sovereign, and the illegal persecution of Tequilla Sovereign and Reubin Flood.

It wasn't important to Reubin—except that it was the only way to clear Tique and insure her future *and* her safety.

A gnurl galloped toward Nodivving. The Prime Minister of Snister leaped into the air in some sort of martial art maneuver and lashed out with a foot. Even Reubin heard the snap of the gnurl's neck. The animal collapsed and plowed up sand.

Nodivving landed on his feet, poised. Two more animals were almost upon him and he whirled out of the way, knife slashing. The gray hide on the neck of one of the beasts streaked with running blood. Both animals skidded to a stop, their hooves cleaving deeply into the sand. They moved swiftly on Nodivving. He stood and faced the attack.

At the last moment, he stepped aside, dodged a cutting hoof, and slammed his fist, bottom edge down, between the eyes of the wounded gnurl. That animal fell as if shot.

Nodivving chased the remaining gnurl who wasn't expecting an attack. Nodivving leaped on its back as it turned to come at him again. The animal ran wildly around the arena, shrieking. Nodivving held on with his knees and one hand. They neared Reubin and the aircar.

As the gnurl began to twist to bite the thing on his back, Nodivving reached under the other side of its neck and drew his knife quickly across. Blood showered. Nodivving kicked away from the beast and, while in midair, threw the knife at Reubin.

It was a deadly throw. But Habu's reflexes reached out and caught the knife, though by the blade, and blood from his hand mixed with blood from the gnurl.

Nodivving stood in front of him. "You and me, snakeman." His voice was taunting. "One on one. This was your idea." He put his hands on his hips. "Gnurls hardly count in one on one."

Reubin dropped down off the aircar. "I thought a little turnabout-is-fair-play would get your attention."

"Come on." Nodivving must have sensed something wrong with Reubin. "I thought you were tough. I thought you wanted to best me. Ha! Habu, sure. Habu is a farce."

Reubin's head hurt so badly he couldn't think of words to induce Nodivving to confess to murdering Alex. Reubin upended the bottle, pouring liquor down his throat. It washed back some of the rushing blackness.

Nodivving was watching him closely. He obviously saw the pain on Reubin's face and he must be connecting the two. Nodivving's knowing grin told Reubin the answer. The Prime Minister flexed his wide shoulders and muscles rippled. "Come on, snake-man."

"I will," Reubin stammered, wondering how Tique was reacting. He hoped she wouldn't try to come to his aid, simply do her job. More than likely, she had her hands full with Constabulary trying to break into the Corona.

"Hah." Nodivving was derisive. "It seems that the notorious Habu is mere talk. Bunk. I didn't believe it anyway."

Reubin managed a grin. "Nodivving, I believe you

would pay with your life for a chance to fight Habu. Habu scorns you.'' Reubin threw the half-full bottle at the man. "You will pay for murdering Alexandra Sovereign.''

Nodivving leaned aside and the bottle whistled past him. He did not respond to Reubin.

Through the persistent pain, Reubin grimaced to himself. He'd have to lose the contest between the two in order to get Nodivving talking. Why couldn't things work out easy for once?

Reubin kicked sand at Nodivving and moved at him clumsily. He knew whether he was faking or not, it was about as good as he could do while fighting the pain in his mind. And the drink had impaired his reaction time.

Nodivving flipped him as he came in.

Reubin hit the ground rolling.

Blackness seeped through his consciousness. The madness had overwhelmed Habu.

Nodivving hit the ground where Reubin had struck, both bootheels slamming mercilessly. He grinned at Reubin.

Reubin rose and faked Nodivving to the right, whirled, and connected with a toe to the man's hip.

Nodivving spun himself, as if to get away from Reubin's attack, but continued the spin and lashed at Reubin's neck with the edge of his hand.

Reubin only partially blocked the blow, diverting it to his shoulder. Pain and weakness swelled through him, agony momentarily overriding the pools of black madness and death growing in his mind. His left side felt paralyzed.

He kicked out with his right foot immediately and took Nodivving by surprise. But the man rolled with the blow and came up in a crouch.

Reubin could not pursue him. He wanted to, but couldn't.

He stood there with his left arm hanging uselessly and his shoulder sloping unnaturally toward the ground.

Nodivving moved on him at once, his arms, hands, feet moving in a blur.

Reubin backed to protect himself but found himself pinned against a wall.

Blows rained on him and he even managed to lift his paralyzed left arm to protect himself. It was smashed away. The internal death was merging with the lethalness of Nodivving's attack.

A kick to his forehead drove him to his knees. Pain erupted throughout his body. His kidneys were mortally wounded. Most of the ribs on each side were broken. None of it mattered.

Nodivving quit and moved back.

Reubin looked at his useless left arm and noted that it was bent in the wrong direction. Blood poured from a laceration on his forehead and his broken nose. The pain in his mind had been washed back, but now came on anew. The pressure built again, building faster and invading his very being.

Reubin knew he was a dead man breathing. He looked up at Nodivving. Only one eye worked properly. "Kill me," he rasped. "As you killed Alex."

"I will," Nodivving said, moving forward. "I will. She told me you would come for her. She laughed in my face."

"You killed her."

"No," Nodivving said. "I will not have you think I did this to her. She died in my hands. I didn't know why—then." He stopped and looked at Reubin. "I regretted I had to take such drastic action, but she had rejected me too many times."

"You wanted her ssecret," Reubin said, blood dripping from his chin.

Nodivving grunted an affirmative. "I'd followed her here. Research was one of my divisions at Omend. Alexandra Sovereign was a neuroendocrinologist on the Long Life Project. She knew part of the hormone and chemical sequence the Long Life Institute uses."

"Power and greed," Reubin said, voice so low it couldn't even accuse.

Nodivving said. "Sure. Why not? Those fools at the Long Life Institute have it. Why shouldn't I wield some, too? There was nothing left for me—'' He paused. ''So what? It will make no difference to you. You're dead.''

Reubin saw the tableau of the two of them displayed on one of the giant screens at the top of the arena. Tique was telling him she'd gotten the confession and taped it. And transmitted the entire thing live to the whole world.

''Where is the woman?'' Nodivving said. ''And the seeds.''

Reubin whispered. ''The seeds are in my pocket. Look above at the screens.''

Nodivving raised his head and eyes; he stood frozen. *''God damn you!''* Nodivving had realized it all in a second. He reached out to Reubin and dragged him forward. The pain was unbearable, assaulting the very fabric of his existence.

Nodivving dragged him to his feet and lifted Reubin above his head.

One last time. Some of the pain went away. *We control. Together.* The blackness remained, creeping slowly through his entire awareness. Come forth, Habu. *Kill.*

He felt strength surge. His mind commanded adrenaline release. His body tensed. Power ran through him.

With his good right hand, he grasped Nodivving's wrist below. He squeezed. The wrist shattered. Habu savored the crunching bones and the scream of fear and surprise.

Nodivving released Reubin and he fell beside the PM. Nodivving held his wrist and kicked Reubin.

He killed Alex, Reubin thought and rose to his feet.

Nodivving was looking at him with horror now. Panic raced across Nodivving's face and obliterated the acknowledgment of Habu's superiority in his eyes. A man next to death and unable to move had come to life.

With his right hand, Reubin reached out and took Nodivving by the front of his jumpsuit. He lifted the Prime Minister off his feet and held him at arm's length.

''Habu ssends you to hell,'' he rasped.

He lifted Nodivving higher.

The man was screaming uncontrollably now, a high-pitched animal wail.

Reubin began twirling Nodivving above his head. Spittle flew about. Nodivving's bladder released and his jumpsuit stained at the crotch. Reubin slammed Nodivving to the ground, headfirst, a most satisfying sound. Nodivving was dead.

What about the others? If there were others. Nodivving had been the key. The PM had admitted culpability in Alexandra's death.

Reubin staggered past the body.

Pride.

Do not die here, planetbound. *Do not let them see you die.*

Too late. Too many imperatives. Too many demands.

The aircar. Take it.

He stumbled toward the aircar.

Tique's tones boomed from hidden speakers, piercing the blackness overwhelming him. "Reubin, I've medical help coming."

He ignored her and fell into the aircar. Somehow he righted himself in front of the controls. He cranked the damn thing and headed it toward the great double doors. The closed double doors.

Come on, Tique, don't fail me now.

The aircar picked up speed. Reubin kicked laser weapons out of his way. He coughed blood and it splattered on the inside of the bubble.

The double doors slid back and he was through them, hurtling so close to the ground that every warning light in the machine was blinking and horns sounding. He pulled back the yoke and the machine climbed. In the rearview screen he saw a horde of aircars and skycycles string out behind him.

He snatched the HUD to his face and locked in on the spaceport. He punched in max speed, governor-override. The adrenaline surge from killing Nodivving was fast rolling back from the onslaught of the darkness.

An aircar mounted laser seared over the bubble-canopy but did no damage. They should know that of all the vehicles on the entire world the PM's would be designed for safety and armored to prevent ambush.

He hoped that the same applied to the spaceyacht.

He hoped he would live that long.

He was out over empty country now, outrunning the enemy. Enemy which ought to be considerably weakened by knowledge they were chasing an innocent man. Except, of course, for the deaths at the settlement and in the groves. They ought to be disconcerted, too, on account of the death of Fels Nodivving, Prime Minister and CEO.

Reubin fingered the seed packet in his pocket.

Pain raked his body and the old pain and pressure returned to his mind. He had no strength remaining to fight it. He had no strength left with which to think straight. He began the last downward spiral into the blackness.

Should the world called Snister pay for Nodivving's mistakes? Was Snister itself responsible for Alex's death?

His head throbbed to the explosion point. Again he remembered Habu's communion with the planet through the wormwood trees. Reubin slumped back unconscious, dying.

Habu came forth. A raging Habu. A Habu unwilling to die. Not now. After so many centuries? Habu pulled himself to a level of control he had never attained. He needed nothing. He would burn the advancing blackness for power and strength. Harnessing the madness, he managed to focus.

He sat up, left side paralyzed. His right hand took out the packet and shook seeds into the same hand awkwardly.

He extrapolated. This world and the wormwood trees would rather deal with kudzu and tangantangan than men, men who *artificially* grew more and more wormwood trees, ruining the delicate balance.

Habu decided it was not his decision. The decision lay with the world below. Allow the planet and fate to decide.

He touched a control and a patch opened in the bubble. The suction caused by the vehicle's speed swirled air within the cockpit.

Habu opened his hand and held it to the opening. Seeds sucked out and streamed along in the turbulent airstream behind him. He shook the rest of the seeds from the packet into his hand and repeated the action. Done.

If the seeds germinated, took root and grew, then so be it. If not, the world itself had decided.

He thought that by now all the human inhabitants of the entire planet knew his destination. Would they stop him? Would the Constabulary catch him? He didn't think it would really matter.

He looked down upon himself. His entire front was covered with blood. His eye was blurry again. Even Habu was dying.

17: CAD

"**H**e's dead," Josephine said aloud. She said it again, clearly. "Fels Nodivving is dead."

Everyone in Operations was looking at her.

Cad watched the change come over her. She was in charge. "What a spectacle," she said in her new, ringing voice.

They'd all watched the battle in the arena—along with everybody else on this screwy world, Cad amended. He admitted it *had* been a spectacular battle, if you were inclined toward those kinds of things. Habu had surprised even him.

Josephine turned to the Duty Operations officer, "Do you agree that you heard Fels Nodivving confess to murder and conspiracy?"

"I did, madam." Cad had found the man very procedure oriented.

"Log it."

"Logged."

"Additionally, Nodivving is dead."

The Ops officer checked a readout. "Confirmed."

"Therefore," Josephine said, voice still loud and clear, "in accordance with Wormwood, Inc. regulations and operating procedures, I assume command."

"Confirmed, *Command One*," said the Ops officer.

"Very well," Josephine said, a satisfied glint in her eyes. "Give me the chase."

A long shot of Nodivving's aircar taken from one of

the chase vehicles appeared on the great screen above and in front of the room.

"Destination?" Josephine said.

"Spaceport, madam."

"That's the way I figure it," Cad said. How could Habu still be going? Nothing could have sustained such punishment and continued.

The Ops officer worked his console. A wide shot appeared from the tower at the spaceport.

"What the hell?" Josephine asked. "Give me a comm link with them."

"Roger."

A side screen activated and a uniformed Constabulary officer came on the screen. Cad guessed the officer was on flight control duty.

Without preamble, Josephine snapped, "What is the corporation yacht doing on the pad?"

"Ready for launch, madam."

"By whose authorization?"

The officer checked and blanched. "Yours, madam."

Her face turned into a storm. "Counterfeit." She paused. "Do not allow it to take off."

"The orders contained your command code and were confirmed." The officer hesitated. "I will try, madam. But the launch sequence has gone past the turnover point of our control. It's now in the hands of the pilot."

"Damn it! Get me the pilot."

The side screen blanked.

Into the picture from the tower came the aircar. It did not slow as it should have. At the last moment it slewed sideways and slammed into a support strut of the launch facility.

Cad knew that the pilot was busy watching the aircar and unable to respond immediately to Josephine.

The side screen came alive. The pilot at the controls. A woman. Wormwood, Inc. jumpsuit. "Yes? What *is* it?" Her attention obviously divided. "*What* is going on?"

Josephine began. "This is—

The screen split. The face of Tequilla Sovereign appeared. "Josephine. Let him go."

"No."

"He's dying, Josephine. Give him that much. Let him die alone. In peace."

"No."

Cad's eyes went to the wide shot again. A body had fallen out of the aircar. It pulled itself to its feet using the smashed strut.

"Zoom in!" demanded Josephine, back in her whisper. Awe dominated her face.

The man faced the camera for a moment. The entire body was soaked with blood. Cad wondered how he was even alive, much less functioning. The strut was dark with blood.

The look on the man's face was that of an untamed creature. Not an animal. Not a man. A creature.

"Jesusgod," whispered Josephine. "The warrior from the beginning of time."

The whole room was captured by a power Cad couldn't define. It was as if they all held their collective breath.

"Madam? Your orders," the pilot said, her eyes glued to her own screens.

Tequilla Sovereign spoke again. "Let him go, Josephine. I've got this broadcasting on every wavelength, on every outlet. The entire world is watching you." The Sovereign woman was persuasive. She was tough and unyielding, unlike the wimpish picture Josephine had painted.

Cad moved up beside Josephine, disappointment deep within him. He wanted Habu's body. There were scientists who would pay much to take it apart and find out what was inside.

But his concern for Josephine took priority. He leaned over and whispered to her. "Everybody saw the arena. Everybody knows what is going on. You can't stop him. It would be political suicide."

She turned to him. "Oh?" Cunning returned to her eyes. "You're right, Cad." Her eyes still reflected her awe of Habu's powerful figure. "But if I don't stop him, you won't have him to collect your commission."

"But I'll have you," he whispered and was rewarded by a sly smile. "Also," he continued, "I will have a galaxywide exclusive. This story will make me a wealthy man."

Cad's eyes went back to the screen.

Habu was staggering up the ramp.

The pilot spoke, hysteria close to the surface of her voice. "Madam, your orders please!" Cad knew starship pilots were hardened. Nothing affected them. But this apparition was enough to shake the most crusty veteran.

"Josephine?" Tequilla Sovereign's voice was urging.

"Let him go," whispered Cad into her ears. "There is no other choice."

Josephine snapped her head around. Cad could almost see her admiration for Habu. It was obvious to anyone who knew her well. She took a breath. "Pilot, I determine there is a lethally dangerous madman who just boarded your ship. I advise you to abandon ship."

"Roger." The pilot rose and disappeared through a sliding panel.

Cad had to admire Josephine's decision. It covered her and accomplished what she'd needed to accomplish. No one could fault her. What a marvelous bureaucrat she was.

"Madam—" said the Ops officer in front of them.

"Hold," snapped Josephine.

Habu appeared on the side screen. He staggered onto the flight deck. The pilot had not disconnected the link. Cad couldn't believe Habu was alive, much less able to move.

"But, madam—" The Ops officer again.

"I said hold," she said, voice of command.

Habu was ghastly. A slaughtered corpse.

Cad watched Tequilla Sovereign see the picture and sob.

The man was white from loss of blood.

There was no intelligence left in his eyes or face. He was a thing.

Cad's attention was split. He saw the pilot fall off the ramp as the ramp withdrew into the ship. The door closed. The wide shot from the tower showed her running across the launch pad.

Habu was punching pads and working the ship's systems. With one hand, slowly and deliberately.

His left lay dead on his lap, forearm horribly askew.

Josephine was watching the picture, mouth open, jaw slack, spittle at the edge of her mouth.

"Mother of God," Cad said to himself. It was impossible for the man to be alive, much less moving intelligently.

"Madam," said the Ops officer.

Habu hit the switch cover and snapped the large, green switch. He fell back against the seat, one eye closed, the other crusted with blood.

The launch sequence took up where it had been held.

"Madam," the Ops officer said, and reached back and shook Josephine by the left elbow. "Madam. Look."

Cad saw what the Ops officer was referring to. "Priority signal" from a ship in space.

The picture from the spaceport tower showed the yacht trembling and then it accelerated slowly, then more quickly. It buried itself in clouds and the picture was no longer useful.

Someone switched the sideview screen view of the yacht's flight deck to the big screen.

Habu lay there motionless. He opened his eye slowly, his good eye. Cad couldn't see the other as it was covered with thick, now hardened blood.

The Ops officer snapped a switch. "Audio only," he directed.

"Wormwood Operations, I repeat, do you copy? Hello, Snister Command Center."

"Roger," the Ops officer said. "I have your transponder squawking now. Long Life Vessel *de Leon.*"

"Wormwood Operations, this is the *de Leon.* I am responding to your emergency priority request."

"What is he talking about?" Josephine asked, turning her head quizzically.

Tequilla Sovereign clapped her hands, the sound oddly muted over the screen. "Reubin's other plan!"

Cad thought swiftly. He spoke conversationally. "When the man ordered the seeds from offworld, he could have requested a Long Life Institute roving ship."

"By his own authority?" Josephine asked incredulously.

Cad nodded. "It's entirely possible. Ask the *de Leon*."

Josephine nodded to the Ops officer.

"This is Wormwood Operations, *de Leon*. Whose authority do you quote for the emergency priority request?"

The voice came back. "Says here the authority came from the Minister of the Interior, one Josephine Neff. Command code confirmed through Webster's, including funding code."

"We're paying for it, too?" Josephine whispered. She sank into a seat.

On a screen Tequilla Sovereign's face had undergone a change. There was no gloating about her triumph over Josephine. Her hands moved. "Reubin. Reubin. Do you copy?"

On the main screen, Habu's one eye swiveled to the comm. He lifted the torn brow of that eye.

"Reubin, there's a Long Life Institute ship out there. Your plan worked. Here, just a second." Her face dipped to her console and her hands flew. "I've got the coordinates, Reubin. Transmitting. Did you get them?"

Habu's right hand reached out from death and touched a button. He nodded, and a droplet of blood fell on the pickup, partially blocking the lower left corner of the view and thus the corner of the large screen in Operations.

Tequilla Sovereign's voice came again. "Hello, *de Leon*. There's a customer in bad shape headed your way. Can you snag him?" Her eyes glinted. "His name is Reubin Flood and he previously made the arrangements on Webster's."

"We'll try."

"Reubin? Activate the course change. Hit the button

again." Tequilla's voice was worried. "Your ship will stop when it reaches that point. The Long Life people will come and get you. Do you copy, Reubin?"

He didn't move.

"Reubin! Do it!" Her voice was stronger, commanding. Intensity leaped from her eyes.

His hand inched out again, slowly moving for the control, leaving a trail of smeared blood behind it. Taking an eternity. Habu looked at his comm console for a space, and Cad thought he was staring into a bottomless hell. But the look softened and Cad guessed it had been for Tequilla Sovereign.

Habu's arm moved as if by decimals. He fell unconscious and his hand barely brushed the control as he collapsed and the picture winked out.

Cad switched his glance to Tequilla Sovereign. Tears welled from her eyes and ran down her cheeks. She moved her hand and her picture died, leaving all but one of the screens blank. The shot of the empty launch facility was as bleak as Cad's mind. So much had happened so quickly. He was still stunned.

Josephine Neff was sitting there, with her face in her hands, rocking back and forth. "Funding authorization? The Company can't afford that."

But Cad knew she was stuck.

Josephine closed her eyes. Her voice was low, but no longer a whisper. "That goddamn woman did it. Somehow she did it."

The pilot's voice from the *de Leon* came through. "Hello, Wormwood Ops. Say, it's our procedure to take anybody who wants to come. If there are any other people down there who want to undergo the Change, now's their chance. Please announce and advertise same. Costs and required medical profiles will follow by data transmission."

Cad knelt next to Josephine. He whispered into her ear. "You know, it's worth considering."

Josephine dropped her hands and looked at him, speculation growing in her eyes.

But he knew her.

She lived for power, power over men. Now she had it. Even though the Company went broke from the expenses of a priority appearance of a Long Life Institute ship, and even though the rogue programs still abounded in the Wormwood, Inc. systems, she would remain on Snister—as long as she was Command One.

Additionally, they wouldn't let him aboard the *de Leon* without her authority and assurances as he did not meet the required medical profile. It also occurred to him to wonder if he really wanted to end up on some godforsaken primitive frontier of the galaxy chasing a new Habu.

Damn.

And, right now, Cad was powerless to leave Josephine. He didn't want to. Nor would he.

Cad let his eyes find the empty screen where Habu had been. One day, one day I will catch you. One day.

EPILOGUE: TIQUE

She walked slowly because of her heaviness.

Tequilla Sovereign was on one of her many outdoor treks.

It wasn't even raining.

She realized she was in an arca she'd never before visited.

A strange and wonderful looking vine stretched across the entire plain in front of her. It reminded her of a grapevine. Purple flowers sprouted from amongst large, lobed leaves. Flat, hairy pods abounded. She didn't have to be a horticulturalist to know they were seed pods.

A giant, green mound to her left. That's it. A hill, totally covered by the plant.

Kudzu, *he* had called it.

She fancied she could see the vine growing right there in front of her.

Only one other plant abounded. A bush. Long flat seed pods. Some had grown past the height of her head. Others clumped and grew as if in hedges.

She realized the plain in the valley was interspersed with kudzu and tangantangan.

New headaches for Josephine Neff. Aw.

Josephine was all right—now. With that man Cadmington Abbott influencing her, she'd become more responsible and her judgments were usually well-founded. But the entire Habu episode had made her more human.

But Cad. The man was obsessed. He'd interviewed Tique in depth on many occasions, wanting to know everything that had occurred between her and Reubin. In minute detail. Everything. How Reubin had reacted to each situation. His serpentine similarities.

Tique found the Habu-dominated situations disquieting, even in memory. Including Reubin's propensity for immediate and lethal action.

She didn't tell Cad a lot. It was none of Cad's business, the relationship between Tique and Reubin. Sure, she fed Cad some things, some obvious stuff. But nothing about their real personal relationship. She didn't tell Cad about Reubin fixing her hair, or of their short time together in the hospital. She did relate the story of Reubin trying to escape, blind and carrying her, smashing into trees and tripping, still trying while under heavy fire. That should give some insight into Reubin's character.

And though Cad had asked point-blank, she'd denied vehemently that Reubin was the one who'd got her pregnant. She'd lied to Cad with a straight and serious face.

Tique had thought and thought about her scheme. She'd realized that she hadn't taken her birth control treatment for a couple of months. At least that long. And his infertility must have broken down much as the Long Life treatments had deteriorated and allowed his mind to begin the short slide into oblivion. An iffy proposition between them, but the seed had taken, just as nature intended.

Tequilla Sovereign would bear Reubin Flood's child. She would not say "Habu's child," though that might well be what would happen.

She'd decided to do it for two main reasons. For Mother. A last gesture. That's the thing that had started Tique thinking about having Reubin's child. It was the one thing she could give Mother *and* Reubin. She'd done it when she thought Reubin was going to die at literally any minute. Neither he nor she had expected him to come out of it alive. So Tique wanted to give Reubin a legacy, a continuation after his death. Something she was certain her mother would have done eventually anyway. Given him a child. Or more.

She'd also coldly decided to trick him into impregnating her to find out if Habu were a psychosis in Reubin's mind—or something which had left its imprint on Reubin's genetic structure.

Did she really want to know?

Was Habu *really* something dredged from the primordial pool? At times, this possibility was easy for Tique to believe as she remembered him rescuing her from the settlement, or blind and killing trained Constabulary and security personnel in the wormwood groves. Those memories were not of an actual human being. Yet she contrasted those memories with him fixing her hair in the wilds. A truly gentle man.

Perhaps his child would prove that Habu might be a result of his severe trauma on Tsuruga—or the child might prove that Habu was something different, *something unique in the universe*.

Either way, she might not ever know. If Habu were an alien mind or presence, it shouldn't show up in the child. But if it were something pure Reubin Flood it should appear in the child. And maybe then, not immediately. Tique wondered how long it would take to show those unique Habu traits.

She'd thought it out. She had perhaps twenty years before her first Change. The kid would still be too young to leave behind, so the LLI would allow her to take the child with her. Then figure another hundred years on a new planet out on the frontier, and she had maybe one hundred and twenty or so years to find out some answers.

The doctor had said that hers was a difficult pregnancy—but these days they could usher her through to term.

Wouldn't Cad trade his next Change to know what she knew? And was hiding from him and the rest of humanity.

Tique had the feeling lately that Cad was becoming restless. She wondered what the effect on Josephine would be when Cad departed upon his never-ending quest. His departure would help her humility. For now, though, Josephine and Cad were a devoted couple. But eventually Cad's quest would resume.

For Habu.

Carefully, Tique knelt to study the kudzu vine. She shook her head. The whole thing was still like a dream. Yet Mother was gone. And now Reubin.

What had Reubin said to her about kudzu? Erosion control. Water retention. Prevents silting. So much for the flood plains. It would take a while, years perhaps. But the deed was as good as done. Tique fingered a vine, pulled it up, and saw that it grew also as a result of root division—in addition to seeds. She bet she could grow a cutting, too. She pulled that part of the vine up slowly. The roots extended deeper than her own height. A couple of meters at least. Yep, water retention and erosion control.

Perhaps the kudzu and tangantangan would reach some accommodation with the world and, specifically, the wormwood trees. She hoped so. She saw birds trying the new seeds. And wind would blow them far and wide.

Josephine Neff would preside over a declining Wormwood, Inc.—maybe.

Tique and Josephine Neff had reached what Tique called "an unarmed truce." Tique had chased down most of her rogue programs and killed them. It had been a hard decision. But in return for Josephine's promise not to plant any more wormwood, Tique had helped fix the computer- and data-system ravagement she'd done at the settlement. Tique thought of the alien tangantangan and kudzu spreading out in all directions as Habu's Legacy. Or one of them, at any rate. Tique thought that allowing this Olde Earthe derived vegetation to continue to grow would give her a lever over Josephine—should Command One renege on her promise. Tique felt strongly about the world as nature had intended it to be. It would satisfy her naturalist curiosity if Josephine had lied to her or later change her mind. In fact, in all her dealing with Josephine, the new Prime Minister no longer treated her as inconsequential. Tique supposed her triumph, then her cooperation, surprised Josephine.

In their reconciliation conversations, Josephine had disclosed what she and Cad had discovered about Fels Nodivving.

Nodivving was an ambitious man. But centuries had bored him. In his current life, he'd risen as high as he could in Omend, Galactic Operations. He was executive veep. In his portfolio was the Research and Development Department. They'd stumbled across endocrinology and neuroscience research. A list of neuroendocrinologists turned up, and he had suspected that list to be an original of those working on Silas Swallow's Project. He'd cross-referenced names and sifted and discovered Alexandra Sovereign was an employee of theirs on Snister—at Wormwood, Inc. Fels had transferred himself to Snister and the rest was now history.

It explained Fels' attempts at romancing Mother. The pressure on Fels peaked and boiled over when Mother returned to Snister to wind up her affairs. Fels couldn't wait any longer. Unlimited power and money were slipping through his hands. A man like Fels Nodivving would see himself as the one man to lead humanity. A new regime, directed by himself.

At least, that's what Josephine and Cad and Tique surmised from what they could learn. The parent megacorp, Omend, G.O., was very uncooperative about the whole thing. Maybe it was because of industrial espionage; more likely they didn't want to be held responsible and liable for Nodivving's actions. An outside possibility was that they were in complicity and Fels Nodivving was their agent in a galactic hunt for those neuroendocrinologists who'd worked for Swallow. You'd have to get that original list and chase it down. Or you'd have to research and discover her mother's hiring and employment history with Wormwood, Inc. There was no way anyone would ever be able to confirm that.

Well, maybe someone with the talent of Reubin Flood.

Reubin had the knowledge, that was for sure. Cad and she had discussed that at length. Reubin had told her he'd worked on a small part of the original project, helping to set up the Long Life Institute's computer systems. As a consultant or something. He'd probably planted a self-updating and self-upgrading program which allowed him access to the LLI programs, operations, and files. Much the same as Tique had installed rogue programs in Wormwood, Inc.'s system.

Which helped explain Reubin's ability to call the LLI ship via that long, coded message to Webster's.

Tique speculated that Reubin muddied his trail greatly each time he went through the Change.

Except this time.

He'd been so . . . wounded. Also, he'd boarded the *de Leon* and undergone long life treatment as ''Reubin Flood'' as opposed to some alias.

A trail. One which, during her conversations with him, Cad showed that he recognized. The gleam in his eye told her that very fact. Reubin was now vulnerable. To Cad. To the Federation. Even to Omend if they wished revenge.

The legend of Habu would certainly grow now. He was already widely known in this sector. Newspeople flocked from all points. She'd refused perhaps two hundred requests for interviews. The Habu legend was no longer a myth. It was truth. Now it was real, for people could say ''Reubin Flood'' as they spoke of Habu. It personalized the legend for them. That point might well soften his image—in this sector at least. Fels Nodivving and the video of the final encounter had accomplished in one stroke what legions of publicity experts could not have done: given the notorious Habu a better image.

Tique pushed herself up and dropped the vine. Had Reubin known she would ''fix'' the damage she'd done in the Wormwood system? Was that why he'd seeded kudzu and tangantangan?

She wondered if he'd done the right thing. She *always* wondered if *she* had done the right thing.

Staying home.

Instead of—

At least she'd have his child. His final legacy.

She wiped dirt from her hands on her maternity trail-jeans. She swung her backpack up with a practiced movement.

She walked on through the alien foliage, continuing her trek. She knew it would rain.

DAW

C.J. CHERRYH
THE ALLIANCE-UNION UNIVERSE

The Company Wars
- ☐ DOWNBELOW STATION   (UE2227—$3.95)

The Era of Rapprochement
- ☐ SERPENT'S REACH   (UE2088—$3.50)
- ☐ FORTY THOUSAND IN GEHENNA   (UE1952—$3.50)
- ☐ MERCHANTER'S LUCK   (UE2139—$3.50)

The Chanur Novels
- ☐ THE PRIDE OF CHANUR   (UE2292—$3.95)
- ☐ CHANUR'S VENTURE   (UE2293—$3.95)
- ☐ THE KIF STRIKE BACK   (UE2184—$3.50)
- ☐ CHANUR'S HOMECOMING   (UE2177—$3.95)

The Mri Wars
- ☐ THE FADED SUN: KESRITH   (UE1960—$3.50)
- ☐ THE FADED SUN: SHON'JIR   (UE1889—$2.95)
- ☐ THE FADED SUN: KUTATH   (UE2133—$2.95)

Merovingen Nights (Mri Wars Period)
- ☐ ANGEL WITH THE SWORD   (UE2143—$3.50)

Merovingen Nights—Anthologies
- ☐ FESTIVAL MOON (#1)   (UE2192—$3.50)
- ☐ FEVER SEASON (#2)   (UE2224—$3.50)
- ☐ TROUBLED WATERS (#3)   (UE2271—$3.50)
- ☐ SMUGGLER'S GOLD (#4)   (UE2299—$3.50)

The Age of Exploration
- ☐ CUCKOO'S EGG   (UE2371—$4.50)
- ☐ VOYAGER IN NIGHT   (UE2107—$2.95)
- ☐ PORT ETERNITY   (UE2206—$2.95)

The Hanan Rebellion
- ☐ BROTHERS OF EARTH   (UE2209—$3.95)
- ☐ HUNTER OF WORLDS   (UE2217—$2.95)

DAW

**THEY WERE THE ULTIMATE ENEMIES,
GENERALS OF STAR EMPIRES FOREVER OPPOSED—
AND WORLDS WOULD FALL
BEFORE THEIR PRIVATE WAR...**

IN CONQUEST BORN
C.S. FRIEDMAN

Braxi and Azea, two super-races fighting an endless campaign over a long forgotten cause. The Braxaná—created to become the ultimate warriors. The Azeans, raised to master the powers of the mind, using telepathy to penetrate where mere weapons cannot. Now the final phase of their war is approaching, when whole worlds will be set ablaze by the force of ancient hatred. Now Zatar and Anzha, the master generals, who have made this battle a personal vendetta, will use every power of body and mind to claim the vengeance of total conquest.

☐ **IN CONQUEST BORN**   (UE2198—$3.95)

The long-awaited new fantasy epic from the best-selling author of TAILCHASER'S SONG.

THE DRAGONBONE CHAIR
Book One of *Memory, Sorrow, and Thorn*

by *TAD WILLIAMS*

THE DRAGONBONE CHAIR is a story of magic and madness, of conquest and exile, and of a young apprentice whose dreams of heroic deeds come terrifyingly true when his world is torn apart in a civil war fueled by ancient hatreds, immortal enemies, and dark sorcery.

Complete with a beautiful full-color jacket by award-winning artist Michael Whelan, THE DRAGONBONE CHAIR opens the way to a world as rich, complex and memorable as any in the great masterpieces of fantasy.

". . . promises to become the fantasy equivalent of WAR AND PEACE."—*Locus*

654 pages   Size: 6 × 9 $19.50
(Hardcover edition: 0-8099-0003-3)

DAW

"Marvelous . . . impressive . . . fascinating . . .
Melanie Rawn is good!"

—Anne McCaffrey

DRAGON PRINCE
Book 1
Melanie Rawn

An epic tale of a land on the verge of war . . . and the one
man who was heir to the power which could save or destroy
it.

THE DRAGON LORD—Rohan, prince of the desert, ruler of
the kingdom granted his family for as long as the Long Sands
spew fire. He must fight desperately to save the last remaining
lords of the sky, and with them a secret which might be the
salvation of his people. . . .

THE SUNRUNNER WITCH—Sioned, fated by Fire to be
Rohan's bride. She had easily mastered the powers of sunlight
and moonglow. Yet now she must survive the machinations
of treacherously cunning enemies and find the one ever-shifting
pathway of light which could protect her lord from the menace
of a war that threatens to set the land ablaze!

With strikingly beautiful cover art by award-winning artist
Michael Whelan.

☐ **DRAGON PRINCE** (UE2312—$4.50)